# THE
# LOCKET

BOOKS BY NATALIE MEG EVANS

# THE
# LOCKET

## NATALIE MEG EVANS

*bookouture*

Published by Bookouture in 2023

An imprint of Storyfire Ltd.
Carmelite House
50 Victoria Embankment
London EC4Y 0DZ

www.bookouture.com

ISBN: 978-1-83790-525-6
eBook ISBN: 978-1-83790-520-1

*This novel is dedicated to anyone, anywhere, who dares to love against the rules.*

# PROLOGUE

Irene wished she'd put on a blouse instead of her jumper. With so many people crowded into the little hall, the curls she'd put in with hair tongs were sticking to her forehead, and even her lipstick was melting. Paraffin lamps were the only source of lighting, and they were pumping out heat. No chance of opening a window, with every pane shrouded in blackout cloth. They must boil away until the dancing ended and the vicar sent them home with his prayers.

Mrs Prentice, the vicar's wife, was playing a waltz on the piano. An old farmhand accompanied her on his accordion, his cheeks fiery with effort. Irene's mum stood at the kitchen hatch, her eyes making pathways in the crush towards Irene, who was dancing with Norman Plait. The most eligible man in the room, being the only one under fifty.

The Saint Bernard's Waltz always kicked off the dancing at the village hall because anyone could do it. Three steps to the side then you stamped your feet. *Bash-bash*. Two steps the other way, then two steps forward. You weren't meant to stamp at that point, but Norman wasn't concentrating. *Bash-bash*. He was going on about the airbase being built on the boundary of their village, between Flixfield and neighbouring Medfold, telling her how he'd caught 'some military type' crossing his fields to find out who owned the lane that ran alongside.

'I told him, nobody owns it,' Norman bellowed in Irene's ear, 'and kindly not to trample my winter wheat.'

'It costs nothing to be friendly,' Irene yelled back.

All the village farmers, Irene's father included, were nervous about the imminent arrival of military personnel, and planes taking off and landing on their doorstep. They hated good agricultural land being torn up for runways, but what could they do? For weeks, grinding and crashing had echoed across the fields as tractors with chains ripped out the hedgerows and flattened an old farm that had been compulsorily purchased by the War Office. Nissen huts had sprung up, rows and rows of them. Then the biggest shock of all... turned out it wasn't the Royal Air Force that was coming but the USAAF – the United States Army Air Forces. 'Army' and 'Forces'. It added up to an awful lot of uniforms heading towards quiet little Flixfield.

She shouted above the piano to Norman, 'If the Yanks are on their way, we'd better make them welcome. We're all fighting the same war.'

'They're already here.' Norman marched her three steps forward. *Bash, bash*. Two steps the other way, then another two steps forward. *Bash-bash*.

'You aren't meant to stamp your feet there,' she told him crossly. 'What do you mean, they're already here?'

'I saw lights glowing across the fields as I walked here. They got turned off all at once, so I expect the Air Raid Warden cycled over and raised merry hell. They'll have to learn to obey the law of this land. Such as, not tramping across my wheat fields.'

'Sounds like we'll soon be outnumbered.' Teasing Norman when he was in this mood was irresistible to Irene. 'They'll be drinking the pub dry of beer. You'll turn up at The Ten Bells and be offered a bottle of pop.'

Norman scowled. Two steps to the right, two the other way. *Bash-bash.* 'Yanks have a bad reputation,' he grumbled.

'For what?'

'Inducing young ladies to break off from their sweethearts. They'll get wrong from me do any of them try it with you.'

'Get wrong' in Norman and Irene's Suffolk dialect meant 'get into trouble'.

'It's none of your business what I do, Norman Plait. Besides, those men have left their country to fight for our freedom. How would you feel if you went to fight in North Africa or Greece, and everyone scowled at you and wished you'd go home?'

In the smeary light of the oil lamps, Irene saw colour rush to Norman's face. She should have remembered that being excused military service on account of him being a farmer was a prickly matter. To mend things, she said, 'If you were abroad, the local girls would fall for you, wouldn't they? It's how it goes.'

Norman nodded. 'I suppose they would.' There was nothing particularly boastful in his comment. He was medium height and solid, with dark hair and blue eyes that made most women look twice. And though he was ruddy-cheeked from his outdoor life, it brushed a little maturity onto his twenty-six years. Six hundred acres and the best farmhouse in the village made Norman Plait a matrimonial catch.

Shame she didn't want to catch him, Irene reflected. She was only nineteen, and the closest she'd ever got to leaving the village was going to secondary school a few miles away, on a bus that brought her back home every night. War had put a stop to any hope of escape, and her life consisted of long shifts at the jam and pickle factory, J.P. Rattray's, down the road. That, and helping out on the farm and going to church twice on Sunday. She wasn't ready to be plunged into marriage.

'Those Yankee boys won't come to our pub.' Norman looped back to their earlier conversation. 'They won't find us in the dark with the signposts taken out.' Content that he'd laid an anxiety to rest, he allowed himself a smile.

Norman had a slow way about him, but Irene never confused that with stupidity. Round here, words were what you produced when you'd thought things through.

Abruptly, he steered her to the side of the room. When they were the furthest they could get from the piano, he said, 'We've been friends, you and I, since you were a nipper.'

'Mm.' She looked towards the exit. Someone had hung a bunch of greenery above the black velveteen door curtains in honour of tomorrow being the first day of spring. She was desperate for fresh air, but you couldn't open the doors unless you extinguished the lamps first. Blackout laws were a danger to health, in her opinion. If you didn't fall in a ditch getting home at night, you suffocated.

'We're good as a pair, aren't we?' Norman persisted.

She guessed where this was leading and tried to step back, but Norman held her wrist. She didn't push him away because not only was her mother looking at them, so was Philippa. Philippa Plait, eight years old and known to all as 'Little Flip', was Norman's sister and while she might seem innocent with her round, forget-me-not eyes, her gaze was burning a hole in Irene.

How to tell Norman once and for all that she didn't love him? And had no desire to be a farmer's wife, tied to the land and the rituals of the seasons for ever and ever, Amen? Or find herself stepmother to Little Flip? Her way of letting him down gently was to say, 'Thing is, we're almost brother and sister, aren't we?'

Norman digested the comment, and half a minute later, he

replied. 'We're nothing of the sort. We're not related by blood, Irene. Not in the last few generations, anyhow. I want you to marry me.' His voice grated with emotion and he squeezed her wrist so tightly, it made her fingers numb.

Nobody had taught Irene how to deal with passion, or such intense proximity, and it provoked her to nervous laughter. She tried vainly to unlatch his fingers, saying, 'I can't marry you because I'm in love with someone else.'

'Who?'

The way the word flew from between his teeth warned her that she was handling this all wrong. But she couldn't retreat now, so continued in an off-handed tone, 'He's called Randolph.' Before the war, which had stopped everything that was fun, Irene and her best friend Sally used to cycle to the local cinema each Saturday. Sucking on sherbet lemons, perched on prickly velvet seats, they'd fallen for a succession of film stars. Her favourite was Randolph Scott, riding tall on a horse in the Wild West and speaking with what the picture-papers called a 'slow southern drawl'. Being carried off by Mr Scott was a silly dream, but Norman wasn't to know that.

His face set stubbornly. 'I've never heard of anyone called Randolph. You've made him up. Your mum wants us to make things official.'

'Well, I'm not ready,' she muttered.

Little Flip was still staring from the other side of the hall. Irene reckoned the child hadn't blinked this last five minutes.

Norman followed her glance and Philippa jumped off her chair and ran to him, throwing her arms around his middle. Nearly nine, with a birthday coming, Little Flip was tiny for her age. She'd arrived late in her parents' marriage, and her mother had died giving birth to her. In a knife-twist of fate, her father had died a few weeks after that. Norman, just eighteen at the time, and finding himself with a farm to run single-handed, had neither the time nor the skill to care for an orphaned baby sister.

A female relation had moved in but it had never gone well, people whispered. The relation hadn't taken to the baby, who'd been a fussy feeder and a poor sleeper. From this bad start, Philippa Plait had grown into a strange little being who loved nobody but her brother. The elderly relative was still at the farm, keeping house and complaining all the livelong day, but to Philippa, Norman was everything. Father, mother, guardian and hero. If Irene married Norman, she'd become the focus of Philippa's hatred, stuck in the house with the child.

Some girls yearned to be mothers. They carried dolls around from the moment they could walk. Irene never had. She liked reading, writing and drawing. Leaving Flixfield was her big ambition.

The music stopped; the dance ended. Men wiped gleaming foreheads. Women dabbed with delicate hankies. They applauded the musicians, and as the clapping faded, the sound of a vehicle pulling up outside became the loudest noise. Gears crashing, wheels on rough ground. A beam of light penetrated the edge of a blackout curtain.

'Somebody didn't pin that cloth tight enough,' Norman observed and when there came a knock at the door, like a burst of Morse code, he growled, 'I hope it's not the Air Raid Warden paying a visit.'

The Reverend Prentice strode past, flipping the door curtains aside and trapping himself in a cocoon of black velveteen. A moment later, he backed out, saying, 'Come in quickly, lads, mustn't show any light.'

Five men in green and buff uniforms, wearing side caps, filed into the hall. A sixth brought up the rear. His green, button-up tunic carried sergeant's stripes. Removing his cap, he took a slow look around before saying, 'Good evening, ladies and gentlemen. The landlord at your public house directed us here, and told us this is where the fun is tonight.'

You could have heard a spider fall. Six young Black American men, two of them stringy-thin, the others with muscles pressing against their sleeves, was a sight nobody there could have imagined they would ever see. For a full half-minute, nobody spoke. The vicar opened and closed his mouth. Evidently, he had not realised who he was inviting in.

Norman broke the silence, muttering, 'I never seen anything like it. Never in my life. Never.'

The six turned towards him and the one with the sergeant's stripes said politely, 'You've seen us now, sir. If you wish us to leave, we'll surely go.'

*A deep southern drawl.* Irene realised that Norman had let go of her wrist. She took a step towards them.

The Reverend Prentice spoke finally. 'You chaps are, um... I believe lately arrived at the base? The first of many, er, friends and allies.'

'That's right, sir.' The sergeant's answer cut through the vicar's wavering address and Irene's heart began to beat faster. 'All the way from Camp Livingston, Louisiana, where we were trained to fight. But that's not our only job. We're engineers, flown in so your guys can hand the airdrome over to us. From now on, we build it and we guard it.'

'Ah,' said the vicar. 'Jolly good. Jolly good.'

It took courage for a stranger to stand firm in front of all these eyes, Irene thought. To stay dignified in the face of forced politeness. When Norman muttered, 'Somebody should have warned us we'd get this lot,' she angrily shushed him. His response was to take hold of her arm.

The man with the sergeant's stripes continued: 'We're mighty sorry to burst in on you, but we hope you can find it in your hearts to welcome some lonely boys into your community.'

Irene stepped forward, freeing herself from Norman's grip. She extended her free hand. 'You're more than welcome. Hello.'

'Why, hello, ma'am.'

Her hand was taken and she stared, fascinated, at the clasp

of dark fingers against her pale ones. She felt embarrassed because he must see how rough her nails were, the tips coral pink from being scoured with soap to get rid of the pickling vinegar smell. Mind you, his hand had the rasp of calluses too. Engineer. And workman? She looked into his eyes. He smiled.

'Sister, d'you like to dance?'

'Sometimes.'

Norman hissed in her ear, 'You're not to. I'm telling you, Irene, come away. What'll people say?'

Plenty, and then nothing. She smiled back at the man whose hand she held now in both of hers, hoping to make up for the cold welcome. Her neighbours weren't unkind. They just didn't like change, or a shock. She tilted her head, saying, 'We don't know any American dances.'

'Then I guess you'll have to teach me yours. I'm Sergeant Theodore Robinson of the 923rd Engineer Regiment.'

'I'm Irene.'

'Irene, fair as a dream. These are my friends, and part of my platoon.' Sergeant Robinson pointed to each man in turn. 'Den, Jake, Robbie, Duke and Fletch.'

The names sang past Irene's ear because she was gazing into the darkest eyes she'd ever seen. She knew she'd get wrong from her mother, from Norman and probably the vicar too, but she didn't care. When someone looks back at you as though they see you, really *see* you, with all your layers, corners and secrets, you cannot go back to being 'Irene who works at the jam and pickle factory, that Norman Plait is sweet on'.

You cannot. And, anyway, you don't want to.

# 1

## RUBY

The taxi reversed down the stony drive. Evening was falling, a sheen of frost on the clay roof tiles of Oak Apple Farm. Its windows were dark, but this would be home for the next however many weeks.

The cab ride from Stansted Airport had cost seventy pounds, but Ruby had had no choice as it was Sunday, and coming by train would have stranded her miles away. At the airport, the driver had tapped the postcode into his satnav and muttered something about 'The back of beyond.' Near the end of the journey, as they drove through ever-narrowing lanes, he'd turned to her, saying, 'We passed a signpost saying "four miles to Flixfield" ten minutes ago. The one just now said "five miles". Am I missing something?'

'No, the locals have a wry sense of humour,' she'd replied. 'Stay on this road; I'll tell you when to take a left.'

She'd tipped him twenty pounds on top of the seventy, leaving herself with ten pounds of the one hundred she'd got from the airport cash machine. Her purse jingled with unusable euros. Lifting her suitcase, because the driveway stones were too deep for its wheels, she crunched towards a five-bar gate. The wind cut through her. What was it her grandad used to say?

'We call it a lazy wind, 'cause it don't go round you, it go through you.' *It goo throo yew.* Ruby could still conjure up Grandad's crusty Suffolk inflection. The last time she'd seen him, he'd been waving her and her mother off at this same gate.

'Keep you well, dears, and come back soon.'

They hadn't come soon enough; their next visit had been for his funeral.

Ruby stood on the wrong side of the gate, remembering that day, and her last visit to Oak Apple Farm during Christmas and New Year, 2019 to 2020, when she and her mother had discovered how frail and disorientated Ruby's widowed grandmother had become. It had been a reality check; Grandma Irene could not cope alone, and choices must be made. While they'd been running through those choices, the pandemic had hit, forcing their hands. Irene had been rushed into a care home before she was ready, dying less than three months later. That summer, Ruby had discovered that the rambling, old house in the middle of nowhere had been left to her.

Two-and-a-half years had passed. Finally, here she was though her mother had begged her not to come.

'The last thing you need is to be on your own at Christmas, darling child. Come away with me or stay in Laurac until you work out what to do next.'

There was the rub. Her life had fallen apart and Ruby had no idea what 'next' looked like – except that she must sell Oak Apple Farm, and now was as good a time as any. And yes, she was dreading Christmas.

The gate seemed to be frozen shut. Ruby gave it a shove and the mailbox attached to it tilted drunkenly, spilling envelopes and fliers onto the drive. She picked them up. In the fading light, she noticed that the farm's butter-yellow walls had cracks, which she didn't remember having seen before. The clay pantile roof looked like the ridge of a sagging tent, pulled up in the middle by the huge chimney stack.

Five hundred years old. The odd crack was to be expected.

Ruby finally got the gate open. As she closed it behind her, she looked back at the road. A ketchup-red sunset glowed behind a line of bare oak trees. Christmas was two weeks away, and as the cab had driven through the village, she'd been charmed by the glittering, ice-crystal lights people had wound through their hedges and trees. Flixfield wasn't flashing-Santa territory. Bring on a flurry of snow, the scene would be magical.

At the front door, she rummaged for the key her solicitor had couriered to her, hoping the outgoing tenants had at least left the heating on a low setting. As the house had been empty since early November, leaving it full-on could have burned a lot of fuel. She hoped she wasn't gripping a final-demand letter from the energy company. Pushing open the heavy front door, Ruby discovered it was colder inside than out. There was no heating on at all.

She groped for a light switch. Located it and pressed. Nothing happened. Had those wretched tenants turned everything off at the mains?

She found her phone and shone its torch. The light picked out solid oak beams. There was no lobby or entrance hall at Oak Apple Farm; you stepped straight into a room known as 'the dining hall'. One end housed a cavernous inglenook fireplace and when the fire was lit and the wall lamps glowed, it was as cosy as a Dickensian Christmas card. But it wasn't cosy now. With dusk melting fast into night, the beams, the panelling and a slate floor sucked up every glimmer of light. A long table with high-backed chairs was skimmed with dust. Flashing her torch at the wood burner and the hearth, Ruby gasped in shock, until she realised she was staring at a Halloween pumpkin, leering at her through vacant eyes. Splodgy, painted Halloween masks were pinned to the bressummer beam above the inglenook. Taking them down, Ruby's foot crunched on something. She'd trodden on some sweets. Huh. Her tenants took the kids trick-or-treating, had a last party, then did a runner.

Tossing the masks on the table along with the mail she'd brought in, Ruby went through the kitchen to the scullery where the boiler lived. Flashing her torchlight around, she located the fuse box. She had to stand on a chair to reach it, but one flick of a switch and the lights came on. Nothing worse than a tripped circuit. She turned the central heating on at the wall. When no reassuring gurgling ensued, she crouched in front of the boiler, listening for the sounds of ignition and pump. The boiler remained depressingly mute.

Had the gas been cut off? She'd like to blame her runaway tenants, but she had to admit she'd ignored Oak Apple Farm for too long, leaving its care to her solicitor, a lettings agent and her great-aunt Philippa, who lived just over the road in an equally old and draughty farmhouse. Age must have caught up with Philippa, otherwise she'd surely have been across, emptying the mailbox. On Ruby's last visit to Flixfield, that Christmas of 2019, Philippa had been in and out of Oak Apple Farm the whole time, handing out her opinions. Bossing Ruby and her mother around, while blocking their attempts to get the frail, ninety-six-year-old Irene to consent to move to Maple Court, a beautifully appointed residential home in the local town. Irene had needed round-the-clock care by then, but Philippa had refused to see it.

She'd call on her great-aunt in the morning, Ruby decided. Right now, she'd light a fire before she froze. Get rid of this damp smell. There were logs, kindling and old newspapers in a basket inside the inglenook. Grandad had taught her how to lay a fire. She remembered him saying, 'You start with paper, scrunched up in balls or you can twist it into sausages, howso-ever you like.'

'Can I do both?' she'd asked.

He'd thought about it for a good twenty seconds. 'You can, dear. Then you lay the kindling on top, like this.'

She crouched down and opened the door to the stove. There were firelighters in the basket. Grandad had despised them, telling her, 'You won't need them if you use dry kindling.' He'd died in the summer of 2001, still firmly stuck in his ways.

Ruby pushed firelighters into the paper and lit them, watching the flame take hold. She thought of the miles she'd covered that day from Gascony in France – getting on a plane at Toulouse-Blagnac Airport, economy flight, three hours, then a delay at Stansted for her luggage to appear. She had watched her suitcase go round twice on the carousel before realising it was hers. The last weeks had been draining and shocking. Late autumn 2022 would always be the season when her career as a restaurant chef, and her relationship, had disappeared in a single weekend of emotional Armageddon. She was thirty-four and back to square one.

She blew on the flames, then closed the wood burner's door, leaving the blaze to get itself going, and went to fill the kettle. The kitchen tap honked and wheezed and she let the water run to clean out the pipes. She was glad she'd asked the taxi driver to stop off at a service station so she could buy a few provisions. Dropping an Earl Grey teabag into a mug, she told herself to look on the bright side. France scored ten-plus for most things food-and-drink related, but Britain was the home of sensible tea, Marmite and that wicked pleasure, sliced white bread. She'd have a peanut butter sandwich, after she'd explored upstairs. Inhaling the bergamot steam rising from the mug, she smiled for the first time in hours.

Carrying her tea, Ruby checked to see if the boiler had fired up. Still nothing. She costed the call-out charge of a heating engineer. A hundred? Two hundred? She was still thinking in euros, but euros or pounds, it would have to wait till morning.

She wasn't going to pay a Sunday night call-out charge. A mere twenty-five minutes back inside Oak Apple Farm had already told her that her dwindling resources would be stretched getting the place ready for sale. But she couldn't go through winter cuddling a dead boiler.

In the dining hall, the stove cast a fierce amber glow. Its cast-iron sides vibrated. Maybe she'd overdone the firelighters? The stovepipe was making popping sounds. The inglenook was made of bricks and mortar, blackened from the open fires of long ago. It could cope with a bit of heat; she needn't worry.

Her phone buzzed in her coat pocket. It was her mum, Amanda, calling to make sure she'd arrived safely. The call kept cutting out. 'I'm going upstairs; stay on the line,' Ruby shouted into the phone. The signal got better the higher you went, she recalled. 'Can you hear me?'

'Just about, darling. Are you all right?'

'Not great. It's freezing and the heating won't work.' At the top of the stairs, Ruby flicked on the landing light. The bulb flared then went out, plunging her into darkness. 'God, now I've blown the upstairs circuit. Mum, I don't think a soul has been inside this house for six weeks!'

Her mother tutted sympathetically. 'Philippa won't have, that's for sure. She's sulking after we fell out in the summer.'

'I didn't know you'd fallen out,' Ruby said. 'Well, no more than normal.'

'I didn't say anything because I was so cross. I rang her last June to wish her a happy birthday and, somehow, we got onto the subject of your gran's jewellery. You know it was all left to me...' The signal broke up, Amanda's voice coming through in static bursts. '...sent surface mail in a box... so idiotic.'

'I know. Crazy!' Ruby was angry about it too. Irene's will had been specific. Oak Apple Farm to Ruby; jewellery, clothes and other effects 'to my daughter Amanda'. Because Irene had died at the height of lockdown, Maple Court had been asked to send all valuables to France by international courier. What they'd done instead was hand everything to Philippa, who had boxed up the jewellery and posted it to Amanda's address in France. It had never arrived.

'We got to talking about it,' Amanda continued, 'and Philippa totally contradicted herself, said she'd taken all Mum's things to a charity shop *on my instructions*! I blew a gasket. Clothes and books, yes, and I can accept never seeing the bracelets and brooches again, but not the locket! And then, Philippa flatly denied it existed.' Amanda, who after years in Gascony spoke English with a slight French accent, slipped into Suffolk brogue to imitate Philippa: '"I never heard Irene speak of any such thing."'

'Philippa's getting old, Mum. Maybe she's growing muddled.'

'Not her. I told her to stop bloody gaslighting me. She did the same thing that last Christmas we were together, when Mum kept asking for her locket. You remember?'

'I do.' The final days here with her grandmother, nursing, feeding and dressing her, had been all the more harrowing as Irene plucked at her throat, leaving marks in her flesh. *Where's my locket? Where've they taken my locket?* Over and over. Ruby had a pin-sharp memory of Great-Aunt Philippa tut-tutting: 'What are you talking about, Irene? My brother bought you lots of lovely bits and bobs, but never a locket.' Gaslighting? Sounded plausible.

'I'll find it, Mum, if it's humanly possible.'

'Thank you, darling – I have to dash. My gate's opening.'

Amanda must be about to get on her connecting flight. She was on her way to Marrakesh to spend the holidays with her ex-husband and the ex's new partner. Ruby had been invited along too, and while she'd been tempted by the prospect of sunshine and seeing the stepdad she missed, worries about Oak Apple Farm sitting empty had got the better of her. It had been a good decision: she dreaded to think what disasters might have struck the farm had it been left unoccupied much longer.

'Safe travels,' Ruby shouted into the phone. Ending the call, she pushed open the door to one of the smaller bedrooms. It would be useful to know if she'd blown all the upstairs lights. Seemed she had: the light didn't come on and when she switched on her phone torch, the battery died. This was turning into a Gothic horror story.

An orange glimmer took her eyes to the bedroom window. At the same moment, she became aware of a noise like bees swarming behind the fireplace. There was no longer a working fire in the bedroom, just a brick niche containing a chest of drawers. The bricks felt warm, and the sound was coming from within them. She went still, recalling another of her grandad's strands of wisdom.

'The first blaze of the winter is the most dangerous.'

She was jerked from stillness by a hammering on the front door. She could hear someone shouting. One word jumped out at her.

'Fire!'

2

Pulling open the front door, Ruby stared into dazzling LED torchlight. Whoever was pointing it stepped back, and she saw it was a man, bulky in winter layers. He told her roughly to get outside. 'Quick. Look up.'

Doing as he said, she saw that one of the chimney pots was gulching black smoke and shooting tangerine stars. Beautiful, in a disturbing way, until a spark landed on her upturned face.

'You've set your chimney alight,' the man shouted over the guttural roar. He pulled her clear as whirling fireflies cascaded onto the brick path.

Panic spiralled through her as she imagined the fire spreading between floors, along ancient timbers. As a professional chef, Ruby had dealt with a few kitchen fires in her life, but this was a different scale. 'What shall I do?'

'Er' – the stranger was pitch-perfect at sarcasm – 'put it out?'

'How?'

'Or ring the fire service. Your call.'

'My phone's out of battery.' She almost wept. 'Call them, please.'

'Done it. I saw the flames five minutes ago.'

'Why didn't you say?' She let her distress flow, not caring that this was a stranger and certainly a good Samaritan. 'When will they get here?'

'About forty minutes. They'll be coming from Ipswich or Lowestoft.'

Forty minutes? An image of Oak Apple Farm collapsing into a heap of smoking timber rocked her but, all at once, a deathly calm descended on her. She heard herself stating the unadorned truth. 'I don't know what to do.'

'We could try and put it out ourselves.'

She saw then that he carried a fire extinguisher. He was inside the house before she could reply, and she dashed after him. Flames raged behind the stove glass. Why hadn't it dawned on her that something was wrong? No fire should burn this searingly, unless you were about to make glass or melt steel. She began to close the front door.

'Keep it open – carbon monoxide.' The man was half-crouched in front of the stove. He was wearing a padded, corduroy-collared jacket with leather patches, the kind of English countrywear she associated with field sports. A waxed Barbour cap and work trousers dotted with pockets implied the outdoor life as did his boots, with their ridged soles. He'd put the fire extinguisher down next to him.

'What are you going to do?' It was probably shock, but she was speaking like an automaton.

'Well, I'm not going up the chimney.' He twisted to look at her. 'Have you got an insulated glove?'

'No.' Why was he asking? Then she realised – the stove door handle would be red hot. She'd left her suitcase by the door, and hurriedly unzipped it. Hurling aside clothes and some kitchen utensils – she'd packed erratically because her mind was still all over the place – she threw blue-and-white-striped oven gloves towards the inglenook. 'Use those. Professional grade.'

Folding them into a thick pad, he opened the stove, rearing back at the heat. He removed the pin from the fire extinguisher and broke the seal. Rolling onto his side, he aimed the nozzle into the blaze, killing it instantly. He then aimed it up the chimney, keeping the flow going for forty seconds or so before slamming the stove door and shutting the damper. 'That's closed off the air supply.'

Ruby released her breath. 'Is it out? Are we safe?'

'Go check outside.'

Anxiously, she peered out. The firework display had ceased, thank God, though the scent of burned tar hung in the air. 'Seems to be out,' she called shakily, going back inside.

Her Samaritan was on his feet. 'It could still be smouldering internally. The fire crew will want to give the chimney a thorough check, and they'll probably take a cherry picker up to the roof. And you know what they'll ask you?'

'Um... pass.' She pushed a hank of dark brown hair off her face. Her cheekbone was sore where the spark had landed.

'They'll ask you, "When did you last have the chimney swept, madam?"'

'Oh.' She had no idea.

He walked towards her. He was tall, fit-looking, with straight features and a strong chin. She judged him to be around her age. A dash of evening shadow to his jaw brought the kick of loss to her heart. She had been so in love with another man's chin, one to which she no longer had stroking rights.

Her voice tight and formal, she asked, 'Were you passing when you saw the fire?'

'No.'

OK. Even given he probably hadn't enjoyed the last ten minutes, he was being studiedly unfriendly. The way the peak of his cap hid his expression didn't help. If you couldn't see a person's eyes, you couldn't read them.

'I'm Ruby,' she said. 'Irene's granddaughter. Do I get to know your name?'

'Will Keelbrook. I'm your neighbour opposite, at Westumble Farm.'

'Westumble?' That's where Philippa lived. Don't say it was 'had lived'. Philippa hadn't died, surely? She and her mother would have been informed. Yes, no?

As if he read her distress, the man said, 'I'm living in the barn. Mrs Gifford still lives in the farmhouse.'

'Thank goodness. Philippa's my great-aunt. My late grandad's sister. How is she?'

He was already halfway out of the door, carrying his empty fire extinguisher, but he paused to say, 'Keep air circulating and when the fire service comes, tell them your chimney hasn't been swept in months.'

'How d'you know it hasn't?'

'Because you had tenants, and they never sweep chimneys. It's the owners' responsibility.'

'It was theirs, actually, under the letting terms.'

He gave a distinctly unimpressed laugh. 'Run after them and tell them that. They left without settling their tab at the pub.'

'They didn't pay their last month's rent either.'

'There you go, then.' Will Keelbrook gave the wood burner a disparaging glance. 'If I were you, I'd get a new one.'

Ruby felt instantly possessive of the stove her grandad had installed. 'It's been here as long as I remember!'

'Exactly. Stoves don't make good antiques. Modern ones are more efficient and safer.'

They were also upwards of a thousand pounds, Ruby reflected. She'd lost her job at the end of November, negotiating the bare minimum of a severance package. The fight had been knocked out of her, and her employer had taken advantage. 'I'll think about it,' she said.

'Don't light any fires until you've had a new flue installed.'

'All right. Thanks for – you know – seeing the flames and being so... um...' She couldn't summon the word because speaking English took conscious thought, and would do until her ear adjusted to the change of country.

'For being handy with a fire extinguisher?'

'Yes, and for coming to my aid. You didn't have to.'

'I did, actually. I was worried about mine and Philippa's thatched roofs. Sparks travel. Keep safe.'

He left then, but she followed, driven by a question.

'How is it you live in Auntie Philippa's barn?'

He turned and dipped his torch so it didn't shine in her face. 'She's eighty-eight.'

Irritation flared. 'Has anyone ever said you have a really strange way of answering questions?'

'What I mean is, she's amazing for her age, but somebody has to look out for her. How long since you or your mother were last here?'

Not since July 2020, after the first lockdown ended and it was possible – finally – to get on a plane and travel. Irene's funeral had happened by that time, a service attended by Philippa and one of the carers from Maple Court. After laying flowers on the new grave in Flixfield churchyard, Amanda and Ruby had stayed at Oak Apple Farm, cleaning inside and threshing the lawn, whose grass had grown thigh-high. After a week of non-stop effort, Ruby had flown back to France, because the restaurant where she was head chef couldn't function without her. Her mother had followed on shortly after, hating being alone in her childhood home.

Interpreting Will Keelbrook's expression as judgement, Ruby volleyed straight back at him: 'You must recall that thing... what was it? Oh yes, Covid. We couldn't get here.'

Without replying, he headed into the darkness. From somewhere distant came the two-tone wail of an emergency vehicle.


The fire crew was sympathetic, telling her that hers was the third chimney blaze of the week.

'October's generally the busiest month,' the crew manager told her as he wrote out a brief report while his colleagues finished inspecting the chimney, 'but we can expect a few in the runup to Christmas. Usually when the second-homers turn up for the holidays.'

As Will Keelbrook had predicted, a firefighter had ridden up in the cherry picker and aimed an industrial-size nozzle down the chimney. The sirens and floodlights had pulled a crowd, people coming up the drive to ask if everything was all right. Ruby had mumbled, 'Yes, fine,' to each in turn.

'Householders light their first fire when the weather turns cold,' the crew manager explained, 'not thinking there might be a jackdaw's nest up there, or hard-packed soot the chimney sweep missed. When did you last have the chimney swept, madam?'

Pre-warned, she had her answer ready. 'Not recently enough.'

'Ah. Is your hubby home soon?'

Ruby swallowed down a sharp retort. No millennial would have assumed a husband for her, but the crew manager was in his fifties and she let it pass. 'He's not.'

'Stuck in London, is he?' The firefighter cheerfully sized her up. 'Well, when he's home and had a nice beer, tell him he needs to get a stove fitter out. That lot in there is condemned.'

'Yes, I saw.' Black-and-yellow hazard tape now adorned the front of the stove, and the lounge fireplace too as it shared the same chimney stack. Her first steps into the lounge, which was off the dining hall, had been accompanied by two firefighters. Volunteers, they'd told her, from Lowestoft.

'Santa needs to bring you a new stove and a new flue, madam.'

'Can't I get them repaired?'

The crew manager shook his head. 'Likely it got up to a thousand degrees before your friend put the fire out.' Ruby had explained about Will. 'They're goners, dear.'

On that note, they left. No sirens this time, and she imagined them laughing about her all the way back to Lowestoft. 'Poor cow, doesn't know a chimney from a cheese sandwich. She'll have a meltdown when she discovers Waitrose won't deliver this far.'

## 3

In the master bedroom where her grandparents had lain together through nearly six decades of marriage, Ruby made up the bed. The tenants had emptied the airing cupboard of the linen Ruby had paid for when the lettings agency took over, leaving only the sheets and blankets from Grandma Irene's time. It brought a lump to Ruby's throat, flinging a double sheet across the bed and seeing a neat, hand-stitched patch on the striped cotton. The worn blankets, and a bedspread painstakingly created from tiny squares of cast-off cloth.

Wearing two jumpers, Ruby crawled under the covers and curled like a shrimp, a hot water bottle at her feet and another cradled to her stomach. The firemen had assured her that every last spark was out. They wouldn't lie. If there'd been any danger, they'd have packed her off to a hotel for the night. She woke in the morning with a headache and a gripe in her stomach. It took a moment for her to realise it was because she hadn't got round to making the peanut butter sandwich she'd promised herself yesterday. In fact, she'd eaten nothing since bolting down a burger at the airport the previous afternoon.

Opening the bedroom curtains revealed a grid of misty

panes. Wiping away condensation, she discovered a white canvas sky streaked with coral pink. For a moment, she wondered where the snowy flanks of the Pyrenees had gone.

'You're in Suffolk now, girl,' she murmured in her grandma Irene's voice.

Suffolk, a place of sharp winds and empty roads, of kindly, thoughtful people from whom Ruby's mother had run the minute she could. Opening the window, she saw a frost-bound wilderness where once there had been a garden. A straggling hedge drew a line between Oak Apple Farm and the fog-bound fields and low hills beyond. Shortening her focus, she saw that somebody had lit a bonfire on the lawn, rather close to the hedge. It could have nothing to do with last night's chimney fire. More likely to have been the tenants having an early Guy Fawkes celebration. Even so, she'd better check.

There was no need to dress as she was still wearing yesterday's clothes. No shower for her until she'd called a boiler engineer. Downstairs, she opened windows to get rid of the smell of smoke, averting her eyes from the stove with its waspy black-and-yellow tape. Her boots left bruised-green prints in the crisp grass as she trudged across the garden. The scorched circle was indeed the remains of a bonfire. If it had been lit to burn a Guy and bake potatoes at the solstice, it had done double-duty as a means of destroying a hoard of personal papers too. Poking about in the blackened mess, Ruby identified bank statements and motor insurance documents. Maybe, knowing they were leaving, the tenants had wanted to travel light.

Very light. Ruby hauled a badly charred object to the edge of the circle using both hands. It was an old-fashioned leather suitcase, which explained why it had withstood the flames. Its brass locks had fused shut.

Unequal to grappling with it before breakfast, she retrieved a partial sheet of paper from the bonfire; a letter, with just about enough wording visible to identify it as a hospital discharge form. From a place called Thewell Park, in Diss.

Diss was a town twenty miles away, and the closest mainline station to here. Ruby knew it well, from visiting her grandparents by train during the years she'd studied and worked in London. Thewell Park was a mystery, however. It sounded like a private institution. She spent nearly an hour hand-shovelling the debris into black bin bags she found under the kitchen sink. Depositing the bags by the dustbin, she then dragged the suitcase to the back door. She intended to open it, somehow, but it wasn't coming in with her. Her hands were sooty and she smelled of bonfire. Keeping to the theme, she told herself dryly.

After a cold-water wash and a change of clothes, Ruby filled the kettle for coffee, broke eggs into a bowl and put bread under the grill. Her phone had recharged overnight, bringing a message from her mother, prefaced with hearts, kisses and folded hand emojis.

*Sorry couldn't chat more yesterday. Have arrived Marrakesh, Charlie sends love and we all wish u were here.*

Me too, Ruby agreed silently. Her ex-stepdad Charles had always thrown brilliant parties, with Christmas his speciality. She hoped her mum would hit it off with his new partner. Even though Amanda swore she never held grudges, it was a potential minefield. 'The Marrakesh Triangle,' Ruby muttered, making a face. 'Maybe I should have gone along after all.' She carried her coffee, toast and scrambled eggs through to the dining hall, finding a coaster to put her mug on. Grandma Irene had been very particular, no hot cups directly on the wood. She'd have hated how the garden looked and Grandad would have raged at the state of the wood burner, taped up and stippled with dry white powder. Ruby briefly entertained a picture of Will-the-neighbour sprawled on his side, jetting retardant up the stovepipe. A man who knew what to do in a crisis. His judgement of her was an equally strong memory. Had she heard right, he lived in the barn at Westumble Farm? Converted, presumably. Most farms in Flixfield had been modernised. Oak Apple Farm would get a makeover in due course, hoovering up a fortune in the process.

All the more reason to sell it and move back home to Gascony.

She fished an old newspaper out of the log basket. It was the local *Echo* and had a pull-out property section where she found an estate agent selling similar properties to this. She rang the number. The woman who took the call sounded keen. Four-bedroom, former farmhouse? Lovely. Any fields or paddocks?

''Fraid not. My grandad sold the land off thirty-five years ago, after he retired.'

'Oh, well, never mind. Clients seeking country life don't always want the bother of land. Their dream is a lovely character property.'

Oak Apple Farm certainly has character, Ruby responded silently. Out loud, she gave the address and her personal details. 'Ruby Plait. P-L-A-I-T. Yes, I'm the sole owner. No, I haven't found a property to move into, I'm not... I mean, I'm resident in France and I'll be going back as soon as I can. I mean, at some point.' Best not to sound too desperate. She hung up, having arranged for an agent to view the house the following day.

*Judas, selling the old place.*

Not *my* old place, she answered the voice of her conscience.

Breakfast plates washed up, Ruby went back outside with a blunt knife she'd taken from the kitchen drawer. She slid the knife behind one of the suitcase locks and, using a stone she found in an overgrown rose garden, bashed it hard. The knife blade snapped. And all she'd achieved were marks in the leather and a painful wrist from hitting herself.

Deciding she needed a better tool for the job, Ruby went to

one of the outhouses, where last time she'd been here she'd admired her grandad's array of meticulously cleaned tools.

Not a single one remained. She recalled her tenants had expressed a desire to grow vegetables. 'Sure,' she'd replied to the lettings agent via email. 'They can use whatever they like, but ask them to take care of everything as there's family history in those sheds.'

'Bastards,' she said out loud. She wanted to cry. First Grandma's jewellery, now Grandad's spades, edgers and forks. Going back to the suitcase, she stared angrily down at it. What would it take, a chainsaw?

Her immediate solution was to go back inside and make fresh coffee. At some point she needed to do a food shop, since she couldn't live long off fuel-station rations. And she must think about getting some transport, because living out here required wheels. She heard the five-bar gate click open, and sighed. Not now. She wasn't feeling up to being polite to any nosy neighbours. Will Keelbrook's terse manner last night, followed by all the discoveries of theft and damage, had made her feel distinctly uneasy. Maybe whoever it was would go away if she stayed in the kitchen.

The choice was taken from her as the door bumped open. To Ruby's astonishment, a large dog lumbered in. It was a Labrador with a coat the colour of treacle tart, and after giving her a friendly glance, it went straight to the fridge and sat down, expectantly.

'No chance,' Ruby said. 'It's unplugged. Cupboard is bare.'

Someone was calling her name. 'Ruby, hello?' It wasn't Will Keelbrook. It was a familiar voice, Suffolk born and bred.

Ruby hurried into the dining hall to greet the diminutive woman on the threshold. Deep-set eyes stared into Ruby's. Blue eyes that were all the brighter for having white brows above them and crow's feet at the corners. A wide forehead, prominent cheekbones and a short chin... it was Ruby's own face with fifty years grafted onto it. 'Aunt Philippa.'

Philippa Gifford gave Ruby a good once-over. 'I thought I'd call, save you the bother.'

'I was going to come later. It wouldn't have been any—' A noise cut Ruby short. From the kitchen came the sound of paws thudding on the floor. 'There's a dog in my kitchen. Did it come with you?'

'"She" not "it",' Philippa said. 'She's Edna and she believes she's welcome everywhere. I hope you haven't left any food out.'

'Only eggshells and toast crumbs.'

'She'll have eaten them. Are you inviting me in, or do I remain a doorstep ornament?'

'Sorry. Sorry, Auntie.' Ruby stepped back, implying a welcome. She could hear the dog crunching heartily in the kitchen. Did Labradors eat eggshells, then? 'I planned to call on you as soon as I'd managed a proper shower.' Ruby indicated her grimy clothes. 'I've been clearing up in the garden. No hot water. I only arrived yesterday.'

'I know when you arrived.' Philippa had made it to the middle of the room. Her liver-spotted hand gripped an aluminium stick with a tripod at the base. Ruby recalled her great-aunt complaining of a painful hip the last time they'd met. Philippa took a long glance around, as if reminding herself of the room's layout, then drew Ruby's attention to a damp patch on the ceiling. 'Looks like you've had a leak. From the roof, I should think.'

'Nothing would surprise me.' Ruby pulled a seat out from the table. 'Sit down, Auntie.'

Philippa stayed where she was. She was dressed for the weather. A rainbow-knit hat was pulled down over her ears, and tufts of white hair poked from under it. A knitted poncho matched the hat and from under its knotty tassels flowed a velvet patchwork skirt. Her feet were snug in flat, fake-fur boots.

Philippa wrinkled her nose at the stove. 'And you set the house on fire and had to be rescued.'

'Well, only the chimney.' Clearly, Will Keelbrook had filed a report. 'Can I make you a coffee?'

'I've never taken to coffee, you should know that. Do you have fig leaf tea?'

'Er, sorry. I'm completely out of it. I'll add it to my shopping list.'

'You won't find it in a supermarket, you have to send off for it, but it's good for the kidneys. I've become a hippy in my old age, like your mother. See?' Philippa tugged her skirt out, showing off its myriad colours.

Ruby said, 'I like your style.'

'Is that what you call it? I put on the first thing I find.'

'Me too.' Ruby thought of the boutiques in the town where, until her world had fallen apart, she'd lived quite happily. Laurac specialised in little designer shops selling beige and pearl-grey cashmere, monotone silks and 'accent' scarves for wealthy women. There was a refreshing honesty in Philippa's mode of dress, but attempt to copy it and you'd look like a jumble sale.

Philippa was still ignoring the chair. 'I stood at my window yesterday evening, listening to the sirens until Will came back and told me the fire was out. I suppose you're in shock.'

'Not really,' Ruby assured her. 'But I am upset.'

'Oh?'

'Someone's stolen Grandad's tools.'

'Hi, anyone seen my dog?' Will walked in.

'I thought she was Philippa's,' Ruby said, deliberately with-holding any kind of 'hello'.

'No, all mine.'

Ruby pointed to the kitchen. 'She's in there, dining on eggshells.'

'So long as there isn't chocolate, grapes or fruitcake in there.'

'Nothing so luxurious.' Ruby wondered why Will and Philippa had come together. To seek after her welfare, or to peer at her, like a new panda at the zoo?

Will went to the kitchen door and whistled. Edna bumbled up to him and he crouched down, ruffling her ears. 'Been scoffing? You'd better not have gone through the bin.'

'The bin's empty,' Ruby assured him. 'I haven't been here long enough to fill it.'

He looked back at her. 'Edna has no manners. Sorry.'

'She was a rescue dog,' Philippa said. 'Will is training her.'

'Will is failing to train her,' he corrected.

He sounded in a better mood this morning, but Ruby wasn't ready to smile, or join in the chat. Something about the two of them suggested some kind of collusion. Philippa was still staring around, as if inspecting the room for change, or deterioration. Will, with Edna at his heel, seemed intrigued by the filth on Ruby's coat sleeves. She could have mentioned the suitcase, but then she'd have to admit she'd broken a knife attempting to open it. Like the firemen, he had almost certainly pegged her as useless.

As yesterday, he was wearing hardy, outdoor clothes. The waxed Barbour cap wasn't pulled quite so low and she saw he had hazel eyes and thick lashes. Glittering white flecks on his shoulders made her look towards the window, and she saw that light snow had begun to fall. She was going to have to swallow her pride and ask this pair to recommend a boiler engineer.

'How was your first night here?' Will asked.

'Fine. Only, I need someone to fix my heating. Who do you use?'

'Davey Stebbins kept me going at Westumble for years,' Philippa said.

'Davey Stebbins... is he good?'

'*Was*. He died of the Covid.'

'Oh. How awful.'

'He'd have done you a proper job.'

Will cut in, saying, 'I had a quick look round the back just now, too, and there's a couple of broken pantiles on the ground. Tiles, off the roof,' he explained. 'You've probably had some rain come in.'

Ruby raised her eyes towards the ceiling. That would explain the damp patch.

Will followed her glance. 'Shouldn't be a huge repair job.'

Good, though whoever did it would want scaffolding, which cost a bomb. Perhaps she should take a trip to the nearby town, enquire around for a builder along with a heating engineer. Will and Philippa seemed unable to answer a straight question between them but she ventured one more: 'Is there still a bus service in the village? I need to go into Hollesford.'

Philippa said, 'Huh!' as if Ruby had asked for a stretch-limo service. 'They stopped the bus five years ago, so unless you've got a car or enjoy a good walk, you'll have to get stuff delivered. Lots of people do. Mind you, I hate those supermarket vans round our lanes.' She consulted Will. 'Do you think she looks ill?'

Will looked embarrassed by the question. 'I don't feel qualified to say.'

'To me, she looks like death warmed up.'

Ruby spoke up. 'I didn't have the most fantastic night's sleep, but once I get the heating going' – she added a heavy emphasis to 'heating' – 'I'll be fine. If I'm pale, it's because it's so cold.'

Philippa's reply came like a spear-thrust. 'You thought it was good enough for Irene.'

*This is what she does.* Ruby could hear her mother saying it. *All sweetness one minute, then before you realise, she's got her teeth in your neck.* She imagined Philippa waiting for her moment to speak those words. Ruby wasn't going to let it stand.

'Remember Christmas 2019, Auntie? Mum and I were

adamant Grandma shouldn't stay another winter here. Even with the heating working, and carers coming in, it was untenable. Mum found Maple Court, and it only became a tussle because you kept telling Grandma that leaving here would kill her.'

'Because this was her home for more than seventy years! And I was right. That place did kill her.'

'It did not; the staff were lovely. Grandma died four months short of her ninety-seventh birthday from nothing worse than old age!' Ruby's cheeks burned with exasperation. 'You must remember saying, "You'll make one hundred, Irene," and her replying, "Please, God, no, I've had enough." She was telling us what she knew, Auntie.'

'What you wanted her to say, you mean.'

Will cleared his throat. 'How about Ruby goes back to yours and makes use of your bathroom, Aunt Flip? Not that I'm saying you need it,' he told Ruby hastily, 'but you do look cold.'

A hot shower would be fantastic, but had the request caught Philippa in her amiable mood, or the stubborn one? Her great-aunt was running her hand along the edge of the dresser, leaving trails in the dust, forcing Will to say, 'Aunt Flip, would that be all right?'

'Mm? Yes, if she wants. She's welcome.'

Ruby murmured her thanks. That was Philippa all over. Anger like a meteor shower, accusations whizzing, then in the blink of an eye, all nice again.

Determined not to be beholden for more than one quick shower, she said to Will, 'If you have the number of a heating engineer… Ideally, one who is still in the land of the living?'

Will said he'd look at the boiler himself, later. 'I've got to ferry Edna to Hollesford first, for her weigh-in. You'll have noticed she's on the large side.'

Ruby had noticed. 'I always thought rescue dogs were generally all skin and bone,' she said.

'There are more forms of abuse than under-feeding.' Will asked if she'd like a lift into town.

'No, I'm fine.' It was a reflex refusal. It would have been useful to go with him, but she was reluctant to build up any sense of obligation to either Philippa or Will.

He didn't seem offended. 'OK. Aunt Flip, ready to go?'

Philippa turned, a framed photo in her hand. She'd taken it from a drawer in the dresser. She looked at it, then at Ruby. 'You take after my brother.'

'After Grandad? Yes, that's what Mum says.'

'Norman's hair was black when he was young,' Philippa continued, ignoring Ruby's comment. 'And his eyes were blue, like mine. There's not a bit of Irene in you, to my way of seeing, nor much of your mother.'

'There has to be something of my father in my looks too,' Ruby said, pushing her hair aside to reveal wide cheekbones. 'It takes two to make a baby.'

'Hm,' Philippa grunted and set the picture down. 'I'll be off, then, and put the hot water on and find you a towel. Bring your own shampoo, if you don't like supermarket brand.'

Will whistled to Edna, who had gone back into the kitchen. The dog trotted in carrying the oven gloves Ruby had thrown to Will last night. They were butcher-stripe cotton, with a shade of blue that had been specially created for Pastel, the restaurant whose kitchen she'd run for four years. Pastel had survived lockdown and the exodus of most of its staff because Ruby had refused to let it fail. She had rebuilt its reputation and, last summer, there'd been a three-month waiting list for a table.

Pastel, Ruby Plait and Laurac had become fused together, as a famous landmark.

To conceal her confusion and disbelief at being here in Suffolk rather than in the pretty medieval town she missed so badly, she bent to take the gloves from the dog's mouth. 'Drop, good dog.'

Edna stared up at her with soulful eyes.

'Edna, drop. Good girl.'

Edna sat. Will released the gloves by pressing each side of the dog's gums.

Ruby accompanied them outside and saw an old Volvo parked the other side of the gate. It was olive green, its sills streaked with mud, and when Will shepherded Philippa towards it, Ruby felt she was seeing something else that didn't quite add up. It wasn't the kind of car she'd associate with any man under sixty. Will Keelbrook was a bit of a mystery, all told.

'I'll walk over in a few minutes,' she called, after Will had seen Philippa into the passenger seat and helped Edna into the rear.

Instead of getting into the driver's seat, he approached Ruby, saying, 'Come round the back with me.'

'What?'

He was already walking towards the side of the house, so she followed. She found him staring down at the leather suitcase she'd left by the back door.

'Did the chimney fire spread into the house?' He looked faintly sick at the idea.

'No.' She explained how she'd found the suitcase. 'My tenants had a bonfire before they left.'

He nodded, thoughtfully. 'I remember seeing flames and smoke on Halloween weekend. What else did they burn?'

'Personal stuff. I want to look inside the case but I can't open it.'

Will inspected the tarnished locks. He then turned the case around, reached into one of the reinforced pockets of his trousers and pulled out a Swiss army knife. Using the blade, he dug out the rear hinges.

'It didn't occur to me to do that.' She crouched down beside him, intrigued. But when Will lifted the lid, she saw only a lot of old books. They reeked of damp, but apart from scorching at the corners, they'd escaped the flames. 'How weird,' Ruby said. 'Why put them in a suitcase? I mean, if you're burning books, wouldn't you just hurl them into the flames?'

Will stood up. 'I don't know; I'm not the book-burning type. Better not keep Philippa waiting. Anything I can get you from town?'

'Er... no thanks.' She hardly noticed him go because she'd discovered that one of the books was a diary, and, on opening it, had seen written in faded ink on the flyleaf the name 'Irene Boulter'.

'Boulter' had been Irene's name before she married.

The suitcase wasn't junk left by the tenants. These were precious things of her grandmother's.

# 4

A Westminster clock chimed two p.m. as Philippa put a mug of fig leaf tea in front of Ruby. They were in the snug kitchen at Westumble, a stove kicking out heat. Still, Ruby was troubled. Before walking over to knock at Philippa's door, she'd taken the contents of the suitcase into the house. Along with a stash of her grandma's old schoolbooks and some charming, naive paintings, she'd found diaries dating from the war years. They were the personal memories of a grandmother whose life had touched hers far too infrequently, and when she laid them out on the dining table, Ruby had felt a piercing sense of loss.

She wanted to ask Philippa how those books and papers had ended up as bonfire fodder and, in a way, she hoped her tenants were responsible. The alternative was that somebody with a key had entered the house, and attempted to destroy personal mementoes. Philippa had a key. She'd had one for years; but would she have had the strength to carry a suitcase full of books outside? And the desire to set fire to it? Surely not. Will? No, unless he was a terrific actor. He hadn't shown a flicker of recognition when he broke the hinges.

Philippa joined Ruby at the table and urged her to try her tea. Ruby took a cautious sip.

'Better than it looks?'

'Much better. It tastes like ordinary tea, only milder. Auntie—'

'Fig leaf tea is supposed to be good for bones. After my Ronnie died, I went on a health kick. No more tea-and-two-sugars, no more cherry brandy of an evening. I still get a fancy for cake and cream, though.'

Ruby made an effort to sound as if nothing were wrong. 'You're looking good on it, Auntie Philippa. Your hair is amazing.'

Without the woolly hat, Philippa's luminous white hair hung in a bob. She touched it and sighed. 'Once you've passed eighty, it's more a case of continual maintenance than glowing health.' She peered at Ruby's chest. 'You've lost weight, girl. You were quite buxom, as I remember.'

It was true. The black jersey she'd been wearing since yesterday had once been figure-hugging. Now it bagged on her. 'I worked flat-out during lockdown,' Ruby said, 'and there's something about being surrounded by food that makes you forget to eat.'

'I'd have said it was the opposite.'

'Well, I forgot to eat.' Before Philippa could probe why she was no longer in her French kitchen, Ruby aired something that had played on her mind since her first conversation with her aunt. 'Did Grandma Irene feel she'd been abandoned at Maple Court?'

Philippa sipped her tea, holding her mug with fingers that showed a faint tremor. At last she said, 'Yes. Because you and your mum went back to France and left her.'

That wasn't accurate. Ruby's mother had begun the process

of relocating to Britain – not a simple matter – only to be caught out by events.

'I had to go back,' Ruby said, 'or I'd have lost my job and my home. Mum intended to move into Oak Apple so she could be near Grandma.'

'Only she didn't. The road to hell is paved with "intended to".'

Ruby put down her mug. 'Let me be clear. Mum went back to Laurac to find someone to look after her house and to organise her finances. She got caught out by the lockdown. She couldn't travel.'

Philippa looked unconvinced. 'That's what they said when I visited Maple Court. Not that I could sit with Irene. That wasn't allowed. I had to wave at her, from outside a window. "Her daughter will come when she can" was the story.'

'Mum was stuck in France, from March to July, and while she was moving heaven and earth to get out, Grandma died.' On 1st May, in the heart of the springtime Irene so loved. 'You have to understand, Auntie Philippa, lockdown rules were even tougher in France than they were here. Mum needed a permit to travel even to the shops—'

'I've heard it all before, Ruby.'

*And you didn't listen then, either!* Ruby drank her tea and shifted in her chair. She could feel ash in her hair and couldn't wait to get under a shower. Philippa had greeted her with the words, 'The water needs another twenty minutes.' She'd peered at Ruby, and sniffed. 'Been raking out the coals?'

'No. Tidying up a bonfire.' Philippa had visibly jumped and, as now, had peered at Ruby as if the comment had provoked a troubling question.

Ruby now asked another, seemingly innocent, one. 'Did you keep a wartime diary, Auntie?'

'What's brought that up? No, never. I was born in '34. I was a nipper when war broke out.' She half got to her feet, then sat down again. 'That water must have come up to heat. I won't show you upstairs. I try not to climb them after I've come down in the morning, not till I go to bed again. I'm not saying I can't...' Philippa's rising tone suggested to Ruby that somebody had questioned her ability to remain in her home. 'It's my choice and I have a cleaner comes twice a week, to keep things tidy.'

'I'll find my way, Auntie.' Ruby picked up the fresh clothes she'd brought along.

'Use whatever you like up there. Towels are in the airing cupboard.'

The shower ran hot and fast, and Ruby could have stayed under it for an hour, except that concern for Philippa's energy bill made her turn it off after five minutes. It felt good, as she towelled herself, to smell of soap and herbal shampoo. She found a hairdryer in a drawer, a modern antique which howled like a ghost but dried her hair in record time. Putting it back, she couldn't resist a rummage. Philippa's cleaner obviously didn't tidy inside the drawers, which were full of lipsticks in old-fashioned tubes, caked mascara and innumerable bijou boxes. She picked up a vanity case, made from Bakelite, the precursor to plastic. It was painted to look like tortoiseshell. *Supremely collectible.* Flipping the lid, the scent of violets swelled up from a swansdown powder puff. Ruby patted some to the back of her hand. Too pale for her. The case had other little compartments, but before Ruby could look inside, a loud bump from below made her conscious of Philippa, alone downstairs.

She dressed quickly in her clean things and went down to find Philippa feeding logs into the wood burner. 'I can manage,' Philippa snapped, before Ruby could offer help.

'Did something drop?'

'Huh? Oh, yes, this.' Philippa showed her a pair of long-nosed pincers, the kind that lifted hot logs and coals. 'I let them fall on the hearth. You look a bit peachier, dear.'

'I feel it. Fabulous shower.'

'Will made me put it in, said my old one wheezed like a village pump.'

Ruby took a long look around the room. Westumble Farm was the same age as Oak Apple, but even more like Hansel and Gretel's domain with its crooked timbers and diamond-pane windows. She must have been here before but she wasn't certain. Perhaps when Philippa's husband, Ronnie, had been alive because she remembered being in a kitchen with a round-faced, red-cheeked man alongside a younger, dark-haired Philippa. What she didn't remember was the sheer number of china teapots, figurines and dolls on every shelf, nor the horse-shoes and brasses attached to every beam. No niche was left uncluttered.

'You're quite a collector. Do you still have cats?' Ruby asked. She'd stroked a pair of purring ginger cats here, or so her memory told her.

'If you're thinking of Tiger and Spice, they're long gone. I feed a few outdoor moggies. Feral ones that come for their food. They do a good job, keeping the mice down.'

'This was where Grandma Irene was born, wasn't it, in this house? I remember her saying once that they used to get mice inside the walls.'

Philippa nodded. 'She was born here and lived here till she married my brother and went to Oak Apple. I was born at Oak Apple, so we swapped places.'

Ruby took a breath. 'Could I ask you something? This morning I went out and found—'

'Hi, you two.' Will bumped the door open, supermarket bags in both hands. Edna pushed past him and made a direct line to Ruby. 'I bought oat milk, Aunt Flip,' he said. 'Couldn't get the almond stuff. Edna, leave Ruby alone.'

'She's all right.'

Edna's coat was deep reddish-brown, her eyes like melting chocolate buttons. As the dog rested her chin on her knee, Ruby wondered how an animal this beautiful had needed to be rescued.

'If you still need to shop, I've got to go into Hollesford again,' Will said. 'The builder's merchant hadn't got what I ordered, but it's arriving after lunch.'

His eyes rested on her hair, which gleamed when it was freshly washed. Ruby was woman enough to be pleased that he was seeing her showered and fragrant, wearing a cashmere top that hung a little off one shoulder. She imagined the scales tipping slightly back in her favour.

'So, would you like a lift?' he asked.

'Yes, OK.' She'd intended to spend this afternoon investigating a broadband connection as the signal on her phone wasn't great. The house needed proper Wi-Fi, as that would be the first thing any prospective buyer asked about, according to the estate agent. Looking at her watch to see what time it was now, she exclaimed, 'Oh, damn.'

She turned her arm to show Will her watch face. She must have cracked its glass trying to break the locks on the suitcase. It was a waterproof quartz which she'd won in a professional cooking contest. The Euro Hoteliers' Top Young Chef Award, to be precise. Swiss-made, as the competition had been run from Zürich, and a proper chef's watch, designed to strap around the forearm rather than the wrist. It was a link to the time when her career had been at its zenith. 'Is there a jeweller in Hollesford?'

'Think so.' Will looked at Philippa, who seemed suddenly guarded. 'I remember you going somewhere to get a battery for your watch, Aunt Flip,' he said.

'Lubbock's on the Thoroughfare,' Philippa said, before adding a discouraging note. 'Only, they close early.'

'In that case—' Ruby got to her feet.

Will said he'd pick her up in fifteen minutes. He went, leaving Edna to stretch herself out in front of the stove.

Ruby thanked Philippa for the tea and use of the shower,

only to be stopped at the door by the words, 'What's really brought you back here?'

She turned and met Philippa's eye, her mind full of the question she hadn't managed to ask: *Who tried to burn Grandma's diaries?* But that could wait. She answered without prevarication, 'The house. I've either got to re-let it or make a more final decision. Tenants are a liability, but empty houses are a disaster waiting to happen.'

'What does your mother make of you getting Oak Apple, and not her?'

'She's fine. Mum specifically asked not to inherit the farm.'

'I know that, but now it's yours I wondered if she'd had second thoughts. There have been Plaits at Oak Apple since the eighteen hundreds.'

This was sounding too *Cold Comfort Farm* for Ruby's liking and she became brisk. 'Mum isn't bothered. She believes property is a tie and that money is energy, which flows through your life, if you let it.'

'Amanda talks a lot of twaddle, in my opinion. What colour is her hair these days? Sky-blue? Pink?'

Irritated at having her mother disparaged, Ruby said crisply, 'It's grey. My plans are to sell the farm. I've already booked an estate agent.' It struck Ruby then that she expected truth from her great aunt, while withholding it herself. An eye for an eye, a truth for a truth. 'You asked me what really brought me back here and you might as well know. I broke up with my partner and, because of the particular circumstances, I suffered a mini breakdown. We worked together and I couldn't face him. Or my kitchen. Long story short, it blew my job out of the water and I needed...' Ruby couldn't finish, because she didn't know how the story ended.

'You needed to run away,' Philippa supplied for her.

'Pretty much.' Let Aunt Flip win this round. It wasn't far

from the truth. 'Auntie, did you know my ex-tenants tried to burn a suitcase full of Grandma's things?'

'Hey?'

'Books, diaries, letters. They had a bonfire and incinerated a lot of financial and medical records, which is their concern. What I do care about is that they somehow got hold of family stuff and I'm confused because Mum and I cleared out Oak Apple Farm. We left nothing important lying around, so how did they come to have Grandma's diaries?'

For a moment, it seemed as though Philippa would reveal something. But then the shutters came down and she gestured towards the door. 'I don't know what you're saying, dear, but you're letting the warm air out, and you mustn't keep Will waiting.'

From her window, Philippa watched her go. Young Ruby got her dark hair and blue eyes from Norman and it looked like she favoured Norman in character, too. 'Dogged' was a good description.

After Irene had been shipped off to Maple Court, and Ruby and her mother went back to France, Philippa had gone through every cupboard and chest at Oak Apple Farm. As Ruby had said, there hadn't been much left. Irene's clothes and shoes had gone to charity shops. Pictures and ornaments and Irene's best china were in trunks up in the attic, wrapped in newspaper. Family photographs were in the dining hall dresser. Ruby and Amanda had gone back to France, leaving her, Philippa, with a key. She'd found the suitcase with the diaries under the double bed in what had been Norman and Irene's room. Philippa had been down on her knees because she'd been searching high and low for something else. And there was the suitcase, pushed so far underneath, she'd had to get almost flat to see it.

Mary Daker, a friend in the village, had got her son to pull it out. Philippa remembered vividly how she'd felt when she had seen the contents. Like a sewing machine was tacking across the flesh of her heart. She'd had Colin Daker lug the suitcase with its contents into the garden, along with some old papers she'd found behind the dresser, and asked him to set light to everything.

'Wind's in the wrong direction,' he'd told her. 'You'll have sparks flying across the road to set your thatch on fire.' Colin had promised to come back and burn it for her once the wind had dropped. It sounded like he hadn't, and that suitcase had sat waiting until those hippy-dippy tenants of Ruby's had decided to have their own bonfire.

If Ruby saw fit to read those diaries, she'd soon be asking questions. More questions.

'Don't fret. She's selling and will be away soon,' Philippa whispered to a china cat she picked off the windowsill. The cat was part of a set she'd bought from an ad in the *TV Times* – 'Charming, collectible feline family' – and paid for in instalments. 'Londoners will buy Oak Apple, and when I'm gone, that's our family book closed. Ruby can badger me all she likes and I'll say I can't remember.' Philippa put the china cat back in its place. 'When you're eighty-eight, nobody argues when you tell them that.'

## 5

Hearing Will hoot his horn from the bottom of the drive, Ruby grabbed her shoulder bag. He was talking into his phone as she climbed into the Volvo beside him, saying, 'Don't dislocate your shoulder trying to open it, Mrs Crouch. I'll be along soon as I can. Maybe tomorrow? No – I understand. I'll call in a couple of hours. See you then.'

'Who's dislocating a shoulder?' Ruby manoeuvred the seat back a few inches. Philippa's short legs meant it had been pulled well forward.

'An old lady on Strawberry Avenue. That's a cluster of sheltered homes just along from the village hall, where the old jam and pickle factory used to be. Her back door has wedged shut.'

'And you're going to open it for her?'

'I'll take it off its hinges and plane it, then put it back. So yes, I am.'

'Wow. Robin Hood?'

He gave a frown and she wished she hadn't sounded quite so snarky. 'I just mean, you seem to spend a lot of time helping old ladies,' she said.

'That sounds really creepy. Would you like to rephrase?'

'Philippa, Mrs Crouch...'

'That's two, and one of them is my godmother.'

'Aunt Philippa's your godmother? I didn't realise.'

'And I've offered to look at your broken heating, so am I guilty of targeting young women too?'

'Course not. You're twisting a comment made off the cuff.'

Will waved hello to somebody pushing a wheelbarrow of logs along the street. 'Mrs Crouch could phone around for a carpenter and wait six weeks before anyone turns up. Meanwhile, she can't let her little dog out into the back garden. We're a small village, Ruby, and we operate as a community. I lend a hand sometimes and, yes, I help Philippa because she means a very great deal to me.' He took his eye off the road for a moment, his glance catching her full in the face.

'Point taken.' She recognised the dig at her supposed neglect of her grandma. As they drove out of the village, she pretended to scroll through her phone for messages. She felt aggrieved. Misjudged. And at the same time, very guilty.

In Hollesford, which was a modest-sized market town, Will dropped her at one end of a pedestrianised street known as the Thoroughfare, where the independent shops were located. He'd pick her up at the supermarket in an hour. 'Which is that way,' he said, pointing to the square church tower.

She found Lubbock Brothers, Jewellers and Watch Menders, next to a newsagent. Despite Philippa's prediction, it was still open, though there was nobody behind the counter. Ruby spent a few minutes looking at a display of vintage jewellery and listening to the unhurried ticking of a clock. Finally, a man ambled in from the back, comically surprised to see a customer. Though it was a quiet Monday afternoon, he wore a collar and tie beneath a knitted jumper.

Returning his 'Good afternoon,' Ruby put her watch on the counter. 'Are you Mr Lubbock? I'm hoping you can replace the glass on this.'

'Clement Lubbock, the more handsome brother.' He picked up the watch. 'Quality. Swiss. Yes, I can get you a new crystal – that's what we call the glass on the front of a watch – but I'll have to order it in.'

'No problem.' Something in the man's easy manner made her act on impulse. Digging into her bag, she produced a small box. 'Do you buy rings?'

'I prefer to sell them,' Clement Lubbock said wryly as he extracted a gold ring with sapphires each side of a solitaire diamond. He gave her a beetling look. 'Engagement ring?'

'It's whatever you want it to be. It cost two thousand euros.' She kept all the inflection out of her voice. 'Before you ask, it's mine to sell. Is it something you'd be interested in?'

He moved his mouth, indicating *Maybe, maybe not*. He was older than she'd first assumed, his hair fine as silk under a slick of pomade. 'I couldn't offer more than three hundred, miss.' Seeing her reaction, he explained that new stock came to him on a sale-or-return basis. 'For me to lay out money, a ring has to be something special.'

She'd thought it was special, when she'd put her credit card across the jeweller's counter in Laurac. 'Three hundred is all you could offer?'

'It's a nice diamond, but when people can buy new rings on easy credit, second-hand doesn't hold its value. Unless it's an antique and—'

'Something special,' she finished for him. She wondered if she ought to walk out, but only in movies did the man behind the counter yell out, 'All right, five hundred, my final offer!' This ring hadn't brought her much luck, had it? 'Would you consider four hundred?'

Mr Lubbock held the ring to the light. 'I'd consider it and say, "three hundred and twenty tops". I have to allow for a mark-up, you understand?'

Yes, she understood commerce. 'All right. Could you

transfer the money straight away?' She was thinking about Will's promise to service her boiler, and that she would insist on paying him the rate for the job. 'I have a few bills coming in.' Broadband. A new stove. The roof.

'I could transmit the money straight away, but I'd need your ID. And an address.'

Her passport was still in her bag and as Mr Lubbock scrutinised it, she wrote, 'Ruby Plait, Oak Apple Farm, Flixfield' along with her bank details.

He looked intrigued. 'Oak Apple Farm rings a bell.'

'Perhaps you knew my grandmother, Irene Plait.'

'Mm, I was more familiar with Mr Plait. Was it Norman?'

'He was my grandad.'

'He was here a lot over the years, buying little things for his wife. I always knew when her birthday was coming around.'

She savoured the tiny insight, and then before she could stop herself, she asked, 'Did my grandma come in to sell anything of value? I'm talking about a few years back. Or maybe someone else did on her behalf, more recently?' She felt bad speaking her suspicions out loud, but Ruby didn't credit the story of Grandma Irene's jewellery going missing in the post. It felt far too convenient.

Clement Lubbock wrinkled his brow. 'Not that I recall. My brother might know – he has the photographic memory. Or he did. He got Covid quite badly, and is still getting over it. Irene Plait...' Ruby sensed him delving deep. 'I've an idea she did come in, some years ago. Not to sell, to have something mended. A necklace or a pendant. Something about it was odd.'

A pendant? Her heart rate stepped up. 'Odd, how?' she asked.

Clement shook his head. 'I'll ask Basil. My brother.'

'And the ring? Do we have a deal?'

'Given your grandfather was such a good customer, all right. I was sorry to hear about Irene's death, by the way. There was a note in the local paper,' he explained. 'That wartime generation is passing.'

'Yes they are, sadly.' But some of them leave diaries behind, Ruby reminded herself, picturing the green, blue and grey books airing on the dining table. 1939 through to 1944, so not the whole span of the war. She'd had a quick flip-through earlier, and discovered that Irene had covered the pages in such tiny handwriting, she'd not be able to read it without help. She asked Mr Lubbock if he sold magnifying glasses.

'No, but I can lend you one.' He found her a rather beautiful one with a wooden handle. 'Bring it back when you've done whatever you're doing.'


Ruby was pushing a trolley into the supermarket when her phone alerted her to a bank transfer. Three hundred and twenty pounds. *Au revoir* engagement ring, thank you Mr Lubbock. She put vegetables, olive oil, coffee beans and flour into her trolley, reading the labels as she went. It wasn't just the brands that felt foreign; the shop's layout confused her – the food organised in different aisles to what she was used to. Her hour was up before she'd reached the wine section. Will was probably outside in his car and if she kept him waiting, he'd think her rude and entitled. More than he already did.

She put back a bottle of Cabernet Sauvignon. On her last trip two years ago, she'd noticed how expensive wine was in England compared to France, and since then it had rocketed in price. She exchanged it for a bottle of low-cost gin and some tonic. It would keep the cold of Oak Apple Farm at bay – though nowhere near as well as an actual boiler repair man. As she walked away from the checkout, a card on a noticeboard caught her eye and she photographed it on her phone. She spotted Will's Volvo at once, as it was the longest, and muddiest, vehicle in the car park. He was leaning back against his headrest, eyes closed. She woke him when she put her shopping behind the passenger seat, next to his from Easifix Builders Merchants.

'Sorry, it took longer than I thought,' she said as she got in.

He stared blearily at her. 'No worries. I go to bed too late and I was grabbing a power nap.'

'What is it you do?' She fastened her seat belt. 'Apart from un-wedge doors.'

'Whatever anybody wants to pay me to do.'

'Like a handyman?'

'If someone pays me to be handy, I'll be handy.'

'I'll remember that.' She was still picking up an edge to his tone.

He asked if she'd found the jewellers'.

'I did.' She declined to say more and he didn't ask. As he drove away, she called the number on the card she'd photographed. A man answered after two rings. 'Hi,' she said. 'That ladies' bike you're advertising, is it still available?' It was, and the seller lived in Hollesford. Ruby turned to Will. 'Do you know a Spindle Close?'

'No, but satnav will. You want to buy a bike, off an ad?'

'I need sustainable transport and it's thirty pounds. "To be sold through no fault of its own, as wife has given up", apparently.'

Will gave a dry smile. 'More likely, the bike's given up.'

'Then I shall love it back to health.'

Ten minutes later, she was standing outside a neat bunga-low, making a transaction with a stranger through her phone banking app. One cheerful ping later, she was the proud owner of an electric-blue ladies' mountain bike, and a hot-pink cycle helmet thrown in for free.

Will looked on as she buckled on the helmet, then pointed to the rear of his car. 'I can fit the bike in; you don't have to ride it home.'

'But I want to.'

'Without having it checked? What if a wheel comes off?'

'I'll figure it out. I like living dangerously.'

He shrugged. 'Your call. What's your phone number?'

She gave it to him, asking why he wanted to know.

'So I can phone you, and if you get stuck, you'll have my number.'

'To rescue me?' The decision to sell her engagement ring and abandon everything it had represented had made her touchy. Tearful, inside. 'I can cycle eight miles without supervision.'

'OK.' Will got into the car, lowering the window to ask, 'D'you still want me to check out your boiler?'

'Yes... thank you.' Was anybody really this nice? Kindness could be passive aggressive, as much a burden as neglect. She said, 'I think it's the gas pressure, which means getting a proper man out.'

'As opposed to a handyman. I'll see what I can do.'

'Or it's possible nobody paid the gas bill.'

He was laughing at her, which felt worse than him judging her. When you've dropped from alpha to zero in the blink of an eye, you don't want to be somebody's light relief.

She waited until his car had disappeared before getting on the bike. She'd cycled everywhere when she'd worked in the big city – Toulouse, in her case – but when she'd taken on the head chef position at Pastel, a car had come with the job. She hadn't sat on a bicycle for ages. A couple of circuits of Spindle Close helped her find her balance. There was a moment of jeopardy when she turned onto the main road and set off on the wrong side and a car swerved, sounding its horn frantically. She pulled over to recover and a message came up on her phone. It was from Didier Frémont. *Putain*, this wasn't the moment to hear from her ex. How weird, as if he knew, subliminally, that she'd offloaded her engagement ring.

The message read, *Ruby, où-es tu?* He'd been to her mother's house, he wrote, and the neighbour had told him that Ruby and her mother had left separately, pulling suitcases. *Call me please – dès que possible.* Soon as you can.

And a follow-up message. *I need those projections you did for Pastel, it's urgent.*

She almost threw her phone to the ground. She was meant to jump through hoops, was she, after she'd found him in *her* bed, under *her* duvet, entangled with Lily Bouchard? Lily bloody Bouchard, whose father owned Pastel, where she'd sweated blood and tears all those many months!

'You can whistle, Didier. I'll call you when hell freezes over.'

Three hours later, her cheeks smarting from cycling into a freezing headwind, Ruby wheeled the bike up the drive of Oak Apple Farm. It was dark, and the moon was up. She could have made it home much quicker if she'd followed the maps app on her phone, but she'd turned her phone off in case Didier tried messaging her again. Sustained exercise had taken the edge off her anger.

Will's Volvo was blocking her gate and she found him in the house, by the kitchen sink with the taps running.

He turned, hearing her come in. 'I was starting to think you might have gone into a ditch.'

'I got lost, but in a good way. Was it the gas pressure?' Her voice was husky from pedalling in the cold.

'No. Because you have oil-fired central heating, Ruby. We don't have gas in the village. Never have, never will. Didn't you know?'

Maybe she had known but had forgotten. 'Oh. Fair enough.'

'I suppose you weren't ever here long enough to work it out.'

'This is getting stale.' She slammed her shopping bags down

on the floor. 'I'm sure Philippa has fed you stories of us neglecting my grandmother, but has she ever mentioned that my mum left home in France to come back here, and was turned back at Calais because she didn't have the correct permit? Mum drove overnight, trying to beat the lockdown deadline. She was fined and given a severe telling-off by the French border police.'

'I didn't know.'

'Now you do. People love to invent myths, and after repeating them a few times, they start to believe them.'

Will lifted a hand, showing a reluctance to be drawn in. 'You've about half a tank of oil; that's the good news,' he said. 'The bad news is I can't get the boiler working.'

She groaned, ready to crouch down and cry.

'It's probably a blocked nozzle, or you need a set of electrodes. I'll give you the name of a heating engineer.'

Ruby looked at the running taps. 'I haven't got leaking pipes as well, have I?'

Will turned off the tap. 'You're fine. The water's been standing in the pipes and round here you get limescale so there's a chance of water-borne bacteria.'

'Now you tell me. I've already drunk from these taps.'

'What – direct from the tap?'

'No, I filled the kettle.'

'That's OK, if it's boiled.' He'd kept his coat on. For her part, she was cooling down fast. Didn't he ever take off that Barbour cap? Perhaps he was thinning on top and was self-conscious. Didier's hair was thick. Coal black, darker than hers. He let it fall forward for his social media profile pictures.

'Could we get that heating engineer today?' she asked.

'Do my best.' Will pulled away from the sink and knocked into her shopping bags. Her bottle of value gin rolled out.

They watched it complete a trundling journey across the floor. Neither of them said anything. Will, after giving her a long look through hooded eyes, left her to it, pulling his phone out of his pocket as he walked off.

'My name's Ruby, and I can't get through a day without gin,' she muttered as she unpacked her shopping. When everything was put away, she went into the dining hall and turned diary pages, knowing they'd dry out faster when she had the heating on. Fetching out Mr Lubbock's magnifying glass, she opened one of Irene's old school exercise books. In the glow of the wall lights, she made out the owner's name easily enough: 'Irene Boulter. Form Two. Hollesford Secondary School'. The first essay inside was entitled 'The Vikings in Suffolk'. If she was going to read through this lot, she'd need an angled light with a decent bulb.

Her phone rang, a number she didn't recognise. A man spoke, local from his accent.

'George Oaks, heating services.'

What, so soon?

'Will Keelbrook gave me your number just now, Miss Plait. It so happens, I've completed a job your side of Hollesford. Want me to come over straight away?'

'Please!' Ruby could have danced with relief and sent heart-felt thanks to Will. Maybe, gruff manner to the contrary, he was what he seemed. Kind.

'This side of Hollesford' probably meant twenty minutes away. She used the time to read the essay her grandma had written at around twelve years of age.

'When the Vikings met the Saxons as were already here, and farming their land, they got mightily wrong from them. My dad once found an axe-head while digging beets.'

Ruby smiled. 'Getting wrong'... God, she remembered that little phrase. It was one of Grandad's. 'Don't you do that, dear, or we'll get wrong from your grandma.' It covered a multitude of bases. Everything from a severe telling-off from the border police, as in her mother's case, or – presumably – a whack from a battle axe. Enjoying this glimpse into her grandma's youthful mind, she separated more pages and out slipped a rectangle of mottled card.

She took it to the wall, so the lights shone right on it. It was an invitation, neatly written in black ink and with a hand-painted design around the edge.

### *The family of Miss Irene Boulter invite you to the engagement party of their daughter*

To Grandad Norman, obviously, though his name was hidden under a layer of mildew. The only other part that was readable was the time and date.

### *4 December 1943*

### *4 p.m. at Flixfield Village Hall*

Ruby did the maths... seventy-nine years plus a few days ago, her grandparents had celebrated their engagement. But for a sturdy leather suitcase, this little fragment would have been lost. Burned to ash.

Because somebody didn't care – or because they cared too much? Hearing wheels on the drive, she put down the invitation and went to let in the boiler man but her mind lingered on this latest discovery. The family of Miss Irene Boulter... *her* family. *Her* people, whom she had never really got to know.

Was it too late; could she dig back through these papers, and finally make their acquaintance?

## 6

IRENE

Irene got off the bus from Hollesford a stop early to see how the new airbase was progressing. She wasn't prepared for the smoking mountain of brick and timber that had once been Boundary Farm. Everything was changed. Even the mossy old gate had made way for a new entrance road where a steel barrier offered a clear challenge: *Halt, come no further!*

A guard turned at the sound of her footsteps. 'Afternoon, ma'am.' He was Black, and he spoke with a drawl like the man she'd met at the village hall dance. Theo. But unlike Theo, he didn't quite look at her, almost as though someone stood next to her and he was addressing that person instead.

She hesitated before asking, 'Is Sergeant Theo Robinson on the base today?'

'I believe I saw him head to the south side with a work detail, ma'am. You want me to pass on a message?' There was no fracture in the immaculate politeness.

She said, 'Just tell him, Irene Boulter says hello.' She spoke slowly because Theo had found her accent hard to follow.

Harder than she'd found his. 'And, um, and please tell him, I enjoyed our dance.'

The soldier continued to stare across Irene's shoulder. 'I'll be sure to tell him, ma'am.'

Thanking him and walking on, Irene dug a sherbet lemon from the bag hitched over her shoulder. In town, she'd treated herself to a quarter of mixed barley sugar and sherbets. The woman who'd scooped the sweets from their jars and inscribed an X on her ration book had told her that more rationing was on its way, 'For anything worth eating, so get these down your throat while you can, my woman.'

A few doors on from the confectioner's, Irene had bought sewing cotton and a bit of blue satin, which didn't need coupons because it was an offcut. Most of her clothing coupons went to her dad, who wore out the knees and elbows of his clothes because of his condition. She knew what she was going to do with the satin.

'You've got the bluest eyes I ever saw,' Theo had said as they danced his first ever foxtrot at the hall. He'd picked up the steps without fuss. They'd foxtrotted twice more, after which she'd partnered Theo's friend Duke in a reel called The Lancers, and then danced a waltz with Fletch, who seemed to know the steps by magic. Then another waltz, this time with Theo again. *Theodore* was his full, proper name. She'd have danced the next dance, and the next with him, except her mother came up, saying, 'The men are getting the trestles out for supper. Lend a hand in the kitchen, Irene.'

'Oh, Mum!' There were lots of helping hands; they didn't need hers.

'Kitchen, please, Irene.'

Her mother's tone had been warningly soft, but, like a schoolgirl downing an illicit glass of alcohol, Irene had discovered defiance. She'd kept hold of Theo's arm and said, 'Mum, this is Sergeant Theodore Robinson. Sergeant Robinson, this is my mother, Mrs Violet Boulter.'

'I'm pleased to meet you, ma'am.'

'Yes, the same, I'm sure.' Violet Boulter barely accepted Theo's proffered handshake and waved Irene towards the kitchen. 'Mrs Prentice wants help setting out the cutlery.'

Irene overheard her mother asking Theo if he'd been introduced to Norman. 'He's over there, speaking with Mr Prentice, our vicar. Norman is Irene's fiancé. Shall I take you over, and make the introductions?'

After that, it was bad to worse. The hall's coal-fired range – there was no gas or electricity in Flixfield – had overheated and crisped the supper's baked potatoes to the point you couldn't get a knife through them. The cheese on them was like melted lino. What was optimistically called 'mixed salad' turned out to be butter beans stirred up with sliced gherkins and beetroot. They were 'seconds' from J.P. Rattray's, Irene's workplace. It all looked horrible, pale beans coated in beetroot juice, as if they'd been rolled in blood.

Theo and his friends had tucked in. Did they not get enough food on the base? They certainly didn't have the smartest uniforms. Duke and Fletch's were worn at the cuff, and a patch on Theo's tunic was the wrong shade of green. Irene's mother had sat next to him, with Irene's father in his wheelchair on the other side. Like they were hemming him in.

What did Theo and his friends make of them all? Looking around her through newly awakened eyes, Irene's neighbours suddenly seemed all the more wind-burned, their hearty, homely chatter utterly dull. Frayed collars, make-do dresses. She laid down her knife and fork, impatient for the dancing to start again. One more waltz with Norman might earn her the last dance with Theo. She wished it might be a slow waltz, so they could talk more, but the last dance of the evening was always the Lambeth Walk, which sent everybody home in high spirits.

Theo had told her he was a 'First Sergeant' in the Engineer Regiment, but not the guy in charge. 'Not by a long shot.' This was his first time abroad. 'From Georgia to Florida, to Louisiana to over here.' He and 'the boys' lodged in Nissen huts, which, he said, 'Might as well be inside out, for all the heat they keep in. We don't sleep too good, so we sit by the stove playing gin rummy. Your country sure is cold, ma'am.'

She'd said, 'Sorry.'

He'd laughed at that. 'Apology accepted.'

His laughter had been like a glass of champagne, or how she imagined champagne would be, bubbles fizzing in your stomach. Dancing with Theo, she'd not stopped looking into his face, so different in tone and colour from hers. From anybody's she knew. His bones were clear-cut and his skin dark like oak, not because it was tanned or weathered, but because he came from that place called Georgia. His eyes were velvet black. He'd called her 'Irene, fair as a dream'.

He wasn't Randolph Scott; he was better because he was real. During supper, as she speared a butter bean that was desperate to escape, she'd thought how stupid they'd all look doing the Lambeth Walk. Nothing like the strutting Pearly Kings and Queens in the film of that name, more like turkeys turned out onto hot sawdust.

She didn't get to dance it anyway, as Little Flip ruined everything by being sick. Philippa was always being sick and it was Irene's mother, and Irene, who'd taken her into the cloakroom and cleaned her up.

'Get her home, will you?' Violet Boulter had wrung out Philippa's dress over a bucket. 'Wrap her in your coat, Irene, and take her back to Oak Apple. It's past her bedtime by a mile.'

'I want Norman,' Philippa had whimpered.

He could have her, too, Irene had thought crossly. Little

Flip was Norman's responsibility, and with him out of the way, she'd have a clear run at dancing again with Theo Robinson. 'He can take her home, Mum.'

'She needs a good wash down, and that's not man's work, Irene. You've had your dancing for the night. And put Norman's nose out of joint. No point making bad into worse. You'll get wrong from him, as it is. Take Philippa home. Then you can come back.'

That wasn't so easy. At Oak Apple Farm, Irene got a telling-off from the bitter old crone who looked after Philippa, as if she'd made Little Flip eat whatever didn't agree with her. Irene was sent to fetch a tin bath from the scullery and seeing how the old woman's impatience made Philippa cry all the more, she had stayed and helped wash the little girl. There were marks on the child's back, which the old woman said Philippa had got by rolling about on the yard, in a temper.

Philippa had not once stopped wailing, 'I want Norman!'

By the time she got back to the hall, Theo and his platoon were gone and the Lambeth Walk had been walked and boxed away for next time. The lamps had been doused; the doors stood open. People were edging down the steps, guided by torches with brown paper over the glass.

Norman pounced. 'You made a fool of yourself tonight, Irene.'

Only one thing was important to her. 'Did he leave a message?'

'Who, that—' Norman used a word that struck against Irene's ear and made her want to lash out. 'Why would he do that?'

'Because he liked me, Norman. He found me interesting.'

'Oh, I'm sure he did.' Norman's clamp on her arm made her feel that, like the lamps, her soul was wrapped in brown paper.

She pulled away.

His tone changed, to coaxing. 'Irene, don't be like this.'

'Choosing who I dance with? You say I made a fool of myself, but better to make a fool of yourself than have somebody else do it for you.'

These words had stalked her over the week, as she laboured at J.P. Rattray's, peeling her way through a mountain of pickling onions. The tears they'd brought were a cover for her anger and confusion and she let them flow. She was the fool, thinking all day about someone she'd had four dances with. Theo Robinson wasn't in a position to come calling in the hope of seeing her. The 923rd Engineer Regiment was a military unit. He'd told her, 'I'm in the pay of Uncle Sam; I take his dollar and he gives me my orders.'

As she finished her sweet, she decided to take a shortcut home across the fields and struck off into the lane called Long Hedge, an old drover's route that separated Oak Apple Farm's land from the new airbase. And there he was – Theo Robinson – standing on the boundary and talking with a white soldier. Other men in khaki overalls stood waiting, as if for orders. These men were Black and their overalls were streaked with the same brown clay that clung to their shovels. Fingerless gloves insulated their hands from the bitter cold. The ancient hedge along the airfield side of the lane had gone and concrete posts marked its former course, piles of stone and soil at their feet like giant molehills. Rolls of chain-link wire were plonked down at intervals. As she got nearer, the men turned in her direction and she recognised two of her dance partners from last Saturday. When she raised a hand in greeting, they all looked away. Their shoulders were hunched, and she guessed they'd prefer to be working, to keep warm.

Theo's voice reached across a ditch which separated British from American territory. There was tension in his voice as he addressed the white soldier, who seemed about the same age as him. He was making a point, with what sounded like extreme care. The white soldier must have outranked Theo because his uniform had no muck on it, and he was wearing a padded jacket and a side cap. Nor did he have a shovel.

'The way it is, Lieutenant Macbeth, sir,' Theo was saying, 'we cannot follow the old hedge line on account of there being concrete underneath it. We keep hitting hard stuff.'

'Ain't no way there's concrete here, boy,' the lieutenant came back. 'Ain't no way. This is a goddamn cornfield. Folks round here don't lay concrete in cornfields. You tell your boys, dig harder.'

Irena was roused to resentment. What did an American know about 'folks round here'? What's more, the many spoil heaps suggested that Theo's men certainly knew how to dig. And hadn't he realised he was making them stand about with their teeth chattering?

Theo did not back down. 'You take my shovel, sir, try for yourself.'

'I ain't doing your job, boy.' The lieutenant's voice grated. 'You want to spend the night in a lockup, shivering your butt off?'

'There ain't no lockup here, sir. We're fixing to build that last.'

Theo's attempt at humour fell flat. His collar was grabbed, his face pulled close to the lieutenant's.

'Don't you give me no lip—' That word again, the one Norman had used, ripped through the March air like a gunshot. Theo was half pulled off his feet. The lieutenant was a big-muscled man, with knuckles that would put up well in a boxing ring.

Theo waited out the assault and when he was released, he adjusted his tunic and looked the lieutenant in the eye. 'We're thinking, sir, to take the fence at a curve, where the soil is looser.'

'You been thinking, boy? At a curve? Well, my, my.' Sarcasm dripped from the lieutenant's lips and it cut through

Irene's paralysis. She hated sarcasm; the foreman at work used it when talking to her and the other women. Sarcasm was like asking a child to put their hand in your pocket for a sweet, only you'd put razor blades there instead.

She stepped to the edge of the ditch. 'Excuse me, but he's right.'

She had an idea Theo had seen her, but the lieutenant turned, peering at her in surprise through the spindly blackthorn stems on the British side of the ditch.

'Ma'am?' the lieutenant said.

'Sergeant Robinson is right. This field was a smallholding and there was a row of pig sheds here. They got knocked down about ten years ago. The bricks and concrete were buried here to help drainage. That's what your spades are hitting.'

'That is mighty interesting to know, ma'am. Thank you for the intelligence.'

'Theo already told you.' She regretted instantly using Theo's name. 'I mean, it's none of my business, but the best person to talk to, if you want to know what lies under this soil, is Norman Plait. That's his land.' She gestured to Norman's fields on the other side of the lane. 'He'll save you a deal of wasted trouble.'

The lieutenant thanked her again. Irene sought Theo's gaze, but he raised his face to the sky like a farmer, judging the likelihood of rain. She got the message and walked on. It had shocked her to hear Theo spoken to like a ruffian, assaulted and called 'boy'. Called worse. The army was no charm school, but what she'd seen had felt like... how to put it? Like a blacksmith taking his hammer to a ladybird, or something equally harmless.

'Ma'am, one moment if you please.'

The lieutenant leapt the ditch and she felt a prickle of fear. She wasn't alone, there were Theo and the rest in calling distance, but would they – could they – help if she needed them to?

'I am Lieutenant Macbeth.'

'I'm Miss Boulter.'

'Happy to make your acquaintance, ma'am.' He spoke in a drawl like Theo's, but it wasn't the same because he only moved his mouth, not his eyes. Those eyes, blue like hers, had a glassy expression. He was younger than she'd thought, maybe twenty-one or two. Too young to be making men stand around in the nipping wind. He said, 'Seems you know Sergeant Robinson.'

'I don't know him; he came to our dance.'

'That so? Well, let me warn you, ma'am. All that land over there' – he indicated the former fields of Boundary Farm – 'is now American jurisdiction and we do things our own way.'

'So do we.'

His eyes flickered in surprise that she'd come back at him. Then he gave a closed-lip smile. 'We're going to be the best of neighbours, I know it. We sure like you folk, and hope you like us. But stay away from those boys.'

'They're men, not boys.'

'They're boys, Miss Boulter, and if any of them hang around with you, they'll get into severe trouble. I hope I make myself clear?'

'You mean, if Theo and I step out, we'll get wrong?'

'You won't "get wrong", Miss Boulter, with your *purdey* face. *He'll* get wrong. All kinds of wrong.' Macbeth gave her a cheerful salute and crossed back over the ditch. Irene heard him shout, 'You boys, get digging like the US soldiers you are. A few lousy Limey bricks ain't gonna stop us putting that fence up.'

Limey bricks? They spoke a foreign language. Still, she'd taken the warning. Stay away from Theo, or you'll put him in line for punishment.

A clod of clay landed on the ground in front of her and broke into pieces. She fancied Theo had thrown it, and it felt like a final message.

*Keep to your side of the fence, Irene.*

# 7

RUBY

The boiler engineer confirmed Will's prediction: Ruby's electrodes had sooted up. Fortunately, he had replacements in his van. By the time he left, the whole feel of Oak Apple Farm had changed. Dank cold was in retreat. The rooms felt less echoing, less abandoned. It was probably psychological, but who cared? George Oaks, oil-fired boiler specialist, was worth every penny of the one hundred and twenty-five pounds he'd charged her.

Wanting to share this small success, Ruby picked up her phone and pressed the first name on her frequent contact list. 'Come on, Maman, answer. *Vite, vite.*'

After three rings, her mother's phone went to message, and Ruby began to ramble, as if Amanda were in the next room. 'Alleluia, the heating's on. Oh, I found something today you'll be really interested in.' She was looking forward to talking about the diaries. 'So, Mum, I had tea with Auntie Philippa. Ever tasted fig leaf? She was by turns kindly and hostile and has a godson living in her barn. Did you know? He's protective of her and swings from being judgemental to really helpful, so I've got two of them messing with my head.' Ruby paced as she spoke. From the day she'd started work in a professional kitchen, she'd lost the knack of sitting down. Chefs have two positions, Didier used to say, upright and horizontal. He'd wanted to be a chef himself, but had found his niche as a front-of-house manager. He was still at Pastel, ensconced with Lily Bouchard in what had been Ruby's flat and, for all she knew, driving her car.

Having implored her mother to call as soon as she could, Ruby went to the dining table and arranged the open diaries in date order. They spanned a time period from January 1939 through to 1944, stopping abruptly in March of that year. Some of the pages were crammed with Irene's miniscule writing, and some were blank but that didn't surprise Ruby. She'd started diaries in her time, and then lost interest, or found herself too tired at night to bother. Worried the drying paper would create condensation, Ruby opened a couple of windows a small way and a cross-draught wafted a piece of card off the table. It was the engagement party invitation she'd found earlier.

## 4 December 1943

### 4 p.m. at Flixfield Village Hall

Her grandparents had married three months later, in March 1944. Had marriage to Norman stopped Irene's diary-keeping? 'Married women have never much time for writing'... Ruby vaguely remembered that from a book she'd studied in sixth form. Though clearly not studied well enough, as she couldn't recall the title. What she knew for sure was that she and her mother had come here in 1994, for her grandparents' golden wedding anniversary. She'd watched the horse racing on TV with Grandad while Grandma and her mum had cut sandwiches for a party in the kitchen. Grandad, who always seemed

to have a box of Maltesers on hand to share, had let her make
penny bets on each race and had paid out whenever her horse
won. 'Go on like this, Ruby, you'll bankrupt your old grandad.
That's three pence you've won already!'

A darker memory intruded, of Grandma coming in, wearing
her apron, every inch of her face a scowl. 'I'm glad you've got
time to sit about, having fun.'

'Isn't our daughter helping you with the tea?' Grandad had
asked.

'Amanda? She's about as much use in a kitchen as a bucket
of smoke.' Grandma Irene had stared at the TV – a silver
monster with a protruding back and the colour turned up too
rich. 'You wanted this party, Norman. I didn't. I never see why
people make such a fuss of being married.'

Grandad hadn't responded. Ruby had no memory of him
ever doing so when Grandma snapped at him.

Philippa was a different matter. Auntie Philippa had ripped
into Grandma as they washed up later, after the party.

'Nothing was ever good enough for you, was it, Irene? Not
Oak Apple Farm, nor fifty years with my brother!'

It had scared Ruby to discover that grown-ups could yell at
each other like that.

What had gone wrong with Irene and Norman, to turn love
into a weary test of endurance? The war? Norman had spent
his war years here. He'd told her so. 'I was in a reserved occupa-
tion. We had to make sure the country was fed, see.' Maybe the
fact that Norman had never put on a uniform had somehow
undermined Irene's love. Assuming she had loved him, of
course.

Ruby turned her arm to check the time, only to remember
that her watch was in the hands of Mr Lubbock, awaiting
repair. It must be late, anyway, as her stomach was rumbling.
She shredded vegetables and root ginger and stir-fried them
with tofu and tamari, a thick soy sauce. Eating at one end of the

big table, she got a blob of sauce on the invitation card. An urgent dab with kitchen paper revealed something she'd previously missed.

The design painted on it wasn't of flowers, as she'd at first assumed. A second look through the magnifying glass showed it to be red, white and blue flags. The Union Jack and the Stars and Stripes. They were crossed, to imply friendship. Or a union?

She glanced at her phone. No – it was far too late to call Philippa to ask what the flags meant and would her great-aunt even let on, if she knew? A good tactic might be to invite Philippa here for morning coffee, or tea... Her aunt had confessed to missing cream cakes. 'That's one thing I can do for her,' Ruby murmured and, with a plan forming, went to check the oven.

It seemed to be working, but could use a good clean. 'No time like the present.' She went at it with a scouring pad, her grandma's crackly radio keeping her company as she worked. She laughed when 'I Will Survive' came on, and wondered what Didier would think if he could see her. Would he despise or envy her ability to get on with her life? At least he hadn't messaged her again.

Taking a break, she peeled off her rubber gloves and went into the lounge, where she'd parked her laptop. She checked inside one of the inner pockets of the computer bag for a particular item. Yes, still there. A citrus-yellow memory stick containing the financial projections for Pastel that Didier wanted so badly. Maurice Bouchard, father of Lily, had asked her to do some figures with the view to opening a sister restaurant in a neighbouring town. Ruby had worked hard on those projections, sitting up into the early hours because she'd assumed she was part of the expansion plans. Didier wanted her to hand over all that research, just like that. Hadn't he realised how deeply he had insulted her? Ruby doubted she would ever erase the moment she'd walked into her bedroom and seen the pair of them together, Lily blinking mascara-smudged lashes and saying in a gravelly, so-what voice, 'Papa owns this building, this flat and your job.' Meaning – you don't count and I've won.

Didier had not leapt to Ruby's defence. Either he'd forgotten he'd once loved her, or he never had. She put the yellow memory stick back into its pocket. He could still whistle.

She returned to cleaning the oven until the music on the radio stopped for the ten o'clock news and a weather forecast warning of heavy rain. Her thoughts turning to the fallen roof tiles, Ruby phoned Will. He went to bed late, he'd told her, but after a couple of rings, she got cold feet and was about to cancel the call when a deep voice said, 'Yeah?'

'Oh, sorry. It's Ruby.'

'I know. I saved your number, remember. What's up, run out of gin?'

'Come off it. I prefer wine, anyway.' She apologised for the late hour.

'Don't worry, I'm still working. I didn't answer at once because I screen calls.'

'Thanks for sending George Oaks. I have warm radiators! Now, I need a roofer just as urgently. We're getting rain.'

'I'll call round in the morning.'

Why did he need to call round? 'Someone reliable and not hideously expensive. Just a name will do.'

'Will Keelbrook.'

It took her a moment to catch up. 'You do roofs?'

'Yup.'

'OK... really?'

'Yes, really. Do you want me?'

She laughed nervously. Not that he was flirting; no man could sound less lustful, frankly, but thinking about Didier had left her edgy. 'I do. I was going to invite Philippa for mid-morning coffee, so maybe you could come then?'

'Philippa doesn't drink coffee.'

She managed not to sigh out loud. 'It's just a way of saying "mid-morning treat". I also bought peppermint tea.'

'OK. See you then. Goodnight.'

Before heading for bed, Ruby propped the engagement card against the kettle, then turned down the heating. It could stay on at a gentle temperature until the house warmed up. The pages of Irene's diaries already felt dryer, and it was so tempting to start reading right away, but Ruby knew she couldn't risk tearing the aged paper by going through them too soon. If she smudged the writing, it would be lost forever.

As she lay in bed on her second night at Oak Apple Farm, Ruby couldn't wait for the words laid down in the midst of a war to become readable, as they encountered air for the first time in decades. The sense of mystery made her fingers itch.

# 8

## IRENE

'The Ten Bells is looking for a barmaid,' Irene's workmate Joyce Fuller said as they walked home together after a long shift. They'd been peeling silver onions all day, so small and slippery, they shot through your fingers like bullets if you weren't careful.

'Are you after another job, then?' Irene replied. It was a lovely evening, the sun dipping behind the factory roofs.

'Not me. Not with my lot at home,' Joyce said. 'I was thinking of you. You're always going on about how you've got no money for lipstick or stockings. The pub pays two bob a shift.'

Two shillings a night... and it was true, Irene was always belly-aching about the fact that everything she earned at J.P. Rattray's either went to her mum, or into her savings account at the post office. 'For her future', whatever that was. 'I could ask,' she said thoughtfully. 'Only, my feet kill me after a day at Ratty's. I don't know about standing another four or five hours of an evening...'

'It'd be worth it to meet some nice fellows.'

'What fellows? Wheezy Cobbold and Billy Gifford?' Not to

mention Norman Plait, who drank and played dominoes at The Bells three or four nights a week. Joyce laughed at her.

'Not them, my woman. Yanks. Those Engineer boys. Haven't you seen them, wheeling down the lanes four-abreast on their bicycles every night? Get a bit of romance under your belt, Irene. Before you know it, you'll be like me, past thirty with five kids. Have some fun while you can.'

Irene thought about that offcut of satin, from which, with careful placing, she'd cut two cap sleeves and the yoke for a blouse. It would be nice to show it off once it was sewn.

*The bluest eyes he'd ever seen.*

She ached to meet Sergeant Robinson again, ask him why he'd gone from liking her to throwing a rock. So, instead of going home, Irene walked on to The Ten Bells, finding it shut. She tapped on the side door and waited.

# 9

## RUBY

TUESDAY 13 DECEMBER 2022

After a quick breakfast, Ruby cycled to neighbouring Medfold, where there was a community shop. She bought free-range eggs, raspberry jam and double cream. As she secured her shopping to her bike rack, a notice in the window caught her eye: 'Kitchen help wanted, apply at The Ten Bells, Flixfield'. One glance reinforced something that had been fermenting since she'd quit Pastel: her time working for other people was over.

Setting off for home, she took a diversion down a leafy track to test out her new bike's suspension. The first mile was a puddle-filled assault course, until a wooden bridge took her into an area of wide stubble fields traversed by a concrete track. Every now and again, other tracks intersected hers, and she felt there must have been a village here, once upon a time. Abandoned buildings disturbed the pencil-line horizon. Silos, or old barns? Stopping, she snapped some photos on her phone, though the only living things were birds of prey mewing overhead and crows – or were they rooks? – feeding on the stubble.

Broad, empty, this was a landscape to inspire feelings of loneliness.

She followed the sound of traffic towards a rusty metal barrier that was almost hidden by brambles. She dismounted and ducked under, and at once her eye was drawn to a neat garden cut into an expanse of verge. Crossing the grass, she saw that the garden surrounded a monument. At its foot was a flower vase packed with flags. Red, white and blue. The Stars and Stripes.

'OK,' she said slowly to herself, 'I'm paying attention.' Wiping eyes that streamed from the cold wind, she read the citation carved into the monument.

### From these fields, from 1943 to 1944, American Airmen joined their British Allies in the Cause of Freedom

### The 699th Bomb Group

### Flixfield, England

She hadn't cycled across a deserted village, she realised now, but a former airfield. What she'd thought were abandoned buildings were probably old aircraft hangars. At school in Laurac, she'd studied the Second World War from a French perspective and later, at sixth-form college in England, she'd learned about the Holocaust. She knew almost nothing about American airmen based in Britain. What did a Bomb Group do? Bomb, presumably. But that must be only part of the story. The plastic flags, rattling in the breeze, and a wreath of red poppies, which must have been laid a month ago for Remembrance Day, spoke of memories kept alive. After taking photos until her fingers were too cold to press the button, Ruby got back on her bike.

As she pedalled home against the wind, her thoughts addressed new territory. Irene's engagement invitation had shown a union of British and American flags, for which there was only one plausible reason: the engagement hadn't been for Irene and Norman, but for Irene and somebody American.

Philippa had to know something. The minute she was home and had turned on the oven for her baking, Ruby looked to see if she had Philippa's landline number on her phone. She did. She must have added it during Christmas of 2019. The number rang fifteen times before Philippa picked up.

'Who's this at this time of the morning?'

'Ruby, inviting you over for tea and cake.' It wasn't that early, anyway. The community shop opened at eight thirty and Ruby had been there forty minutes ago.

'What, cake now?'

'At eleven. Victoria sponge with cream. The heating's on. You won't freeze.'

Philippa huffed a bit, then said, 'I don't think so, but thank you.'

'Will's coming.'

'To see you?'

'About the roof. I shall invite him in for cake too.'

That seemed to do the trick. 'All right then,' Philippa said. 'But I'll bring my own teabag.'

## 10

Philippa's first comment as she came in, leaning on her stick, was directed at the diaries, which Ruby had turned over to dry their backs. 'You won't have read those yet.' It was a question disguised as a statement.

'Only the odd line so far.' Ruby turned to Will, who came in behind. 'No Edna?' She'd put the cake on top of the fridge to cool, out of the dog's reach.

'She's sleeping off a walk across the fields. I'll need a long ladder to get up to your roof, Ruby.'

'Course you will. I should have asked about that last night.'

'Last night?' Philippa looked sharply from Ruby to Will. They had all progressed into the kitchen.

'I mentioned, Will's sorting my roof,' Ruby replied.

'I know that. I didn't know you'd had a nighttime chat.'

'I wouldn't call it a chat.' Ruby glanced at Will, to gauge his reaction to Philippa's comment, but his face gave little away.

'The ladder's in the haybarn,' Philippa said. 'I had it chained to a wall and padlocked, so thieves wouldn't get it.'

'Like they did Grandad's tools,' Ruby said sadly.

'Norman's tools? They're still there, I hope. I had them

stored on the upper floor of the barn, where they'd be safe. The key's in the dresser, middle drawer.' Philippa pointed towards the dining hall. Without waiting for Ruby, she went into the next-door room and opened the drawer herself. 'Here we are.' She held out a bunch of keys to Will, then turned accusingly to Ruby. 'What made you and your mother shut all these photographs up in here?'

'Because tenants don't want to look at other people's family pictures.'

'But you're here now. They should be on show, or they'll get mouldy.'

Will took the keys. Ruby followed him out, curious to discover if her grandad's tools really had survived. The ladder was where Philippa had said it would be, padlocked to brackets along one wall of the haybarn. Will released it and lifted it down.

'Did she mean the tools are up there?' Ruby glanced at a set of dusty, rickety stairs.

'That's what Aunt Flip said. You don't have to come up, though.'

'Yes I do.' She wasn't having Will think her squeamish. Her reward for dirtying the hems of her jeans was discovering a time-capsule of vintage tools and farm implements, locked inside some metal feed-bins. 'Wow. I was convinced my tenants had pinched them.'

'One thing you'll learn about Aunt Flip, she's deeply protective of Norman,' Will said. 'Even though he's been gone over twenty years.'

Protective of the past, too. Returning to the house, Ruby found Philippa reading one of Irene's school exercise books. The dresser had been freshly dusted – Ruby had done it once already – and a cluster of framed photos was arranged on top. Turning as Ruby came in, Philippa read out loud, '"Irene Boulter, form two. Botany". Fancy her keeping this stuff. I chucked mine 'cause I didn't like school.' Philippa put the book down, open at an illustration of a horse chestnut twig. Fruit, leaf and flower, with neat labels describing 'inflorescence, axillary bud, leaf-scar'. A teacher had written 'Very good' at the bottom.

'Grandma had talent.' Ruby thought of the decorated engagement card and wondered if she should show it to Philippa now. Maybe better to wait until the cake was on the table. 'Did Grandma Irene enjoy art?'

'I wouldn't know,' Philippa answered. 'You forget, she was starting secondary school when I was born and by the time I knew what to ask, she'd left school and was earning a wage at Ratty's.'

'Ratty's?'

'J.P. Rattray, the jam and pickle people. They had a factory down Hut Lane, where the sheltered bungalows are now.'

'Hut Lane?'

Philippa rolled her eyes. 'You don't know much, do you? By rights it's Tithe Barn Lane, but once the village hall was built, which we all called "the hut", we changed it to Hut Lane. Your grandma worked for Rattray's from when she left school to when she married my brother, and then went back a few years later, till it shut down some time in the 1960s.'

'Irene got engaged in December 1943. To Grandad, right...?'

Philippa stepped into the trap. 'That's about right. The war was still going hammer and tongs, and I wasn't much aware of it on account of having the chicken pox. Later on, I was supposed to be bridesmaid at their wedding. I had a little yellow dress, but I wouldn't wear it.'

'Why not?'

'Oh, I don't know.' Philippa stroked the old bedsheet Ruby had put underneath the books and diaries to accelerate their drying, and protect the table's surface. 'Where exactly did you find this lot?'

'Didn't I say? Outside, in a suitcase. Someone had tried to burn them.'

'Sounds like the best idea. If I were you, I'd finish the job.'

'Not likely. I'm glad you saved Grandad's tools, Aunt Philippa, and I'm delighted I found these mementoes of Grandma. I want to find out everything I can about Irene and Norman.'

That triggered something in Philippa. 'You oughtn't to go reading private things.' Her aggression had come from nowhere. Fear-based, Ruby thought. What was Philippa afraid Ruby would find out? Knowing she'd gain nothing by pushing, she invited her aunt to go through to the lounge. 'Give me your teabag and I'll put the kettle on. Go make yourself comfortable.'

Philippa stepped into the lounge, then came straight out again. 'I've never liked that room.'

'Let's sit in the kitchen, then, where it's nice and warm.' Ruby pulled out a folding table and Will, who had put the ladder against the back wall and come inside for his tool bag, fetched in three dining chairs. Ruby brought out the cake and his eyes widened in pleasure.

'You weren't wrong, Aunt Flip. She's a top chef.'

'Actually, I learned to bake a sponge at school,' Ruby said. 'My professional style was more edgy.'

'I can believe it.'

She cast Will an enquiring look. 'What makes you say that?'

'The lingering smell of spices around the cooker... lighting fires without checking the chimney liner. Cycling along dark lanes without planning a route. Edgy.'

'Is that good or bad in your opinion?'

'It's better than being boring.'

She laughed. 'I'll take that.' With anybody else, that exchange might have signalled a desire to flirt, but nothing in Will's manner suggested he found her attractive. Today, he was wearing a black woollen hat pulled down past his temples and

he hadn't shaved. Well, he lived in a thatched barn in the back
end of nowhere. He was probably high-risk for growing a beard.
She invited Philippa to sit down as she brewed a mug of fig leaf
tea. 'Coffee or tea for you, Will?'

'Neither yet, I'll get the job out of the way. Coffee when I
come in, please.'

As she made coffee for herself, Ruby saw Will through the
window, climbing the ladder. 'Should I go out and hold the
base?'

Philippa sniffed. 'Could you keep it upright, if he fell off?'

'Probably not.'

'Then let him get on with it. He's got a head for heights. My
brother, Norman, bought that ladder to mend the chimney
stack, years ago.'

*My brother, Norman.* Protective. Possessive.

Philippa regarded her steadily. 'Are you giving me that tea,
Ruby, or are you going to stand there holding it?'

'Sure.' She sat down and served the cake. 'D'you want a fork
or are you happy with fingers, Auntie?'

'Fingers are God's forks, aren't they?'

It was a good cake. Ruby was critical of her own food,
always looking for improvements, but this one had a springy
crumb. Fruity jam and whipped cream made it rich and
Philippa was enjoying it. Above the kitchen roof came the occasional thump and every so often a broken tile clumped to the
ground.

'I hadn't realised Will's your godson until he said,' Ruby
commented.

'Why shouldn't he be?'

'No reason. Just that godparenting is an old-fashioned thing
these days.'

'Ha.' Having chivvied up her tea, Philippa had left it to
cool. She lifted her mug, two-handed. Ruby took note: buy some
lightweight china. Or offer tea in a cup. 'Will's grandma was my

oldest friend,' Philippa explained. 'Me and Doris were chums from when we were this high.' She raised her palm to table height. 'We left school the same day and went to work in a shoe shop in Hollesford. She was my bridesmaid when I married Ronnie, and I was her maid-of-honour a bit later. We always promised we'd be godparents to each other's children, only I never had any.'

It was spoken matter-of-factly, but Ruby was not deceived. Being childless had hurt.

'Will was Doris's grandson, not her son?'

'That's right. Soon after Doris married, her husband wanted to live in Canada, so they emigrated.' There was bitterness in Philippa's voice. Ruby read the subtext: *They left me.* 'She had a daughter over there,' Philippa continued, 'but there was no point me being godmother to the little girl with all that ocean between us. Still, we kept writing, Christmas and birthday cards, for over thirty years. I knew when Teresa – her daughter – married an Englishman who'd gone out there to work in the forests. He was a no-hoper.'

'In what way?' Just nosiness, Ruby told herself.

'The outdoors type, the sort that forgets to go home. They split up and, out of the blue, I get a call from Doris saying she and Teresa are coming home. Doris had lost her husband and wanted to be back here near her family. Would I look for a house.'

'Will was born by then?'

'He was. He was about two when he came to Medfold. A dear little chap, all smiles.'

Oh? What had gone wrong since?

'Only he hadn't been baptised, so once they were settled, we arranged it and I stood godmother to him, and my Ronnie was his godfather.'

'What about his mum, and Doris?' Will hadn't mentioned family in the next village.

'Doris died not long after they came home. I think moving was all too much. She's buried in the churchyard here alongside her brothers and sisters, and I look after the graves, to help Will.'

'And his mother?' There was a sad twist coming; Ruby saw it in Philippa's eyes.

'When Will was in his last year at primary school I used to pick him up and bring him to my house for his tea, to help his mum. She was working in Hollesford, see. One night six o'clock came and she didn't arrive, so I took him home and I found Teresa on the floor. It looked like a stroke, but it was a brain tumour. Inoperable. She was only forty-one.'

'That would make Will ten or eleven when his mum died.' Poor boy. 'And the father?'

'Him?' A fragment of terracotta tile plummeted past the window, landing with a shattering clunk, which blotted out Philippa's judgement on Will's father. 'We tracked him down, but he didn't want to know.'

This triggered Ruby to try and summon an image of her own father. As always, she saw an empty picture frame. She'd never known him. 'Will didn't have to go into care, I hope?'

'No, because Doris had been one of six and there were sisters still living. Will was placed with one of them.'

An elderly great-aunt? 'It can't have been easy.'

'No, and Will came to us at Westumble often as he could. My Ronnie let him help with the forge, and with the horses. You know how my husband was a farrier?'

Ruby nodded. Somehow, she had known that.

'For a while, we thought Will might be his apprentice. But Ronnie said to me one day, "That boy's got a good brain; he can make more money with that than with his hands." His mother's life insurance meant he could go to a boarding school. He was sporty as well as clever and it was the making of him. He'd come here for holidays, and always for Christmas.'

Not Christmas 2019, or Ruby would have met him. 'I'm glad you took Will to heart. He's very loyal to you.'

'As I am to him,' Philippa said and Ruby sensed a warning. *Don't you mess with that lad.*

I won't, she vowed silently. I'm over men.

Footsteps on wooden rungs told them that Will was descending. His coated, hatted shape darkened the window. Ruby got up to make his coffee, thinking that, perhaps, she now understood him better. He'd lost his mother at a vulnerable age, and had a father who didn't care, which felt worse than her situation, having a father who didn't know she existed.

Will came in, shrugging off his jacket. 'There's a millimetre of frost up there.' He took the coffee she handed him. 'Fabulous.' His gaze travelled along the worktop. 'Glad you left me some cake.'

'You can take some home. You too, Auntie Philippa.' Ruby made fresh coffee as she doubted one mug would warm him up. 'More tea?' she asked her aunt. 'I bought peppermint teabags yesterday, and chamomile.'

'Peppermint, then.' Philippa's attention was on Will. Checking for damage, Ruby thought.

She asked what he'd found up on the roof.

'Six pantiles lost, a few frost-damaged and some ridge tiles need replacing. The parging underneath is flaking. That's why they blew off.'

Ruby looked at him blankly.

'The lime mortar that keeps the tiles in place. They shift and the wind gets under them.' Will pulled off his hat and Ruby was shocked to see his hair was shaved to an army crew-cut. She'd assumed his hat-wearing was to conceal a thin patch, but nothing about Will's head implied male pattern baldness. Chemotherapy? A friend of hers in Laurac had undergone treatment and had shaved his head before he lost his hair.

'Storm Maggie-Anne gave your roof a mauling,' Philippa said, interrupting Ruby's thoughts.

'It was Storm Marion,' Will corrected, 'which hit at the beginning of November. We'll get matching tiles from the salvage yard and seal up that hole.'

'I will insist on paying you, you know that?'

Will gulped his coffee and made a face. 'Could I have sugar? Sorry, I should have asked. I'm happy to do it if you want me to and you can pay for the materials.'

And his labour. She'd insist. 'I'm worried about you climbing that ladder. In case you fall. Should I get some scaffolding?'

He took the sugar she offered. 'Up to you. Full-height scaffolding costs about a hundred pounds to hire.'

'All in, or plus VAT?'

'A hundred per day, plus VAT.'

Dear heavens. 'How many days would we need it?'

'Three, four. Depends on the weather. If the rain sets in, it could still be costing you at Christmas.' He looked at her from under his lashes. 'You have to decide how much my wellbeing is worth.'

That was unfair, and to avoid answering, she cut a large slice of cake and handed him the plate before sitting back down. She'd been aware of Philippa fidgeting during their exchange and searched for something inclusive to say. 'I discovered the old airfield this morning. It felt utterly deserted.'

'It is,' was Philippa's response.

'D'you remember when it was active?'

'How old do you take me for? I was five when war broke out, and eight when the Yanks arrived and they weren't interested in me.'

No. But they were in Irene. One was, at least.

'I wasn't suggesting you were hanging about the place, Auntie Philippa. I asked if you remember anything.'

'Planes thundering over, day and night. They'd shake the roof and the shadow of them would cross a room. A lady in the village kept rabbits, and the poor little things died of fright. You fastened your hands over your ears if you were outside. And I remember a massive explosion when one came down short of the runway. That would be end of 1944. My brother was out in the fields, and was first on the scene.' Philippa dashed away the memory. 'All at once, before VE Day, the Yanks went home. Some local girls went over as war brides. That was the talk of the village.'

'Did Irene know any of them?'

Philippa didn't appear to hear. 'The buildings were left to fall down and the land was sold. Norman wanted it, it was good land for wheat, but Irene wouldn't have it.'

'Why not?'

Philippa shrugged. 'In the end, some farmer from Medfold got it for shillings and you still see their harvesters going by every year.'

Ruby put the engagement party invitation in front of Philippa. 'I found this in Irene's history book.' Now she thought about it, the schoolbook predated the invitation by some years. Irene must have hidden the card where she thought nobody would look.

Philippa picked it up and emotion scuttled across her face. 'I need to get home. Will, when you've finished?'

'Sure.' Will put down his plate. He'd only half eaten his cake. He picked up the invitation, tilting it to catch the daylight. '"The family of Miss Irene Boulter invite you to the engagement party of their daughter to Sergeant Theodore Robinson." Who was he?'

'Say that again!' Ruby demanded.

'Sergeant Theodore Robinson, fourth of December—'

'Yes, 1943, but the name. I didn't see it before.' Ruby took the card, half-suspecting Will was playing a joke. But no. When she also angled the card towards the light, she saw it quite clearly. 'Auntie—'

Philippa was leaving the room. 'Where's my walker?'

Ruby followed her. 'Auntie, who was Sergeant Robinson?' Philippa reached for her walking stick and her coat, and Ruby went to help her. 'Was Grandma engaged to someone else before she married Grandad, someone who died maybe?' You only had to walk around a war memorial to appreciate the crushing statistics for young men in conflict.

Philippa called out, 'Will? I'm ready to go.'

Will thanked Ruby for the coffee and said he'd be round later. Could she leave the ladder where it was. 'I'll fix a tarp on your roof, in case it rains today.'

He returned a couple of hours later, with a roll of tarpaulin and ropes. He gave Ruby a letter from Philippa, which Ruby suspected had been dashed off in some agitation.

*Irene would make things up when she was young. Girls pretend about being married and I suppose she liked imagining herself with a handsome Yank called Theodore or some such. Please throw away those diaries. Irene wouldn't like you going through her things.*

Or is it that *you* don't like me going through her things, Ruby mused. Her grandmother had indeed been a private person, yet she'd kept these books in a suitcase. Irene must have known someone, sometime, would find them.

Her phone pinged, bringing another message from Didier. No words, just a sad-faced emoji with a tear in its eye. Fury raked through her. This was what he did when he wanted something? Fatuous, emotionally stunted man-child. Did he know how many actual tears she'd cried after their break-up?

She fetched Clement Lubbock's magnifying glass from her bag, and selected Irene's 1943 diary. The paper must be dry enough now. She'd begin with this one, reading everything leading up to the engagement party at the tail end of the year. Opening it at the flyleaf she saw – 'Property of Irene Boulter. If ever I find you reading this, Little Flip, I'll turn you into a frog.'

Ruby burst out laughing, the words a shot of anti-depressant. Once upon a time, her grandma had possessed a sense of humour.

Ruby turned to 1 January 1943 and held the magnifying glass over the pencil jottings. The first line wasn't much of an opening hook: 'Did nothing much. Dad having a rotten day and Mum cross with everything.'

Saturday 2 January: 'Half-day shift at Ratty's. Only one tea break. Foreman breathed beer all over us. I hate pickle even more than I hate jam.'

Oh dear, Ruby thought. Six diaries' worth of this would be heavy reading. A few pages on: 'The onion lorry got stuck in the lane. Nellie H. sat with me at dinner time and told me her leg-veins hurt from standing. She wanted me to look at them. I said no thank you.'

Her grandma's voice flew from the page. Sharp. Unsympathetic. What if she ended up not liking the young Irene? Or discovered her to be deadly dull? Ruby flipped pages. The hairs on the back of her neck rippled as a name jumped to her eyes. *Theo.*

Sunday 21 March: 'Can you fall in love all at once?'

A week later, Irene had written something that drove away Ruby's dread of the diary being in any way banal.

'Saw Theo again, getting wrong from a man called MacBeast. Theo threw a rock at me.'

*Overpaid, oversexed and over here.* Wasn't that what they said about American servicemen in Britain during the war? Nobody had mentioned anything about rock-throwing. Irene was in love with this man?

And who was MacBeast?

There were few clues, as the rest of the month was blank. Not until mid-April had Irene picked up her pencil again. Her thoughts seemed to move faster now, the writing forward-leaning, each letter impatient to merge with the next.

Sunday 25 April: 'I have my eye on some fancy stockings and now I'm in with a chance of affording them. Joyce tipped me off about them needing a barmaid at The Ten Bells and I'm working there Friday and Saturday nights now. Who knows who I might meet, working behind the bar????'

Ruby smiled at the enthusiastic question, while fuming on Irene's behalf over the workload placed on the young woman. Nine-hour shifts at the pickling factory yet unable to buy a pair of stockings without taking bar work! Ruby thought guiltily of the wardrobe full of clothes she'd left at her mother's. Wheels on the drive took her to the window. Who was interrupting her at this cliff-hanger moment in Irene's life, and driving a shiny hybrid? Then she remembered – 'The estate agent!' Swooping on the diaries, she put them away in the dresser drawer and whipped the old sheet off the table. She gave the dining hall a swift glance.

She hadn't hoovered or washed up the coffee things, but hey-ho. How much did she care anyway, when all she wanted was to learn if Irene had got her wish, and made contact again with the rock-hurling Theo Robinson?

## 11

# IRENE

FRIDAY 23 APRIL 1943

Mr Scattergood showed her how to pull a pint using the tap handle. 'Draw it down slowly. Tilt the glass or you'll put too much head on it. My customers don't like paying for froth.' He had her stand the glass on the bar. 'Wait till it settles. The head should be no more than the width of your thumb. See? Now you try again with this.' He fetched out a half-pint glass.

'We're a tied pub,' he told her after she'd got the knack, 'and we mostly sell Lacons bitter and mild beer from the barrel, but we stock different kinds of stout, brown and light ale in bottles.' He pointed to the shelves beneath the bar. There wasn't much to see. Irene had heard Norman complaining that his favourite beer, Mackeson Stout, was only occasionally available.

'With those, you flick the tops off with a bottle opener, and the tops go in there.' The landlord tapped a metal bucket with his toe. 'That's so they can go back to the plant to be melted down.'

The bottle opener was attached to the bar by a chain. Mr Scattergood drew her attention to bottles arranged in front of a mirror. 'Whisky, gin, brandy. You won't get asked for them often, on account of the price. Ladies like to drink port' – he lifted a squat green bottle – 'though, quite often now, they drink beer like the men. We serve them in half glasses. Never serve a lady a pint glass.'

'Aren't our mouths big enough?' Irene wasn't much of a drinker.

'No, dear, it's because we have a beer quota and when it's gone, it's gone. If I let the women drink all they want, there won't be enough for the men.'

Irene wouldn't relish telling the likes of Joyce Fuller or Nellie Hibbert to limit themselves. Why were women treated like they deserved less, by nature? She'd heard Ratty's foreman joking with the lorry drivers, saying, 'You got it easy, *bor*. I'm surrounded by a lot of clucking hens.' Even though the women did more work than him for a tenth of his wages, he still slated them.

'Sorry, Mr Scattergood?' She was being asked a question.

'I was saying, are you sure you can take a further job? They work you hard at the factory, don't they?'

'I want more money, see. I have plans.'

'Do you, now?' Mr Scattergood gave her a one-eyed look. His left eye had a way of closing, as if he'd got lemon juice in it. Or he'd spent years on a ship, peering through a telescope. His nose had a wart on the side. Irene wondered what it was like for Mrs Scattergood, waking up to that every morning. 'What plans?' he asked.

'To buy some nice things. A new dress and have my hair done occasionally. How much will you pay me, Mr Scattergood?'

'Oh, you want money too, do you?'

'Course I do.'

He laughed, his gummy mouth opening wide. 'Only joking. You'll have to get used to a bit of ribbing, standing behind the bar. It's two shillings a shift, with sixpence bonus since you'll work Friday and Saturday. Young girls don't want to work those nights, because they're out courting. Do your parents know you're here?'

'Yes. Mum kicked up a dust, but she always does. I had to promise her I'd keep helping around the house.'

'That's as it should be, Irene. Do they know I get Americans in here? The Engineer boys.' Mr Scattergood didn't say 'Black soldiers', but she knew from the way his eyebrows moved, that's what he meant.

'I expect Mum knows,' she answered. 'My dad won't care.' I don't care either, she told herself, though it wasn't true.

'And what about Norman, dear? What does he think about you pulling pints?'

Irene wished people would stop mentioning Norman Plait as though he was her owner. 'I don't know what he thinks, Mr Scattergood, and I'm not going to ask.'

The landlord scratched his ear. 'So long as there's no bother. When the Yanks are in, my locals won't expect to be served last, or in a hurry.'

'Yes, Mr Scattergood.'

'The boys from the base, well, they want to see a friendly smile and a pretty face. I'm not all that much to look at, see.'

'No, Mr Scattergood. Sorry, I mean—'

He laughed. 'You mean, you've seen better-looking frogs. Now you tell me something. What do you want out of this job?'

'Like I said, extra money.' She'd worked it out. Seven pounds by the end of next year might be enough to get her away from Ratty's and into a hairdressing course in the big town, plus those silk stockings to start with.

'You're after an American sweetheart, maybe?'

Taken off-guard, she reddened. 'No. I'm not in the market.'

'Good. 'Cause there's three things you should know about Yanks, Irene. One, they don't care if you're already stepping out with a good, honest English lad – they'll still try charming the socks off you. Two, when this horrible war is over, they'll all go home.'

'I know that.'

He raised a finger. 'Three – and this is the most important...'

Irene bit her lip, anticipating a reference to the Engineers, their colour, and how they stood out in this rural niche.

'Three,' the landlord repeated. 'They like their beer a lot colder than we can ever serve it, so be prepared for gripes. Under no circumstances *ever* refund the price of a pint.'


This evening, her first, was quiet for a Friday. Only locals came in, most of them farmers or farm workers. They all asked after her dad, sighed and said things such as, 'It's a bad do, him getting that Arthur-itis and all.'

One said, 'You're a lot easier on the eye than the landlord, Irene.'

'And the landlady,' muttered Wheezy, who'd spent his life digging ditches and laying hedges and spoke in a kind of cracked whisper.

Irene whispered, 'Shh, Mr Cobbold.' She'd heard the Scattergoods talking about her in the kitchen a short while ago. The landlady had wanted her husband to appoint a strong youth to help heave the barrels from the cellar. Irene had heard her mutter, 'Girls spend more time flirting than serving beer. All it'll take is one American winking at her, and you'll have a melting jelly on your hands. Violet Boulter won't thank you for it. She doesn't want her daughter going off the rails, things being as they are at Westumble.'

*Things being as they are*, Irene had echoed inwardly. Was it never allowed for a girl from her background to change *how things were*? As the evening progressed, she became adept at pulling a pint with the prescribed head of froth, and flipping the tops off bottles without taking skin off her thumb. She was quite enjoying herself by home time and the best thing of all – there had been no sign of Norman. No Americans either, but she could be patient.

As she put on her coat and bade the landlord and landlady goodnight, she congratulated herself on a plan put into action. 'See you tomorrow.'

It was around eight the following night, Saturday, that the sleepy ambience of The Ten Bells got a shake-up. The sound of a vehicle outside cut short a good-natured argument between two domino players. All eyes swung to the door. There were two vehicle-owners in Flixfield, the doctor and the village bobby, and they could all tell by the deep thrub that this vehicle belonged to neither. Irene nervously touched her collar, checking that only her top button was modestly undone. She'd sat up nearly all night, sewing blue satin sleeves and a yoke onto the body of a blouse cut down from one of her mother's.

Heavy cab doors clunked shut. Her heart began to thump.

Billy Gifford, one of the domino players, nudged his neighbour. 'Reckon it's those airdrome boys, come to teach you how to dig a proper ditch, Wheezy.'

He was right. The first through the door was Jake, followed by a man Irene remembered as Robbie. They nodded politely. They were dressed as they had been at the spring dance, in uniforms that were firmly the wrong side of smart. Duke and Fletch came in next.

Billy Gifford invited them to a game of dominoes. 'I'll take you on one man at a time. Losers buy the next round.'

Fletch grinned. 'You got it,' and he pulled a chair up to Billy's table. Duke joined him and Robbie sat at an adjacent table.

Irene's heart sank low in her chest. No Theo? Hardly was the thought released when the door swung open and in he came, followed by Den. Theo took off his cap, chucked his vehicle ignition key up in the air and, seeing Irene behind the beer pumps, missed his catch.

The keys hit the floor, and Fletch cried, 'You dropped that can of corn, sergeant! What took your eye off the ball?'

Irene knew from the way Theo swiftly bent to pick up the keys that he was embarrassed. Because she was here, the stupid girl who had got him into trouble? But when he straightened up, Theo had found his smile. He held up his palms as a riposte to Fletch. 'I've been handling grease all day.'

She wanted to ask straight out, 'Why did you lob that rock at me?' but Mr Scattergood came in, drawn by the commotion. 'Five pints of Lacons for you lads?' he boomed.

'What did you give us last time?' Theo asked.

'Light ale, but we're out of that. Try the bitter beer. Irene will do the honours.'

Hands shaking, Irene slowly pulled down the pump, holding the first glass under the flow. Over the gentle pouring sound, she heard the landlord politely asking Robbie and Den to move to another table. He indicated one in a far corner. 'You'll do better at that one, over there.'

Irene saw Theo's profile harden. In the level voice she was starting to recognise, he asked, 'Is that on account of the colour of our skin, sir?'

'Hey?' Mr Scattergood scratched his head. 'No, *bor*, it's on account of the tables and settles this side all having their regulars.' He touched the back of an empty seat. 'This one is Toby Fuller's and was his old dad's before him. The table that side is for the church wardens and that' – Mr Scattergood pointed to a high-backed settle alongside the fire – 'is for the men that work at the flour mill.'

'Unwritten rules?' Theo suggested. To Irene, he sounded tired.

'That's right,' agreed the landlord. 'The nearer the fire, the more a seat belongs to some other old boy. T'ain't nothing to do with skin. All are welcome, but my regulars will be buying my beer long after you've moved on. Anything else you need, ask Irene. It's her first week here, but she can fetch me if she doesn't know the answer.'

With a nod of acceptance, Theo took the empty table. Den and Robbie brought chairs over to join him.

Irene carried their beers over but none of them spoke or even met her eye. It was so different from the night at the village hall. Impulsively, she said, 'Mr Scattergood told the truth. It's not about who you are, just that he'll get wrong from all quarters if he changes how things are done. If they didn't like you, you wouldn't be invited to a game of dominoes.'

'I guess so,' Theo conceded. His hat was on the table, the inside facing up with a pocketful of coins shining on it.

Irene watched them pick up their pints. The beer came up the pipe a bit cooler than the palm of her hand. Would they think it too warm? She waited while Theo took the first mouthful and wiped the froth from his top lip.

Wheezy, tapping a coin on the bar to get Irene's attention, called out, 'If you don't like froth, *bor*, blow it off afore you drink. Lacons don't improve for sippin'.'

Theo raised his glass in a wry toast, then took a gulp.

'He should take a leaf out of my book,' Wheezy croaked as Irene walked back behind the bar. 'Half of mild, dear.'

After she'd filled his glass and Wheezy had gone back to his seat, Theo approached.

'Did that gentleman call me boring?'

'Wheezy? No, he called you "bor". It means "friend".'

'You certain?' He leaned towards the bar, his expression at once playful and mistrustful.

'Course. It's a compliment.'

'Would he call you "bor"?'

'No, because I'm a girl. He'd call me a "little ol' mawther".'

'That don't sound too much like a compliment to me.'

'What do you call somebody you like?'

He shrugged before he smiled. 'I might call them Miss this-or-that. May I call you "Miss Irene"?'

'I suppose. Though nobody else calls me "Miss". Not round here.'

'I'm not from round here. Tell me what goes into this beer, Miss Irene.' Theo held up his pint so the light shone into the clear, tawny-brown liquid. Mr Scattergood kept his barrels well, the regulars said.

'Beer is grain, water and yeast.' Irene helped her mother make a barrel or two for home drinking though it never poured as clear as pub beer.

'I know what beer's made from, but this don't taste like what we get at home. It's...' Theo twisted his lips. 'Kinda bitter.'

'Well, it's bitter beer with a lot of hop in it.'

'Hop... like the Lindy Hop?'

She laughed. 'I don't know what that means. Hops... that grow on poles. They go in with the beer to make the froth and give the flavour. Don't you like it?'

He put the glass to his nose. 'Guess I'll get used to it. I'm having to get used to a great deal over here.'

'Like the weather?'

'And remembering which side of the road to drive on.'

Did they drive on a different side in America? Why would they do that? She reached under the bar for a dimpled bottle and released the screw top. 'My dad takes a splash of lemonade in his beer these days, to make it sweeter. Taking medicine has changed how things taste to him. Shall I?'

Theo put his glass on the bar. 'Make it sweeter, I'm yours forever.'

'There's no such thing as forever.' She needed to know more about Theo Robinson before she allowed him to talk such nonsense to her. She poured, her hand shaking. Mixing beer half-and-half with lemonade was for boys who hadn't learned to hold their alcohol. But it was fine to add a quarter of an inch. It was all in the measure. 'There, try that.'

When he curled his long fingers around the glass, she saw how his nails were broken so short, you could see the skin of the nail bed. It looked sore and she pictured him scrubbing ingrained dirt off his hands before coming out. The cuffs of his green tunic were a lighter colour where they folded over. It dawned on her that the coins in the hat were because the five men had pooled their money. She'd heard people say that American GIs earned twice as much as their British counterparts, but looking at Theo's cuffs, the brass buttons polished down to the base metal, it didn't seem like it.

'Does that taste nicer?'

He gave it some thought. 'I like it better now. What do I ask for next time – Irene's very own mixture?'

'That won't help if I'm not here.'

Mr Scattergood appeared at her shoulder. Irene wondered if she should have charged Theo for the splash of lemonade.

'You ask for a pint of bitter with a lemonade top, sergeant,' the landlord said. 'So long as we haven't run out of beer or lemonade, that's what you'll get. All well, Irene?'

'Yes, thank you, Mr Scattergood.'

'That's dandy.' The landlord reached across the bar to take a pint glass from Billy Gifford. 'Fill it up again, *bor*?'

Theo seemed in no hurry to return to his corner. Irene burned to explain her clumsy behaviour in front of that Lootenant MacBeast. Theo's men blamed her, she could tell from the way Den and Robbie talked in low voices, keeping veiled eyes on their sergeant. When Billy Gifford stumped back to his dominoes with his glass recharged, and Mr Scattergood went to collect the empties, Irene leaned towards Theo.

'Why did you throw a mucky old rock at me?'

'I didn't throw any rock, ma'am. Why d'you say that?' Theo had a way of looking at her from under his lashes, and she wondered if he was as fascinated by her as she was by him. Or was he afraid of looking at her?

'Well, someone lobbed it, and if it had hit me it would have hurt.'

He put an elbow on the bar and leaned in. '"When I walked you home, the moon was a silver dollar. A silver dollar – a lucky silver dollar".' He was half-speaking, half singing. 'Where is my lucky silver dollar, Irene?'

She shook her head. 'I haven't the foggiest what you're talking about.'

'When a man needs to say something, and he can't speak, he throws his money about. Ain't that true?'

Not in her world.

'It was clay, Irene, it wasn't a rock. And I made sure it didn't hit you.'

'So you did throw it!'

The pub door opened. Irene's spirits plunged. Norman had arrived. He looked straight at her, a hesitant smile cutting across his face. Then he noticed Theo at the bar and his expression turned thunderous.

Theo followed the direction of her eyes. 'Is that the man your mother says is engaged to you?'

'No. I mean, he is but I'm not.'

Theo glanced at the door. 'All the same, Miss Irene, he doesn't seem to like me much.'

There was nothing Irene could say in contradiction, not with Norman heading their way with a look on his face that suggested he was ready for battle.

## 12

Norman laid his hands on the bar, his fingers splayed wide. The look he gave Theo boded ill, but, to Irene's surprise, he spoke with a forced, bantering tone. 'What are you doing here, boy, supping our beer? We haven't enough for ourselves.'

'There's a full barrel and he's no more a boy than you are, Norman.' Shame fizzled up from Irene's feet, seeking her cheeks. 'If you've mislaid your manners, you'd better go home.'

'I'm not going any place, unless the landlord tells me.' Norman thrust out his jaw, saying to Irene, 'I didn't know you'd taken a new job.'

'Why should you? It's my life.'

'I know it's your life.'

'So stop acting like it isn't. What are you drinking?'

'The usual.'

She sighed emphatically. 'It's my second night. How should I know what your usual is?'

'Because you do know. Bottle of Mackeson.' Norman cocked a sideways glance at Theo's elbow, which was resting on the bar.

Convinced Norman was going to shove him, Irene became

clumsy and snagged her thumb on the serrated edge of the Mackeson top. She sucked off the blood, angrier than ever. 'There,' she said, thumping the bottle on the bar. 'Anything else?'

Muttering, 'Not right now,' Norman paid and took his drink to the domino table. Irene heard him greeting Billy and Wheezy in a bluff style. 'Either of you boys fancy being beaten hollow tonight?'

'All in good time, Norman.' Wheezy indicated the game with Fletch still in progress. 'And there's another in hand.' Duke had yet to play him.

'If you say so.' Norman chose a table on its own, sat down and glowered into his glass.

Theo returned to his table. One of his colleagues came up and placed a coin on the bar. 'What's this one, miss?'

'A two-shilling piece. You're Robbie, aren't you?'

'Last time I looked, miss.' Robbie made a quick move of the mouth. It could have been a smile. 'Is it enough for another round of beer with – what is it? Lemonade hat?'

'Lemonade top. Erm... not quite.' Beer was sixpence a pint. 'One more sixpence.'

'I'll stand the lads that.' Billy Gifford, who was the village farrier and happened also to be Joyce Fuller's brother-in-law, put six pennies on the bar. 'Price of beer goes up every month. You lads won't keep count any more than I do.'

'I didn't mean to impose on you, sir,' Robbie said.

'I didn't see no imposing, *bor*. We're all in this mess together. How's the shovellin' *uvver* at Boundary Farm?'

'He means at the airbase,' Irene explained, seeing Robbie's confusion. 'He's asking how the digging is going.'

Robbie half-closed an eye. 'Good and hard and keeps us hungry. Thank you for your generosity, sir. Next time, it's on us.'

Billy watched him go, then drew Irene's attention to where

Norman sat gloomily contemplating his ale. 'He'll stay there all night, so he can walk you home. That's love, that is.'

Pulling the first of five pints, Irene muttered, 'It's six hundred steps to my front door. I don't need to be walked home like a schoolchild.'

Billy Gifford's grin showed his single peg of a front tooth. He'd been kicked shoeing a donkey as an apprentice. 'My missus don't need me to buy her a rose at Easter, but I do all the same. Norman *wants* to walk you home, dear.'

Fletch lost his dominoes match and, after that, Wheezy Cobbold made short shrift of Duke. 'Next time, we'll play for coin,' Wheezy chortled.

Theo and his friends drank up and, after bidding everyone goodnight, battled their way past the blackout curtains at the door. Theo paused long enough to catch Irene's eye. She felt he wanted to say something, but couldn't.

At ten o'clock, Mr Scattergood helped her take the empty glasses to the scullery. He hung a lamp on a hook so she could see to wash up, muttering, 'When they put electricity in Hollesford, they promised it would get here in two years' time. That was in 1923.'

As she rinsed the beer glasses, Irene stared out at a waxing moon above a ridge of trees. Yesterday had been St George's Day, an important marker in the farming year because if the April showers had penetrated a spade's depth into the soil by then, the harvest should be good. Behind the ridge, some half a mile away, ran Long Hedge Lane. And behind that, the airbase.

'The moon was a silver dollar...' she sang. What had Theo meant by, 'When a man needs to say something, and he can't speak, he throws his money about'? *He could not speak that day.*

Her hands stilled. 'Irene Boulter, you are the stupidest—'

Mr Scattergood brought in more glasses. 'You can go when you've finished these. Shall I tell Norman to put his coat on?'

'No. No! And, Mr Scattergood, if you don't mind, I'll slip out the back.'

Lamplight reflected off the landlord's bald scalp. 'And I'm not to tell Norman, right?'

'Please.'

'Don't fall over the empty crates, then. Are you back next Friday, or was tonight not to your liking?'

'I'm coming back. I want to work here, Mr Scattergood.'

'Then mind how you go,' the landlord said, a phrase that generally meant little, but to Irene, whose mind was racing ahead to Long Hedge, it sounded like both a challenge and a warning.

# 13

## RUBY

Ruby and Will were at a salvage yard, somewhere east of Hollesford. She'd lost her bearings soon after he took a back lane out of the town. She left him discussing clay pantiles with an assistant, lured into a magnificent tithe barn by an arrow saying, 'More treasures this way'. Irresistible. Perhaps she ought to have stayed with Will but he was incredibly thorough, and it had been bitterly cold in the yard.

This weather made her miss Laurac, whose climate was far from perfect – baking in summer, frigid in winter – but what you didn't get there was icy rain driven from skies the colour of wet sacks. Inside the tithe barn, she meandered past the window frames from a Victorian chapel, and threaded around islands of farmyard bygones. A kitchen table stacked with enamel pans held her attention for several minutes. These were the sort of pans Irene would have cooked with after her marriage, and which were discarded in their millions in the 1970s. Ruby picked up a pea-green one with a red rim. Pretty.

It was also £65. The estate agent had estimated a price for Oak Apple Farm roundabout where Ruby had expected, and she had arranged visits from two more to be on the safe side. But until she sold, she had to watch her spending. She wandered around, stroking wooden handles and riveted knobs as a medieval carol played over a speaker. *Gaudete, gaudete!* Rejoice, rejoice!

Reading Irene's diary late into the night, there'd been a moment she'd mentally kicked herself. *T'aint nothing to do with skin*, the landlord of The Ten Bells had said and that was when Ruby registered that Theo and his friends were Black. Irene might have hinted at it or even stated it previously, but Ruby's hard-wired presumption that American GIs were square-jawed, gum-chewing white dudes from Ohio and Kansas had got in the way of her realising. Call it perception bias. Though if she was hard on herself, she might call it casual racism.

Twenty minutes later, Will found her. 'OK, that's done, except the paying part.' When she didn't answer, he said, 'Have you got stove envy?'

She was standing by a massive wood burner whose glass peephole shimmered red. She laughed. 'I'd give my eye-teeth for one of these.'

Will gave it a thoughtful appraisal. 'You want one half this size. George... boiler man? His father does stoves. He'd find you a reconditioned one, though you'd still need a new flue.'

'That sounds promising.' She followed Will to the site office to pay for her roof tiles, wondering if she'd always been this cagey about accepting help. Was it the legacy of Lily Bouchard's triumphalism – 'Papa owns this building, this flat and your job' – that she was determined never again to be vulnerable or under obligation? That thought flowed into another: Irene, rejecting Norman's attempts to control her, yet marrying him a year later. A lot could happen in a year. Irene's diaries were proving addictive. She'd left her grandma staring out at the moon. A moon like a silver dollar. 'Straight home after this?' she asked Will.

'Yes, but via Hollesford, to call in at Easifix. I need—' He broke off as her phone chimed a message. 'Bad news?' he asked a moment later as she peered at the phone screen.

'Good news. Amanda has finally made contact.'

'A friend?'

'My mother. Sometimes she's "Mum", but right now, having gone under the radar in Morocco, she's definitely Amanda. It's what she does, and it never fails to worry me. Didier used to accuse me of infantilising her.'

'Didier?'

'My ex.' Ruby supposed she ought to explain more, but the checkout assistant was proffering the card reader. She paid and helped Will load the tiles in the back of his Volvo. As they drove back towards town, Ruby read her mother's message. It made little sense.

> *Dreamed last night I found Mum's locket in the oven.*
> *Remember how it was the only thing she wanted to take to*
> *Maple Court? Any luck in your search for it?*

Ruby had forgotten her promise: the diaries had diverted her attention. She texted back: *No luck yet. Will check oven.* Her mother placed a lot of faith in dreams. Ruby dug out Lubbock Brothers' card and saw that they stayed open until three. Clement Lubbock had mentioned Irene bringing in a necklace, or pendant and something odd about it had lodged in his mind. He'd undertaken to talk to his brother and hopefully he had.

The sky had darkened, and rain hit the windscreen like dried peas, forcing Will to navigate carefully along the single-

track lanes. Ruby let him concentrate. They'd reached Hollesford by the time the cloudburst had spent itself and she felt she
could speak.

'Any chance of me calling in at the jewellers'?'

'Course. You can do it while I drop in at Easifix.' He drove
on for a while, then glanced at her. 'I hope you don't mind me
asking, but was there anything in what Didier said about you
and your mother?'

'That I infantilise her?' She considered for a moment. 'I look
out for Mum, for sure.'

'Didier minded?'

'He was jealous. Mum put their mutual antipathy down to
her being a free-wheeling Sagittarius and he a secretive Scorpio.
Take out the astrology, the truth, he didn't want to
share me.'

'So it was serious between you and him?'

It had been, for her. 'I was making plans for buying our first
home and of us opening a restaurant together. If you can judge
seriousness by the time one half of a partnership spends
scrolling through commercial estate agents' details, then it was.
Very.'

'It didn't bother you that he and your mum didn't get on?'

It had bothered her. 'I wanted to be a daughter to Mum and
a partner to Didier, not an umpire while they slugged it out.
When Amanda doesn't like someone, she goes all sweet and
flaky while also being passive aggressive.'

'No, you're going to have to explain that,' Will said.

'OK. One day, we arrived and she'd prepared his favourite
Japanese sushi. Plates of it. While we were eating, she let a dog
she was looking after chew his Kitsuné sweater. After that, he
stopped coming with me to see her, then tried to stop me going
too.'

'You've told me a lot about Didier in four sentences.' Will

pulled over to let a pickup go past. 'Though you lost me at Kitsuné.'

'Upscale menswear. I had to buy him another.'

'Had to?'

'Yes...' She broke off, thinking about the engagement ring she'd sold to Clement Lubbock. She'd bought that, too. Why? Didier had earned as much as her. Will was looking directly at her and she gave an awkward laugh. 'Don't take everything I say seriously. I use humour to dilute stress. And, you know, it's funny, my boyfriend disapproving of my mother. Demanding to know when she was going to settle down and get a proper job.'

'What does Amanda do for a living?' They had left the country lanes behind and Will was taking back streets towards the town centre.

Picking up her bag so she'd be ready to jump out, Ruby said, 'She makes bangles and earrings from found items. Sea glass is a favourite.'

'That figures. Aunt Flip calls her "the original hippy".'

'She's not far off,' Ruby agreed. 'Amanda quit school in 1967, the Summer of Love, and spent ten years picking grapes, and travelling between festivals. She's never worked in what you'd call a sensible job and is certainly not your usual senior citizen.' Guessing from Will's silence that he was doing the maths, Ruby saved him the time. 'Mum's seventy-two. Thirty-eight when she had me. She hadn't wanted children. She believes the world is overpopulated.'

'She told you that?'

'Course. We're close.'

Will only spoke again as he pulled up illegally on double yellows. 'Will this do? Back in half an hour.'

Ruby said as she got out, 'In case you're wondering, I was a happy accident and there's never been a moment Amanda hasn't loved me. She makes a point of telling me, because she felt unloved in childhood.'

It was only as she headed up the Thoroughfare towards the jewellers' that it dawned on her that she'd said the most tactless thing possible to a man who had lost his mother at age ten.

## 14

'Hi, remember me?'

'The lady who sold her engagement ring. How could one forget?' Clement Lubbock peered at Ruby over his half-moon specs. The innards of a clock were laid out in front of him. 'I'm afraid your watch isn't ready yet.'

'Actually, I came in to see if you'd remembered any more about Irene Plait, and her necklace. The pendant?' *Or locket.* Ruby wasn't going to say the magic word yet.

'Ah, yes.' Clement Lubbock put down the brass cog he was holding, and nodded encouragingly. 'I mentioned your grand-mother to Basil, and after some head-scratching he remembered where her file was.'

'You keep files on people?' This was sounding a bit MI5.

'Call them records. In 2002, we hired a lady to explain the concept of a computer to us and began to, er, digitise our records. For the previous ninety or so years, going back to my grandfather's day, every transaction, purchase and repair was annotated by hand, copies kept on carbon-paper. Such as this.' Mr Lubbock took something from a drawer to show her. It was a square sheet that had been torn from a perforated pad. 'The customer got the top sheet and we filed the carbon copy under the first letter of their surname.'

'And kept them all?'

'And kept them all. Give me half a moment.' Mr Lubbock went into the back of the shop and returned after a few minutes with a similar sheet of paper in his hand. 'Here you are.'

Ruby read what was written on it. The date was 12 June 2001. '"Mrs Plait. Modification to silver locket…"' She took a sharp breath, the hairs lifting on the back of her neck. '"For repair of chain. Sent to…"' She shook her head. 'I can't read the rest.'

'Sent to Grimmonds and Sons. Basil's shorthand is a mystery to most. They were gold- and silversmiths in Hatton Garden, London. We always sent our delicate work there until they closed.'

Ruby read the ticket again. 'Grandma's locket went for repair. Is that what you were trying to remember when I was here before? You thought there was something a bit odd about it.'

Mr Lubbock agreed. Something odd, which had nibbled at his memory. 'Mending a chain is bread-and-butter. It's the modification that was interesting.'

That's what the ticket said. 'Modification to silver locket'. 'What was done to it?'

'Take a look at this.' Mr Lubbock took a gold heart-shaped locket from a cabinet of vintage jewellery. 'This is a traditional Victorian piece.' He prised it open and showed her what was hidden inside: a miniature of a man with Prince Albert-style waxed whiskers. 'Some gentleman gave his beloved a picture of himself, and she placed it inside this locket, along with a coil of his hair, see?'

She did indeed see: a delicately plaited curl of brown hair. 'And she wore it round her neck to remember him?'

'An act of intimacy. In an age before instant photos, when

one didn't advertise one's feelings, a locket was a discreet way of keeping a loved one close.'

'Did my grandma's locket have a picture inside?'

Mr Lubbock couldn't recall. 'Our records show that we sent it to Grimmonds and contacted your grandmother when we received it back.'

'She collected it?'

'We received payment in full, so yes, she would have done. The thing that stuck was the alteration your grandmother demanded. The whole point of a locket is that it opens and closes.' The jeweller clicked shut the one in his hand. 'She wanted hers welded shut.'

'Why?'

'That is a mystery, my dear. And if the glint in your eyes is anything to go by, it's one you will do your darndest to find out.'


Back at Oak Apple Farm, Will and Ruby stacked the tiles in the haybarn. Will would start the job in the morning, if the rain kept off. The tarpaulin he'd lashed over the hole in the roof billowed against its ropes, but it was doing its job. Will had to go.

'Work to do. See you tomorrow.'

As darkness fell, Ruby mixed herself a G and T and picked up Irene's very first diary, from 1939, when Irene would have been fifteen. The writing in this one was larger, as if Irene had not learned to keep secrets, nor felt the need to shrink her script to baffle prying eyes. Its content was suitably innocent: mentions of a friend, Sally Mickleson, and the cycle rides they went on. Every Saturday, they biked to the cinema in Hollesford, enjoying the freedom of empty lanes that few teenagers today would experience. Every film Irene had watched was named.

'Me and Sal saw *Hound of the Baskervilles*. Ever so scary, biking home in the dark!'

And *Gone with the Wind*. 'I cried all the way back. Sally thinks Scarlett O'Hara only had herself to blame.'

There were references to a film star Ruby had never heard of. She'd look up Randolph Scott when she got her broadband. According to Will, the best internet in the village was trans-mitted from a mast on the church tower. He'd given her the number of a local provider. Tomorrow, she'd call them and also investigate a reconditioned wood burner. She hoped Will didn't presume she needed her hand held in perpetuity.

With no TV and no internet to distract her, Ruby quickly became immersed in her grandmother's 1939 world. A poignant entry on 3 September, the day after her grandma turned sixteen, ran:

'Had the rottenest birthday in the whole world. Mum said no to me going to hairdressing school. Thinks I'm too young. She went to Ratty's yesterday and got me a job there, so I start Monday. And war started today. I could cry.'

The following day was blank, and the day after. On 6 September, Irene had written: 'I expect I will care about the war in time but right now, my life is over. I hate Ratty's. I hate jam.'

Ratty's. What a name for a food manufacturer. She'd never known poor Grandma's dream of being a hairdresser and reflected on a conversation she'd had with her mother when she was maybe a year older than Irene had been. 'Mum, I've been thinking. I don't fancy university. I want to be a cook. Well, a chef.'

Her mother's reaction?

'How wonderful, darling. Shall I ask around, see where the best courses are? Do you want to study in Britain or France?'

Ruby hadn't known how lucky she was.

On 9 September, Irene's entry foreshadowed sorrow and

trouble to come: 'Dad fell off a ladder today. His legs went all weak, he says. He mentioned the other day how his knees hurt, like they were burning. Mum says it's because he worked all day in the rain, in wet things.'

And the day following: 'Dad is in bed, doctor called. There is something up with his back now and he has fever. I never heard a man cry before. Mum is sure he'll pull through. I don't know.'

The diary then fell empty, implying that Irene had been too busy helping her invalid father, or too dispirited to put pencil to page. Ruby put that diary aside, going back to the one for 1943. She was impatient to pick up where she'd left off that morning, with Irene washing up at The Ten Bells, asking if she could nip out the back to avoid a confrontation with Norman.

'With her mind full of Theo and the moon.'

*The moon was a silver dollar, a lucky silver dollar.*

On impulse, Ruby googled the lyrics. A song, 'The Moon Is a Silver Dollar' had been released by Lawrence Welk and his Orchestra in 1939. A wartime song, then, but listening to it with her phone to her ear, she couldn't match its lyrics to the words Theo had sung across a pub bar to Irene. Perhaps Theo had not been singing the same song at all, but passing on a message of his own, not wanting to rouse suspicion.

Whatever the reality, Ruby reckoned that Irene's next action had been to set out in the moonlight, on a mission of her own. She propped up the diary so she could shine her phone torch directly on the page. The opening words, written the day after Irene's second shift at the pub, supported Ruby's hunch.

'Well, I got away without Norman knowing. I was fixed on finding that silver dollar.'

# 15

## IRENE

Irene didn't need her torch as she crossed the fields behind The Ten Bells. St George's moon was so bright, when she passed a cow pond she could have peeled its reflection off the water. Looking back the way she'd come, the village was a dark-blue cut-out on a ridge, every lamp and candle shrouded behind blackout curtains.

She thought of Norman. He'd soon be asking the landlord where she was. She had a feeling Mr Scattergood was on her side and wouldn't say. Or maybe he would. Men were usually on other men's side, weren't they? Anyway, she was three fields clear and nobody knew she was here except the moon and Norman's cows watching her pass. Their breath spread silver haze in the night air.

Reaching Long Hedge Lane, it felt safe to switch on her torch. The moment the light touched the tree branches, roosting pigeons took flight. She froze until she was sure nobody was around to notice. Long Hedge was an ancient right of way, but there was a chance of guards patrolling the fence on the American side. They might think she was chasing Theo, and then he'd be in trouble again. If she was able to put his dollar in his hand, he'd know she understood and cared.

'When a man needs to say something, and he can't speak, he throws his money about. Ain't that true?'

He'd encased his silver dollar in clay and lobbed it. That's what he'd meant, she was sure. And she'd find it, but talk about a needle in a haystack! Where ought she start?

That day last month, Theo and his comrades had been digging holes for posts. These posts now stood tall, with chain-link panels filtering the moonlight, like milk through a sieve. She re-pictured the moment the lieutenant had jumped the ditch to give her a talking-to. He had come through a gap between blackthorn stems. A month of growth meant the blackthorn was in full leaf and there were no gaps any more. In the end, she walked all the way to the village road, which she'd left that particular day to take the short cut, and began working her way from there.

Holding her torch inches off the ground, she crept along. She searched side to side in case the coin had bounced and rolled. When she'd gone past the spot she knew was beyond her search area, she repeated the process in the opposite direction. No luck. No dollar.

She tried to picture the moment from Theo's point of view. He'd have seen her walk away, snatched up a clod of clay, squeezed it around the coin from his pocket, and hurled it. Before the lieutenant saw what he was doing. The lump had broken a pace or so in front of her feet. Thinking about it, the dollar wouldn't have bounced or rolled, because the ground had been wet. It would have bedded itself in the track, or in the grass growing along the middle.

Irene changed the scope of her search, getting down as low as she could without actually going on hands and knees. A slinky shape crossed the lane in front of her and she smiled.

Those Americans thought they'd erected an unscalable fence, but Mr Fox had already found a way under.

What was that noise?

It came from the direction of the village. She stood up, listening hard. It was men's voices, like a hunting call. *Ay-ee. Ay-ee. Ay-ee.*

Perhaps the breeze changed direction, or they were travelling fast towards her because suddenly she knew they were calling, 'Irene!' A search party.

She had to get out. Get home before they found her.

She dropped her torch and it went out. Groping for it, she felt something cold and flat. She held it up to the moonlight.

*Where is my lucky silver dollar, Irene?*

In my hand, Theo. In my hand.


Irene made it to her back door and there she stood, with the sense of an escape pulled off, waiting for her breathing to subside. Quietly as she could, she dragged her shoes across the boot-scraper. She'd crossed one of Norman's sugar beet fields, where the young tops were showing through the clay, and her shoes felt as though they weighed at least five pounds each. She placed them beside the others in the lobby, and tiptoed through the dairy, then through the kitchen, lifting the latch on an internal door with the delicacy of a man defusing a time-bomb. Her eye went to the light beneath the sitting room door. Her father had a bed in there as his rheumatoid arthritis meant he could no longer climb the stairs.

Her mother's high, tense voice cut into the silence. Violet, speaking to her husband. 'I know what your feelings are, but as I see it, we haven't any choice.'

Choice of what? Irene crept closer.

'I don't want this any more than you, John, but Norman's offer—'

John Boulter cut in on his wife. 'I'm not ready to sell our land to Norman Plait. Enough, now.'

Irene had often wished she had a penny for every time her mother sighed. The sigh that slid under the door would be worth threepence at least. Her mother had the last word, as usual. 'We'll speak about it when that dratted girl has been found. I tell you, John, she gets more headstrong every day. Norman's sure she's gone up to the American base.'

Irene's mouth turned down in disgust. When had she ever been headstrong? Every day of her nineteen years, she'd done as she was told. Left school. Worked at Ratty's. The only thing she'd ever said no to was Norman.

She crept upstairs. In her bedroom, in the dark, she undressed, folding her clothes onto her chair. She put on her nightdress. There was water in the jug on her washstand and she soaped her hands, scraping the dirt from under her nails.

'"When I walked you home, the moon was a silver dollar,"' she sang in a whisper as she squeezed toothpaste from a metal tube, rubbing it on her teeth because brushing was too noisy and might alert her mother. She would slip into bed, like a good, obedient daughter, and beat Norman at his own game.

Hanging up her coat, she took the silver dollar from the hip pocket. There was a fireplace in her room, and one of the bricks at the back was loose. She lifted it and slid the coin into the gap. There. Hidden.

Without a hot water bottle, her bed was icy and her teeth chattered as she hauled the blankets up to her chin. When she heard feet on the stairs, she rolled over, her back towards the door. The feet stopped. Irene could hear her mother's breathing, then the door opened a crack.

'Irene, are you in bed?'

'Uhh,' she mumbled and shifted as if disturbed from slumber.

The door closed and Irene let go of her muscles. Had her

mother felt under the blankets, she'd have discovered a cold bed. The house went quiet – until resolute knocking penetrated a dream. Irene dragged herself to the window. Even in the dark, she could see who stood at the front door. Norman Plait. Like a Traveller's dog set to chase a rabbit, he never knew when to give up.

Hearing her mother come out of the master bedroom, Irene pushed her arms into the sleeves of her dressing gown. She'd act innocent. Norman couldn't prove she'd been on Long Hedge Lane, could he?

After giving her hair a quick brush, in case of any black-thorn blossom in it, she followed her mother downstairs, standing back as Violet opened the front door of Westumble Farm, and Norman's outrage spilled in.

# 16

---

## RUBY

Frustratingly, Irene's recounting of what Norman had said and done was written in such faint script, Ruby's tired eyes quickly gave up. She'd read it later, in better light. The next clear entry, on Monday 26 April, ran to a single, tantalising line:

'Went to evening service at church yesterday. Norman looked at me all angry, and I'm that angry too I don't care.'

On Tuesday 27 April, Irene mentioned that Mr Scatter-good had sent a note to ask her to do an extra night at the pub the following day. His back 'had gone' – presumably, lifting those barrels. 'Worked four hours, till Mr S. let me go at half ten. Only Billy Gifford and the domino players came in, one being Norman. I ignored him.'

Billy Gifford... father to Ronnie, who some years later had married Philippa? Apples didn't fall far from the tree in these parts, Ruby reflected. Course, Irene would have been hoping to see Theo Robinson, to return his silver dollar.

Her thoughts switched to the other person in this three-way tangle. Grandad Norman, depicted in the diary as perpetually angry and red-faced. Bumbling through the Saint Bernard's Waltz, stamping in the wrong place. He and Irene must have worked it out in the end. The grandad Ruby had known had been visibly fond of his wife. All that jewellery he'd bought. Little tokens of love. Getting up off her chair, she took one of the framed photos off the dresser. It was Irene and Norman's wedding picture, the bride in a flower-print blouse tucked into a high waistband, Grandad in his Sunday suit, a rose in his buttonhole. He was looking towards his bride, half-smiling. Grandma wasn't smiling at all. The photograph, which had been hand-tinted over its original black-and-white, was inside a cardboard mount which tantalisingly hid Irene's hands. Odd, Ruby thought, to frame a wedding picture so it concealed the ring on the bride's finger.

She went back to the diary, leafing through every page of that summer, catching the occasional mention of Norman, and references to Theo. Intriguingly, the pages from 30 August to 6 September 1943 appeared to be stuck together. When Ruby tried to prise them apart with a knife from the kitchen drawer, it was clear they'd been glued.

Diary pages stuck. A locket welded shut.

Maybe Irene's mother had been right to be alarmed all those years ago. By the age of nineteen, Miss Irene Boulter had learned to keep secrets.

## 17

## IRENE

30 APRIL 1943

Irene was just hanging up her jacket for her Friday night shift at The Ten Bells, when Mrs Scattergood popped out of the kitchen.

'Sorry, dear, but we don't have the hours for you.'

Irene stared back. No hours? 'But your husband told me you were short-handed.'

There was something steely in the landlady's smile. 'I don't know why Mr Scattergood would have said that.'

'Well, he did. Short-handed, and that was before he put his back out. He said it right here.'

'He never should have! We have all the staff we need.'

Irene knew that wasn't true, just as she knew who was behind this sudden dismissal. Coming round to their house, banging on the door like a Victorian landlord after his rent.

Irene said bitterly, 'I bet Norman's been saying as he'll do his drinking in the King Alfred at Medfold unless you cut my work.'

The landlady's cheeks turned muddy red. 'That's enough, young lady. I don't have to take your impudence.'

Mr Scattergood, all this while, was polishing tables not ten feet away. Irene looked him full in the eye. He mumbled something about paying her for the time she'd done. Her three measly shifts.

Walking towards home, she cried with disappointment. She'd been convinced that Theo would come in tonight. She had his silver dollar in her pocket, wrapped in a square of tissue paper. On impulse, she veered off the village street and took a path across the fields to Medfold. Her aim was vague; she simply wanted to get as far away from Flixfield as she could. She had to see Theo again. But how?

She reached Medfold as the sun began to set, and seeing the blinds being pulled down in the post office windows felt like a call to action. She darted inside. 'Can I buy some notepaper, and borrow a pen? I'll be quick.'

The postmaster was a distant relation, a Jessop on her mother's side. He tut-tutted and checked his watch. 'If it was anybody else, dear... Go on, but don't make it a three-volume novel.'

So, with the postmaster rattling his door keys, she dashed off some words, no time to think them over or to be clever.

*Dear Sergeant Robinson,*

*I hope you don't mind, but I've got something of yours I feel you would like to have back. Here is a hint. Should you look at the moon some night, you might think of this. I lost my work at the pub, and I suppose you will soon find that out. Whatever they say, it is blasted Norman's fault. I shall wait each evening, six thirty, in St Christopher's churchyard, Medfold. That's the village nearby Flixfield. I shall stand by the yew tree, near the back fence. I shall understand if you cannot come but I hope you will.*

*Yours,*

*Miss I. Boulter*

She addressed the envelope to Sgt T. Robinson, United States Airbase, Flixfield, and ran the flap between finger and thumb to make sure it was stuck down. Mr Jessop let her buy a stamp, and she watched him put the letter in a sack.

'That'll be on its way in an hour from now, dear.'

On Saturday 1 May, Irene completed a shift at Ratty's, then made the three-mile walk to St Christopher's, where she spent an hour waiting beneath the soaring yew tree. She made the same journey again on Sunday and Monday too. And Tuesday, Wednesday and Thursday. If her factory friends, Nellie and Joyce, put two and two together when they saw her take the footpath out of the village, instead of heading home, they said only, 'The pleasures of an evening stroll, Irene!'

Her letter should have reached Theo by Monday latest, so the obvious explanation for him never being there was that he didn't want to see her. On Friday 7 May, she was determined to give it one last go. At five that evening, she stripped off her white overalls and was almost out of the door when the foreman called her back. He pointed to her, Joyce, Nellie and another and said, 'We're going too slow on the lid-basher, so you lot can stay and catch up.'

Lid-bashers turned flat metal discs into jar lids with 'J.P. Rattray finest preserves' on the top. To sit there with the birds singing, and the fragrant scent of broad bean flowers drifting in through an open window, going smack-crunk-chuck, filling a basket with new lids, was nothing short of torture. He finally let them go at quarter past six. It felt like fate was against her and she was doomed never to see Theo Robinson again.

Arriving at St Christopher's as dusk made lollipop shapes of the trees around the graveyard, Irene wondered how many people had noticed her racing through the village... but she had her excuses ready. If anyone followed her into the churchyard to ask what she was doing, she would say, 'I'm paying my respects to my kinsfolk' and wave the primroses and pussy willow stems she'd grabbed on her way here. She placed the untidy bouquet on a Jessop tomb, and picked her familiar path towards the rear boundary. There she slumped beneath the yew tree, her nose filling with the scents of decaying leaves and sappy new growth. Rooks cawed around the church tower, until silenced by the boom of a plane. The skies were getting busier, and would be busier still once the Flixfield base was handed formally to the Americans.

Why didn't she just go home? Theo wouldn't come. All that 'Irene, Irene, fair as a dream' was a lot of old tripe, to make her smile at the time. She closed her eyes, thinking, I'll post the dollar to him, without a note.

When I walked you home, she sang in her head, the moon was a silver dollar, a lucky silver dollar.

It hadn't brought her much luck. Seven shillings was all she had to show for her time as a barmaid. Two shifts at two shillings and sixpence and on the Wednesday night when she'd dropped everything to help Mr Scattergood, she'd earned the midweek rate at sixpence less. The silk stockings she hankered for cost nine shillings and three clothing coupons. Mum had pooled all their coupons to buy a new overcoat and hat for Dad, so that was that. The blouse she'd made from the satin offcut had been given one outing, and nobody had noticed it.

The crunch of shoes on the church path brought her out of her gloomy spiral. She half stood. Theo? Two figures were heading into the church, and she quickly crouched down, hearing the great door open and clank shut. A moment later, light flared behind a lancet window, dying instantly. Somebody lighting a lamp, then pulling the blinds. Even churches had to obey the blackout. More people came, ladies wearing smart hats, talking in *phwah-phwah* voices. Probably the choir meeting to practise. They weren't bellringers; church bells had been banned since 1940. If you ever heard them across the fields you'd know the Germans had invaded.

Time to go, she told herself. Her mother might wander down Hut Lane and see Ratty's closed and dark and 'dratted girl' would turn into 'Irene's going off the rails!' Only, more people were arriving so she had to stay put. It definitely had to be the choir. After ten minutes passed with no more comers, she was hesitating whether to make a dash to the gate when the crack of twigs alerted her to someone's approach. Whoever it was was picking their way around the graves.

'Who's there?'

'Irene, that you, sweetheart?' came a sharp whisper.

The way 'Irene' was spoken, with an upward slide, could come only from source, one voice.

## 18

Irene waited, lamed by shyness. When she spoke, her words bore no relation to her feelings. 'Theo Robinson, you're a whole week late!'

'A week? Irene, no. I've been here the last two evenings, since I got your letter.' Theo came towards her, his figure in a tunic and military side cap cutting in and out of the shadows. Something about the way he stopped a pace or two off suggested he was uncertain too. 'I obeyed you *to the letter*, and waited, wondering if Irene is the kind of high-instep young lady that invites a man to meet her under a tree, then don't show.'

'I was here every night since... *days* ago!'

'And I've been waitin', patient as an ox, under the old yew tree... by the side of it, at any rate. I wasn't eager to crawl underneath in case there were ants.'

Crawl? She gestured to the mighty boughs above their head. 'This is the tree. Which one were you waiting by?'

Theo's expression was lost in the darkness, but he made a click in his throat. 'This is a yew tree?'

'Course it is!'

'Ain't no "course". Where I come from, there was never a yew bush this tall.'

'Because it isn't a bush. I wrote "tree".'

'So you did.' He came close enough to hold out his hand, and she shook it in a fumbling way. 'Seems we've been wasting a lot of good meeting time,' Theo chuckled. 'I'd better buy a book on English shrubs and trees.'

'I'll lend you one. And I'm glad you're here.' Next time, Irene suggested, they should meet next to a gate. 'Gates must be the same wherever you come from. If you want to meet again. You might not.'

'I would like us to meet again.'

His words vibrated against her neck, above the collar of her work blouse, and Irene was suddenly conscious that she was meeting a man, in the darkness. Not going off the rails but edging that way. She said primly, 'I brought your property' and held out his dollar, like a shopkeeper proffering change.

She felt Theo's fingers close around it. 'That lucky dollar, the same one?'

'Yes. I looked for it after I saw you last, and it got me into a lot of bother.'

'I'm truly sorry for that. It's too dark to be sure, but I'll take your word that it's mine.'

Never far away these days, disappointment replaced pleasure. Had he any idea what she'd gone through to find the coin? Not only breaking fingernails, the indignity of Norman Plait seeing her in her dressing gown, then having the gall to demand to inspect her shoes. Norman had stood at the door after her mother had opened it, saying, 'I'll know if she's tramped across fields to get home, rather than come by the road like she ought to have done. The clay on my land don't come out easy from the welts of shoes. I should know.'

Irene had felt her blood boil, all the more when her mother

had instructed Irene to fetch her shoes. Thank heaven, her dad had got himself from his room, wanting to know what was going on. When Irene told him what she was being accused of, God bless him, he'd told Norman Plait that one man and one man only had the right to order Irene around in this house: 'And that man is not you. Norman, go home.'

Irene's voice was sticky with emotion as she said to Theo, 'If I thought that's all the thanks I'd get, I wouldn't have bothered.' She felt childish for showing how she was so easily hurt.

'Oh, Irene.' He caught her as she strode away from him. 'I'm sorry, sweetheart. I get stupid sometimes when I feel too much. It's why I sing, and my friends tell me to button the heck up. You found my dollar; I'm more honoured than I can say. My momma gave it to me and told me to keep it safe always.'

'So why throw it at me?' She shivered because Theo had put his arms around her and she wondered if that meant they were properly courting, because you didn't stand this close to a man who wasn't your dad or grandpa, unless you were stepping out together.

'I threw it 'cause I didn't know how else to speak with you. And Lieutenant Macbeth... he was on his way back, remember?'

*Macbeth*, not MacBeast. She'd better remember that.

'He was wanting to remind me to adhere to the Jim Crow laws.'

Jim Crow? Irene had no idea who that was, though if that lieutenant had anything to do with laws, they'd be rotten ones. 'I thought you were chucking a rock at me. I supposed you were angry.'

'Why would I be angry with you, Irene?'

His mouth was so close, Irene felt the bristles of his upper lip, a wiry growth that spoke of a day's work, started early, and no time to shave. She knew the Engineers turned out first thing because when she went to feed the chickens before breakfast, she'd hear the throat-clearing rev across the fields of the machine that laid the concrete runways. He must be ready for his supper and to get some rest, except he was here.

Time hung, their pulses and their breathing locking step. Nearby, a creature scuffled among the leaves, a hedgehog probably. From the interior of the church, carolling voices pushed a top note.

'I always knew that dollar was lucky for me, Irene.'

Theo bent his head and Irene experienced her first proper kiss as the sun slipped down behind the roof of Medfold church. Not her first kiss, but the first one she had joined in with. Her friend Sally's brother had come home on leave a year back, taking Irene to the pictures and had tried to kiss her on the bus home. She hadn't liked it. She liked Theo's kiss because it didn't go like a bull at a gate.

In the films, when the violins began, girls being kissed threw their heads back, so she did too. Theo drew away.

'You want me to stop, sweetheart? I can stop if you tell me.'

'I – I don't want you to stop. I'm only – I mean, I'm not very good at it.'

'You're doing just fine.'

When Sally's brother had kissed her, her hands had got stuck between her chest and his, awkwardly, like a pair of wooden spoons. With Theo, her hands knew where they wanted to be. Around his shoulders, her fingers spreading. He was taller than her, but not overly, and when she pressed her hips forward, they fitted against his.

He broke away again. 'Now, baby, we're in deep danger. I gotta go.'

'Can't we walk back together?'

'Not to Flixfield, seeing the boys and I don't billet at the base no more. It's why I didn't get your letter till two days back.

The huts were too cold even for us, so we're in housing outside a town called Eye. You know it?'

'Yes, I've been there. My dad calls it "Eye-Eye".'

He laughed. 'Well, my boys are in the truck, waiting for us to go back there. Irene, I want to see you again. I don't want to leave it so long.'

'Me neither.'

'There's a dance at the Volunteer Hall in Hollesford. Can you come? You told me you don't work at the pub now.'

'When?'

'Tomorrow. Most folk can go out on a Saturday night, right?'

Yes, but most people didn't live at Westumble Farm, with an invalid father and a mother whose favourite word was 'no'. Violet Boulter had tolerated Irene going to the cinema with Sally before the war but going out with a man would be a different matter. Even if Irene fudged, and implied she was heading out on her own, Violet was now afraid of the military traffic on the roads. Not just because of dimmed headlamps, but because those trucks were full of sex-starved soldiers. Not that Violet put it like that, but Irene knew it was what she feared. Oh, she so wanted to dance with Theo again, without Mum, Dad and the vicar breathing down her neck!

Hang on though… A chink of light dawned. Sally was at home just now. Her father, who was the village doctor, had been seen driving to pick her up from the railway station. 'Can I bring a friend?' she breathlessly asked Theo.

She felt the vibration of his laughter. They were still locked together.

'Sure, if it's another girl. I don't want you bringing no other boy along.'

'It's not a boy, I promise!'

'The more the merrier, then. Hey, I gotta go.'

The waiting truck had blasted its horn. A last, lingering brush of the lips. Theo said, 'Shall I go first?' Another blast of the horn made the decision. He let her go. 'Hope I see you tomorrow, Irene...'

'What time?'

'Can you do eight? You're sure your folks don't mind?'

'They won't mind.'

Because they wouldn't know who she was meeting. Sally could keep a secret just as well as Irene could.

## 19

'The Volunteer Hall, in Hollesford? I suppose you can go, since it's with Sally.' Violet paused on her way to her husband's downstairs bedroom. 'There won't be any drinking?'

'No, Mum. Only pop.' Irene had been round to Sally's, and secured her friend's compliance. 'We'll go on our bikes, and ride home together.'

'Mm.' Violet narrowed her eyes. Irene held her breath. This wasn't going to be a simple 'yes'.

'You wouldn't lie to me, Irene?'

Irene crossed her fingers. 'Course not, Mum.'

'I didn't tell you,' her mother went on. 'Norman came round the other morning while you were out doing the hens. To look at your shoes.'

'My shoes?' Down came the sensation of being shut in a box with no air-holes.

'I let him look,' her mother said.

Irene's fingers turned into fists. 'You never should.'

'It didn't matter, Irene, because I'd already cleaned them. Didn't you notice? I stayed up after he came knocking the other night and a mighty lot of elbow grease it took, getting wet clay out of the stitch-holes. If I had any imagination, I'd say you'd run across a sugar beet field in them.'

Irene felt the slow boil of a blush. 'Oh.'

'Oh, indeed. Your dad didn't like the way Norman spoke to you and nor did I. If you don't fancy him as your intended, you'll hear no more from me.'

'I don't fancy him, Mum.'

With a nod that implied, *That's that, then*, Violet Boulter went to tend to her broken husband.

At six, wearing her new blouse, a flowered skirt, a cardie knotted over her shoulders and fresh white ankle socks, Irene cycled to Sally Mickleson's house on the outskirts of the village. Sally was waiting with her bicycle in the driveway, her glossy curls protected by a headscarf.

With a half-day shift at Ratty's behind her, then cooking her dad's tea, Irene hadn't had time to faff with curl-papers, and instead had braided her hair around the crown of her head. She felt dowdy compared to Sally, who was wearing a dress under a shoulder-padded jacket. Bright lipstick too.

Sally caught her expression. 'Here.' She produced a gold applicator. 'Montezuma red, all the rage up west.' Sally sounded posher after her year away from the village.

'West... you mean Puddock's Green?'

'The West End, silly. London. Shall we go? Pops and Mops say I'm to be back by eleven, so the clock's against us.'

Pops and Mops. That was new. In any case, Irene's mother was expecting her back at ten thirty so the clock really was ticking.


They parked their bikes at the back of the Volunteer Hall, which was on the edge of town, near the railway station. There were a dozen bikes there already, and even more motorbikes. Military green, mostly, some with side cars. That meant plenty of men, not like some of the dances Irene had attended in the early months of the war with women dancing with women, and a few codgers and pimply lads watching on.

There was home-made bunting slung across the entrance that spelled out 'May Day May Day'. Bit late for May Day, Irene thought.

'Isn't that the international call for assistance?' Sally joked. 'I hope we won't need to be plucked to safety!' With her new-found London confidence, Sally walked straight in and surveyed the scene.

Irene shuffled in behind, looking for Theo and his friends. She saw a sea of RAF blue, young airforce men with ties tucked into their shirt fronts, hair glistening with grease. They stood four-deep at the bar. The heat of bodies intensified the smell of beer. Swing music played above the cheerful racket of voices. Irene recognised a tune from the wireless.

'I like this one,' she said in Sally's ear, her nerves showing in the pitch of her voice. 'It makes me want to dance.'

'Glenn Miller,' Sally said with the ease of one who haunted West End night spots. 'It's a gramophone record.'

'I know,' Irene muttered. Did Sally think she'd supposed the American band leader had come to an old hall in Hollesford on a magic carpet?

They hadn't progressed far when some men at the bar turned, holding their pints clear of the crowd. Spotting Irene and Sally, their expressions lit up.

'Ladies, your prayers are answered,' one of them blared out. They were quickly surrounded. There were other girls present, some in WAAF uniform, most in civvies. Red lipstick and sausage-roll curls, eyes wide and rabbit-like with the hope of a good time. No danger they wouldn't get one, Irene thought. With this many RAF crowded in, even Little Flip's nasty old aunt would get spun around if she showed a leg here.

A pilot officer with gingery-fair hair and a straight side-parting, silver wings on his tie, bagged the first dance. 'Name's Peter. You look like a Mary to me.' He sounded quite plummy.

'I'm Irene.'

'Fancy a drink, Irene? You have a choice of beer, beer or beer.'

'I'd better have beer, then.' Oh, Lord, her mum would smell it on her breath. When she accepted a pint glass, it almost slipped through her hand, it was so beaded with moisture. She sipped it hesitantly. To be honest, she'd have preferred a cherry wine. Peter laughed because she got froth on her upper lip and, when she realised he wasn't laughing at her, she joined in.

'Come on,' he said, 'let's shake a trotter. Your pretty friend is still choosing between Martin and Lubomir. The dancing's about to start again.'

'Lubomir?' What kind of name was that? Czechoslovakian, it turned out. Not that she knew what that was either.

Peter and many of the others were based at Mendlesham, he told her, a distance away, training Czech pilots to fly Spitfires. It all felt absurdly glamorous. She hoped Peter wouldn't ask what she did for a living.

She was nervous about dancing to swing music, but Peter was a good leader, and she discovered a quickstep could be adjusted to the tempo. There was an awkward moment when she tripped over his foot and he leaned close and asked, 'Who is it you're looking for? You keep searching the room. Do you need the ladies, or do I have a rival?'

'No, nobody. Just, I don't meet so many folk, where I live.'

'Where is home, Irene?'

She told him, Flixfield, Westumble Farm, and though he said how thoroughly nice it sounded, she suspected he found her... what was the word? Quaint. He sounded like the man on the wireless who talked to the housewives fashioning pies out of turnip and sawdust, saying, 'Bravo, what clever little women you are!'

The clock above the bar stood at two minutes to nine. Theo was late – unless she'd brought Sally to the wrong place. Not that Sally would mind. She'd selected Martin and they were dancing.

By nine thirty, Peter had invited another girl to dance and Irene was on her third partner. She thought he'd introduced himself as Oliver, but with all the racket, he might be called something else. He too had fair-gingery hair, and a moustache that wiggled because it was combed through with some kind of wax. She suspected that behind the moustache he was quite young.

Theo still hadn't come. When the music stopped, Irene made her way to the ladies where she discovered her cheeks were apple pink. Her lipstick had stayed on, which was something, and her plaits were surviving better than Sally's curls, which had probably been set with sugar water.

She fastened a button on her blouse. Some girls were wearing sweetheart necks revealing the edge of satin brassieres. Something else she'd planned to buy with her pub earnings. How much longer would she have to keep laundering her last pair of white socks? She wasn't the only girl in ankle socks, of course, but other women had clearly had time to dust face-powder on their legs and run a seam up the back with eye pencil. She'd read about doing that in a magazine.

When she walked back into the hall, the music had stopped and the din had subsided to a low hum. There were new arrivals.

Den, Jake, Robbie, Duke and Fletch in their best uniforms, which still looked poor beside the service dress of the British airmen. Theo was lifting the gramophone onto some staging and she watched him show a record in its sleeve to some of the RAF lads. He put it on the turntable and out flowed 'American Patrol', a song she loved. Dancers surged onto the floor, and Theo assessed the various jerky versions of the quickstep being performed, until with a shake of his head, he lifted the gramophone arm off the record.

Cries of 'Hey!' and 'What's going on?'

Theo got up on a chair. 'That ain't no way to dance when Mr Glenn Miller's band has the stage. People, are we gonna have to teach you how to do a Lindy?' He looked around. 'Shall we show 'em, Jake?'

Jake, who Irene would later learn was Theo's best friend among the regular companions, grinned broadly. 'Sounds like a plan, sergeant. Am I the girl, though?'

'You surely look more like a girl than I do, Jakey.'

To laughter and cheers, simpering and shimmying, Jake took up his position. He waited for Theo to get the record turning again. Braying saxophones in close harmony played the opening and everyone watched, spellbound, as Theo and Jake performed a spinning, gyrating dance that looked random, but which couldn't be because, somehow, they kept repeating the footwork.

I can't do that, Irene thought desperately. When Jake was flung over Theo's back, then pushed through his legs as Theo kicked, there was loud applause. At the end, silence fell, then everybody cheered. Theo gestured towards his panting partner. 'I give you the undisputed king of the Lindy Hop, Jake Hendrick.' He too was out of breath.

'You ain't too left-footed yourself, sergeant.' Jake grinned.

Theo called the crowd to order. 'OK, ladies and gents, find your partners, please. We're gonna take this slow.'

Any number of girls vied to be his partner. And then Peter cut off Irene's attempts to get near him. 'Come on, sweetie, let's show 'em.'

She pretended she hadn't heard, because Theo had seen her and made a move, only for Sally to plant herself in front of him and shout above the music, 'I already know how to Lindy Hop.

I've been in London for ages, and got shown by one of your people.'

'Then let's see how well *my people* taught you,' Theo answered, sparing Irene a lift of the eyebrow. He took Sally onto the floor, and Peter pulled Irene after them.

You started side by side, that was the easy bit, kicking your leg forward in time to the beat. Only Peter never managed it when she did, and when she changed her timing to match his, he kicked on a different beat. It was Norman and the Saint Bernard's Waltz all over again. By looking at Theo's feet, and Jake's and Duke's, she worked out that the basic step was a kind of rock step and kick. Then you did a little march on the spot. Theo and Sally were mirroring each other's moves, making turns and slides...

Irene gave up. 'The foxtrot's a lot easier,' she said into Peter's ear.

'But nowhere near as fun. Fancy a stroll outside? You're looking flushed.'

'I'm all right.'

Memories of Sally's brother on the country bus had left Irene convinced she wasn't cut out for this sort of thing. Romance. Dates. Peter was young; they were all young despite the moustaches and greased hair. Men doing a dangerous job, so of course they wanted to spend their evenings with nice, fun girls. That just wasn't her.

She was also upset that Theo had invited her specially, then come late so she was stuck with Peter. Stuck here until Sally decided she wanted to leave. Her friend was now dancing with Duke and looked just as happy as when she was twirling with Theo, which made Irene feel a little better at least.

'Excuse me, may I cut in?' Theo tapped Peter on the shoulder.

'I'm not sure, old thing.' Peter looked ready to object, but

Irene's change in demeanour must have been obvious. 'Oh, all right, I get the picture. Good luck, old bean.'

'What is an "old bean" exactly?' Theo asked as he steered Irene into the dancing.

'It means "dear boy" or "old chum". It's not rude, anyway.'

'Glad to hear it. Now loosen up, sugar. You can't Lindy Hop if you're stiff as a roll of canvas.'

'Thank you, I'm sure. I don't know how to do it. That's why I'm stiff.'

'It's the intention, not the footwork. That'll come later.'

'*You* are late, now we're mentioning it. Eight o'clock, you said.'

He made a regretful flinch. 'Since we moved billets, we've got a whole lot further to come and we have to sign up for a truck and a driver. What should take an hour takes two. But I got here, and so did you.'

'Sally and I have to set off at ten. Leastways, I do.'

'Then let's make the most of it. Hey—' Theo shouted at a group of servicemen without partners standing in a huddle. 'One of you cats wind up the gramophone, else we'll be doing the funeral march.'

She and Theo danced three dances, and by the third, she was getting the hang of it and had finally begun enjoying herself.

But then Theo said, 'You better give some other man a chance, Irene. We'll have tongues wagging otherwise.'

'I want to keep dancing with you.'

'We'll practise some time. Soon enough, I'll be throwing you over my shoulder.'

And catching her again, she hoped. She couldn't believe she'd ever get to that stage. Sally was showing off, doing side rolls over Duke's back, giving everyone a glance of her knickers on the way over. Was that a London habit?

'Go dance with those airforce boys, Irene.'

'All right. I'll wink at the one who has probably parked his desk outside.' The beer had got to her, for otherwise she'd never have said such an unkind thing. She marched up to a shy-looking serviceman wearing glasses, announcing, 'I'm Irene and I'm not quite the worst dancer in the room.'

This one, James, qualified for the title of the worst. Still, why should it matter? It was dawning on Irene that a night like this was to let these men forget for a while what life had become. For some, it was sitting in a shuddering cockpit at ten thousand feet, being shot at. James had a safer role as a welfare officer – but it was his sorry job to write letters to grief-stricken parents and widows, after the telegrams had been delivered. She was getting a glimpse of what it must be like for these boy-men, teetering between life and death. She suddenly wished she'd let Sally's brother kiss her. He was in the Navy, in the convoys. One kiss wouldn't have hurt.

At ten, the dancing paused and they ate stodgy sausage rolls, drank the last of the beer, and there was a collection for the town's Spitfire fund.

As money clinked into a box shaken by a cheerful townswoman in a velvet hat, Theo murmured in her ear, 'How exactly are you getting home tonight? Only, when I went outside a moment ago I heard your friend accepting a lift in an RAF boy's side car.'

'Oh, God. We came on our bikes. I'd better go and see what she's up to.'

Theo came outside with her. He'd been out before to smoke a cigarette. She hadn't realised he smoked, but she shouldn't be surprised. Practically everybody did. Canteen breaks at Ratty's generated enough fug to kipper them all. The women said it made you forget how hungry you were. She'd probably smoke too, except her dad's lungs couldn't stand it.

She spotted Sally and a pilot officer sharing a cigarette and walked up to them, still influenced by the beer she'd drunk. 'Does your mum know you smoke, Sal?'

'Darling Mops? Only if you tell her,' Sally came back. She cocked a glance at Theo's hand on Irene's waist. 'Are you going to tell yours?'

'Yes. At some time.'

Sally smiled up at her companion. 'This is Lubomir, Lyubo to friends, and he's taking me home. You don't mind, Irene?'

Irene looked over at the parked motorbikes. Room for one only in a side car. If she demanded a lift, she'd have to go pillion, hanging on to her skirt. She'd make her own way. A thought struck her. 'How will you get your bike home, Sally? I can't ride two.'

'Why not ask your friend?' Sally pouted Montezuma lips at Theo.

'Because then he'd have to walk all the way back to Eye,' Irene said before Theo could make his feelings known. 'He'd be going all night.'

'So? Nobody will see him in the dark.'

'Stop it, Sal.' Irene didn't look to see how Theo took this remark, but she was disappointed with Sally. Making jokes about people's skin was what washed-up comics did at end-of-pier shows, when they'd run out of decent jokes. 'I don't mind riding home on my own but you'd better work out what to do with your bike.'

Theo finally spoke. He didn't mind a walk, he said. Five, ten miles, was all the same to him. He didn't sleep too good in the stately home they were putting up in. 'Too much creaking and footsteps in the night. And, hey, we've got the moonlight, Irene.'

'We don't,' she said, glancing up. 'It's the dark of the moon in three days.'

Laughing, he began to sing, '"When I walked you home, the moon was a silver dollar..." Escorting you, ma'am, is my poor way of saying "Thank you".'

'What for?'

'Reuniting me with my lucky charm.'

They had to raise the seat on Sally's bike to accommodate Theo's longer legs. At twenty-five past ten, with Irene doomed to get wrong for being late, they set off. She'd been right about the moon. Its waning crescent dipped in and out of cloud, useless for lighting the way. But Irene knew the lanes and there was no traffic once Sally and Lyubo had roared past. She and Theo cycled abreast, their down-directed front lamps carving a tunnel in the dark. With the owls screeching and, once, a nightingale fluting from a thicket, the journey felt intimate. Romantic. They talked over the squeak of their wheels and sang. Theo made up words to one of Glenn Miller's songs.

*Irene's this girl I'm glad I know,*
*sweet as the morning dew, hey man,*
*she kinda likes me too, least I think so.*
*Irene, she found my silver buck, gave back my luck,*
*leastways I truly hope so.*

He caught rhymes from the air, his voice deep and sweet as a clarinet. The peace was broken by Lyubo, coming back the other way, casting a watery beam on the road as he swerved past them.

Reaching Flixfield just after eleven, they wheeled their bikes along the street, and, as Westumble's roof came into sight, leaned them against a hedge. Folded in darkness, they kissed.

'Does this make us serious, Irene?' Theo asked when they pulled apart.

'Are you serious?'

'I reckon.'

'Then I am too.'

It was a simple statement, which felt terrifyingly important, like making a vow while cutting a vein to make the blood flow. It not only committed her, it would cause ructions. Irene knew what her mother would say. She could well imagine Norman's reaction too. Her dad, mild as he was, would also take it hard. 'Why couldn't you find a local boy, Irene? Like your mother did with me?' Yes, she knew instinctively that this heady first drink of love would be poisoned by others.

'We don't know much about each other,' she said faintly.

'True, but it's good too.'

'Is it? See, I know everyone in Flixfield, and most things about them. Even what some of them pray about, and whether they like liver or not.'

'Well, I don't like liver, Miss Irene, but I want to find out all about you. It will be like getting into a book, a page at a time. Don't you want to know all about me too?'

Yes, she did! Everything he thought, and liked, and his life before here. And more than that, she wanted to explore the giddy feelings she got when he held her and kissed her. She began by moving closer and raising her face. 'Page one,' she whispered.

## 20

A few days later, Irene and Theo were caught kissing in the churchyard at Medfold by the man who cut the grass. He stood with his scythe, gawping at them like the Grim Reaper. They needed somewhere safe and private to meet and Irene knew the very place.

Dunbury was an abandoned village between Flixfield and Hollesford. Deserted back in the plague-times, it had a ruined church, St Margaret's. In the echoing nave, lit by candles Irene brought from home and with an audience of flitting bats, Theo taught her to Lindy Hop. They got round the lack of music by Theo making percussion in his throat. Irene would sing, inventing absurd lyrics. Laughing and laughing. Kissing among the fallen slates and the wormy pews. She learned how to take her weight on the balls of her feet, and do lightning-fast foot-work, swing-outs and jazzy improvisation. At one point, Theo stopped calling the dance the 'Lindy Hop' and began talking about 'Jitterbugging'. She learned to flip over his arm, do lifts and to cartwheel, to slide through his open legs and roll over his back.

On the fourth or fifth visit, they were trying a new move

and she crashed to the floor, pulling him down with her. Laughing like drunks, they lay on the cracked tiles of St Margaret's nave, until something changed in his eyes.

'I can't hold back no more, Irene.'

'I don't want you to, Theo.'

'It's not right, baby, 'cause I can't make things formal, how I'd like.'

Irene's reply was to wriggle off her knickers and pull her skirts above her hips. Opening her mouth to Theo's kiss, she guided his hand between her thighs, and felt him shudder. She knew all the rules that were made for girls like her, and she was breaking them.

And in church.

She didn't care a candle's flicker, because these sensations taking her over were blissful and urgent and completely, utterly right.

## 21

## RUBY

THURSDAY 15 DECEMBER 2022

*Phew.* Grandma.

Ruby turned the page, feeling like a voyeur.

Irene had written again the next day but must have revealed thoughts too intimate, or erotic, even for her own viewing as they were crossed through in heavy pencil. 'The diarist redacted her own words,' Ruby said, as though to a court hearing.

When Irene wrote again, it was in a matter-of-fact tone, as if the girl who'd grappled with her lover on the floor of a deconsecrated church was nothing to do with her. The big news in Irene's life at this point was that the Volunteer Hall at Hollesford had become out of bounds. Ruby read Irene's words with growing unease:

'Two RAF bases near Hollesford have been turned over to the United States, and the crews have arrived. White GIs won't share a room with Black servicemen, not even a public hall. Theo and the others can't go to the Volunteer Hall any more.'

At the beginning of June 1943, Irene wrote:

'Didn't see Theo last night 'cause they're behind building the emergency runway and leave is cancelled. Theo has the date for the first deployment of the 699 Bomb Group.' 'Deployment' was printed hesitantly, suggesting it was a word outside Irene's scope. It must refer to the imminent arrival of US squadrons at Flixfield. Pilots and aircrew. White GIs, in other words.

'They're coming mid-August, though we can't know the exact date. Mum must have heard something about me and T. as she said in a funny way today, "Staying home tonight?" I asked what made her think that and she said, "'Cause you haven't powdered your legs yet." She followed me upstairs, saying, "I hope you are being careful, girl. Some things you can't hide under a gooseberry bush, least of all in a village like ours." I pretended I didn't know what she meant.'

Norman's name had become markedly absent from the diary since the business with the shoes. Did he know how serious things had become between Theo and Irene? Ruby wondered. And what about the US authorities? Had rumours of a liaison between a local girl and a Black engineer spread as far as the airbase?

'...if any of them hang around with you, they'll get into severe trouble,' Lieutenant Macbeth had told Irene. White and Black didn't mix. *Couldn't* mix under American Jim Crow laws, which would follow the white crews to Suffolk and which spelled 'segregation'. Certain that catastrophe was lurking in the pages ahead, Ruby tried again to prise apart those her grandma had deliberately stuck together. She succeeded only in tearing the fragile paper. How would Will respond if she asked to borrow some razor blades? Remind her, probably, that men used disposables these days, or electric razors. There was an art supplies shop on the Thoroughfare in Hollesford, though, opposite Lubbock's. They'd have craft knives. Tomorrow morning, she'd cycle into town.

She marked her place again in the diary and put it aside. She was in danger of forgetting she had a house to sell. Another estate agent was due later this morning. She had skirting boards to wash, perfume to zhoosh around to disguise the persistent whiff of damp paper...


'You have to have a new wood burner,' was the second estate agent's parting comment. 'A lovely, warm glow sells a property like this better than anything.'

'Should I borrow a Labrador to lie in front of it?' Ruby was sure Will would loan Edna for an hour or two.

The agent, who seemed very young to Ruby and was so tall he'd hit his head on a beam, failed to pick up on her humour. 'I really wouldn't. You'd be surprised how many people are allergic to dog hair. You need Bob Oaks.'

Suppressing the desire to ask if he meant she should ask Mr Oaks to lounge about on a rug, she told him she already had his number somewhere. Bob Oaks was George the boiler man's dad and Will had found his card among his collection of tradesmen's details, and read the number out to her on a phone call. The third and last estate agent, a woman with expensive-looking highlights, made exactly the same point about a new wood burner.

'It's an absolute must at this time of year.' She also mentioned the name Oaks and Ruby, though still baulking at the expense, gave in.

'All right, I'll call him though I can't suppose he'll get here before Christmas.'

'Oh, just tell him you're freezing and you've nowhere to hang your stocking,' the agent said breezily. 'I'll come back to you with a valuation, soon as I've had a think.'

Ruby had written Bob Oaks' details on the bottom of a supermarket receipt, the nearest bit of paper when Will had phoned. She called him and it went to message: '*Professional stove fitters, twenty years years' experience, leave your message after the beep.*'

'Hi, Ruby Plait here, Oak Apple Farm. I'm freezing and I need a new, or reconditioned, stove by Christmas or I'll have nowhere to hang up my stocking.'

Let's see where that got her. Reported for sexual harassment, potentially.

She now had a choice what to do with the rest of the day. Clean more of the house, or... Ruby looked at the diaries, then at the rain-pocked window. Cycling into town for a craft knife to open those stuck pages felt less than inviting. Her mind travelled beyond the gate of Oak Apple Farm. Will Keelbrook, possessor of a Swiss army knife and a trade card for Easifix, would surely own one. Asking to borrow it was a perfectly acceptable reason to call on him and finally see his place. As she walked up Westumble's drive, the farmhouse door opened and Philippa appeared, dressed to go out, in rain mac and matching waterproof hat.

She frowned slightly at Ruby. 'Will's taking me into Hollesford so I can buy my Christmas cards,' she said.

On cue, the back end of the olive-green Volvo emerged slowly from the rear of the property.

'Could I bag a lift?' Ruby asked, swallowing her disappointment that she wouldn't, on this occasion, get to see Will at home.

Was that annoyance on Philippa's face? However, Philippa said she had no objection. Will said, 'No problem,' and drove up to her gate so she could grab her bag and purse. In town, along with a craft knife, Ruby picked out two Christmas cards in the art shop, one for Will, one for Philippa. Last Christmas, she'd signed eighty-five cards to friends and customers. How things changed.

At home, after putting the tofu and Chinese cabbage she'd

bought at the deli on the Thoroughfare into the fridge, she took a craft knife blade from its packaging and inserted it between the first two glued pages of Irene's diary. With a sound like seed heads popping, the blade severed the dried glue. Monday and Tuesday 30 and 31 August 1943 lay open. Ruby's eye fell on a single word.

*Locket.*

## 22

## PHILIPPA

She stared at the object in her hand. A broken coil of silver chain with a heart-shaped locket at its end. All at once, the case flew open and out buzzed a fat blowfly. Philippa screamed and threw the locket at the wall. 'Horrible thing!'

She woke up in her armchair by the stove, which had gone out. Ugh, that fly had been so real. Slowly getting up from her seat – these days it took a minute to find her balance – she hobbled over to the far side of the kitchen and switched the kettle on for tea. In truth, she knew exactly what had prompted the nasty dream. It was going up the Thoroughfare in Hollesford.

Will had helped her with her food shopping, then driven into the town centre to pick up Ruby, who was buying art supplies or something. You could take a car up the pedestrian street if you had a disabled badge, and hers lived in Will's glove-compartment. He'd bought that car to make things more comfortable for her. He was a love.

They'd crawled past Lubbock's, bringing memories back to Philippa of a June afternoon, and the shame that came with it.

2001. It had been four days after Norman died, and

Philippa had been tending her roses in the front garden, the tears running down her cheeks. She'd seen Irene go past, a basket on her arm, heading for the bus stop. They'd still had a bus service back then. She and Irene weren't speaking. They'd quarrelled badly, but it didn't stop Philippa wondering what the bus trip was about. Irene didn't need food. All the women in the village were taking little offerings to the new widow: soup, cake, biscuits and the like. *I know where she's going.* It was pure instinct, but Philippa had always had a knack for guessing right. She'd mopped her tears with her sleeve, fetched her handbag and was on the bus ten seconds before it drew away. Irene had turned her face from her.

When they got off, they went separate ways, but Philippa made sure to notice what direction Irene took. Straight to Lubbock's, the jewellers', just as she'd thought. Irene came out again a few minutes after and headed off towards the mini mart. Philippa entered the jewellers', and found Basil Lubbock in charge. She'd said, 'Mrs Irene Plait left something with you a minute ago, and she wants it back.'

'She wants her locket back?' came the surprised response. Just her luck it had been starchy Basil there that day and not his brother Clement, who had a more obliging way about him.

'That's right,' she'd said. 'I'll take it, please.'

Basil wouldn't hand it over. 'If Mrs Plait comes in herself, that's a different matter.'

'But I'm her sister-in-law!'

'Indeed,' Basil Lubbock had intoned, without moving an inch.

'Then let me see it. I need to look inside it.'

Philippa remembered the expression that had spread across Basil Lubbock's face. Disdain. *I know what you want. I know what you are.* He hadn't said it out loud, of course, and he'd remained polite. As she'd walked out of the shop, Irene had come out of the mini mart. They'd stared at each other before turning in different directions.

'I never did see that blessed locket again,' Philippa muttered, opening a box of nettle leaf tea. She'd run out of fig leaf. 'She must have got it back, then hid it. Where? Because I looked high and low.' Even under the beds at Oak Apple, which had made her knees ache for a week.

In the last months of her life, Irene had spoken of it, as if she'd just that moment put it down. 'Where's my locket? Where have you put it, Little Flip?'

Back to childhood, calling Philippa that old, old name. 'What locket, Irene?' she'd said, feigning ignorance. 'I don't know what you're talking about.'

That had been unkind, but the world was cruel, wasn't it? The only antidote to Philippa's shame now was the certainty that if she couldn't find the wretched locket, then neither would Ruby.

## 23

### IRENE

'Sorry, Philippa, I can't take you with me; it's your teatime.'

'Where are you going?'

They were standing in the road, halfway between their homes. Irene had wheeled her bike up Westumble's path and was about to get on board.

'Not your business, Little Flip. Go in, before you get wrong from your auntie.'

They could hear the nasty old woman shouting from the door of Oak Apple Farm. 'Philippa, d'you come here this minute or you'll not get a bite of supper!'

Elsie Binney was her name. Irene pictured her with her fists wedged against her hips, her grey bun wobbling with each inflation of her lungs. What put the old dragon in such a filthy temper always?

'Go on, love, or she'll shout herself hoarse.'

'What's in that bag on the back of your bike, Irene?'

'My dancing shoes. I'm going out, but I can't pedal in them because the soles are too thin.'

Philippa turned the information over; you could see her teasing out the meaning. Then she asked, 'Are you gally-vanting off with that darkie soldier? You are, I know you are.'

If Irene hadn't been holding her handlebars, she'd have grasped the child by her cotton print collar. 'Philippa Plait, who said such words to you?'

'Norman did. My brother is that cross with you he won't speak to you till you 'pologise for leading him up...' – cogs turned in the child's brain – 'up the garden path and I know what path that is.'

'Do you now.'

'A slippery path, Aunt Elsie says so too.'

Irene had hitched up her skirt ready to get on her bike, but let it fall as thoughts of her and Theo played like a film in her head. His lips on her breasts... her legs around his waist. Dear God, don't let anyone else know of it!

Philippa pulled hawthorn leaves from the hedge, scattering them onto the tops of her sandals. It was August, the air sticky and full of little flies. 'Auntie says you're light.' Philippa gnawed her bottom lip with her small teeth. 'What does light mean when it's a person?'

It meant a light-skirt. A gadabout. One who took her pleasure from life like the bees searching for nectar.

'Am I light?' Philippa nagged.

'Light means happy. Always cheery.'

'Then I'm not. Auntie says I'm miserable as a wet Sunday.'

'Never mind what she says.' Irene mounted her bike. 'Don't use words like "light" and calling the American servicemen what you said a minute ago; that's not right, dear.'

'It's what Norman calls them.'

'They've come to fight for our freedom. Each one of them left his home to be of service to us. They deserve our respect. Now go in for your tea.'

Philippa shot off, but not towards Oak Apple Farm. She'd

spotted Norman bringing home a laden haycart. Irene knew the child would repeat their conversation word for word and so she cycled off as fast as she could. What could Norman do, call the police and report her for going to a dance? She wasn't giving Theo up. There were no segregation laws over here, though as Theo had pointed out, attitudes travelled more easily than men, and the airbase was now home to over fifteen hundred of them, with another thousand expected imminently. All but a couple of hundred of them were white. 'And if there's a white American GI who respects a Black GI,' Theo had said, 'he's the one I haven't met yet.'

Tonight, she, Theo and the others were heading out to the coast. Finding somewhere they wouldn't cross paths with white GIs was getting harder. Reaching Dunbury and the abandoned church absolutely panting for breath, she threw her bike down into the long grass and lay next to it, swatting thunder bugs off her arms. When she heard the grind of a truck, she sat up. It sounded like a military vehicle. She crept forward and peered out onto the road, checking for the double wheels and the familiar white star on its front. Only when it was close enough for her to read the number plate did she step into the road, waving her arms.

Lil' Roy, the driver, halted with a nervous grin. *In quick*, said the jerk of his head. Theo jumped out of the back, helped her over the tailgate, and lifted her bike in. Hands reached for it, whisking it out of sight and in less time than it took to say the first three lines of the Lord's Prayer.

The first time Theo had insisted on picking her up, there'd been consternation.

'You gotta be crazy, brother!'

Jake had said, 'If the lieutenant sees a white girl riding along with us, he'll lynch us one after the other, till he runs out of rope or trees.'

Lil' Roy would say nothing because he had all the same

reasons to hate Macbeth. The Black engineers loathed a man who knew less than they did, and used his authority like a stick to beat them.

'Ready to dance, Irene?' Theo asked as she sat down at the back, where she wouldn't be seen.

'In this heat? Maybe I'll sit outside sipping iced tea.' She was picking up their ways of talking, and 'iced tea' got her a laugh. It was airless under the canvas roof. They called the truck 'Kelly', because the letters on the front were KLL. Kelly must have been left out, gathering in the day's heat.

Lil' Roy pulled up short of their destination, in a stretch of silent countryside, and Irene climbed out. Her bike was handed down and she mounted it then followed the truck. Theo always waited for her. These days, he rarely danced with another girl. Nobody could move her feet like Irene could and, besides, they were serious.

Reydon village hall was packed. Men off duty from the coastal defence stations stood around in their khaki service dress. They were a different breed from the Brylcreemed RAF lads with their laconic talk. Their partners were local women, land girls, a few ATS in uniform. The arrival of the Engineers of the 923rd brought a round of applause. Theo and his crew were known as bringers of the latest music and of a good time.

Irene, when she took to the floor with Theo, also created a stir. Spinning and swinging out, her light blonde hair catching the light, she garnered admiration, even envy. It didn't feel real. Except that Theo, handsome and smiling, his velvet glances only for her, told her that it was. 'Real as real, Irene. More so than any other time in my life.'

Tonight, he wore a silver pin on his tie, which, like all the men, he tucked into the front of his shirt so it wouldn't flap as he moved.

She looked closer. 'Hey, that's your dollar!'

'I reckoned the best way never to lose it again was to have a pin soldered on the back. Safer there than in a pocket. Ready, Irene?'

She was.

'American Patrol' swelled out from the gramophone. Irene and Theo strutted into the space created for them, coming together like magnets. They danced four songs in a row, and afterwards, Irene could have wrung out her blouse. She was getting a taste for beer and drank two straight pints to moisten her throat. Theo hoisted the dust cover off a piano in a corner and began a jazzy riff, keeping the tempo slow so the older folk could have their moment. He was an accomplished player, needing no sheet music. He began to sing, improvising. '"When I walked you home, the moon shone bright as a dollar, a lucky silver dollar..."' He was working on that song, he'd told her, but still didn't know how it finished. All at once, he put down the piano lid, indicating that he wanted to take her outside. They stood by a wall, shoulders touching, listening to the grumble of thunder out to sea.

Irene said, 'That sound always reminds me of spuds being tumbled into the back of a cart.'

'Me,' said Theo, 'I'm put in mind of a freight train lugging pig iron. My momma, she always says that the pig iron train takes so long to lumber past, you got time to cook up a hoecake on a skillet and sell it to the man in the guard-van.'

'What's your mother's name?'

'Ruth-May. And your mother is Violet. Maybe one day they'll get to meet.'

'I think they will.' Two pints of beer, she was ready to believe anything.

'Irene, tip your head forwards.'

'Why?'

''Cause I'm asking.'

She did so and felt him move the damp curls at the nape of her neck.

'Hold still, honey.'

Coolness against her skin, then a weight slid down the front of her blouse. When he said, 'Done,' she thought he'd dropped a pebble between her breasts – until she pulled out a fine chain, and found it was attached to a silver heart with a curved top.

'It's a locket,' he told her, 'and you can put inside it whatever you choose, but I hope you'll keep this in there for now. Hold out your left hand.'

Her breath came so shallow it scratched her lungs as Theo put a ring on her fourth finger. A gold band that gleamed when she held her hand up to the twilight.

'Does this make us... you know?'

'It makes me promised to you, sweetheart. You get to choose for yourself.' Theo kissed her. 'I'm kinda hoping it does, Irene.'

'It does. But I thought we couldn't.'

'You're right, it has to stay secret, because I can't be seen to be engaged, least of all to a white English girl. You get what I'm saying?'

'Can I tell Mum and Dad?'

'Maybe not yet. They need to get used to the idea of you being with me. Do they know?'

'Not really.' They must know something, of course, since the gardener in Medfold churchyard had obviously yapped to all and sundry. If Elsie Binney had heard, then the weathercock on top of the church tower would know about them kissing too.

'The ring fits into the locket,' Theo was telling her. 'I made sure of it.' He slid the ring off her finger to show her. 'You nestle it in, then you close it shut so only you and I know it's there.'

'I hope you didn't spend too much,' she said.

He laughed, a sound between humour and desperation. 'I spent everything I have, but the assistant in the jeweller's saw my uniform and my pain and struck me a deal.'

They were being called back inside, for the ritual of eating sausage rolls and emptying out their pockets into the Spitfire tin. Soon, she was back on the floor with Theo, thinking, This is my first dance as an engaged woman.

She was jitterbugging to 'Bugle Call Rag' when a flash half-blinded her. When she'd stopped blinking, she saw a bearded man in a trilby hat training a camera on her, his flash gun ready to go off again. 'You didn't ask,' she protested, thinking – I know him from somewhere.

He knew exactly where they'd met, and when the music had stopped, he told her. 'You're the pretty one at J.P. Rattray's who I asked to hold up a jar of pickled beetroot. Remember?'

Oh. Yes. He'd turned up at Ratty's a few months back to take pictures for the local newspaper, for an article entitled 'Suffolk Feeds the Nation'. She and three other women had stood in a line, each holding up a jar from J.P. Rattray's range. Their picture had appeared a week later under the headline: 'These girls aren't in a pickle, they're jam-packed with determination to keep our favourite food on the shelves'. Joyce had been pulling faces at her and the camera had caught her mid-snort, so she'd looked boggle-eyed.

'So, you and this fellow.' The photographer gave Theo an up and down look. 'Front page material, I'd say.'

Irene said quickly, 'Please don't. My folk wouldn't like it.'

'Ah, but our readers will. Remind me, you're Irene... Irene what?'

'Smith.'

'Boulter, isn't it? In my line, you don't forget a name. You, my friend?' The photographer whipped out a notepad and pencil, and smiled expectantly at Theo.

Theo plucked the pencil and tucked it in the man's hatband. He'd drunk a few pints. 'Ain't no call to write down my name, sir.'

For all that, when the *Echo* dropped through the front door of Westumble Farm a few days later, there were Irene and Theo on the front. The photographer must have asked around because they were both named.

Her mother plonked the paper down on the breakfast table. 'So it's true, what Elsie says. You *are* stepping out with one of those coloured Yanks.'

'I am. And we're serious.' Irene touched her jumper to feel her silver locket, hidden beneath.

'What's this?' Irene's father had come out of his room, using two sticks.

Irene got up to help him. 'I'm stepping out with a man called Theo, Dad, and I want you both to meet him.'

John Boulter looked around. 'I don't see him. Has he gone invisible?'

'Very funny. He's not here. He works at the base. He's an American, Dad. May I bring him to tea, soon as he can?'

She saw her parents exchange glances. It was her mother who answered.

'I suppose, though God alone knows what Norman will say.'

Irene was long past caring about Norman. She cared that her mother was looking at the picture in the paper, though, as if she wanted to cry. Violet Boulter rolled the newspaper, and rammed it into the range where she set it alight.

'Are you upset because Theo's Black, Mum?'

'No. He can't help that. It's you, front page of the newspaper, showing your you-know-whats!'

The photographer's flash had gone off as Irene performed a spin that made her skirt flare, revealing a good deal of well-honed thigh. If that was the worst of her mother's worries, things could only improve.

Everyone in the village took the *Hollesford Echo* and when Irene arrived at Ratty's for her next shift, there were cheers and whoops from the other women. The foreman leered aggressively. 'No more secrets now, Miss Boulter.'

Norman hammered on the door of Westumble Farm. Irene was out at the time, but her mum warned her, 'Don't bring your Theo here yet. I never saw a man more angry than Norman when he called on us, with that newspaper in his hand.'

Irene meant to follow the advice, and keep Theo away from Westumble. Only, events got in the way. The thing she most feared happened.

The following Saturday night, she, Theo and the others somehow drove all the way into Flixfield instead of stopping a mile short. They'd been dancing in Southwold, by the sea, and the intention was to drop Irene off with her bike, then double back to their accommodation near Eye. Only, they were singing and talking so happily, Theo forgot to knock on the partition to alert Lil' Roy.

They turned a sharp bend, and the brakes went on so hard, they lurched sideways into each other. The roadside was awash with light.

Lil' Roy rapped from the other side of the partition and they heard him shout, 'Irene, get out right now. MPs up ahead.'

She had no idea what that meant, but from the way Theo and the other men hustled her towards the truck's rear exit, she knew they needed her gone. She'd have made it out and run away across the fields except that her skirt caught on the tailgate and she fell. Putting her arms down to save herself, excruciating pain speared up her wrist.

Theo vaulted out to help her up. 'It's MPs. Military police. Irene, you gotta go!'

She tried to get up, only someone shouted, 'You there, don't move!' Hard footsteps approached. A torch shone in her and Theo's faces.

In a silky drawl, the owner of the torch said, 'Well, lookee here, First Sergeant Robinson and his little white tramp.'

## 24

'We heard you got a girl in the truck, Robinson, in violation of the rules and natural law.' The military policeman let that sink in. 'Looks like our intelligence was sound.'

There were other men too, and one came to stand behind Irene. Another took up a stance beside the officer shining the torch, while yet another manhandled Lil' Roy out of his cab. Lil' Roy was pitched over the tailgate to join the occupants in the back of his own truck.

Held breath had its own sound, Irene discovered. It was a clicking in the throat, and repeated swallowing while the stomach clenched with dread.

The officer shining the torch named himself as First Lieutenant Jackson, and the man standing behind Irene as Officer Resnik. Irene was aware of another man in uniform, shifting his feet on the road but faceless in the darkness. Jackson told the MP who had brought Lil' Roy to drive the truck back to base. 'You boys?' Jackson pitched his voice to the scared, silent men in the rear. 'You stay good and quiet, see you don't give no trouble.'

Theo spoke up. 'This lady's hurt, officer.'

Why weren't they putting Theo in the truck? A coldness

crept through Irene despite the sticky heat of the night. The torch beam was burning the back of her eyes and whenever she moved her head, it followed her, it seemed, deliberately. It was hard to keep standing up.

Theo tried again. 'Lieutenant, this lady needs somebody taking care of her.'

'Oh, we'll take care of her.' It wasn't First Lieutenant Jackson who spoke, but the one who all this time had waited in the shadows. Seeing his face, Irene let out a gasp. Macbeth. Had he summoned the military police? If so, who had betrayed them to Macbeth?

The truck moved off, pumping exhaust fumes and making her cough. She watched it bump across the verge to get around the military police vehicle, the men inside picked out in the red tail lights until they rounded a corner and were gone.

The torch beam swung on Theo.

'What's that you're wearing on your tie, Robinson?' First Lieutenant Jackson demanded.

'A tie pin, sir.'

'Looks like a dollar to me.'

'It's a silver dollar, sir; I had it made into a pin. It's kinda lucky.'

'You don't say. Did you know, soldier, it's illegal to melt, destroy or tamper with United States currency?'

'I ain't tampered with it, sir, nor melted it. Just had a man put a pin on the back. Goddamn!' Jackson had snatched the pin off, ripping Theo's tie, before hurling it. They heard it land on the road.

'It ain't worked for you, soldier, 'cause this ain't your lucky night.'

Resnik seized Theo, jerking one of his arms high behind his back. As Theo breathlessly asserted his right to a court martial, Lieutenant Jackson stepped back and said, 'All yours, Macbeth, you get first go.'

Irene had never imagined what it was like to hear a man being beaten. Like the thud of the threshing barn floor, with gasps and cries of agony that started loud, then weakened as the assault went on. And on, Resnik holding Theo's arms behind his back as Macbeth rained blows on Theo's face, stomach and every unprotected part of him. Meanwhile, Jackson kept Irene back with one hand. His other hand shone the torch, showing Macbeth where to aim. Theo's knees gave way, and then he was vomiting, his cries reduced to the pulsing whimper of a man who was ready to bleed into the road.

Irene had screamed the whole way through, incoherent with fury and grief. She now sank down, sobbing, pressing the heel of her good hand against her locket until the chain bit into her skin. The other hand, her left, lay in her lap, weirdly bent and shooting pain into her shoulder. Resnik and Jackson dragged Theo to their vehicle, pushed him inside and started the engine. That left one figure in the road beside her.

Torchlight hit Irene's face.

'Well, now, little lady, I warned you we got rules.' Macbeth offered a hand to help her up.

She stared through tears, seeing only the man's stocky outline. 'Why did you do that? It's evil. You didn't need to do that!'

'Sometimes, you gotta teach a boy a lesson. And now, miss, I'm going to teach you one too, which in due course, you'll thank me for.'

# 25

## RUBY

What 'lesson' was coming? The pages Ruby had prised open, from the 21st August to the 27th, had shown how Irene's life had opened up. Dancing, excitement, an engagement ring and a locket.

*The* locket. It had to be.

The 28th August detailed Theo's beating, but the day after was blank. Ruby used her craft blade to separate the next two pages, 30th and 31st. Blank too. The first two days of September were also empty, and she wondered why Irene had sealed them. So she never again had to look at them, and into the abyss of despair?

*Down in Alabama with its vicious racists...* Martin Luther King's words had been spoken, by twisted coincidence, exactly two decades after Theo and Irene's ordeal. Only, theirs happened on an English country road a stone's throw from where Ruby sat now. Poor, poor Irene, alone in the dark with what sounded like a broken wrist and a hate-filled man looming over her. She must have been terrified, and probably imagined Theo was dead.

Which he might have been. Irene might have stuck the following pages together in an act of silent remembrance... But Theo couldn't have died, since there was an invitation to an engagement party in December 1943. Unless it had been, as Philippa implied, the creation of a delusional young girl? A grieving one...

There were four more pages to slice open, but Ruby had lost her courage. Maybe some things were better not to know.

Ruby woke next morning when it was still dark and, after a snatched breakfast, ploughed past her repetitive thoughts by hoovering the house, attic to ground floor, and then hand-sweeping the skirting boards. When she'd finished, her grand-mother's unfinished story was still going round in her head. Raw and early as it was, she felt the urge to get out of the house. It was driving her demented, not knowing what Irene had gone through, or if Theo had survived. How about another go at visiting Will at home... though could she confide in him, under the circumstances?

Because somebody had betrayed Irene and Theo, and the prime suspect, in Ruby's mind, was his godmother's beloved brother, Norman.

As she walked across to Westumble, she admitted that she was starting to hate her grandad. The American military police had not been lying in wait for Theo's truck on the off chance. Macbeth, clearly, had masterminded the assault, but Norman had to be the most obvious betrayer.

The front garden of Westumble Farm was full of bare-stemmed roses in large, circular beds. This had been Irene's first home; this was the pathway she'd wheeled her bicycle along, preparing to meet Theo for a dance in a place called Reydon.

*'Are you gally-vanting off with that darkie soldier?'*

Ruby shook the words from her head. No. She didn't want to imagine Philippa feeding tales to Norman, and her amiable grandad tracking down Macbeth, to lay information against Theo and Irene. She skirted the farmhouse, passing under a mellow brick arch into an empty farmyard whose clay-tiled roofs were silvery with frost. Will's car was parked next to a black-weatherboarded building whose clean, smart lines came as a surprise.

What had she expected? An outhouse, swept clean, and a camp bed in a corner?

She went up shallow limestone steps and peered through a glass entrance door. A ship's bell hung from a bracket. Ruby over-pulled it and cringed at its jangling peal. Edna arrived, barking at her through the glass, her tail beating side to side. Ruby hoped Will was the kind of person who got up in a good mood. 'I don't want to get wrong from him again,' she murmured in Irene's voice.

What time was it, exactly? She couldn't kick the habit of glancing down to check, realising for the hundredth time that her watch was still at the mender's. It must be getting on for eight, because it was almost fully light. Even so, that was rather early to be clanging Will's bell like a bailiff.

Ah – movement. Edna ran away barking towards a curving, metal staircase. Ruby stepped back and smacked moss off her body-warmer, unsure how it had managed to stick to her on the short walk over. She hadn't dressed for this. Hadn't expected to be entering a designer interior.

He was coming. She saw him raise a hand in greeting as he recognised her. He wore a loose white sweatshirt, black sweat-pants. Pyjamas? He punched numbers into a security panel and the door clicked open a couple of inches. She pushed and it stuck. Will pulled. They wrestled until she let go.

'It only needs fingertips, Ruby.'

She apologised. 'Oak Apple's front door has to be kicked open and rammed shut.'

'Because it's swelled and needs planing off.'

Edna pushed past his legs. Ruby bent down and rubbed the silky warm spot behind the dog's ears.

Will said, 'Off you go, do what you need to do.'

It took a second for her to realise he meant Edna, who lolloped away to a patch of grass, sniffing as she went.

Ruby crossed the threshold into delicious warmth. Taking off her boots, she asked, 'Underfloor heating?'

'Yup. Air source.'

'Very green. And a stove too.' It was at the far end of the open-plan space, obsidian with an industrial-sized flue. 'You're not scared of sparks setting your thatched roof on fire?'

'Take a look through the window.' Will gestured to his kitchen, which was this end, a panorama of glossy grey doors and concrete countertops. She leaned across a matt-black sink and saw, outside, cannisters in a cage.

'LPG?'

'Correct. My wood burner runs on gas.'

'I used LPG in Laurac, in my kitchen. I miss the speed of gas. Grandma's cooker feels like it ought to have a crank handle, it's so ancient. It takes fifteen minutes for a rasher of bacon to think about sizzling.' She was saying whatever came into her head, because he was bound to ask her why she'd come, and what could she say? *I read something truly awful and don't want to be on my own today.*

'There's no point upgrading the oven,' he said, filling the kettle, even though he hadn't mentioned coffee. 'Whoever buys your farm will rip everything out and start again.'

The idea left a little dent in her feelings. He was right, of course, but somehow she minded.

He'd opened the cupboard door, reaching for a metal caddy. 'I'm presuming you'd like coffee?'

'Please. I hope I'm not intruding. Is it very early?'

'Depends what you call early. It's seven-fifty.'

'Sorry. I feel so stupid.'

'Don't worry. I was up late last night and didn't get to sleep till about two.'

'That's meant to make me feel better?'

'It's simply reality.'

Now she looked, his feet were bare. 'Did I wake you?'

'Not really. Is there a problem? Your roof isn't leaking, I hope.'

'It's fine.' She wasn't ready to open up to him. Maybe after a slug of coffee. She began with a lie. 'I, er, wanted to tell you that I've called Bob Oaks... about my wood burner?' She'd come over the road to tell him that? He'd think she was mad.

'You won't regret it.' Will poured dark beans into a grinder. Blades whirred and the kitchen filled with a smell she loved. He looked over his shoulder. 'I take my coffee strong. I got the taste when I worked in the UAE. Is that OK for you?' His gaze had the soft focus of someone who hadn't quite woken up.

'Strong is good.'

He took a brushed-steel cafetière from a drawer that opened with a touch of the knee. Ruby asked, 'Did you design this space yourself? *C'est chic, c'est vraiment cool.*' 'Cool' came with a strong French accent.

He smiled. 'I forget you're not really English because you don't sound French.'

'I do when I'm over there. And if I speak English in Laurac, I sound like a Frenchwoman who took English classes. Don't ask me why.'

He poured the boiling water. 'A friend designed the whole interior for me. Milk, sugar?'

'Dash of milk.' Will's gaze felt like a weight against her skin, and she pretended to be fascinated by the barn's ceiling, which reminded her of a Viking longship she'd seen in a

Danish museum, ribs and arches of ancient wood. An ivory-white wall displayed some statement art. In front of the stove, two massive sofas created a room without walls and enough sitting space for a delegation. A crash and a 'Damn' made her turn. Will had knocked over the coffee beans and was sweeping them off the surface, back into the container. She went to help and they dropped the last dozen beans in rhythm. He dropped one in, she dropped one in, until they'd got them all. Over the coffee aroma, she detected another scent. 'You were being polite earlier. I woke you up, clanging the guts out of that bell.'

'How did you guess?'

The smell of male skin, that musky cocktail. Frankincense, lemon, salt. Getting out of a warm bed, no time to lather it off with shower gel. These thoughts were deeply her own. She said, 'You're in your jim-jams.'

He laughed. 'No. I put these on before I came down. We don't know each other well enough for the alternative.'

Their eyes made contact and Ruby later thought – if she hadn't felt so scruffy, if she'd been the confident, French, after-hours version of herself, they would have kissed. She would have instigated it. Probably. She had always been partial to love-making in the morning. Inevitably so, as for most of her adult life, she'd dragged herself to bed in the early hours and unhurried wake-ups were a Sunday luxury. Had she tilted her head and brushed his hip with her hand, Will would have responded, she was sure.

A flurry of barking at the door reminded them that Edna was still outside.

'Would you?' he asked, in a way that told her he had stepped back from danger. 'The code is one-nine-eight-eight.' Will poured their coffee into white mugs, setting them down on the breakfast bar.

She jabbed in the number and the door clicked. Edna, who

must have been fully accustomed to this method of entering, waited until the gap was wide enough before rushing inside.

Ruby took a stool on one side of the breakfast bar. It was satin smooth. 'Real concrete or a clever fake?'

'Real. I made the moulds and poured it myself.'

She stroked again. 'Then sealed it.'

'Two coats of sealant, then a lacquer, then a buffing wax.'

She'd never realised how sexy a man could be, reciting from a construction handbook. 'It works.'

He said thanks and looked at her thoughtfully. 'This getting up early habit... I reckon you're going off your head here, missing your work. Right or wrong?'

She laughed nervously. Bull's eye. 'Though I wouldn't go back to Pastel – that was my life before November. I've worked from the age of nineteen almost without a break and, you're right, it's killing me, having nothing to do all day.' Except tidy up Oak Apple Farm and read Irene's diaries, of course. She was beginning to see why she'd got so immersed in them.

'What drove you from your job?'

'It's complicated, but I hit a kind of emotional wall, fell ill as a result and was replaced while I was recovering.' She made a face. 'French employment law is rigorous; I could have demanded my job back, but I didn't want it.'

'Because?'

'I made the classic error of working alongside my life partner and when that ended there wasn't room for both of us.'

'So you left, not him?'

'Yes.' Put like that, maybe she had bailed out too quickly.

'And came here for a change of scene?'

Ruby tried to work out if an accusation was on its way: something about 'Grabbing your inheritance while you were at a loose end.' But Will was drinking his coffee, looking past and not at her. She agreed with him, saying, 'This is an interval, while the scenery is shifted on stage.'

Will got up because Edna was nosing at his leg. 'Mind if I feed the wolf?'

'Course not.' The dog's eyes followed Will's every move. 'She's lovely.'

'Some people can't cope with dog food. The smell.'

'I grew up with it. My mum loves dogs and she does holiday care for friends' pooches. My stepdad had a huge great dog called Banjo.'

Will measured out a beaker of dry biscuit and then opened another pouch of wet food. 'I didn't know you have a stepdad.'

'Had. Name of Charlie. He and Mum split about six years ago, but they've stayed friends. In fact, it's him she's staying with in Morocco right now, him and his new partner.'

'Brave.' Will put the bowl on the floor. Edna leapt on it, scoffing the contents before pushing the dish across the floor of riven slate to get every last speck. The noise blocked out conversation for at least a minute.

'I haven't heard you mention your actual father,' he said, when Edna had finally given up.

It troubled Ruby, discussing her biological father. People made judgements. Will seemed to pick up on it, and moved on, telling her he had a favour to ask.

'OK.' It would be about Philippa. *Be nice to her. Call on her.* She was wrong.

'Would you take over tending the Boulter and Plait family graves, in the churchyard? I've been doing it for a while and I don't mind, but I don't know who most of them are, and it feels a bit impersonal. And I have to see to my mother's grave – she's buried at Hollesford crematorium. Would you mind?'

Relief flooded in, being asked something she could easily say yes to. 'Course I'll do it. While I'm here.'

'Because you're going back to... where is it?'

'Laurac, in Gascony. About fifty kilometres from Toulouse. Actually, I may not go back there. I might get as far as Paris for a while. Could you show me the graves, so I know where they all are?'

A beat of silence passed. 'You don't know?'

She felt the atmosphere chill and made a motion of her hand. 'I know where Grandma and Grandad's are, but the wider Boulter tribe... sadly, no.'

'You weren't at Irene's funeral,' Will said.

Here we go. Her voice took on a steely note. 'Because she died in May 2020 when I couldn't travel.' She felt the burgeoning sympathy between them diminish. It was a shame. She'd discovered she fancied Will Keelbrook, and there was plenty to like, so it followed that she wished him to think well of her.

'You'll find Boulters and Plaits on the churchyard's north-east side, pretty much in a line. Your gran is laid next to Norman.'

'Were you at his funeral?' she asked, remembering back to a solemn June day in 2001. Norman had died on the eighth of that month, aged eighty-four, and his funeral had taken place towards the end of the month. 'Did we meet?'

Will shook his head. 'That summer was my first at boarding school and I'd made the junior cricket team, and Aunt Flip didn't want to spoil it for me by pulling me home to a funeral. Uncle Ronnie wrote after it was all over. I didn't appreciate the impact on Aunt Flip until I saw her when I came home. I had no concept then what it meant to her to lose Norman.'

'You call him "Norman",' Ruby said, 'as if you knew him.'

'I did. I practically lived at Westumble after Mum died. Not officially, as I was fostered by my great-aunt in Medfold, but she was nearly eighty and she was acting out of duty. I'm sure she was relieved to pack me off here, as often as she could. When I went to boarding school, I'd come here for the holidays. Aunt Flip and Uncle Ronnie pretty much adopted me, which suited everyone. Norman was always popping over, helping in the forge. He and I would hold the horses and when Ronnie started the mobile forge and got his van, Uncle Norm would travel with him.'

Uncle Norm. It impinged on her powerfully how little she'd known her grandparents.

'I think your grandad was bored once he sold his fields and got rid of his milk quota,' Will went on. 'He sold it when he hit seventy. Farmers shouldn't retire.'

Ruby accepted a refill of coffee. 'I should have been around more. Was he... was he unhappy?'

Will's answer was less pointed than it might have been. 'Sometimes, but he knew he was welcome here, if he needed a break.'

'From Irene? Don't answer that. But I'm seeing a different picture, reading my grandma's diaries. The image she paints of Norman, before they married, is not...' She couldn't find the word. 'It worries me.'

*Oh?* said Will's look.

She lost her nerve, saying blandly, 'Philippa clearly gets a lot from having you here.'

'She does, and I love her back. Thank God for Flip and Ronnie, my surrogate parents.' He paused, as if something puzzled him. 'Ruby, why didn't you ever visit?'

'I did, but infrequently because Mum moved us to France shortly after I was born.'

'France isn't Australia. You can be here in a day, even from the south. It broke Norman's heart. Irene was harder to read, but it must have hurt to lose touch with her only surviving child. What was the deal?'

'Mum never felt part of this world—' *Hang on.* 'You said, only *surviving* child. What do you mean?'

Will uncoupled his gaze from hers. He reached out to stroke the dog.

Ruby planted her elbows on the breakfast bar. 'You can't unsay it.'

Will put his elbows on the bar too so their faces were inches apart. 'Philippa told me after your gran died that she – Irene – miscarried a child some years before your mum was born. I take it you didn't know.'

'You take it right.' Amanda had never said a word!

Will was watching her, reading her face. Her focus blurred, she felt her chest clamp and her breath shorten.

'Ruby?' There was concern in Will's voice. 'Look at me.'

She couldn't focus, and knew what was happening; she'd had her first ever panic attack the day after she'd found Didier in bed with Lily Bouchard, when it had truly hit her that her world had crashed. She gripped the breakfast bar and heard a scrape as Will jumped up. He came round to her side.

'Did I make the coffee too strong?' He held her and she stared up into his eyes, which were full of worry. 'Ruby? Was it telling you about Irene's miscarriage? I shouldn't have. Sorry. It wasn't my place.'

A baby. Whose baby?

*Sometimes, you gotta teach a boy a lesson. And now, miss, I'm going to teach you one too.*

'Breathe, Ruby. Breathe.'

She could hear the dog whining. She was upsetting Edna. Dogs picked up emotions. Will wasn't going to let her fall to the floor, and knowing that loosened her muscles. Her pulse subsided. Will helped her to one of the sofas, sat beside her, and she tilted her head back, eyes closed. It took a moment for her to realise she was gripping his hand. A short while later, she was able to ask, 'Do you have internet?'

'Sure. You want to use a computer?'

'I'd like you to look someone up for me. I need to know.'

'OK. What do you need to know?'

She moved her head against the sofa cushion. 'If somebody

lived or not.' She knew she wasn't making complete sense, but Will accepted her request.

'Let's do it. My office is upstairs.'

She let him help her up, and only thought the next words, because it would shock him and he'd hate her: *I have to know if Grandad Norman was a racist who caused his love-rival to be beaten to death.*

## 26

Will suggested she go ahead of him to the mezzanine level. He didn't say why, but Ruby guessed it was in case she fainted and he had to catch her.

'I'm OK now.' She hated displaying physical weakness. Nothing had surprised her so much as discovering how shock and betrayal could act on the body. Reading Irene's testimony had triggered sensations she'd hoped were behind her. Will's revelation a moment ago had brought them back, like a landslide.

Her hand caressed the bannister as she climbed the stairs. On the upper level, the room doors ran in a line. Will went ahead to open the middle one. She followed him into an office and her eyes went straight to the window in front of a desk, out past Westumble farmhouse to Oak Apple Farm. That's how he'd spotted her chimney fire. He'd told her he'd seen the flames from his house. He must have been working. There were two computers on the desk, one with an oversized screen. Will turned on the smaller one and offered her the bentwood work-chair.

'What are we looking for?' he asked.

'It's "who". Sergeant Theo Robinson.'

'Irene's romantic fantasy?'

'He was no fantasy, Will, and I need to know what happened to him.'

A screensaver flashed up, an upscale building complex overlooking a harbour. Will typed in a password then summoned a search engine before moving the keyboard over to her. 'Go ahead.'

'You do it.' Her fingers felt as though they didn't belong to her.

He pulled up a second chair and did as she asked. His internet connection was fast, and suddenly there was a name: Theodore Talbot Robinson. A click of a link and a picture appeared, a thirty-something Black man in a sharp suit and fedora hat, descending the steps of an American Airlines plane. 'Is this the man you're after?' Will enlarged the picture. A strong, handsome face. Serious. Confident.

'I don't know.' She hadn't picked up that Theo's second name was Talbot. Irene hadn't mentioned it. 'It took me some pages of Irene's diary to realise the soldier she was writing about was Black. She didn't state it directly. But why should she? She was pouring out impressions and feelings, not writing a report...'

She waited for Will to speak, but he didn't. Obviously, he was leaving all this to her. This was her search. 'Would you type in "First Sergeant Theodore Robinson", please?'

A moment later, the page of a wartime newspaper appeared. It was the *Hollesford Echo*, and the photo of Irene and Theo, dancing the Lindy Hop opened up. Ruby breathed, 'That picture caused no end of trouble for Irene.'

'How d'you know?'

'Her diaries, Will. I've read pages and pages. Would you go back to the first picture, and read out the caption?'

He did as she asked: '"Theodore Talbot Robinson, arriving

at Baton Rouge, Louisiana, sometime in 1955. Unknown why he travelled separately from the other members of the group." What group?'

She shook her head. 'But the date, 1955, would be such good news if it *is* him. What else does it say?'

'Nothing. It must have been taken from a longer article, or another website. Are you afraid that Theo died in the war?'

'Not in the war, no. He was beaten up in Flixfield. Savagely so.'

'By...?'

'White military police.'

'American?'

Ruby nodded. 'They'd gone out to a dance, Theo, his friends and Irene. They got stopped on the way back.' She related how Irene had fallen out of the truck, Theo coming to her aid and then the two of them being isolated on the road as the others were driven away. She spared Will none of the horror of Theo's beating and heard the change in his breathing.

And then she said it. 'I'm frightened it was Grandad Norman who set him up for it.'

'Why? Why would he?'

'Out of jealousy. Irene was in love with Theo Robinson. She didn't want Norman, and he couldn't come to terms with it. I have to face the idea that my nice grandad was a bully. A racist. A coward.' When Will returned no comment, but sat rigidly still, Ruby grabbed the keyboard. She refreshed the search, typing Theo's name, and 'Georgia, USA'.

It brought up—

An obituary.

Tears sprang into her eyes as she read it aloud. '"November twelfth, 1987. The death has been announced of legendary jazz pianist and Black Civil Rights activist Theodore T. Robinson, at his home near Savannah, Georgia, following a short illness. He was aged seventy-one and was for many years the pianist with the Jake Hendrick Five."

'Jake was his best friend!' Ruby cried. 'Maybe he became a musician, after the war. He played the piano and wrote songs. He improvised. It could have been him, coming off the plane at Baton Rouge.' She read the rest of the obituary: '"He is survived by his wife, Millie, and their daughter, academic and political writer Sabrina Robinson-Chase."' Emotion made her scalp tingle. The obituary was thirty-five years old, meaning – 'He died a year before I was born. He married somebody else. Had a daughter. I wonder if Irene knew?'

'How far do her diaries go?' Will spoke tightly.

'Through the war years.'

'She probably wouldn't know, then. Before the internet, when people separated that was pretty much it. I doubt his death was reported over here, except maybe in the music press.'

Which her grandma wouldn't have read, Ruby reflected. Could she reach out to his daughter, Sabrina?

*Hi, you don't know me, but my grandma loved your father.*

*Good evening from England. You don't know me, but I hope we can be friends…*

*Dear Ms Robinson-Chase, forgive the intrusion, but there is something I feel you'd like to know…*

Will interrupted her private musings. 'Have you mentioned your fears about Norman to anyone else?'

She shook her head. 'Not to Philippa, if that's what you mean. But she was in part to blame.'

Will got up, his chair sliding backwards. He put his hands on the desk, and Ruby felt penned in by his anger. 'How the hell is Philippa implicated in the beating up of a Black GI by white segregationists? She was a little girl.'

'Who told tales to her brother.'

'Which makes her guilty of what, exactly?' Emotions radiated from Will that he was struggling to hold back.

Ruby got up and ducked past him. 'I'd better go.'

He didn't stop her, but he did follow her downstairs and when he punched in the code to let her out, he stopped the door before it was wide enough for her to get through. 'Don't you dare confront Philippa. I mean it, Ruby.'

'I have to know if my grandad set Theo up for an assault which, from Irene's description, could have ended in his murder.' Ruby had yet to read how the night ended for her grandmother, but, whatever had happened, Norman was complicit there, too.

'Of course he didn't!' Will was still preventing her from going. 'I knew the man a damn sight better than you.'

'He lost Irene a job at the pub. He had form. Would you let me out, please?'

Will had more to say. 'You're convicting Norman from a few lines in a diary.'

'Not lines. Pages, like I said. Irene downloaded her feelings, her passion, onto every line.'

'My point exactly. Irene grew up in a rural bubble, totally unprepared for the American influx. She fell in love and everything changed overnight.'

'She's not to be believed, then, because she was a young, unsophisticated woman?'

'No.' Will shook his head. 'But from what you said, Irene was living dangerously. I agree somebody must have tipped off the military goons, but it could have been anyone in the village who resented a white woman and a Black man going out together. Or someone on the airbase. You don't think military personnel spy on each other?' The gentle light in Will's eyes was gone, replaced with the burn of anger. She could see from the way he passed his hand over his cropped hair how agitated he was. 'Leave Aunt Flip out of this, Ruby. I mean it.'

He opened the door for her and she walked away, wrapped in bleak feelings of loneliness. She'd blown it with Will. He wouldn't come calling again. He was fiercely protective of Philippa. She appreciated that – but it didn't mean her instincts were wrong.

'Damn, and I just bought him a Christmas card.' The joke to herself fell flat. She wanted to cry.

## 27

After lunch, as Ruby cleaned out the last of the kitchen cupboards, she heard footsteps at the side of the house. A grating sound took her to the window in time to see Will, in a woollen hat and work gloves, positioning the ladder against the back wall. Running outside, she saw him pick up a roll of tools and start his climb.

'Hi,' she said.

He glanced at her, nodded and carried on.

'Be careful,' she called, and because he took his free hand off the ladder to indicate he'd heard, she left it at that.

Going back inside, she opened the broom cupboard and stared unfocusedly at its uninspiring contents. After coming back from Will's, she'd lain on her bed and slept solidly for an hour. She still felt wobbly from her panic attack. Was Will's reappearance an olive branch, or was he simply fulfilling his promise to mend her roof so he could then shut her out with a clear conscience? As she was about to close the cupboard door, she noticed lines and numbers marked on the inside. It appeared that Irene had recorded Amanda's height as a child. Ruby recognised her grandma's particular way of writing the number 2, like a capital Z. Amanda's height was marked at two, three, four and five years, with a distinct growth spurt between four and five where Amanda must have shot out of her clothes. Tracing the marks with her forefinger, Ruby wondered about the child Irene had lost. A child of whom she'd known nothing until four hours ago.

She rang her mother and left a voice message. 'I heard something today about Gran. Call me, we need to talk.'

Conscious of Will levering up tiles two storeys above her head, she didn't pick up the diary but, instead, took another look at Irene and Norman's wedding photo. The colourisation must have been done after the print was developed. By a studio photographer? Clearly, one who didn't know the couple very well, as their cheeks were several shades too rosy. Irene's eyes were bluer than life, as if the tinter had felt obliged to add some radiance. Grandad was half-smiling, his face almost in profile as he looked at his bride. Irene stared blankly towards the camera.

Had Irene been forced to marry Norman?

'... *some things you can't hide under a gooseberry bush.*' Her grandparents had married in March 1944, but Irene had got engaged to Theo Robinson around four months earlier.

Hearing feet descending the ladder, Ruby hurried to tap on the kitchen window. She mouthed, 'Coffee?' as Will stepped onto solid ground. She turned away before he had a chance to decline. She put the kettle on and opened a packet of biscuits and when he came in, bringing in a burst of outdoor chill, she said, 'Go sit in the other room. I'll bring this through.'

He didn't move. 'I'm sorry about earlier.'

She kept making the coffee, an excuse not to turn around, because the unexpected apology made her tearful again. She said roughly, 'I wasn't my best self, Will.'

'Me neither.'

'And I didn't expect you to come to do my roof, to be honest.'

'I said I would, and the weather's turning bad tomorrow. Plus, I felt awful after you'd gone. You'd learned something traumatic about Irene, and hadn't had time to process it. I shouldn't have let rip.'

She did turn then, her radar tuned for inauthenticity. Will stood at one end of the kitchen, as if unsure if he ought to come right in. He hadn't shaved, and his cheeks were pinched from the cold. With his hat off, his eyes dominated his face and he was obviously troubled.

'It's OK,' she said. 'Your anger came from the right place. You're protecting those you love. I understand. Don't imagine it gives me pleasure to think that my grandad, who I also loved, might have done something unforgiveable.'

'I don't think that. Ruby, are you sure it's a good thing, burying yourself in those diaries? I mean, you're getting over a break-up and you've lost your work. Maybe you should cut yourself some slack.'

'Read escapist fiction, you mean, or watch TV box sets?'

'Yup. I could lend you *Game of Thrones* on DVD.'

She laughed, and it felt good. On impulse, she stuck out her hand. 'Friends?'

Instead of taking her hand, he placed both of his on her shoulders and kissed her on each cheek, continental-style. His lips were cold, his upper lip giving the touch of sandpaper. Ruby closed her eyes, but he stepped back.

'I don't want to have to choose,' he said.

She didn't get what he meant, which must have projected itself.

'Between you and my loyalties,' he explained. 'So, please, don't make me.' The dark sweep of his lashes suggested he was finding this hard. It wasn't a threat. He meant what he said. It would kill him to choose. Did that mean he cared about her? The thought made her shaky. Happy. Afraid. And inevitably, doubts made her say the wrong thing.

'Tell me how much I owe you for the roof.'

He gritted his teeth. 'Nothing. I do other stuff for money. Being handy, as you called it the other day, is my contribution to global happiness. Good karma, if you like.'

'OK.' Her mother would approve, Ruby thought. Amanda walked other people's dogs for free, for the same reason. 'But can I still talk to you about Irene and Theo sometimes?' she pleaded. 'I need another mind to bounce off.'

'So long as we leave Aunt Flip out of it.'

'Deal.' She took their drinks and biscuits through to the lounge. The first thing she saw was Irene's 1943 diary lying open on the coffee table, with the magnifying glass beside it. 'Ignore it,' she said.

In a contrary move, Will picked it up and frowned at the miniscule writing. 'You'll get a squint, trying to read this.' He sat down on the sofa.

'The pages you're looking at were glued together. I think what happened at that point in her life, after the attack on Theo, was too much for Irene to deal with. She was blocking it out.'

'What did happen, in the end?'

'I don't know yet. Not sure I want to.'

'What d'you know about Theo Robinson, when he was here on British soil? I mean, the indisputable facts?'

He was steering her away from the emotional to the objective, she realised. That was fine, and probably useful. 'OK.' She sat down, gave him his coffee. 'Theo was a little older than Irene. He was Sergeant Robinson of the USAAF. Actually, *First* Sergeant, a rank above. He was from Georgia and, I would say, a loyal soldier but he came across as cynical from a lifetime of discrimination. You know about the Jim Crow laws, and segregation?'

Will nodded. Of course he did.

'They were still in place in much of America when Theo

met Irene and they followed him to the UK. He didn't encounter too much discrimination from the locals here, but segregation on the airbase was in full force. From Irene's descriptions of him and his friends, I get the idea that they were paid less. Their uniforms were worse, as were their living conditions. She drew the flags of both countries on their engagement card, so he must have had pride in America. He joined up, he did his bit; perhaps he hoped it would change things.' What else could she say? 'He was a fine pianist, like I said before, and a better dancer. He was intelligent. Actually, he sounded better educated than Irene. From what they experienced in the summer of 1943 and the timing of their engagement, I sense their relationship got more complicated as autumn set in. Yet, by the following spring, in 1944, Irene was marrying Norman.' Putting down her mug, Ruby fetched the wedding photo from the other room. 'Did you ever see a copy of this?'

Will took it from her. 'No. But...' He screwed up his eyes. 'The rose in Norman's buttonhole could be from Aunt Flip's garden. Wow, Irene looks as if she's been given a life sentence.' He narrowed his eyes. 'There's something a bit off about this picture.' He held it a few inches away for a different perspective. 'Maybe just a bad photo. What are you doing for Christmas?' The question was asked casually.

Ruby hadn't given it much thought. 'I've always worked over Christmas, then gone to bed on Boxing Day and slept for forty-eight hours. This is the first year in God knows how long I'm not employed. You?'

'Edna and I have a date with Aunt Flip. I'm sure you'll be invited and I'd like you to join us.' He darted her a glance. Uncertain, but laced with humour. Challenging her not to hold a grudge.

'If she invites me I'll say yes, with pleasure. What did you mean about the photo being "off"?'

'Not sure yet.' He put it flat on the table and hovered the

magnifying glass over it. 'Ha. There's a patchwork cushion in one of Flip's bedrooms with the material Irene's blouse is made from. Rosebuds with pointy leaves. Must have been home-made.'

Ruby bent for a closer look. He was right. Rosebuds. The blouse had squared shoulders and a V-shaped collar. Buttoned down the front, it was modest as a convent school uniform. 'Woah, hang on. Give me that.' She thrust out her hand for the magnifying glass and pulled the photo towards her. Yes... a fine chain was just visible on one side of the blouse collar. She gave the magnifying glass back to Will so he could look.

He saw it too. 'And there's something on the end of the chain. See the shape of it under the fabric? Something old, something borrowed?'

Ruby reached for a biscuit. She could have said, 'I think it's the locket that Theo gave her,' but that was dangerous territory, the cause of bitter friction between Philippa and Ruby's mother. Rather than mention it, she said, 'Grandma had some nice bits of jewellery, collected over the years, but it got lost being posted to France.'

'How did that happen?'

Because Philippa got the address wrong, or wrote 'jewellery' on the front of the parcel, Ruby thought sourly. But she said none of that. 'It just did. We have to accept it. What are you doing?'

It was obvious what he was doing. He was taking the back off the photograph. 'I've worked out what's odd about this picture. The size of the mount. It's too big.'

'D'you know, I thought that too?' Ruby's phone rang. The number began +33, which meant France. Leaving Will to dismantle the photograph, she took the call, but instead of giving her name, she muttered, '*Qu'est-ce que tu veux?*' What d'you want?

She was expecting Didier but a woman spoke.

'It's Lily, Lily Bouchard. Ruby, please don't end this call. Didier has sent you many messages and about twenty emails. Will you please, please answer them?'

A walnut-sized nuclear bomb went off in Ruby's forehead. 'Why are you calling me?'

'We know you have read his text messages, Ruby.' Lily sighed.

*We.* A merry conclave of two. Her voice splitting from stress, Ruby told Lily to tell Didier that she was going to block him on her phone. And she hadn't seen his emails because she had no broadband. She shut off the call.

'You can read emails on your phone, you know,' Will said.

'Speak French, do you?'

'Enough to understand that.' He was carefully extracting the glass from the photo frame. 'When do you get your broadband?'

In a few days, she told him. 'But I won't read Didier's emails.'

'There.' He put the photograph face up, free of its intrusive mount. They could now see that Irene's hair was rolled in a very 1940s style, and her blouse was tucked into a gathered skirt whose waistband was pulled up higher than Ruby would have thought fashionable at the time. Because Irene's figure was slender, the swell beneath the skirt's gathers was obvious.

'I'm guessing we know why they chose an oversized mount,' Will said.

'Grandma was pregnant when she married Norman.'

Not pregnant with Amanda, though. Ruby's mother had been born six years later, in 1950. Was this the baby that died? There was only one person in the world who could provide Ruby with the answer. But Will, who was clearly thinking the same thing, gave her a look. Philippa was a no-go area.

## 28

On Tuesday 20 December 2022, and for the first time in its five-hundred-year history, Oak Apple Farm acquired a broadband connection. The engineer came as Ruby emptied a bag of her grandmother's clothes on the dining hall floor. She'd discovered it at the back of a cupboard.

'Jumble sale?' the man asked.

'Or a vintage treasure trove.' To her eye, the clothes were from the 1950s and had one unusual feature: labels in the back – not designer tags but plain ones with the initials IRP. Irene Rose Plait. Laundry marks, perhaps?

After an hour of drilling and running cable, the engineer set up the router and invited Ruby to check her connection. She'd charged up her laptop overnight, changing the language from French to English. With the engineer looking over her shoulder, she typed the most anodyne word she could think of into the search engine. Up came the Wikipedia page for 'cabbage'. 'An annual crop with a dense, usually green, head.'

'Seems to work,' said the engineer.

'It's a bit slow.' Slower than Laurac, at any rate. Slower than Will's too.

'You've got fifty-four megabits per second. That's not bad for round here.'

'Then I will give thanks.' She smiled. 'Cup of tea?'

He had another job to pull in, so no. 'To be honest, I get through the day on Red Bull. Have a lovely Christmas.'

After he'd left, she took a breath and opened her emails. Three hundred and seventy-eight to read. They couldn't all be from Didier.

They weren't. Most were junk, though some were from the staff she'd left behind at Pastel, asking when she was coming back.

'*Salut, Ruby. Pas de nouvelles?*' What's going on? Didier was telling them nothing.

One, from her sous-chef, jerked a pained smile from her. 'Lily took over the kitchen after you went. *Quel merdier!* She tried to filet turbot with a bread knife.'

No. Her world! Her stainless-steel-topped empire. Her pantry cupboards smelling of cloves and vanilla. Her cork board and potted garlic; her window boxes. Her team, Alix and Moussa, the trainees and the kitchen porters, the waiting staff and her loyal clients. She missed it all so badly, even stumping home in her Crocs and creased whites at two a.m. to shower off the odours of cooking and oven degreaser. She pictured languid, manicured Lily hacking at an innocent turbot with the incorrect knife. The right knife was in the block, to the left of the gas burners. Ruby's knives, her precious property, left behind because she had assumed, erroneously, that she couldn't take them in hold baggage on the plane. Virtually everything she owned was either in her old flat, which she could no longer access, or in the restaurant kitchen she had abandoned. She should have kicked Didier out and stayed in her job, as Will had implied. Of course. Hindsight was a wonderful thing. She found an email from Didier, sent early that morning.

'You need to collect all your stuff, Ruby. Why is it you do not come home? I know what you think you saw—'

*Think* I saw? Even with the duvet over you, you and Lily looked like two of those wonky parsnips they sell cheap in the supermarket, a fused middle and sticky-out legs. She deleted the email, then searched Didier's name in her email account and performed a mass-delete. Her mum still hadn't phoned, she thought sadly. Must be having too much fun to call. Well, good that one of them was happy.

She wondered how Christmas Day with Philippa and Will would pan out. Should she offer to cook, or would it be deemed an insult? Ruby simply couldn't guess, and rather than dwell on it, she reached for the craft knife, and severed the final glued pages of her grandmother's diary.

# 29

## IRENE

**THURSDAY 3 SEPTEMBER 1943**

Yesterday, I turned twenty. Mum gave me a nice card and some cloth, enough for a blouse. Pretty, with rosebuds, and she tried to make me laugh, saying, 'Shall we measure you up against the broom cupboard, or are you taller than the door now?'

My lips hurt. I scrubbed them with Domestos bleach.

I can't stop the words in my head. Can't stop seeing him and I keep dreaming about what he did. If I write it, perhaps it will stop. It happened five days ago now, Saturday 28 August. They had taken Theo away and I couldn't hear him any more. The silence was worse than hearing him cry out.

Lieutenant Macbeth looked down at me, because I couldn't get up, and he said, 'I'm going to teach you a lesson about how white girls don't whore themselves out to Blacks. I respect your country, but I don't get why y'all want to mix. Where I come from, we have laws that keep Black and white separate. We're happier that way. You don't put fine cattle in with goats, now do you?'

Irene had kept quiet. Who were the cattle, who were the

goats? Her left hand had lost feeling, all the pain concentrating in her forearm, and she suddenly thought, What if I can't use my hand again, with Dad unable to walk? That'll be two of us, unfit for anything.

And Theo, in the truck, with those men. Don't let them hurt him more. Please, God.

'You hear me, sweetheart?'

'I need to go home. You've no right to keep me. You're not the law here.'

'Well, now, that's not quite so, ma'am. I am the law when it comes to the conduct of members of the United States military and if I find a young lady leading one of my boys astray—'

'I've not led him astray, and I don't need lessons from you.'

'You're surely going to get one.' Macbeth had stepped closer and unbuckled the belt of his pants.

## 30

Macbeth stepped closer until his crotch was against her face. His belt buckle nicked her as he gripped the back of her head, tipping it back so her neck curved upwards to the night. He twisted the chain of her locket, until it was hard for her to breathe. The locket came open and she heard the chink of metal on the road. Her ring.

Macbeth scooped it up. 'Who gave this to you?'

'Nobody. Give it back.'

Macbeth took her chin between his fingers and now all she could see was the runkled flies of his trousers and the line of his belt. 'Did Sergeant Robinson give you a ring? You better tell me the truth, girl, or I'll go beat it out of him.'

'Yes. He did.'

'How did he come by it, 'cause it looks like gold to me. There's only one way a man on his pay gets a ring like this. You better speak truth, girl.'

'He bought it for me.'

'No way he did. He don't earn enough in one year to buy gold rings. You're lying.'

Her frightened brain chased the answer that would spare

Theo more pain. 'Yes, yes I am. I paid for it. I work at the factory and I bought it from Lubbock's. They're a shop, a jewellers', in town. He said he'd pay me back.'

'Made you buy your own engagement ring?' A thick laugh sent spittle onto Irene's upturned face. 'That I do believe. That's the kind of low-down trick a boy like that would play. You believe you're engaged, miss?'

'Yes.'

'Well, you ain't. One, it's against the law. Two, he's using you the way a dog uses a tree, to relieve himself, you get my meaning?'

'Please let me go.'

'See, I could have you right here in the road, but I won't put my manhood where some lazy cotton-picker has put his.' Macbeth must have realised he was slowly choking her, because he released the locket chain, and grabbed her hair instead. It had come loose around her shoulders. His other hand plucked at his flies.

'I'll tell my dad. I'll tell the vicar. And our policeman.'

'That so?' He struck her so violently across the mouth, she tasted blood. He pulled her head towards his crotch.

She clenched her teeth, knowing what he wanted from her.

'Open your goddamn mouth, girl.' When she wouldn't, he drove his thumb and finger against each side of her jaw, the way a brute makes a horse's mouth open to take the bit.

She gagged, and struggled as her lungs screamed for a breath she couldn't snatch. Lights swam in front of her eyes.

She gave in because she realised she didn't want to die. During the days after, she scrubbed out her mouth with household bleach. Opening her diary, she wept onto the empty pages, until, driven by shame and rage, she finally poured out her truth. Then glued the sheets together, locking her tears away forever.

SATURDAY 11 SEPTEMBER 1943

It was done. Norman had signed papers with her dad and twenty-four acres of cornfield and meadow behind Westumble Farm had left Boulter ownership. Bought at forty pounds an acre. Irene's father was out making one last circuit of a favourite field, with Norman's help.

In the kitchen, Irene's mother was making blackberry jam. Irene sat at the dining hall table, staring at nothing. Her left wrist was in a cast halfway to the elbow. When Lieutenant Macbeth had let her go, however many days ago, she'd stumbled home and Mum had run for Doctor Mickleson.

Her wrist had been dislocated, not broken, and the doctor had reset it there at the table. She'd almost passed out from pain, glad for the excuse to close her eyes and block out the questions.

*What on earth happened to you? Why were you out there, alone, in the first place?*

*What are those bruises on your face, Irene?*

*Who cut your lip?*

*Irene? Irene? Speak to us, what's got into you?*

She wouldn't be back to work for ages, but you could pick blackberries one-handed and so she'd scavenged the hedgerows every day since, filling boxes with them, which a lad from Ratty's collected each evening from the end of the drive. Her fingers were mauve-tipped. It got her out of the house where she could express her hatred of that man, Macbeth, in bouts of weeping and unfettered anger. She'd heard nothing from Theo. There was bruising inside her jaw, and her throat was swollen, so she couldn't eat. Her neck was ringed with red weals, where her attacker had twisted her locket, half choking her.

Her mum and dad chose to believe her story, that she'd tumbled off her bicycle. 'Where is the blasted thing?' her mother kept asking. 'In a ditch, so you say, but what ditch, Irene?'

'I don't know. Somewhere. Just a ditch.'

She would always be grateful to old Wheezy Cobbold, coming along on his unlit bike, whistling through the gaps in his teeth. Without him disturbing them, Macbeth wouldn't have stopped. She'd been at the point of thinking her chest would explode from lack of air and didn't doubt that afterwards, he'd have dragged her body into a thicket or rolled her into the ditch. Wheezy had chuckled as he creaked past on his ancient cycle. 'Take care, my lovelies!'

He'd thought Irene and Macbeth were courting.

Her mum would keep glancing at her, sighing. 'First the land, and now you, moping and off work. I suppose you had a falling-out with your young man.'

Violet knew nothing of how that hideous August night had ended. Irene's nightmares were the silent kind. She'd wake in a sweat, screaming, 'Leave him alone!' except no words came out. Dr Mickleson had also accepted Irene's story of her bike wheels skidding on some oil on the road.

Footsteps outside made her turn, expecting it was Norman bringing her father home. Seeing instead a dark head and dark neck above a buff-coloured collar, she hurtled to the door, thrusting up the latch one-handed. 'Theo!'

It wasn't Theo. It was his pal, Jake. Wheeling her bicycle, which had gone away with the truck that night. She stepped out, pulling the door behind her. 'How is Theo?' *Please say he's all right.*

'In the sanatorium. He ain't good.' Jake rested her bike against the farmhouse wall, as a sob tore from Irene. From the set of his face, she knew he part-blamed her. He listed what had been done to Theo. 'Broken nose, jaw, they left him with abdominal injury and knocked out two teeth.'

'I'd walk any distance to see him, except it would put him in danger.'

'You ain't wrong there,' Jake replied. 'Best you can do is leave him be.'

Tears, held in for days, brimmed and ran down her cheeks.

Jake ran his hand across his head, leaving trails in his cropped hair. 'What you had meant a lot to him, but there's some things you can't change. Walls you can't push down.' Seeing Irene's wrist-cast, his expression tightened. 'Can I tell Theo you're good?'

What could she say?

'Can I tell him you got away safe that night? You sound husky. You been ill?'

She dug her teeth into the cut on her lip that she wouldn't let heal. 'Tell him I'm fine. And he's going to be all right?'

'I guess. Though they're badgering him on and on, about some ring. You know anything about that, Irene?'

Instinctively, she sought the locket, touching it like a talisman. When her mother had bathed her neck with salt water, exclaiming over the lesions to the skin, Irene had refused to let her undo the clasp, and take the locket off her. She still had her ring, too. Before he left her on the road, Lieutenant Macbeth had pushed it into her mouth. 'Don't go swallowing that, miss.'

'Can I write to Theo?' she asked Jake. He was right, she was still husky and raw-voiced.

'Best you don't, Irene. Letters get opened.'

'Then tell him I love him, but even more, I want him to be safe.'

Jake stepped back. 'Being safe ain't easy for those like us. His momma raised seven single-handed, and Theo worked like crazy to get himself through college, to an engineering qualification. In the army, he climbed a cliff-face to get his stripes. And what do they have him do? Dig holes. Me, I write music and I'm a dental technician, and they got me digging holes too. That's life for us, Miss Irene. In the state of Georgia where we come from, if you're Black, you can have a mind like Solon of Athens, and you still dig holes. You coming along with us set Theo up for a beating.'

'Don't say that.'

'Ain't it the truth, though.' He gave a jerky bow but Irene stopped him going.

Between sobs, she told him what Macbeth had said, about Theo stealing the engagement ring and locket to give to her. 'I know he didn't, but I'm worried they'll make out he did.'

'I wouldn't put that past them.' Jake spoke fast because her father was coming up the drive, supported by Norman, who had certainly spotted them. 'Theo put a down payment on them,' he said, 'but I guess he's missed a payment, being laid up. I'll talk to him when I can.' Jake walked away, then turned and came back. 'I can't do this.'

'What, Jake?'

'Leave on a lie. Theo loves you, and he says, when he's got his strength back, he'll meet you round at Meg's.'

Meg's...? St Margaret's? She rubbed her tears away with her sleeve. 'When?'

'When he's fit to get on a bike, being about the same time as you can do a handstand, Miss Irene.' He lifted her wrist, the one in the cast. 'Reckon you better start doing your bone-strengthening exercises so he doesn't get to Saint Meg's and find he's all alone there.'

## 31

October that year, the fourth of the war, was fine and dry, plums and damsons fit to pick almost to the third week. Trucks offloaded mountains of them at Ratty's, along with tons of apples. Irene had returned to work before Dr Mickleson had given formal permission. Peeling and stoning fruit was her bone-strengthening regime. As she and her colleagues laboured to cope with the influx, transport aircraft thundered overhead. They were bringing yet more American personnel to the base and their engines blotted out the foreman's patrolling footsteps.

RAF Flixfield, now under the command of the US Eighth Air Force, was operational, its concrete runways, hangars, Nissen huts and service blocks complete. A bristling control tower changed the view across the fields. Heavy bombers began arriving in a sustained concussion that made the factory's tin roof shudder. When they came in low, a rumour went round that they carried five-hundred-pound bombs. It scared the women working at the benches.

Midway through October, Theo's Engineers moved on. An RAF base near Beccles was being turned over to the United States and there was digging to be done, concrete to be laid.

Theo hadn't written, nor had he shown up at their meeting place. Irene didn't dare write to him to tell him what she'd done on his behalf: gone into Hollesford, taken out all her post-office savings and paid off the outstanding instalments on the ring and locket. Her mother would make merry hell, should she discover that Irene had spent her nest egg, but so what? Theo's wellbeing mattered more than anything in the world.

Weary of lies and evasions, she told her mother where she was going each time she set off to St Margaret's, to wait for him under its fractured roof.

Violet was dismayed. 'I thought that was all over! What if you fall off your bike again and lie stranded? Or worse, get seen creeping through the dark? You've burned your bridges with Norman; there'll be nobody to speak up for you, save me and your father.'

Irene assured her mother that she'd go carefully. 'My wrist is almost good as before and there's hardly any traffic on the road.'

Nobody could get petrol, apart from the military and a few others, like the doctor.

Realising there was no point arguing, Violet had only one request: 'Say nothing to anyone until you've brought that young man home to meet us.'

'May I?'

'I think you'd better.'

Irene kept her nightly vigil at St Margaret's. As the evenings darkened and the temperature dropped, she took an old paraffin stove to the abandoned church. Once there, she'd boil a tin kettle and make cocoa, wait an hour before writing the day's date and her initials in chalk on the back of a pew. She rubbed out and rewrote the date fifteen times in a row.

The clocks went back, and arriving in dense dark on the first night of November, she shone her torch on the worm-eaten pew and saw scrawled on it:

*TR was here too. Where are you, sweetheart?*

'Theo?' She lifted the candle she'd lit, sheltering its flame with her palm, hardly daring to believe he'd finally come. 'Are you here?'

A figure came towards her from where the altar had once stood.

She could feel her pulse in her throat. 'Theo?'

'I'm here, Irene. I've been praying this last hour.'

'There's no point,' she answered stupidly. Her heart was tearing itself in pieces. 'The church is deconsecrated.'

'The Almighty won't care. He looks out for us.'

Irene threw herself at him, stumbling on a cracked flagstone. He gasped, and she recoiled, terrified she'd re-broken his ribs. 'I'm sorry. I'm sorry, Theo. Are you better now?'

'Bits of me still feel they got whopped with a meat tenderiser...' But he said he didn't care so long as she held him. 'You're still my girl?'

Shaking from emotion and cold, she nodded, then realised he wouldn't see by the light of a single candle. 'Here.' She put his hand against her throat, so he could feel the locket. 'The ring's there too.' Breathlessly, she told him how she'd paid for it, using her savings.

'I know. I went to the jewellers', and the girl behind the counter showed me the "Paid in full" ticket in the book. Said a sassy blonde girl put the money down. Reckoned it must be you.'

'Course it was.'

'I'm going to pay you back every penny. Can't have my girl paying for her own engagement ring.' He paused for a moment, then cleared his throat. 'The thing is, 'cause I missed a payment when I was laid up, the shop wrote to me and Macbeth got hold of the letter.'

'Are you in trouble?'

'I'm always in trouble with that man. He put a cross against my name the first time I looked him in the eye and disagreed with him.' Theo's fingers tightened against her shoulders. 'Macbeth uses any way he can to torment me. Like, yesterday, he said how you and he got to know each other in the dark – really know – after they took me away.' Theo's voice took on a strange note, and Irene's heart began to thud, as shame made its familiar creep along her skin. He stammered as he asked her, 'Was that true?'

She denied it, smacking away the memory of Macbeth holding her head, pushing himself at her, forcing her mouth open... 'He was nasty, that's all, Theo.'

Theo told her that as he lay half-conscious in a locked room in the early hours, Macbeth had come and tried to make him swear he'd never see or touch Irene again. 'You can see how well that worked.' He traced the outlines of the locket beneath her jumper. 'I was crying out for you.' His breathing had deepened and his hand moved to her waist. He buried his lips against her neck and Irene stared up at the vaulted roof. I won't let that pig of a man spoil what we have, she vowed. He's not worth it. She helped Theo lay out their coats on the ground and sank down with him.

# 32

## RUBY

*Hi, Will. Ruby here. Any chance I could drop by tonight? Something I need to run past you.*

She sent the message shortly before five p.m. as she arrived home from a trip into town, where she'd bought Christmas gifts: hand-made honeycomb chocolates for him, artisan jams for Philippa, a bag of beef jerky for Edna. The moment she'd pressed 'send', she wished she hadn't used the phrase 'run past you', which, to her mind, was criminal corporate-speak.

A message came back a few minutes later.

*Working atm. Drop by for a glass of red around 9 p.m.*

Good, she thought. Wine would help because what she had to put to Will might make him angry all over again. Cycling back from town, she had realised she was passing Maple Court, where Irene had lived out her last weeks. Windows ablaze with

Christmas lights had seemed to beckon. She'd pedalled to the front door, gone inside and asked to speak to the manager.

A manager full of Christmas goodwill, who had proved very helpful.

Ruby filled the following three hours washing every lampshade in the house. Amazing how they collected dirt! At 8.55 p.m., she put on her coat and a hat, and went out into a sleety wind. As she walked, she texted Will.

*On way, eta 3.5 mins.*

He was waiting and let her in before she pulled on the bell. The barn's underfloor heating was like a swansdown embrace, and Ruby immediately discarded her padded jacket, her boots and hat. At the far end, the convincingly real gas stove flickered. In front of it lay Edna on a tartan rug, her ribs rising and falling in time with her light snores. It felt perfect, cosy, comforting. She desperately hoped she wasn't going to crash the atmosphere.

Will invited her to sit at the breakfast bar while he uncorked the wine. There was a laptop open on the bar, its screen filled by a glass and marble building overlooking a lake, merging with its own reflection.

'Your next holiday?' she asked.

'My current project. Do you like Bekaa Valley wines?'

'Er, great. Your project... this is your building?' The man who only yesterday had daubed the last of the lime cement under the pantiles of her roof, motivated by goodwill alone?

'Not exactly.' As Will put wine glasses on the bar, he touched the screen and the photograph turned into a 3D model.

'You're an architect?' The slick interior of the barn began to make sense.

'Again, no. I'm a materials engineer. I work with architects, sourcing materials, and run the programs to see if they'll work on their designs.'

She took some mental steps. 'Like me in the kitchen, working out if five layers of flaky pastry can take all those raspberries and Chantilly cream.'

He smiled. 'Totally the same.' He poured red wine. 'On this particular job, I had to tell my client they couldn't use zinc, because it would fry everyone inside the hotel in one-hundred-degree summer heat. Architects sell dreams to clients, then I come along and spoil everything.'

She remembered him saying he'd come back from the United Arab Emirates. 'Is this silver palace being built in the desert, then?'

'It's nowhere yet. It's a computer-generated image of a hotel planned for Al Rayyan, in Qatar.' A touch of the screen summoned a different elevation, a cascading garden above which a building seemed to float. 'I'm working for the architects who won the contract to build it.'

'Freelance?'

'Yes, ma'am.'

'From Flixfield in a thatched barn, for clients in Qatar? That's pretty crazy.'

'It works. The architects are in New York, as it happens.'

'Huh, but I've noticed, you have faster broadband than me.'

Will sat down and his eyes, fringed by their enviably dark lashes, shone green-brown. 'Mine's better than yours,' he teased. 'I'm closer to the telephone exchange. Your telephone wires straggle across the fields at the back of Oak Apple. Haven't you seen the poles?'

'I didn't even notice the central heating was oil, not gas, so you can answer that question.' She took a short breath and blurted out what she'd come to say. 'This evening I had it confirmed that Maple Court parcelled up my grandma's jewellery to send to Mum in France. Philippa persuaded a junior member of staff to give the parcel to her.'

'To post, because she didn't trust the home to get it right.'

'It makes no sense, Will. The home had already paid an international courier to deliver the parcel. Philippa took it an hour before it was due to be picked up.'

'What are you saying?' He wasn't angry; there was no chilling in the hazel eyes. If anything, he sounded afraid.

'That I don't believe it was ever Aunt Flip's intention to send it. I think she kept Irene's jewellery for herself. Holding on to the things Norman had bought.' Ruby pulled in her shoulders, preparing for an attack.

Will picked up his glass, savouring his wine. Ruby did the same. It was very good, full-bodied and bursting with unexpected flavours.

'OK,' he said at last. 'But I'll do the asking.'

She let out her breath. 'Thank you.'

'Just promise me again that you won't run straight over to the farmhouse. Aunt Flip can't cope with accusations. I need to know you understand.'

'I promise.'

'Good. How are you, by the way?'

'I'm fine.'

'Have you eaten?'

'Not since lunch.' Was he inviting her to supper? She was ravenous, having done a twelve-mile round trip to Hollesford and back on crispbread, sliced apple and cottage cheese.

It seemed he was. 'Let's see what's in stock.' Will got up and opened the double doors of a silver fridge, bringing out cheese and charcuterie, unsalted butter, lettuce hearts and, from a cupboard, olives and bell peppers in oil.

He could almost be French, Ruby thought. She couldn't resist joining him, saying, 'We could do a sharing platter.'

'We could.' He was looking at her, smiling slightly at the

change she knew had come over her as she surveyed the raw ingredients. 'You want to whip up a dressing?'

For some reason, she giggled. 'D'you have honey?'

'Better than that. I have honey from beehives in Flixfield.'

'And bread?'

He fetched a half-loaf of sourdough from the crock and watched her slice it as he put together a medley of bite-sized food on a serving plate. 'Let's eat on our laps, by the fire.'

When they were seated, an arm's length from each other on one of the enormous sofas, the food laid out on a smoked-glass coffee table, he said, 'I am duty bound to book a table at The Bells before Christmas, to support the landlord. Would you like to come with me?'

He meant The Ten Bells, of course. 'I'm not sure.' She hastened to explain. 'Irene got sacked after three shifts at the village pub, and it was so unfair. They treated her like an expendable commodity.'

'That would be eighty years and five sets of landlords ago, Ruby.'

'I know. Course I'll come. I expect it's totally different inside, anyway.' Feeling a change of subject was a good idea, she asked Will what made him leave the UAE.

He told her he'd been working in Doha when lockdown struck and he thought he'd be stuck there for a few weeks. 'In a five-star hotel, what could possibly go wrong? Only it went on and on, didn't it? The pool was closed; so was the gym. Meals were left outside on a tray, we were only allowed out, masked, for a few minutes a day and my world became my balcony, staring out over an abandoned building site and a line of frazzled palm trees. I'd have gone mad if I hadn't had friends to call.'

'Did you just sit there, making calls?'

'Not at all. I downloaded books, improved my Arabic, bought a guitar like everyone else. I could still do my paid work, too, minus the meetings. I was lucky, but it gave me time to think. What did I want from life? What was really important to me. What about you?'

'The opposite, really.' Pastel had shut its doors on the morning of 17 March, the day after the French president had announced a total lockdown. 'I planned to use the time conceiving a cookery book and a website,' she said. 'Three days in, I got a call from the town's mayor. Could I help deliver food to some of the older residents? Actually, the mayor meant, "Could you cook it too?"' Her meal-delivery service had taken off rapidly as the restaurant's customers caught on to her enterprise. 'It was part social service, part commercial venture. I called myself Plat de Ruby. Ruby's platter, a play on Ruby Plait, though that was lost on most of my customers.'

'You made good use of your time.'

'It helped me feel relevant, and I discovered I could work for myself and make a living. Didier was enthusiastic and we planned to launch a business. I would work another year at the restaurant while developing the side-line.'

'But?'

'I made a classic mistake.'

'Oh?' Will piled peppered salami onto his bread, added stoned olives, a wing of lettuce drizzled with her dressing and was about to bite into it when she answered.

'I came back early from a conference and found him under the duvet with the restaurant owner's daughter.'

Will's open sandwich became a casualty, and they raced to pick olives off the sofa and blot the fabric with kitchen paper. Edna woke and came over to salvage stray bits of salami.

When they were once again settled, Ruby picked up her wine and motioned towards Will. 'To life, and all other forms of carnage.'

'I'll drink to that. My relationship broke up too – while I was in the Emirates.'

'Is that why you fled home?'

'I'd already decided I wanted to live a different life. That caused our split. Kimmy loved it out there, though she was stuck in England, in her family's home, during lockdown. She couldn't wait to fly back to join me. The idea of moving to Suffolk, living in a barn while I renovated it around her, horrified her. Like suggesting to a fish it would enjoy hanging out on a hot patio, or vice versa, I suppose, as the UAE is like a hot patio, and a fish would survive better in Suffolk...' He gave up on that.

Ruby guessed the split had been more complicated than he implied. She said, 'We're allowed to change. Even to fall in love with other people, so long as we're honest about it.'

'I was honest. Too much so when Kimmy asked, "Do you love me enough to give up your dreams?"' He cringed at a memory.

'You said "No,"' Ruby finished for him. 'Most men would have asked her to define love exactly, or dodged the question.' She was crossing a boundary, unsure she wanted to risk hearing an unwelcome answer, but she asked anyway. 'Is it over? Have you moved on?'

'Yes. What about you?' Will reached out and shifted a wing of hair that had fallen over her brow. She didn't flinch from the touch. 'He hurt you, your ex.'

'He broke my heart. My pride was collateral damage.' Lily, blinking insolently at her with her fair head next to Didier's dark one, was an image she simply could not dislodge. Ruby described how, after finding the two of them together, she'd staggered into her lounge where she'd listened to agitated bickering coming from the bedroom. She'd heard Didier repeating, 'Just get dressed, leave me to explain.' As if he could.

He'd come in, pulling a jersey over his head, which angered her. Couldn't he have put on his clothes first? His opening words had made lightning flash in her head.

'You weren't supposed to come home till the day after tomorrow.' She'd been to a chef's conference in Corsica, supposedly a three-day trip.

'A storm broke; you must have heard it on the news,' she'd said, driven to explain her unexpected return. 'Everyone was saying that planes would be cancelled, so I packed and left rather than get stranded.'

'But you didn't call!'

*I wanted to surprise you!* 'Just get out,' were her actual words. 'And take her with you.' Lily Bouchard had come to stand in the doorway, as if this was all a great bore.

'Lily, please go,' Didier had said softly.

'I will when you've told her it's over,' Lily replied.

Ruby had shoved past her, going into the bedroom. She picked up scattered pieces of clothing and hurled them at the lovers. 'Both of you, get out.' It was her flat, though Didier had pretty much moved in. After they'd left, she'd dragged out a spare duvet and lay down on the sofa. She never slept in her bed again. In the night, she'd woken feeling she couldn't breathe.

'It was shock, I think,' she told Will. 'I couldn't go into work.' She'd lain on the sofa for hours, sweating, ignoring the ringing mobile phone and Didier rapping at her door.

'Ruby? Ruby? We have customers at tables. What are you doing?'

She'd ignored him the next day and the next. On day four, around midnight, she was woken by him entering the flat.

'Ruby, if you don't go in tomorrow you're going to be fired. They told me tonight.'

'They can't. I'm ill and I have a contract.'

'They'll make you fight it in court. Lily's father will pay you three months' salary and he'll let you keep this flat till the agreement runs out. But first, I need the numbers you wrote down.'

It had taken a slow moment for her to realise that Didier was not here for her welfare. He wanted the financial projections she'd done for Pastel. Twelve months' detailed costings for Maurice Bouchard, Lily's father, done in her own time.

'You have no right to be here,' she'd said weakly. 'It's my name on the tenancy.'

'Maurice gave me permission to enter, on the grounds that you might have harmed yourself or taken an overdose.'

'Oh, don't flatter yourself, Didier. I could call the police, report you for breaking in. Put your key on the table.'

'All right. Now give me the figures, Ruby. I need them.'

'Over my dead body.'

All the time as she'd told her story, Will had kept his eyes on her. He now spoke. 'Telling somebody they'll get something over your dead body is risky.'

'I wasn't thinking logically.' Ruby looked down at her feet, resting on the rug. She'd taken off her shoes to avoid bringing the outside onto Will's immaculate floors, but now realised she was wearing unmatched socks. She curled her toes. 'Didier didn't attempt murder, in case you're wondering, but he flew into a rage, which was intimidating.'

'I'd like to have been there,' Will said gravely. 'Did you give him the figures?'

'Not yet. They exist only on a memory stick, which I brought with me.'

He turned that over in silence, then said, 'You haven't blocked his number – why?'

She often asked herself why too. 'I suppose, because blocking people is what angry thirteen-year-olds do.'

'Adults do it when they know something is finished. Or is it not finished between the two of you?'

'It's dead. Over.' She'd left her flat within days of Didier's visit, taking only what she could pack into a couple of suitcases, and had gone to her mother's. Everything else, the mementoes of the countries and cities she'd worked in, a pebble from a Hebridean beach and an irreplaceable bergère sofa she'd bought

in an antiques mart, were still in the flat where Didier now lived
with Lily Bouchard. Losing her chef's knives hurt most. They
fitted her hand through years of use, and their scalpel-sharp
blades could precision fillet. 'I can't bear the thought of somebody else hacking away with them.'

'Why not offer Didier a deal? He sends the knives; you send
the memory stick.'

Will had a point. Only—

'I don't feel ready to offer him a deal, frankly. I know you
think I'm being childish.'

'I think' – he took her plate and put it on the low table next
to his – 'you're human.'

They had moved closer to each other on the sofa until their
thighs touched. Will's lips found hers with a simple tilt of the
head. It was a leisurely, exploratory kiss and afterwards, there
was no awkwardness, and no sense of pressure from Will.

'I've wanted to do that for ages,' he said.

'Me too,' she said, 'since you came downstairs the other day,
warm from your bed.'

'I've wanted to kiss you since Aunt Flip showed me a
picture of you in one of the Sunday supplements. You were in a
feature on—'

'"The foodie secrets of Gascony". A photographer trailed
me through the market in Laurac, while I tried to look natural.
He pictured me leaning forward to smell a cantaloupe melon.'

'Of such things dreams are made. I burned to kiss you then,
the real woman, only Aunt Flip told me you had a boyfriend.'

The spell broke, the reminder that not far away was somebody who would mind deeply that Ruby more than liked Will,
and that the feeling appeared to be mutual. 'I ought to go. It's
late.'

'I suppose. Seems a shame.'

She saw the longing in his eyes, and feared it was in hers
too. She jumped up, rather fast, and Edna barked.

'I'll walk you home,' Will said resignedly.

In the end, they ran because the rain had started again. Ruby happened to look back at Westumble Farm and saw an upper window lit, and movement behind it. You've seen us, then, Philippa, she projected silently. This time, you can't tell tales to Norman.

## 33

'I can't think why you didn't just ask me straight out where those pieces of Irene's had got to,' Philippa said, having directed Ruby to go up to the main bedroom and feel around on top of the wardrobe. 'When Will asked me about the jewellery this morning, he said you and your mum were quite upset about it.'

Ruby might have been flummoxed by the blatant volte-face, except that she was growing familiar with Aunt Flip's tactics. When caught out, Philippa simply adjusted reality.

Will had texted Ruby a short while ago, saying she should call at Westumble. *Had a word with Flip this morning, and she has the jewellery. Go see her but please tread carefully. Sorry to sound like a broken record.* He'd signed off with 'W' and three kisses.

Certain she was moments from having Irene's locket in her hand, Ruby had run across the road, frustrated when Philippa took several minutes to answer her knock.

When the door finally opened, Ruby had thought for a moment that she was seeing a stranger. Instead of the neat pageboy hair, Philippa's head was swathed in a tightly knotted silk scarf. One glance was enough to realise that beneath it, Philippa was bald. The white bob must be a wig and Philippa must at some point have been really quite ill. Ruby recalled Will mentioning that his godmother had suffered a breakdown. The denials, the obstructiveness, made more sense now and brought a rush of sympathy. Ruby had listened patiently while Philippa made her fantastical explanations and invited Ruby to look upstairs.

Standing on a chair in Philippa's bedroom, she searched the top of the wardrobe, which was chock-a-block with craft kits and half-finished cross stitch. An old-style Clarks shoebox felt the right weight. Ruby lifted it down and took it to the bed. Inside was a glittering cache. Necklaces, pendants, earrings, bracelets, rings. Some, Ruby recognised. There were several boxes marked 'Lubbock Bros'.

Ruby laid each item in a line, but even before she'd finished, she knew the locket was not among them. Downstairs, she found Philippa shakily pouring boiling water into a mug. The steam smelled like peppermint.

'Are there any of these pieces you'd like?' Ruby asked, putting the shoebox on the kitchen surface.

'They're all to go to your mother,' Philippa said matter-of-factly. 'That's what Irene's will said.'

'Yes. Thank you for keeping everything safe, but please say if there's anything you fancy. Mum has so much jewellery of her own.'

'I might as well have what she doesn't want?'

'No.' Ruby was trying to be diplomatic, but disappointment was getting in the way. 'That's not what I mean.' She sighed, giving up. 'There's something Irene was given before she married Grandad. To do with her engagement. A sort of pendant.'

She waited, willing Philippa to take the bait. Philippa was

pushing her teabag down into her mug with a spoon, stabbing at it. She'll split it, Ruby thought.

Philippa removed the teabag and turned to face Ruby. 'I haven't heard you ask where Irene's wedding ring is. My brother wasn't dead two days and it was off her finger. What do you make of that?'

Broadsided, Ruby floundered. She hadn't realised the wedding ring was missing and tried to think if her grandma had been wearing it when they'd last been together. She'd washed Irene, and filed her grandma's nails, and had no memory of soaping and drying around a wedding band. So perhaps Irene had taken the ring off as Norman died, as Philippa seemed to be saying. 'Where do you think it is, Aunt Flip?'

'Lost. Properly lost.' Without the white hair framing her face, Philippa looked all of her eighty-eight years. 'Irene was a dark one, who went her own way. My brother could have done better.'

Ruby was stunned by the bitter tone. It was incomprehensible, in hindsight, that Philippa had fought Ruby and Amanda's attempts to get Irene into a care home when it was blindingly obvious that it had to be done. Irene had become a prisoner of Oak Apple Farm, unable to feed or care for herself and falling constantly. They'd assumed Philippa had been hanging on to a person she loved. But it seemed the opposite was true.

Philippa had kept a white-knuckle grip on someone she hated.

'I always thought you and Irene were close,' Ruby said.

'I loved my brother. I rubbed along all right with your gran, in the end, but it's hard to love a person who doesn't know how to love back.' Philippa's wrist suddenly wilted and Ruby moved quickly to take the mug from her. She took it to the table, and helped Philippa sit down.

'I'm sorry,' she said, 'about everything.'

'It's not your fault, girl. I am tired. You got what you came for, so please go.'

'Of course.' Ruby picked up the shoebox, but at the door, spurred on by the slight softening in Philippa's tone, she risked one last question. 'Where's Irene's locket, the one Theo gave her?'

Philippa shook her head. 'I don't know what you're saying.'

'It existed, Auntie. Theo Robinson gave it to her.' Ruby waited for a response. There was none and she couldn't resist one last push: 'Irene wore the locket on her wedding day.'

Philippa jerked violently. Ruby hurried back to her, but was slapped away.

'I was there the day she married my brother. Were you?' Philippa levered herself up using the table. 'I watched Irene's mother help dress her. I held the bouquet. There was no locket, and if you're stirring up trouble I've spent my life trying to forget, shame on you.'

This reaction was precisely what Will had feared. Philippa's nostrils had thinned; her cheeks were bloodless. 'Auntie, please sit down. I'm sorry.'

'When Irene married Norman and came to Oak Apple Farm, she became sister and mother to me, till she tried to leave us.'

'Leave us' was expressed as a howl that cut Ruby to the bone. 'Auntie, all I want is to know more about my grandma's life, not to rake up misery.'

'That's what you've been doing from the moment you arrived!'

'Not true. I've asked some questions, that's all. What are you hiding?'

Philippa shook a finger. Her scarf had slipped, to reveal a patch of moon-white forehead. Her eyes were wide, scared, pupils darting. 'You rake up the past, you'll wish you hadn't. Now go, and shut the door behind you.'

.   .   .

At home, Ruby put the jewellery in a safe place. At some point, she would present it to her mother. Guiltily aware of the emotions she'd unleashed at Westumble, she powered up her laptop. A search of 'Theo Robinson, Flixfield' brought up a website devoted to the 699th Bomb Group – 'A debt of gratitude and the hand of friendship'. Theo's name was among a roster of others, credited with building the base in virgin green fields.

The website's author was local, judging by the peppering of Suffolk dialect in the text. Ruby scrolled down to a page headed: 'High Times and Misdemeanours' and came across a grainy version of the photograph of Irene dancing in some hall or other. Definitely a 1940s night out, judging by the hair and the necklines, the square uniform shoulders of the men. Here was her grandma, living in the moment. Her partner, in a military tunic and paler coloured slacks, was a younger Theo Robinson than the one pictured descending aeroplane steps at Baton Rouge. But definitely the same man.

The photo's caption had all the cheesy style of mid-century journalism. 'No wallflowers at this Friday night hop as US boys teach their fair partners a dance called "The Jitterbug". Eyebrows might rise at the wildness of the dancing, but local lass Irene Boulter and First Sgt Theo Robinson of the 699 don't care a jot!'

From the ecstasy on Irene's face, damn right she didn't care a jot.

But others had. They'd minded enough to set Theo up for a bludgeoning and Irene up for oral rape.

'You loved Theo,' Ruby whispered. So much, Irene had suppressed a serious sexual assault to spare him distress. She'd worn the locket he'd given her when she went to church to marry another man.

That's what Philippa couldn't cope with. Her obsessive love for her brother made Irene's love for a different man unpardonable. But what was she missing? Philippa's reaction earlier, spitting like a wounded creature poked in its burrow, suggested trauma. Secrets. And guilt.

For Ruby, physical work was always the antidote to overthinking. She set up an online account with Easifix and ordered paint-rollers and litres of white emulsion. That done, she put on rubber gloves and started washing the downstairs walls. Five hours in, she lay down on her bed and shut her eyes.

Her phone woke her. Muzzily, she took the call, saying in English, 'Sod off, Didier.'

'It's me, Will.'

'Oh, hi.' *That kiss.* Not the last, she hoped, but the first of many. Her warm bubble instantly burst.

'What the hell, Ruby? I told you not to lay this on Aunt Flip, yet you went over and blindsided her.'

'What? No. It wasn't like that.' She sat up, putting her phone to the other ear. 'Will!'

'I'd intended to be over at yours today, giving a final check to your roof, but I won't make it. I'll be with Aunt Flip at the hospital.'

'Hospital...?' She put her feet to the floor. 'What's happened?'

'She collapsed.'

'Oh, Will. Can I help? Shall I come over?'

His answer was halfway between a snort and a growl. 'You managed to stay away most of your life, so I suggest you leave us alone.'

The call was cut, leaving Ruby feeling she'd been mugged. Will's car was backing out of Westumble as she panted across the road. Philippa was in the back seat, her head resting against a cushion. The silk scarf was still around her head. Waving violently, Ruby got Will's attention. For a moment, she thought he'd drive on, but he braked and lowered the window.

She peered in. Philippa's eyes were closed, her breathing shallow. 'What can I do?'

Will looked as angry as he'd sounded on the phone, but he said, 'Could you fetch Edna, and keep her with you till I'm back?'

'Course I will.'

'You remember my door code?'

'Nineteen eighty-eight. Where are you taking Philippa?'

'A&E.'

'Right.'

'And could you dig out Mary Daker and ask her to do a bit of tidying up for Aunt Flip? The house is chaos. Mary's is the third bungalow after Oak Apple.'

'Third bungalow. Got it.' She let him go.

She went first to check on Edna, who was fast asleep. Making sure there was water in the bowl, Ruby left. She'd come back later, find kibble and bring the dog home to Oak Apple Farm. Instead of going to Mary Daker's, Ruby decided she'd do any tidying that was needed. Neighbours asked questions, and Ruby wasn't keen on the whole of Flixfield discovering that she'd driven Philippa to a state of collapse.

The kitchen at Westumble Farm looked much as usual, full of china plates and knick-knacks. Ruby washed up a couple of mugs and left them on the drainer. The lounge looked fine, but upstairs was a different story. In Philippa's bedroom, plastic bags spilled their contents all over the carpet. Hundreds of picture cards, which had been issued by Brooke Bond tea back in the 1960s, covered the floor. Philippa's collecting zeal must date back a long way, Ruby thought, and she obviously liked postcards, as there was a heap of them too. Mostly from English seaside resorts, one or two from Spain and Portugal. One from

Canada was signed 'Doris', reminding Ruby of Will's early history. Doris, his grandmother, had been Philippa's best friend. *Till she left me.*

Was that the source of Philippa's anger and pain, that those she loved left her? She'd hinted something about Irene trying to leave at some point. It wasn't surprising if Philippa had some kind of abandonment complex, having been orphaned within weeks of her birth. She must have come up here after Ruby left that morning and dragged out these bags. Marks on the carpet suggested they'd come from under the bed, so once she'd gathered up all the cards, Ruby pushed them back there. She'd missed one postcard. It was on the bed, an ink sketch of a manor house captioned 'Thewell Park'.

Wait a mo – that was familiar. There was a blank space next to the picture, for an address, and somebody had written, 'Plait, Oak Apple Farm, Flixfield, Suffolk'. On the back was a printed message:

*Your relative/patient has arrived safely and is in good spirits.* 'Patient' had been crossed out.

For some reason, it struck a chill. *Thewell Park.* Where had she come across that name?

Downstairs, Ruby put away the mugs she'd washed earlier, and Philippa's peppermint tea. The pantry cupboard had an entire shelf of home-made jams and chutneys, with handwritten labels. None of them touched. Better keep the jams I bought her for Christmas, Ruby decided, and get her something else. The cupboard reflected the house, full to bursting with speciality foods, mostly unopened. Clearly, Philippa liked buying herself gifts – Ruby had seen several delivery vans pulling up since she'd arrived in the village. The fact that Philippa had been hoarding Irene's jewellery made even more sense now. *She can't let go.* And I've made things worse. If there's any good reason for me to have come to Oak Apple Farm, Ruby thought, it's so I can help heal our family trauma.

But where to start? Offering to declutter? That wouldn't go down well. On the pantry cupboard's topmost shelf, far too high for Philippa to reach without a stepladder, Ruby found a vintage stone pot. Its label read 'Moutarde de Meaux'. French mustard, the lid stuck fast. Turning it upside down to look for a sell-by date, Ruby saw something flutter to the floor. It was a handwritten note dated Wednesday 31 May 1950. It came from St Peter's Vicarage, Flixfield, and the message that followed read:

*Dear Mrs Boulter,*

*I write to thank you for your kind help with our Whit Monday parade and tea at the village hall. We are at our best when we pull together and there was much praise for your lovely lemon sponge. It was delightful to see dear Irene looking well again. So blooming.*

*Maude Prentice*

Prentice was the name of the vicar from Irene's diary. Maude must be his piano-playing wife and goodness... the note was addressed to Mrs Boulter. That was Irene's mother. Ruby was holding something her great-grandmother had touched. What was it doing here, at Westumble?

Something Philippa had said that morning came into focus. When Irene married Norman, she'd moved across to Oak Apple Farm. But when Irene and Theo Robinson had met in 1943, this place, Westumble, had been the Boulter home and must have remained so for some years.

1950 was significant. Ruby's mum had been born in December of that year.

She read Mrs Prentice's note again and looked up 'Whit Monday' on her phone. There was a reference to Whitsun, part of the old church calendar, which fell seven Sundays after Easter. Whit Monday, the day following, was now rebranded as May Bank Holiday. Maude Prentice must have organised a village party. She came across on paper as the rah-rah, games-mistress type.

*Delightful to see dear Irene looking well again.*

Ruby imagined her great-grandmother reading this, perhaps over a lunch of ham and tomatoes, and it sticking to the mustard jar, to be consigned forever to a too-high shelf. Moutarde de Meaux. A just-visible price ticket showed two francs. If she hadn't been holding the jar, Ruby might have scratched her head. How had mustard bought in France, before the dawn of the euro, made its way to a cupboard in Flixfield?

She put the jar back and replaced the note. Philippa had looked awful in the car. She'd text Will, when he'd had a chance to reach A&E, and see how she was doing. He'd sounded frazzled as well as being stony-faced, which wasn't surprising as the nearest hospital was thirty-two miles off. When her grandma had fallen out of bed, and Ruby had found her ice-cold on the floor, the distance to the nearest A&E had hit home. Remote villages were not for the old and immobile. They'd been right to get Irene into Maple Court and, at some point, Philippa would have to review her life here in this old house with its steep stairs and uneven floors. Maple Court was lovely. It was lockdown that had left Irene marooned there, feeling abandoned.

So much to make up for, if only it wasn't too late. Ruby let herself out and went to fetch Edna. She was walking the dog back to Oak Apple, a bag of kibble in one hand, when it came to her why Thewell Park was familiar.

A letter with that name on it had been among the debris on the bonfire, which she'd piled into a sack her first morning here. She hadn't thrown it away yet and while she didn't relish digging into the sack, the coincidence was too striking to ignore.

The robotic-sounding message on the postcard played on her mind.

*Your relative-stroke-patient, delete as appropriate.*

It had the touch of prison about it. It had been sent to 'Plait, Oak Apple Farm'. Which Plait, Norman or Irene? Or Philippa, who had been a Plait before she married Ronnie Gifford?

## 34

Ruby fed Edna immediately, to help the dog settle in. She then called Will and left a message. He was probably sitting in A&E, chewing his nails. Putting on rubber gloves, she went out into the darkening afternoon. Edna was happy to mooch around the garden while Ruby rifled through the burned papers, looking for the remains of the medical discharge letter. It was horrible work, as the rain had got into the sack.

Her mobile rang and, assuming it was Will, she dragged off a glove and swiped up, asking without preamble, 'Are you still at the hospital?'

'*Non*. Why do you ask?'

God. Didier. 'I don't want to talk to you. Haven't you worked that out?'

'Ruby, speak French, please.'

She hadn't realised she wasn't. She switched language, telling him to stop bothering her.

'I'm doing it because you won't allow a conversation. You are making this so difficult.'

'What's difficult? You cheated; I caught you. Now you've

got my flat and the boss's daughter so go away, Didier. We're done.'

'No, please, listen. We get that you're angry. Lily feels so bad.'

'Well, that's all right then.'

'I'm trying to say, Lily feels we should have explained and apologised. We just...' Didier made a sound, implying the whole business was too complex for mere words. 'I don't know.'

'No?' She spoke coldly. 'I know what happens under a duvet so let's not go there.' She remembered, just then, something she'd said to Will only last night.

*We're allowed to change. Even to fall in love with other people, so long as we're honest.* Was this honest, punishing Didier, fanning the flames of her resentment? It certainly wasn't liberating her. 'Cut to the chase,' she said. 'What do you want?'

'You know what I want.'

'I want to hear you say it.'

'I need the figures you did. Lily's father keeps asking me when I will present them, and I cannot keep telling him that I'm gathering new data.'

'Fine. Now ask me what I want.'

Reluctantly, nervously, he did.

'I want my knives, so I can work. Sounds like we have a deal, Didier.'

'All right.' *That was easier than I thought*, his tone implied. 'Come to Laurac and we will make an exchange.'

'I haven't time to come to Laurac.'

'You can't stay in England forever, Ruby.'

'I can. I have dual citizenship.' Another call was coming in. Ruby took it, without saying goodbye to Didier. 'Hi, Will, how's Philippa?' He didn't answer. 'Will, are you there?'

'Yeah. Lousy signal, I'm leaving shortly.' It sounded as though he was phoning under water. 'They think it was a panic attack, but they're keeping her in overnight. I thought she'd had a stroke. Can I drop round when I'm back? There's something I need to say.'

'Fine.' He was going to blame her. Deservedly. 'See you soon, and I've got Edna.'

'Great. See you in a bit.'


Will arrived an hour-and-a-half later, complaining, 'They're always closing the back roads, putting up diversions and never explain why. I was sent eight miles out of my way.' He stroked Edna's ears. 'Did the nice lady feed you?'

'Nice lady' sounded encouraging. 'Kibble and half a tin of sardines,' Ruby said. 'Omega three is good for female hormones.'

'She'll be here for lunch every day now.' Will looked wrung out and she told him to go through to the lounge. 'I'll make tea. No – sorry – coffee.' She had an idea he didn't like tea.

He'd arrived as she'd been scrubbing her nails under the kitchen tap having given up trying to find the letter from Thewell Park. Everything at the bottom of the binbag had turned to black porridge. However, an online search had revealed that Thewell Park had been in its time a private mansion, an orphanage and, from 1940 until its demolition in the 1960s, a psychiatric hospital. The fragment she'd discovered on the bonfire, though she hadn't seen a date, almost certainly came from the period when it had been a hospital and hadn't belonged to her runaway tenants. No. From the postcard on Philippa's bed, the person discharged had been surnamed 'Plait'.

She found Will standing in front of the cold fireplace in the lounge. 'Bob Oaks is coming tomorrow,' she said. 'I should have a stove and a working fireplace in twenty-four hours.'

'That's good.' Will seemed distracted, unsurprising since he had left Philippa to endure an overnight stay in a hospital bed.

He went to a nook beside the fireplace and opened the doors of a painted pine cupboard. 'Have you ever looked inside here?' he asked.

'Once.' A quick glance, enough to smell the damp and see a spider scuttling into a corner.

'Would you like to get inside?' Will asked.

Ruby's pulse jumped and she wondered if she'd misread this situation. Did Will Keelbrook get off on putting people in small, suffocating spaces? 'No,' she said, very firmly.

'Me neither. There have been mice in there at some point. Now imagine a child shut inside, for hours.' Anger vibrated through the words.

'What are you saying, Will?'

'Philippa told me as we waited at A&E, as though she was repeating a nightmare. She was shut in there as a little girl.' He crouched down and she saw him run his fingers across the inner side of the door. 'Yes. As she told me.'

Ruby joined him and saw scratches on the painted surface. 'Are you saying what I think you're saying?'

'Philippa would take off her shoe and bash its buckle against the door, trying to get someone to hear.'

'How old was she?'

'Three. Four. Five. Until she was too large to shove in. Her aunt Elsie did it whenever Philippa was naughty or broke something. Into the pitch dark, no food or water. Ask any social worker, home is often the most dangerous place for little children.'

Ruby remembered a throwaway reference of Irene's, about marks on Philippa's back, which she'd noticed when bathing the child. Marks explained away as being due to Philippa rolling defiantly on the ground. Really? 'Aunt Elsie' was the 'nasty old woman' who made regular appearances in Irene's diary.

'She was Elsie Binney,' Will said, 'and was the widowed sister-in-law of Norman and Philippa's father, so not a blood relative. A pillar of respectability, church twice on Sundays, Bible by the bed. Elsie rooted herself here on the death of Philippa and Norman's mother, and after the father died she became indispensable. You know Flip's mother died days after giving birth to her, and then her father went two weeks later? Bit of a crappy hand of cards for Little Flip, all told.'

'What about Norman?' Ruby burst out. 'Where's he at this point?' Her trust in her grandad was rock-bottom. Whatever Will said, she still believed he'd summoned the military police to ambush Theo's lorry. 'He was almost adult when Philippa was born. Surely, he could have defended his baby sister.'

Will closed the cupboard. 'Far as I can tell, he was glad someone took on the housekeeping and a squalling newborn. He was a farmer, out from early dawn to last light. Maybe he didn't see.'

'Or didn't want to.' Ruby looked back at the sofa, where once she'd sat with her grandad to watch the horse racing. She'd bonded with him far more easily than she had with Irene. A slow-talking countryman. Patient. Soft-hearted. But was he really? Within hours of his death his wife of fifty-seven years had removed her wedding ring. She looked again at the cupboard, picturing a small Philippa hunched inside. 'Children don't tell, do they? They haven't the words. But what about Irene and Violet, Irene's mum? Why didn't they see?'

Will shrugged and picked up his coffee. 'Wasn't Irene's father crippled with rheumatoid arthritis? She and her mum were his carers. Not that they'd have called it that, but looking after him, and everything else, probably took their eyes off what was happening here. And Elsie was clever, Philippa says. Have you lived with a controlling bully?'

'No, but I've worked with a few.' One chef in particular had emotionally mauled every new young member of staff, reducing them to tears, before putting an arm around them and assuring them he was only trying to toughen them up... 'Did Philippa tell you all this today?' she asked.

Will nodded. 'Waiting in A&E, it came out like a primal stream of consciousness. I should have realised before. When I got Edna, she was called "Elsie" and Philippa experienced breathing difficulties just hearing the name. That's when she first told me she'd been afraid of her aunt.'

Ruby nodded. 'I'm guessing Philippa has spent her life clinging to anybody and anything that offered her an escape, starting with her brother. My grandma writes about Philippa's ice-cold stare whenever anybody else had Norman's attention.'

'Any woman Norman fell for would have been a rival,' Will agreed. He sat down, and let Edna rest her jaw on his knee. He stroked her head. 'Philippa resented Irene for not loving Norman as she ought, but if she had, Philippa would have been up in arms. Irene couldn't win. And Philippa was always inside that marriage, causing ructions.' He gave a slight smile. 'I'm not unaware of what Aunt Flip does, but you have to remember, Oak Apple Farm was half hers, and she felt unfairly ousted, sent to live at Westumble.'

'I get confused, the yo-yo-ing back and forth between Oak Apple and Westumble. I know it's only over the road...'

'It's complex,' Will agreed. 'The Boulters owned Westumble but, during the war, Norman bought all its land, less a few acres. After he and Irene married, Norman bought the house and the remaining land, to ensure that Violet would have a home for life when John died. John Boulter passed shortly after the end of the war and Philippa moved to Westumble, permanently. After Philippa married Ronnie, the couple lived there with Violet until she died in 1970. Norman had gifted Westumble to Philippa and Ronnie as a wedding present, keeping Oak Apple for himself. That's how Aunt Flip comes to own Westumble, and not you.'

'I'm relieved I don't! Oak Apple Farm is more than enough

for me.' Ruby told him about the postcard she'd found in Philippa's bedroom, the façade of a house called Thewell Park, and the chilling message on the back. 'As though nobody could be bothered to send a personal letter to the relations back home, to reassure them. You told me that Philippa had suffered a breakdown. Did she spend time in a psychiatric hospital?'

'To my knowledge, never.'

'It would have been sometime between 1940 and 1968.'

'Pass. If she did, she has her reasons for not telling me.'

'What caused her hair loss? It wasn't cancer, was it?'

'No.'

He was holding out on her. In a moment, he'd blank her. 'I want to know what happened in this family, Will. I'd like to put some ghosts to rest, but I keep falling over new mysteries and secrets. I want to understand Philippa better.'

He patted the sofa. 'Sit down, then, because you're putting me on edge, rocking from foot to foot.'

She sat, with Edna sandwiched between their knees, and Will began to speak.

'It was after Irene had died, and I was still locked down in UAE. Philippa came here to put things into boxes, and she found a cleaning firm in the house, doing the job themselves.'

'Mum appointed them. We couldn't just leave the place empty.'

Will's nod told her he understood. 'But Aunt Flip felt pushed out again, unwelcome in what had once been her home. I'm pretty sure she had a stand-off with the cleaners.'

Ruby gave a dry laugh. 'They left and we had to find others. I should have guessed it was Philippa.' She gave Will a quick look, anxious in case her last remark had riled him.

He caught the look. 'It goes without saying, Irene's death deeply upset Aunt Flip and affected her health. I wasn't there, but when I came home in July 2020, she weighed seven stone and her hair was falling out. I got her to a clinic, and medication seemed to help – until suddenly, her hair just all fell out, in a week.' An involuntary movement of his fingers to his army-style crop cleared up an unanswered question on the spot.

'You shaved in support,' she said. 'Will!' When she'd first seen him without a hat, she'd feared he'd gone through chemo. 'To keep her company.'

He acknowledged it. 'Not that you ever can. *Choosing* to shave your head means it grows back. The best thing I did for Aunt Flip was persuade her to have a lady round, to fit a wig for her.'

'It's a good wig.' Ruby reached across the dog's head and laid her hand on his. 'You're kind, and I bet it really helped Philippa to know that someone cared enough to go that far.'

'Maybe.' Praise seemed to make him uncomfortable.

Edna suddenly ducked under Ruby's legs and loped out of the room, and a moment later, they heard her noisily drinking from the pan of water Ruby had put down for her. Without the dog's panting heat, the gap between Ruby and Will suddenly felt significant. She inched closer before pulling back. He was locked in thought, and Ruby wasn't certain she was forgiven for tipping Philippa into a new crisis. Not that it had bothered Philippa that Ruby had found the missing jewellery. It was the locket. Always the locket.

'You know what I hate?' Ruby said.

Will pulled himself back from wherever he'd wandered. 'Spam fritters? Sugary tea? I don't know. You tell me.'

'I hate it when I feel you're judging me, and that I've fallen short. I don't mean I want to grovel to please you; I'm not that kind of woman. But being thought callous really gets me.'

'Because there's truth in it,' he said slowly. 'You and your mother let two old people struggle on alone. I'm talking about Irene *and* Philippa. Both widowed. Growing old and frail without family. It *was* callous. I get it, you grew up in France, and you never acquired the habit of thinking of Irene, Norman and Philippa as your family, but your mother hasn't that excuse. She chose to exile herself, and I don't doubt she had her reasons. But they grew old, Ruby, and deserved some compassion.'

Ruby looked away and, for a moment, did the unthinkable and blamed her mother, though not out loud. Excuses and explanations piled up in her head, dismissed one after the other. 'It's too late, isn't it?'

'No. Philippa is still alive and all she's ever wanted in her entire eighty-eight years is to be loved.'

Ruby swallowed. A painful lump sat in her throat.

'Can we do a deal?' he said.

'You sound like Didier,' she answered bitterly.

'It's a simple one. I won't judge you, if you do the same with Philippa, and your grandad.'

'That's tough; the evidence is against them.'

'Innocent till proven guilty.'

During this batting back and forth, they had moved closer. 'I thought you rather liked me yesterday,' Ruby said.

'I rather like you today.'

Their lips met. His jaw was bristly, and Ruby made an audit of his day: up early, quick shave, discovery that Philippa had collapsed, urgent dash to the hospital. No wonder he was a little rough around the contours. She opened her lips and felt his reaction, a slight intake of breath, a shifting of his weight towards her.

His phone buzzed. It was on the table and he couldn't stop himself looking at it.

'God, it's the hospital.' Will left the room and Ruby stayed, to give him privacy. He came back a minute later.

'What is it? Stroke, heart attack?'

'Neither. She's told them she's discharging herself because she can't stand it a minute longer. I have to go and pick her up.'

## 35

## PHILIPPA

The fuss they made in this hospital over her hair loss! Was she living with cancer, what medications was she taking? When she answered, 'Fig leaf tea and aspirin if my arthritis plays up,' they'd looked at her as if she'd lost her marbles.

She'd said to the man-nurse with the concerned eyes, 'Marbles all present and correct, dear, but the hair went AWOL.' She had to explain that AWOL was 'absent without leave'. What did they teach youngsters these days at school?

They'd done all the tests, and she'd been taken to a side room and helped onto a trolley bed which was so hard, it was like lying on packing cases. Even so, she'd slept a bit. And dreamed.

Now, she was waiting for Will to come. And couldn't stop nodding off. So hot in here!

Again, she dreamed. This time, she was walking along a shady avenue and there it was, the house with its mushroom-colour walls and tall windows that opened onto a terrace. The lawns had lines of wooden daybeds wheeled out for patients, because fresh air was everything at Thewell Park. There was a gate set in a high wall that encircled the gardens, and a man had to let you in and the same man chose whether or not he let you out. In her dream, she paced towards the front door with pillars where a woman was waiting.

The woman waved. 'Hi, Mrs Gifford, I'm Barbara and I need to talk to you.'

*Go away!*

'Mrs Gifford? It's Barbara and we have to talk.'

*Go away, you don't exist!*

'Mrs Gifford!' Her arm was being touched. 'Mrs Gifford!'

'I'm not talking to you. Go away.'

'It's your nurse, Mrs Gifford.'

Philippa woke to a face leaning over hers and it made her scream. 'Sorry, sorry, sorry. I didn't mean to send you to that place. I didn't mean it. It wasn't me; it was the others.'

'Mrs Gifford, it's Afia, one of the nurses.'

'Not Barbara?'

'I'm not Barbara.'

'Where are you from, then, dear?'

'I've just come on duty and I'm checking up on you, Mrs Gifford.'

'Did you come from London?'

'London, no. I live here, in town. Before that, I'm from Ghana. That's West Africa.'

'Have you got Irene's locket? They all want it, and I can't find it.' Philippa felt her brain switch to a fast wash-cycle. The danger moment. She pulled herself back from falling into the spin. Breathe, breathe. She was in Ipswich hospital. Will had brought her and was coming to get her. 'It's all right,' she muttered. 'I got confused for a moment.'

She'd meant to burn that postcard of Thewell Park, like the rest of the stuff. She oughtn't ever to have kept it. It'd go on the fire, soon as she was home. Nobody must see it. You could look up places these days, on the web, and learn what they used to be.

*Your relative/patient has arrived safely and is in good spirits.*

'I need to go home, Afia.' Her voice wobbled like a child's.

Nurse Afia didn't recommend it. 'Your blood pressure is raised, Mrs Gifford. We'd like to keep you overnight, to be on the safe side.'

Almond-shaped eyes, full of care. *Darkly troubled eyes looking into my soul.* Philippa found her strength and pulled herself up from her seat. 'I am discharging myself. My godson is already on his way.'

## 36

RUBY

Will had asked Ruby to hang on to Edna till he got back, and she'd taken the dog for a walk. The dark and cold ensured it was a quick one. Now, with Edna slumbering on the rug nearby, Ruby opened her laptop, and found the website dedicated to the 699th Bomber Group. She took a long look at the photo of Irene and Theo dancing, training her magnifying glass on it in the hope of detecting a locket around her grandma's neck. The picture was too blurred.

A paragraph under the caption referred to Theo Robinson's time at Flixfield where, 'In 1943, an altercation with authority seems to have cost him his sergeant's stripes.'

'Altercation'? That was a euphemism of some magnitude. 'How about, "beaten senseless by racists while your girlfriend weeps"?' Ruby muttered.

There was nothing else about Theo on that website. Next Ruby googled 'Jake Hendrick Five'.

'A Georgia-based band formed in 1949, originally playing traditional jazz and swing before becoming pioneers of the post-war "cool jazz" sound.'

She assumed that Jake Hendrick was Theo's best friend of

that name, who had danced with Irene in the war years, and wheeled her bike back to Westumble Farm. It felt likely. Theo had written songs for the band, the article said, and one of his compositions had hit number one, staying at the top for seven weeks. That song was titled 'Irene'.

'Oh, my stars,' Ruby breathed. Proof, surely.

'Irene' was released New Year 1951, recorded in Theo and Jake's hometown of Savannah, Georgia, 'with a B-side entitled "Canary Bird"'. Inspired, the article said, 'by Theo's time in prison'.

'What?' Ruby jabbed her keyboard so aggressively, Edna woke up. 'Sorry, sweetie. Oh, damn!' She'd accidentally closed the document and had to find her place again. Prison? She read frantically to the end of the article, muttering, 'No, no, no,' over and over.

Will arrived, to pick up Edna. He didn't have time to linger. 'I'm going to make Aunt Flip carrot and ginger soup. Any tips?'

'Sweat your veg first in butter. Low heat.'

'Low heat. Got it.' He kissed her cheek. His lips felt chilled.

When Will called by the next day, Ruby's new stove and flue were being installed. Over the clattering and banging, she shouted at him, 'Theo went to prison.'

Will didn't look as shocked as she'd expected. 'Four years' penitentiary,' he agreed. 'I looked him up the other day, after you'd gone. I didn't say anything—'

'Because you feared I'd race over to see Philippa, flinging questions she couldn't answer.'

'I didn't say anything,' he continued patiently, 'because it was for you to discover in your own way, in private.'

Ruby sighed. Fair enough. 'How is Philippa?'

'Wrung out. Upset, but glad to be home. She's at the age

where a trip to hospital can be a one-way event, and that scares her.'

'How was the soup?'

'Pretty good, actually, though I practically had to spoon-feed her.'

'Would she like a cake?'

He laughed. 'Probably not a whole one, but I'll help out with any leftovers. Did you note that the article mentioning Theo's jail term didn't say what he was sent down for?'

Ruby had hit that particular brick wall. 'I googled his name in every way possible, and read reams about his musical and political activities, but nothing directly about prison. Maybe there were no records, or he suppressed them.'

'What about his daughter? What was her name...?'

'Sabrina Robinson Something. I can't ask her such a personal question.' It would feel like stalking.

But Will thought that was overscrupulous. 'What if she has a website? People put their stuff online knowing it'll be looked at. Shall I search, to save you the guilt?'

They were on the sofa, as before, Edna gazing at an untouched plate of biscuits. Ruby pushed her laptop towards Will. A few keystrokes later, a Black woman with grey hair, wearing a yellow linen pantsuit and leaning against a tree, filled the screen. A cloudless sky arched over her. It was the website of Professor Sabrina Robinson-Chase.

Theo's daughter had written about her speciality, which was neurodivergence in the African American community, but a page was dedicated to her dad's activism and music. There was a short essay on his prison term, which Will read while Ruby sat back, listening.

'Theo was sentenced to five years for theft and discharged from the military for gross insubordination. To say Sabrina is angry is an understatement.'

'Theft of what?' Ruby asked. 'Does she say?'

'No.' Will closed that website and made a search on Jake Hendrick. The Jake Hendrick Five had played together, with the same three core musicians from 1949 to 1970 when one of the founding members, Henry 'Duke' Scotland, had died. Jake had been honoured for a lifetime of musical achievement two months before his death in 1991. Will closed the laptop. 'They've all gone, Ruby. It's tough.'

She wasn't sure if he wanted to go, and if his sympathy was a sign-off line. 'Stay if you want,' she hedged, 'but if you have work to do...'

Bob Oaks came to the sitting room door just then to tell her about a couple of loose bricks in the inglenook. 'Alongside the salt nook, Mrs Plait, and there's a crack in the bressummer. Just so you know.'

*Ms* Plait, though she didn't correct him. She wasn't sure what he meant by 'salt nook' but a crack in the fireplace's supporting beam was a different matter. 'How bad a crack?'

Bob made a half-inch gap between two fingers. 'It goes into the heart wood.'

That sounded bad. 'Will it get worse?'

'In time.'

'How long?'

'Oh... you've got about three hundred years before you need to worry.'

He'd been having her on, but she couldn't force a laugh because she was filled with anger at discovering that Theo, having dug holes in the freezing cold Suffolk wind for months, had been imprisoned as a thank-you. Sounding rather crisp, she thanked Mr Oaks for the heads up.

'No probs. Forewarned is forearmed,' he agreed cheerfully. 'We'll be done in a few hours, but we'll have to have a gander at the fireplace in this room, if you don't mind.'

That was Will's cue to go. He needed to continue a conversation he'd started yesterday with his New York client. With him and Edna gone, Ruby felt her isolation pressing on her, despite Bob and his assistant noisily ramming a new flue up a resistant chimney. In search of peace, she took Irene's diary up to her bedroom. Sitting on the edge of the bed, she released the last of the glued pages, from the 4th to the 6th of September 1943.

Ruby found a dense carpet of words across two pages with hardly a space between them, as if the choke on Irene's voice had finally been released. Her grandmother was reporting an incident that Ruby thought at first was some kind of courtroom scene, or a military court martial. It took close reading to realise that Irene was describing events that had taken place across the road at Westumble Farm. To be precise, in the dining hall of Oak Apple Farm.

'He told us how Theo and I could never be married. He made Mum and Dad listen, like they were naughty children, who had brought me up wrong.'

'He' had to be Lieutenant Macbeth. Who else?

Ruby's skin crawled. Meeting *that man* on paper once again was bad enough. How must Irene have felt, facing her attacker at close range, in her own home?

## 37

## IRENE

FRIDAY 26 NOVEMBER 1943

Winter was round the corner, short days, dark nights and enveloping fogs. Irene and Theo made a date for the last Friday night of November, but not at St Margaret's. Even with a paraffin stove going full pelt, the old church was too cold.

Nor would they be dancing. Irene didn't feel up to it, and Theo couldn't swing her around with his ribs still hurting, even though his beating was weeks and weeks ago.

They headed out to the coast. Their new haven was the cinema in Southwold, on York Road. They'd cycle into Hollesford independently, meeting at a bus stop on the edge of town, then ride the bus to the coast. The first time they'd done that, Theo had asked anxiously, 'You're sure I can sit alongside you, Irene? I don't have to go sit at the back?'

The question had shocked her. 'Course not!' On this particular evening, seeing him look towards the rear seats, she asked him why he was always so nervous, sitting next to her as though he hardly knew her.

''Cause back home, we Black citizens have to go to the back

so we don't breathe the air reserved for white passengers. Least-ways, I think that's the reasoning. It can't be because it's noisier and bumpier at the back, since we pay the same fare.' His smile was short-lived.

'It's wrong, Theo. All wrong, and I would hate to live where you live.'

He sighed, and she regretted her words. She wouldn't like it if he said insulting things about Suffolk. But before she could frame an apology, Theo sighed again and said, 'Thing is, Irene, if you'd been brought up in the state of Georgia, you'd have sat at the front of the bus and thought nothing of the Black folk stomping past you to the rear.'

She protested, she would not! 'I'd have something to say about it!'

'Sugar, you would keep quiet, I promise you. The world we're born into, we all believe is the real one and we obey the rules... when they work in our favour. Being white, Georgia would be kind to you. Pretty Miss Irene with her blue eyes wouldn't look twice at me.'

'No. I'd look three times.'

He laughed, but with a fleck of grit in the sound. 'Then you'd get me in one hell of a fix. I'd get a date with the lynching mob.'

Hadn't Jake, or one of his other friends, spoken of 'lynching', in connection with Lieutenant Macbeth? 'What's a lynching mob, Theo?'

But he didn't want to talk about it. Instead, he pointed out of the dark window to a glinting patch of water, asking if that was a fishpond.

'Just marshes, I think,' Irene said. 'It's different land here, because we're near the sea. Are you upset with me, Theo? I'm sorry I was unkind about your home.'

He shook his head. He still didn't put his arm around her, but he edged closer and whispered, 'Today, I saw Macbeth on the 'drome we're digging.' He meant the airfield outside the town of Beccles, where he and his men were now working. 'Walking and talking with other white officers. I don't mind saying, it gave me a kick in the gut 'cause I thought I'd left him behind me.'

It gave Irene one too. Just the name 'Macbeth' made her feel breathless and trapped. She squeezed Theo's hand, hard.

As always at the cinema, they headed for the anonymity of the back row. Usually, they'd sit through two showings of whatever film was on. *Casablanca*, *Mrs Miniver* or a cheaply thrown-together comedy, along with the Pathé newsreels. The film wasn't the point; the cinema was warm, private. They could hold hands without anybody looking curiously at them.

This evening, the film was *Lassie Come Home* but unfortunately Lassie stayed lost because, halfway through, the reel broke and the projectionist couldn't fix it. To whistles of disappointment from the audience, Irene and Theo slipped away and bought chips for themselves before heading for the bus stop.

That was when he drew her closer and said, 'Ain't it time I met your folks?'

'I suppose,' she said, sounding hesitant. She'd prepared her parents for a meeting... sort of... but how would she introduce Theo when it came to the moment? 'My friend' or 'My intended'?

What if Mum and Dad took against Theo, or he made a poor account of himself when her mother asked searching questions, as Violet most assuredly would?

'I guess you don't want me at your place,' Theo said, picking up on her uncertainty.

'No, I *do* want to take you home. It's only... my parents can be fusspots. Mum in particular.' She pulled herself together. There was never going to be an easy moment to introduce Theo at Westumble Farm. And since fate had stepped in, stopping the film early, tonight was the night.

## 38

They reached Westumble Farm shortly before ten. Night and dense fog meant that even Irene had taken a couple of wrong turns on the cycle back from Hollesford. Still full of misgiving, she led the way round the back of the farm where they propped up their bikes. 'Help me open this door,' she said. Her courage had suddenly drained. She was grasping for a way of delaying the moment she took Theo into the house. Her solution was to take him into the haybarn instead. 'Shh! Don't disturb the cows.'

'Your folks live in with the cattle?'

'No, course not. This is where we store the hay. It's nice and private.'

'Are you leading me astray, sweetheart?'

'Bit late for that. Just follow me and don't fall over anything.' Irene guided Theo around islands of old sacking, and tools that her father could no longer handle, and up a set of wooden stairs. Under the ancient thatch, among the sweet-smelling hay, she sank down, bringing him with her. 'I want it to be like it'll be when we're married.'

'Laying in a haybarn?'

'Lying down, somewhere soft. We can pretend it's our bed.'

She pulled his head towards her, kissing him with her eyes tight closed. Theo knocked a pitchfork over with his feet, and they gripped each other, their ears pricked for any sounds that would show they'd been heard.

'We're going to make love before I meet your parents?'

'Yes.' She was impatient, her blood up, and she used every wile to override Theo's reluctance. Her lips, her hands... until he gave in. In her frantic climaxing, she forgot about her mother, who would be peeling aside the blackout curtains, to see if her daughter was coming home. Irene forgot about Macbeth, and what he'd made her do. Theo climaxed inside her. Usually they were more careful, but this time she held him tightly, not letting him roll off her. They lay exhausted in each other's arms until the rustle of mice made them pull their clothes together and stand up.

'My parents will be long asleep by now. You'll have to meet them another time.'

'And that was your plan all along, Irene.'

Yes, if not exactly with forethought. 'I'll make you some cocoa, to warm you on your way.' They crept out of the barn and picked their way through the kitchen garden. The kitchen windows were shrouded with blackout cloth, but Irene was confident her parents would have retired for the night. She eased open the back door, which was never locked. 'Shh!' She giggled, drunk on love and loose-limbed despite the icy-dank night. They went through the dairy, into the kitchen.

'Mum!'

Violet was standing by a table-top oil stove, watching steam float from the kettle's spout. She spun around. 'Irene! What time d'you call this?' She stared at Theo, clearly trying to assemble a name from memory. 'Um...?'

Irene stepped in. 'It's Sergeant Robinson. Theo. I've brought him to meet you.'

Theo nodded politely. 'Good evening, ma'am. It's good to see you again.'

'But it's so late!' In the oil stove's jumping flame, Violet's complexion had a sickly cast. 'What kept you?'

'The film broke down and had to start again so we missed our bus.' Irene flushed at the lie, hoping the malty smell of hay on their clothes wouldn't reach her mother's nose.

'It broke?' Violet asked stupidly.

'Yes. Snapped and the reel flapped about while the projectionist tried to grab it.' Irene was aware of Theo shifting his feet. He respected truth, and she curled her fingers in his as if to say, *This is for both our sakes.* 'Is the tea for Dad?' Dad never usually drank tea after six in the evening, or else he'd be getting out of bed all night.

'No.' Violet dropped her voice to a whisper. 'We've got a visitor.'

Oh, don't let it be Norman, sniffing them out.

'It's the vicar,' Violet said and passed her a milk jug. 'Take this in and mind your manners. Oh, and two cups and saucers from the Sunday china.'

'I thought you said there was one visitor.'

'Just do it, Irene.'

What had brought the Reverend Prentice over at this hour? 'It's not Dad, is it? He's not had a turn?'

'Your father is in bed, as well as he ever is.'

With an apologetic glance for Theo, Irene took two gold-rimmed cups and saucers from the dresser. In the sitting room, Reverend Prentice got to his feet. A second man also got up from a chair and Irene dropped the cups.

No. Not him. Not here.

Violet rushed in, drawn by the breaking of china. 'Oh, Irene, my best things!'

Irene couldn't speak. She knew her mouth was opening and

closing. She wanted to warn Theo, who had lingered in the kitchen to speak with Violet, but was too late. He came in, holding the sugar bowl. The shock of seeing Lieutenant Macbeth in front of him showed in the way he stalled, and the alteration in his breath.

Completely unaware of the terrible undercurrents, Violet fetched fresh crockery and when she came back in, she shut the kitchen door, closing off their means of escape.

## 39

The vicar spoke first.

'Irene, I have apologised to your mother for intruding so late, but my mission cannot wait.' Reverend Prentice was a tall, spare man who had been an army chaplain before taking on this country parish. He was somewhat deaf from serving at the Front, amid the guns, in the last war, and as a consequence projected his voice loudly.

Irene stared mutely at her mother. *What's going on?* Though of course she knew. What else would it be about, but her and Theo?

Violet began to pour tea. 'Reverend Prentice is here for your moral welfare, Irene.'

The vicar addressed Theo. 'Sergeant Robinson?' He'd spoken affably to Irene, but now sounded stern.

Theo, who had taken up a ramrod stance as Violet relieved him of the sugar bowl, met the vicar's eye. 'That is correct, sir. I met you when you were kind enough to allow me and my friends into a dance. Way back in March, I believe.'

'Er, yes... quite so.' Reverend Prentice appeared surprised by Theo's confident reply and cast a glance towards Lieutenant

Macbeth, who stood silently, his thoughts and purpose quite unreadable. The reverend asked them if they'd been enjoying a night out.

Irene's mouth was filling with saliva, a precursor to being violently sick. She tried to calm herself by digging her nails into the tops of her legs, until she felt the pain through her dress and her underthings. She let Theo answer the question.

'Sure, we've been out tonight, sir. We watched *Lassie Come Home*. Leastwise, we tried to.' His eyes were fixed on the opposite wall and though he was talking to the Reverend Prentice, he might have been addressing a section of the oak panelling. 'Only the reel snapped.'

'I see. Any good?' asked the vicar.

'In what way, sir?'

'*Lassie Come Home*. Is it worth a trip to the cinema?'

'I guess so, if ever we get to see the end.'

'I thought you did,' Violet said, handing tea to the vicar. Macbeth had declined any refreshment. 'Irene said you watched it a second time.'

Theo gave a kind of shrug. Irene looked at the floor. Violet sighed. 'Do sit down, reverend. And you, Lieutenant, er, Mac...'

'Macbeth, ma'am. Thank you, I will stand.' Macbeth addressed Reverend Prentice. 'Reckon we'd better get this matter over with, reverend sir.'

It's about the ring, Irene thought, and my locket, and them thinking Theo stole it. But she could prove he didn't because she had the receipt saying it was paid off. Theo was paying her back, four shillings a week. He'd insisted, but they didn't need to know that.

The vicar asked Violet if it might be possible to fetch Mr Boulter.

'My husband's in bed,' Violet replied. 'You of all people know how he keeps to his room, but rest assured, I apprise him of everything.'

*Apprise.* Her mother was using what Irene called her 'Sunday best voice'. Violet was nervous, but her mother hadn't the first idea what the other white man in the room had done to her daughter. Nobody knew, but her and Macbeth himself. He's thinking about it now. Irene felt it. He's picturing what he did to me... she put her hand over her mouth and retched.

Violet stared at her, appalled. Theo took her hand and pressed it.

'Is Irene of age?' the vicar asked.

Violet frowned. 'She's just turned twenty.'

'Then she is not of age, and both you and Mr Boulter must be present to hear what I am to say.' Violet was too much in awe of church and clergy to refuse a second time to fetch her husband.

Getting John Boulter into a dressing gown, into his wheelchair and from his downstairs bedroom took several minutes. Normally, Irene would have helped but she could not move. Sweat was creeping down her back. *He's thinking about pulling my head back, forcing my mouth open.* Please God, don't let him speak it. Don't let Theo ever know, or Mum. And please God, not Dad. Not my dad.

The tension in the room seemed to have a smell, a texture, which made Irene's gorge rise every few moments. She breathed through her mouth to control it.

'Can somebody open the door?' It was Violet, and Theo opened it and helped steer John Boulter's wheelchair into the room.

'Over near the fire, please,' Violet told him. 'I don't want my husband catching cold.'

John, meanwhile, glared around at the strangers. 'What's this in aid of? Something Norman Plait's got up to?' A shaky finger pointed at Macbeth. 'He likes you lot, Norman does.'

'Lieutenant Macbeth has called about Irene,' Violet said,

laying a blanket over her husband's shoulders. 'It's about her and her... um, friend.'

John gave Theo a tilted look. 'You, at last. What's your story, then, *bor*?'

'Depends on what your question is, Mr Boulter, sir,' Theo replied.

John hmphed and addressed the vicar. 'Speak up, then, reverend. This must be important for the womenfolk to drag me from my bed.'

Reverend Prentice said that indeed it was. 'I want your permission to ask your daughter important questions.'

'You have it.'

'Irene.' The vicar pulled himself straight, as if he were up in his pulpit. 'Are you involved in a liaison with this man?' He indicated Theo, though without looking at him.

'No.' Irene gasped out the word and felt Theo's shock. She saw her mother's relief, and Macbeth's eyes narrowing. 'No. It's not a "liaison"; we're engaged to be married.'

She heard her mother's, 'Oh, Irene!' and her father's grunt of surprise.

Macbeth slowly shook his head and Irene's stomach contracted. She leaned against the wall for support. Groping again for Theo's hand, she clasped fresh air. His gaze was again fixed on a point on the far wall. Like her, he knew he was being slowly backed into a corner.

The vicar asked his second question. 'Irene, are you proposing this engagement should, at some juncture, become marriage?'

'That's usually what happens when you're engaged, isn't it?' John Boulter got in while Irene summoned a response.

'John!' Violet chided. 'The vicar didn't ask you.'

'I don't see how any of this is the reverend's business, Violet.'

Reverend Prentice clearly disliked being challenged. 'It is

my business, Mr Boulter, because today I received a visit from a staff officer charged with discipline at RAF Flixfield where Sergeant Robinson was based until recently. The airfield, as I'm sure you know, rests under United States jurisdiction but it borders my parish.'

'Course I know,' John snapped. 'The ruddy thing got planted on six hundred acres of prime farmland. It don't explain why you're in my house, scaring my daughter. Look at her. She's white as a sheet.'

'It's not my intention to frighten anybody. I'm here to help you avoid a serious situation, Mr and Mrs Boulter. A very senior officer from the base called on me to alert me to the fact that a young woman from the village is consorting with an American serviceman. I was politely asked to warn her family of the potential consequences.'

'What about him?' John Boulter aimed a jerky glance at Macbeth. Though his voice was weak, Irene felt her father was determined to assert what was left of his authority.

'Lieutenant Macbeth represents the US Air Force, and was asked to come along to remind Sergeant Robinson of his duty and obligations.'

Irene gave a low sigh of anger. How dare this churchman preach duty and obligation, when she'd endured physical humiliations he could never imagine. *If I were to tell him* – all of them – *how I was abused and forced, and mocked and shamed... if I had the words to tell them, would any of them ever look me in the eye again?*

She said harshly, 'Theo and I already know what the US Air Force thinks about us.'

'I doubt it.' The vicar spoke gravely. 'In the state of Georgia, where Sergeant Robinson comes from, marriage between Black and white is illegal. Not frowned upon. *Illegal*. It is against the law.'

'I know what illegal means.'

'In America as a whole, I am told, mixed marriage is heavily opposed. You wouldn't understand, Irene – why should you, growing up in England? I'm here to help you and your good parents see the danger.'

'I'm not asking anyone to help,' Irene rasped. It took all her strength to get the words out. She felt as if somebody had bolted an iron corset on her and was tightening the screws. 'Marrying Theo isn't illegal here. I can wed who I like, so long as he's not already married, and Theo isn't.'

'You can't marry who you like,' Violet said shrilly. 'You aren't of age. You need our consent and, from what the vicar's saying, I don't think we can give it.'

In answer, Irene tugged out her locket. Fumbling with the catch, she tipped the ring into her palm, pushing it onto the fourth finger of her left hand. She held that hand up so they could all see.

Reverend Prentice's expression grew hard. 'Irene, listen to me. You may be at liberty to choose whom you marry, but Sergeant Robinson is not. You merely need to persuade your parents, while he has to obtain his commanding officer's consent. And I am empowered to tell you, he won't get it.'

'Then why are you here?' Irene's father demanded.

'Because the United States authorities do not want to be seen to badger a British civilian, Farmer Boulter. However, be in no doubt, this situation will not go away. How would you feel if a Women's Air Auxiliary Force welfare officer were to come to your door, to deliver a lesson on moral conduct to Irene and your wife?'

A vein pulsed in John Boulter's forehead. 'Keep your preaching for Sunday, reverend.'

'John!' Violet beseeched her husband. 'You're speaking to a man of God!'

'God? I gave up with him time past. What kind of God makes a man a farmer, then stops him being able to so much as pick up a spade?' John moved his shoulders so his blanket fell off him. 'You don't scare me, Preacher Prentice, and nor does that wooden soldier over there.' John pointed a bent finger towards Macbeth.

But Irene knew her dad was scared. And she sensed that Theo was afraid too. They could object all they liked, but they were like three blind mice in the path of a threshing machine. When Theo spoke directly to Reverend Prentice, his voice vibrating with anger, she felt an uprush of pride and the chill of foreboding.

'Sir.' Theo moved so that he was directly facing the vicar and Macbeth. 'You have told me nothing I do not already know and, with respect, I do not need to be informed of the realities of segregation and discrimination by an Englishman, even a man of God. Allow me to tell you something: I don't know where I'll be in three, four or five years' time. I don't know where the army will take me, or when I might see home again. If I ever do. I asked Irene to become engaged to me, that is all. Engaged. Neither the United States Air Force, nor the Royal Air Force, nor you, can tell me that I may not pledge myself, any more than you can tell me which side to butter my bread or which hymns to sing in church. Irene has done me the honour of agreeing to become my fiancée and all I ask of her is that she waits, so that in due time, when I leave the military, I can come and find her.'

Reverend Prentice's silence, and Macbeth's, empowered Irene. Once again, she stuck out her left hand. 'You do it,' she told the vicar.

Taken off-guard, Reverend Prentice shot a glance towards Violet.

'Don't ask her for help, reverend,' Irene rasped. 'I'm asking you. If you reckon I shouldn't marry the man I love, because of the colour of his skin, you pull off my ring and throw it away.'

'Now you're being ridiculous, Irene. I said nothing about the colour of this man's skin.'

'Say his name. Say "Theo Robinson".' Irene stepped forward. A minute ago, she'd felt so browbeaten, she'd all but vomited. Now she knew without doubt that she would be separated from Theo. They'd find a way. But they wouldn't break her, or him. And one day they would marry. 'What you're thinking is written all over you, Reverend Prentice, and I'll tell you something. I don't want to come to your church and listen to you blather on about fellowship and "suffer the little children" and all about him' – she pointed at the ceiling, her thoughts travelling past the roof of Westumble Farm as high as heaven – 'being the God of all, when really, you only mean he's the God of people like you.'

'This is outrageous!' The vicar's face was red.

'Irene, please,' Violet begged.

Irene rounded on her mother. 'If you're on the side of Lieutenant Macbeth and our vicar, you pull off my ring and chuck it, Mum. I dare you.'

Violet clapped her hands at her daughter, as she might try to scare off a stray dog. 'You're being hysterical.'

'Ten more months, Mother. Next September I'll be of age and I won't need anybody's consent. I'll wait for Theo, even if this war lasts forty years.'

'Three acres.' John Boulter spoke into the pulsing silence. They'd all forgotten about him, but now they turned like a choreographed chorus. Irene's heart sank with pity and sorrow as her father repeated, 'Three acres.'

Violet went to him. 'Let's get you back to bed, John.'

'That's all I got left.' John waved his wife back. 'Since I had to sell most of my land. I've nothing much to leave my daughter and the man she marries. But they can have that three acres I got left. Put chickens on it, lad,' he pitched at Theo, who blinked. 'When this bloody war's over, people will still want to eat. They'll all want a chicken in the pot. You can get four big sheds of poultry to an acre. Make you a tidy living.'

Irene dashed across to her father, took his gnarled hand in hers, and sobbed against it. 'I love you, Dad.'

That was when Lieutenant Macbeth walked up to Theo. 'Boy, Uncle Sam needs his best sergeant back on form, so why don't you see sense now, and take a ride back to base with me. I'll get you safe home to where you're billeting now. Ain't no chance you're gonna marry this girl.'

'You're wrong, sir. I am.'

'Uh-uh?' Macbeth directed a complicit grin at Reverend Prentice. 'Why, you couldn't even pay for the ring you gave her. You defaulted, sergeant, and the good folk who sold it were forced to write to our commanding officer. You got any notion how deep that brought the United States military into disrepute?'

'The debt is satisfied, lieutenant,' Theo replied. 'You know well why I couldn't go to town and pay my dues. You put me in the hospital.'

'Shut your mouth, Robinson; I'm doing the telling. And I'm about to tell you why you won't want to marry this young lady. Step closer.'

'No, sir.'

'Step closer, boy, that's an order.'

'Don't, Theo.' Irene knew what was coming. Macbeth's shoulders had gone back, as if he was preparing to throw a punch. Irene shoved herself in front of him. 'Get out. Get out of our house.'

'Let me hear him.' Theo firmly pushed her aside. He took a step until his face and Macbeth's were inches apart. 'Say what you gotta say, lieutenant.'

'Theo, don't listen to him!' She knew without doubt that Macbeth had come here with one purpose. To degrade her to the man she loved.

Irene heard Macbeth say, 'I'm sure bustin' to tell you, boy. I got the best time off your gal. Those *purdey* red lips, I invite you to picture them around—' His voice became a whisper, and what word was dropped into Theo's ear, Irene could not catch. It brought a change to Theo's face.

Without warning, he drove his fist into the lieutenant's belly. Macbeth doubled over, gasping, and had no time to recover before Theo took him down, beating him in the face while Violet screamed, 'Stop, stop!' and the vicar tried frantically to drag him off.

## 40

RUBY

Ruby stretched, wincing at the click of cervical vertebrae. She'd been hunched on the sofa, reading for three hours solid. Will would tell her she was getting too sucked in, and he'd be right. At some point, she'd ceased to view Irene's chronicling of a year of her life as a trip back to the past and had begun experiencing it viscerally.

What had happened to Theo, after he'd assaulted Macbeth? Prison, for gross insubordination and theft?

Disturbingly, Irene had not said. That catastrophic night was followed by two blank diary pages.

Irene had written again on 29 November:

'Dad tells me I need to be busy so I'm knitting Theo gloves and a hat. Grey and red wool. I've heard nothing from him.' At which point, Ruby had closed the diary, her eyes almost crossing from reading Irene's ant-sized script.

Hungry, she made herself mushrooms on sourdough toast, and ate it walking around. Two phone messages had arrived while she'd been curled up with the diary. One from her mum:

*Nightmare times, darling, realised Christmas with an ex is BAD IDEA. On way back to Laurac, will call soon.*

Oh, no. Just as Will had implied, when Ruby had told him of her mother's festive plans.

The other message was from Clement Lubbock:

*Your watch is ready when you are. Kindest regards.*

Ruby surveyed her new wood burner, whose installation had finally been signed off at nine p.m. It was a solid black cube with a square of immaculate glass. How about she mess it up a bit by lighting its first fire? She laid it with kindling and logs but, at the last moment, didn't dare put a match to it. What if she set the chimney alight again?

Unable to settle, she mixed herself a gin and tonic, and fetched out Irene's engagement invitation.

### *The family of Miss Irene Boulter invite you to the engagement party of their daughter to Sergeant Theodore Robinson.*

### *4 December 1943*

### *4 p.m. at Flixfield Village Hall*

How was it that less than two weeks after the showdown between the young lovers, the church and the US military, Irene had been able to throw an engagement party?

Sipping her drink, Ruby reopened her grandmother's diary to the day of the party. The page was blank.

So was the page after that, and the ones after, all the way through December until the 23rd – seventy-nine years ago to the day – when Irene broke her silence with the words: 'I want to die.'

## 41

## IRENE

CHRISTMAS EVE 1943

Irene guided the peeler around the knobbly end of a potato, before adding it to the others in a pan. Her job was to make potato salad for a party tonight at the village hall. That would also mean finely dicing onions, as if she didn't chop enough onions in her life.

Whatever her life was, these days.

At the pull-out table in the kitchen, her mum was fiercely mashing almonds in a bowl, making imitation marzipan to go on top of the make-do Christmas cake. Four ounces of boiled butter beans to every half-ounce of almonds and a slug of almond essence whose pithy scent filled the air. There'd be no white icing on the fruit cake, but who cared?

Irene turned around as the kitchen door bumped open and Little Flip tottered in. She was in her nightdress, dark curls stuck to her forehead, her cheeks red from crying. Elsie Binney had gone down with chicken pox. Irene hadn't thought old folk got it, but Elsie was really bad with it and the doctor had insisted Philippa stay at Westumble, to be safe.

'I'm poorly,' Philippa grizzled. 'I want Norman. Where's Norman?' She opened her small mouth and howled.

'Oh, Irene, dear, pick her up,' Violet said in a harassed voice.

Dropping her peeler, Irene did so and gently rocked the screaming child, her back pressed against the cold sink.

'Coo-ee, may I come in?'

Footsteps across the dining hall, a little rat-a-tat at the inner door that Philippa had left open. All very polite, as one would expect from Mrs Prentice, the vicar's wife.

'Sorry to come calling, Mrs Boulter, Irene dear, but I wanted to let you know as soon as I could that the party is cancelled. Doctor's orders. There are four more cases of chicken pox in the village. The Gifford lad came down with it yesterday and all three Newland girls.' Mrs Prentice peered at Philippa, who was still sobbing in a choking, desperate way. 'Oh dear. I think we have case number five, right here. Take her to bed, Irene. I'll call on the doctor.'

When Irene came back down, Mrs Prentice was still there, talking to Violet in a low, confiding voice. '...yes. Today I believe. Shocking business, but quite out of our hands. And one has to let our American allies conduct things their way.'

'Our allies? What's this about?' Irene strode into the kitchen, meeting Mrs Prentice's flustered look, and Violet's astonishment. These were the first words Irene had spoken since the military police had come to the farm and dragged Theo away.

'I was telling your mother' – Mrs Prentice gave her brightest smile – 'if there's any potato salad spare, you could take it to poor Mrs Newland, who has her hands full with three little patients to look after.'

'Don't you tell lies,' Irene hit back furiously, earning the inevitable, 'Irene, manners!' from Violet. Irene ignored her mother, and Mrs Prentice's slow flush of mortification. 'You were talking about Theo. What's happening?'

'We don't know.' Mrs Prentice nodded stiffly at Violet, preparing to make an escape, but Irene stood between her and the door.

'You know more than me,' she told the vicar's wife. The pull-out table was inches away and the sharp smell of almond rose up from the bowl. Irene thought, I'll always hate marzipan from now on. I'll think of this moment, every Christmas, for the rest of my life.

'Irene, let Mrs Prentice go.'

'Not till she tells me. I'll follow her home and sit on her doorstep till she says what she knows.'

'No, it's all right.' Mrs Prentice gestured to Violet, who had come forward. 'She ought to know, I suppose. Your... friend... was arrested for striking a senior officer—'

'Who beat him senseless on the road. Who kicked him time and again, in the belly. Macbeth got his just deserts!'

'Sergeant Robinson is to be sent back, Irene.'

'Back where?' she echoed helplessly.

'Home, to the States. You cannot help him.'

'But I'm knitting him some gloves.'

She knew, even before she saw the pity on Mrs Prentice's face, how feeble-minded that sounded. The floor beneath her feet wasn't solid any more. It felt like the gooey mud at the edge of a pond. She was going to sink right in, over her head. She leaned both hands on the pull-out table and again, the smell of almond flooded her nose.

'Get off me!' She thrust helpful hands away, rushed to the sink where she'd been peeling potatoes and was violently sick.

## 42

CHRISTMAS DAY 1943

A few yards short of the service road into RAF/USAAF Flixfield, Irene dismounted from her bike, resting it on the verge. She wore an A-line skirt and an ivory cardigan, and her blouse with the sapphire satin collar and sleeves. All hidden under a waterproof mac. She'd dusted copious amounts of talcum powder under her arms because she was terrified, which made her sweat.

She shrugged off the mac, dropping it on top of the bike, though first, from its pocket, she took out a vanity case. It had been a gift from her parents, wrapped up for her at breakfast that morning. It contained a powder compact and lipstick, with other little compartments for money and combs and stuff. She patted powder onto her cheeks, which had been whipped pink by the icy wind, then applied the crimson lipstick. She'd slipped out of Westumble Farm while her mother was making sage and onion stuffing. Hadn't been able to abide the stink of it. Mum would be searching the house by now. 'Irene? Irene?'

Two guards stood behind the barrier today. Both were Black

Americans, toting guns that looked nothing like her dad's old rabbiting rifle that she used to hear pop-popping across the fields, back when Dad could still hold and aim it. Get wrong from these guards, you could be cats' meat in seconds. Overhead, a huge grey silhouette threaded through the clouds. A bomber was coming in to land. The air rolled and vibrated around it, and the ground shook.

One of the guards shouted above the din, 'Hold still, ma'am, put your arms out to the side where I can see them.'

Overpowered by the grinding noise, she'd balled her fists against her hips. Unclenching them, she held out her arms obediently. The guard dipped under the barrier, and came towards her.

'I need to see somebody,' she said but her voice got lost in the din.

It seemed that the guard could lip-read. 'You got a pass, ma'am?'

'I... no. I don't need a pass, I'm visiting.'

'Y'all need a pass to enter.' From the distance came the bumping impact of a successful landing, the roar of wheels on concrete. Men's voices were heard, shouting. The guard touched her arm. 'Ain't I seen you before? Sure I have – you're Theo's girl.'

Looking at the guard more closely, she recognised the deep cleft in his chin and a light-coloured scar on his cheek. 'Yes. We met at one of the Hollesford dances. I'm Theo's fiancée.' She thrust out her left hand where her engagement ring shone defiantly.

The other guard was coming over, but the first one jerked his head to keep him back. 'Fiancée or not, there ain't no way you can come in, nor see Theo. It ain't gonna happen.'

'I have to. Please, please.'

Since the humiliation of throwing up in the sink in front of the vicar's wife, cold reality had seeped in. Her mother's face had reflected Irene's own fears. Mrs Prentice had murmured, 'Oh, dear, dear, dear. This could be very difficult.'

'I need to see him,' Irene pleaded. 'I have to talk to him.'

'No way. He's under strict guard, ma'am.' The man checked nobody was about other than his colleague. 'When a Black soldier lays fists on the likes of Lieutenant Macbeth, he's good as wove himself a rope, you get my meaning?'

Cold sweat gathered under her clothes. 'What – hanged, you mean?'

'I mean,' the guard clarified, 'Theo is property of the military police now. Ain't nothing you or I can do.'

Irene sank to her knees, and then, impelled by a wave of fury, she stuck her bare, cold legs straight out in front of her. 'I'm not moving till someone takes me to see him.'

'Then I'll call someone to pick you up and take you home. You don't want that, honey. Get up, please.' The guard put a hand under her elbow, exerting pressure.

The memory of Macbeth leaning over her, on a different part of this same village road, flooded back and she screamed, 'Don't touch me!'

The guard jumped back, and his partner came over. The two men conferred, in low voices.

'We wanna help,' the first one said, 'but you gotta stand up. Can't have you sitting here like a drunk lady. You understand?'

She got up and the second man went to the guard hut. She saw him speaking into some kind of receiver. The icy Christmas wind pierced her layers and chilled the sweat on her skin.

The guard saw how she shivered. 'Lady, where's your coat?'

'I wanted to look pretty, for Theo.' And because she'd thought her close-fitting blouse, tucked into her waistband, would help her get past the barrier. That's how girls in films got their own way. But this was real life.

The throbbing whirr of aircraft propellers from one of the runways masked the sound of approaching footsteps and Irene only saw the two new arrivals as they reached the barrier. She recognised Jake by his long stride, the way his thumbs were tucked into his belt. His companion was Henry Scotland, known as Duke. A heavy plane lifted off, the roar of its engines rolling across the flat ground, congesting her ears, her head. The aircraft climbed before making a wide turn that would take it over Ratty's factory. Seeing it side on, Irene made out a row of windows on its fuselage.

Jake and Duke reached her.

'Irene, he ain't here no more,' Jake shouted.

'Yes he is. This man says he's locked up.' She was conscious of four men staring at her with concern and pity.

'He ain't here,' Duke echoed.

Fear fluttered to life, becoming an immediate, intense pain. 'Duke, Jake, you have to take me to him. There's something I must tell him.'

Jake took his thumbs from his belt and clasped Irene's shoulders to make her face him. 'They're sending him back. He's charged with gross misconduct and insubordination. He lost his rank, and they'll throw him out of the army. 'Less he gets some good lawyer to help him, they'll put him in jail.'

Irene stared into Jake's eyes, sharing the hurt and the rage she saw there.

Jake pointed in the direction of the plane that had taken off a minute before and was now a shape on the horizon. 'He's on that bird, Irene, in handcuffs.'

It finally got through. Macbeth had won. For Theo, the price of loving her was ignominy and jail. And never knowing what she had come to tell him. Her head emptied of every thought but that. She fell to the ground, screaming his name, thrashing until her blouse, skirt and her ivory cardigan were plastered with dirt.

Jake tried to get her up, but she writhed out of his grip, and beat her knuckles against the concrete until the skin split. She wanted to die, and no longer exist or feel anything.

'Come on, Miss Irene.' Jake got a hold of her under one arm, and Duke the other. 'We'll see you back home. My, you look like a dog that's rolled in the ditch.'

They got her to her door and she ran inside in time to be, once again, violently sick. Her locket slipped from inside her blouse, and clinked against the china lip of the sink.

'Lord help us,' Violet murmured as she sponged Irene's face. Jake and Duke had gone. 'Whatever were you thinking of?'

'He's gone, Mum. Theo's gone.'

'That's right, but I reckon he's left something behind.' Violet placed a hand on Irene's belly. 'What on earth do we do now?'

Irene knew what she would do.

While her mother was tending to John, she walked to the haybarn and climbed the wooden stairs, just as she had with Theo the last time they were together. Taking a breath, she turned around at the top and hurled herself off. Her mother found her an hour later, lying in a puddle of blood from a wound to her head. Violet ran for Dr Mickleson and, within hours, the doctor had made arrangements.

'Clearly, Irene has lost the balance of her mind and is a danger to herself, Mrs Boulter. We must do what is best for her and, if your fears are correct, we must prevent harm to her unborn child.'

## 43

## PHILIPPA

Will had helped Philippa up to bed, but she'd not let him do more than that. 'I don't need a carer, and I've had enough of nurses, thank you.' She lay in her bed, unable to get warm despite the two hot water bottles Will had done for her. That came of being old. Your blood got slow.

A name was buzzing around in her head. Wouldn't leave her alone.

Barbara.

Barbara Parkinson.

'I'm Barbara Parkinson, and I'm looking for an Irene Plait.'

Philippa's heart had jumped, as though she'd touched a live circuit. But she'd pulled her wits together. 'Nobody of that name here, dear. I think you've got the wrong house.'

'No, this is the address I was given. I've been doing some investigating, following up... this is difficult. I was born in 1944, here. This is the address.' The woman had turned a sheet of paper, to show Philippa. 'Oak Apple Farm, Flixfield.'

'Well, this is Oak Apple Farm, but I don't know of an Irene Plait, or anyone of that name, dear.'

That conversation had happened back before Will had come into her life. Before he'd been born, even. Philippa's cool-headed reply had done the trick. Barbara Parkinson had gone away and never come calling again.

She, Philippa, had never had to confess what she'd done.

# 44

## IRENE

They still expected you to go outside, even with snow on the terrace. The lawns were frosty, and the air hurt as it went into Irene's lungs. They'd allowed her some paints and a book with blank sheets, and for the first time in her life she was able to finish a picture without Mum coming in and saying, 'Put that away now, dear. The washing won't take itself off the line, and then there's the carrots to scrub.'

Instead of Mum bothering her, it was Dr Mickleson doing his best to break her concentration. She wished they hadn't let him through the gate.

'When did you last menstruate, Irene?'

She didn't answer, and made a careful line in blue paint on the page in front of her.

'I could ask your mother. I'm sure she'll know.'

'End of October last.' She knew the date. She'd begun her monthly the day a delivery of pumpkins at Ratty's had arrived, for pumpkin-and-ginger jam. November had come and gone, with no bleeding, and she'd put it down to shock, from what she'd been through with Lieutenant Macbeth. Then nothing in December, or January either, and now there was no doubt. 'I've been through what they call trauma, doctor.' She didn't look up, and rinsed her paintbrush in a jar of water.

'I know that, Irene. Shock and pain can interfere with menses, but so can pregnancy.'

Everyone knew the answer to her vomiting and nausea, and the absence of monthly bleeds. So why was he asking?

'Do your breasts feel tender?'

'Maybe.' She dipped her paintbrush into a puddle of red paint, let it drip for a moment onto a cloth, then delicately coloured in one of the red stripes on the flag she was painting.

'Irene, would you put your brush away for a moment? I have the permission of the matron in charge here to give you an internal examination. She or another nurse will be present.'

'No.'

'I'm afraid I am going to have to insist.' Dr Mickleson reached over and took the paintbrush from her. He put it into her water jar. 'Let me see your picture.'

She let him, and looked away towards the high brick wall that separated Thewell Park from the town beyond. This was a kind of prison, even if they called it a hospital. They locked you in, didn't they? They wrote your initials in your clothes, so other patients... inmates... call them what you like, wouldn't steal them. They'd taken her locket off her, first thing they did after they checked her hair for nits. 'In case you hurt yourself with it,' they'd said. The marks on her neck, which Lieutenant Macbeth was responsible for, they thought she'd done to herself. She'd get her personal things back when she left.

Soon as she walked through the door at home, she'd hide her locket where no snooper would ever be able to find it.

Irene sensed Dr Mickleson drawing his brows together as he studied her painting.

He read out, in a strained voice, '"The family of Miss Irene

Boulter invite you to the engagement party of their daughter to Sergeant Theodore Robinson. Fourth of December 1943—" Irene, that's almost three months in the past. *The past.* It didn't happen and you have to snap out of this. Your young man went off, leaving you to deal with the awful consequences.'

'He didn't go off; they made him go.'

'Now listen.' The doctor crouched stiffly next to her wooden daybed, putting himself level with her. Irene was sitting with both legs on one side of the bed, a cushion behind her back. 'I know this is hard. I know how much it pained you, but you must put it behind you. You don't want to spend the rest of your life here at Thewell Park, do you?'

'No.' No, no, no, or how would she ever see Theo again?

'There you are, then. Throwing yourself down the steps at home made you look like a suicide risk. I had to intercede with the authorities to stop you from being sectioned. So now you must do your part, and stop the fantasy, stop the nonsense.'

'It's not nonsense.' Irene looked down at her engagement invitation. She still had to colour in all the Union flags. She was doing the Stars and Stripes first. 'If I don't finish this, they'll have won.'

Dr Mickleson sighed. 'Tell you what, if you allow me to examine you, I'll have a word with the doctor in charge here and ask if you can do your painting in the library. Out in the cold, paint never dries properly. Shall we go in?'

She saw suddenly that his cheeks were chapped, and the tip of his nose was white. She was used to being outdoors, as a farmer's daughter, but he travelled around in a snug car, or sat in his surgery where his wife kept the fire blazing. 'All right,' she said.

Afterwards, as she adjusted her skirt, the doctor pulled up a chair and said, 'I calculate you are almost four months pregnant. You must have conceived some time in November.'

St Meg's, in the candlelight. Or the hay loft. Passion and incaution. This was her punishment.

The doctor went on, 'Because you're slender, you aren't showing yet, but you will soon. Do you understand your situation?'

'I know what pregnant means. I'm having Theo's baby.'

'You are having an illegitimate baby. One with a Black father. An *absent* Black father and we need to decide what to do.'

'I want to be with Theo.'

'That isn't possible,' the doctor sighed. 'Even if he meant to do the decent thing, he has no ability to do so now. Irene, don't cry.'

But Irene couldn't stop the tears pooling over the rims of her eyes. 'He would never have left me to face this alone, if he'd had a choice.'

Her mother, the vicar, Mrs Prentice and Aunt Elsie had all taken their turn with her. Even her father had reproached her. All taking different tones, but the message was the same. Irene had made a false step, and they would all pay dearly.

'Well, we'll never know.' Dr Mickleson returned his stethoscope to his case as Irene wiped her eyes on the bedcover. 'I've already informed your parents of a mother-and-baby home where you can remain throughout your pregnancy, because you cannot give birth here. Nor at home, for obvious reasons.'

'Why not at home?'

'Because you are not married and you won't wish to inflict disgrace on your parents. The place I recommend is in Southend-on-Sea, in Essex. Have you heard of Southend?'

'Yes. People go on holiday there.'

'It's close to the seafront, and you can have your baby there and be given the courtesy name of "Mrs Boulter".'

'And then we can come home?'

The doctor cleared his throat. 'You will stay with your baby until he or she is weaned and adoptive parents can be found.'

'No, no. This is my baby, and Theo's. I'm not giving it away.'

'My dear girl.' Dr Mickleson seemed to draw on his last reserves of patience. 'You cannot bring up an illegitimate, mixed-race child in Flixfield, as an unmarried mother. Think of your family reputation. Your own good name. Think of the child, always to be known as the by-blow of an opportunist GI who abandoned its mother.'

'Theo didn't abandon me! He was shipped out. Beaten and kicked, and put in the cooler. He didn't stand a chance.'

'As I understand, Sergeant Robinson showed violence to a superior officer after he was accused of theft.'

'That was made up! And it wasn't theft. It was because of what Lieutenant Macbeth made me do. Theo didn't steal anything. It's not fair, doctor, it's not fair.'

'I agree, it probably isn't, but you are old enough to grasp that life does not always turn out the way we hope. You've behaved with a lack of self-restraint that at the very least demands humility and acceptance on your part. Think of your poor mother. If Sally were to present in this condition, I don't know how I or Mrs Mickleson would bear it.'

You may yet have to, Irene thought, staring miserably at her feet. Sally had written to her, which was kind, though the letter had been all about Sally's life in London. She was still seeing her Czech airman, while also dating an American, and she'd described a 'daring fling' with a Free Frenchman, whatever one of those was. Course, if pure-as-the-driven-snow Sally was to catch for a baby, whoever the father was would be expected to propose, no dithering. The difference? Sally's boyfriends were white.

'The stark reality,' Sally's father was saying, 'is that you're still underage. Your mother and father will decide what becomes of the child.'

'You mean I give birth, but I don't have any say over my own baby?'

'Exactly. Nor over your body, as it happens. If you were to stop contractions during labour, and require a caesarean section, it would be your mother and father who would give consent, not you.'

'I'm twenty. Girls younger than me join the Wrens and go on ships that get torpedoed. Are you saying they'd still be treated as children?'

'I cannot speak for the Navy, Irene. I urge you to ready yourself to leave for Southend. I am willing to drive you, though it's rather a distance, and your mother will accompany you.'

She'd got up off the bed, but now sat down again, feeling the springs creak beneath the thin mattress. 'I can't give away this baby. I'd rather both of us die.'

The doctor took her hand. 'I'm told there is an alternative, Irene. A way through this.'

She looked at him, hope glimmering through a blur of tears. 'What way?'

'Marriage.'

'To Theo?'

'Of course not to Theo! To *Norman*. He's here, in the waiting room. Should I send him up?'

# 45

## RUBY

So that, Ruby thought, closing the diary, was how Grandad Norman came to win the hand of fair Irene. He found her forced into a corner, virtually suicidal, and seized his chance.

She had read Irene's diary until past midnight last night, giving up only when she'd fallen asleep and woken to find her forehead resting on its open pages. Her first impulse on waking was to get back to the story, though she'd taken a few breaks along the way to stretch her cramped muscles, to have breakfast and start making the cake she'd promised for Philippa.

A click told her that the oven was up to heat. She popped the sponge in and set the timer. She was expecting Will in twenty minutes. He'd be on his way back from Hollesford, where he'd carried out a couple of commissions for her.

Edna arrived first, butting her head against the front door. The moment Ruby opened it, the dog rushed past, beating a familiar path to the kitchen. 'No luck, Edna,' Ruby called after her. 'I'm one of those annoying types who wash up as they go.'

Will was closing the gate behind him, hatted, coated.

'How is Philippa today?' Ruby went out to meet him.

'She was fine when I left, maybe a bit agitated. For the first time since Ronnie died, she didn't really want me around.' Then, sounding brighter, he asked how she was getting on with her wood burner.

Ruby confessed she hadn't dared light it.

'Not good enough, Ms Plait.' Inside the house, he took a box from his pocket. 'Your watch, and Lubbock's invoice, which I paid. And this.' He gave her a bag with the logo of Boots the Chemist. 'One last-minute Christmas gift for Philippa.'

Ruby thanked him, asking him to please text her his bank details.

'I will.' He was now free to admire the new stove. 'Nice. Good size too. And you've already laid it, so what are you waiting for?'

More confident with him standing by, Ruby struck a light and held it to a scrunched ball of paper. It was reluctant to catch light. There was one firelighter left, and she looked up at Will before adding it. 'Is this cheating?'

'Whatever works, Ruby. Make a wish.'

She laughed shakily. 'They always say beware what you wish for. But OK. I'd like to find my place in the world again, and to wake up each morning happy.'

Edna bounded in, from a successful scavenge in the bin, judging by the empty flour bag between her jaws. While Will removed it, Ruby gazed at the flames leaping behind the stove's glass.

'Seems a shame that somebody else will get the benefit of this, when I sell,' she murmured. 'But I have to,' she answered herself, walking into the kitchen to check on her cake.

Will followed her. 'You need the money to start again, I get that.'

'I do, but I also believe it's time Oak Apple Farm got away from the grip of the Plaits. All the sadness its walls have absorbed!' Five more minutes, she decided after sliding a knife into the sponge and inspecting the blade.

'Do walls do that – absorb sorrow?'

'I'm coming to that way of thinking,' Ruby said. 'Poor Little Flip, shoved in a cupboard. Then Irene, coming here as a wife, having spent the weeks prior in a psychiatric hospital.'

'Irene did?'

'She had a breakdown after Theo was repatriated. Thewell Park. Remember, we spoke about it?'

He nodded. 'You asked me if Aunt Flip was ever sent there. I saw a postcard of the place on her bed when I helped her upstairs yesterday, so I wondered if maybe she had.'

'No, it was Irene. I found some of her old clothes the other day, and couldn't think why they had her initials written in the seams. But it makes sense, if she went to an institution. She had a complete emotional collapse after Theo was taken away, and found she was expecting his child.'

Will absorbed this. 'That must have been hard.'

'It was catastrophic. Under laws of the time, she was a minor. She couldn't choose to keep her own baby. Can I ask your advice?' She fetched her laptop and located a draft email she hadn't yet sent. 'I'm in two minds. You see, Sabrina Robinson-Chase has a Facebook link on her website and I sent her a friend request.'

'When did you send it?'

'Late last night and by this morning, she'd accepted. I have no idea if she knows my name somehow, or if she glanced at my profile and thought, "hell, why not?" I've begun a message and I want your opinion. If you think it's too much...'

Will invited her to read it to him.

Ruby cleared her throat. Stupid, but the last time she'd had butterflies like this, she'd been waiting in the wings to accept her prize as 'Euro Hoteliers' Top Young Chef', as its first ever female winner. 'Here we go. "Dear Sabrina, thanks for accepting my friend request. I hope you're well. We should talk. My gran loved your dad and, I have reason to believe, never forgot him. This is my mobile number.'"

Will leaned over her shoulder and pointed at a word. 'First, change mobile to cell. Americans use cell phones. Second, are you going to tell her about the baby?'

'In time, but I want to give her a chance to react first. It isn't a happy ending, Will. The baby didn't survive. There is no half-sibling to tantalise Sabrina Robinson-Chase with.'

'Who says?'

'You did.'

'What? When? I said that Irene had lost a baby. *A* baby.'

She took his point. 'Shall I send the message or not?'

Will put his hands each side of her face. 'You are one of the most independent, clear-sighted people I know. You will make that decision.'

'I'm worried she'll write back saying, "Get lost." Or worse, not answer at all.'

'That's the risk you take. Life is messy. All I can say is that my life was made immeasurably better by knowing some complicated people called Philippa, Ronnie, Irene and Norman.'

So Ruby made a few changes and pressed 'send'.

Will put his forehead against hers. 'Can you Edna-sit while I go up on your roof?'

'I thought you had finished.'

'I want to check the lime mortar has taken.'

'Sure.' So meticulous! Or maybe it was an excuse to come over and see her. Her heart gave a little salsa step when he kissed her and said, 'Don't let your cake burn.'

While he was up the ladder, she whipped up butterscotch icing and turned the cake out onto a wire rack to cool. She put coffee beans in the grinder, knowing Will would come in numb to the ears. And she couldn't stop herself – she checked Messenger to see if Theo's daughter had replied.

She hadn't, and Ruby googled the time difference between the UK and Georgia. It was ten in the morning, UK time. OK. Sabrina would still be fast asleep. Feeling the urge to connect in some way, she opened Professor Robinson-Chase's webpage again. The image of Sabrina leaning against a tree struck Ruby more powerfully this time. Nobody chose their online image by accident. Sabrina's stated, I'm independent. Smart, educated, and I own my roots. I'm a strong woman of colour, seventy-one years old since you ask, though you won't know it unless you search me on Wiki.

Sabrina's Wiki page gave her birthdate as 12 August 1951, making her nine months younger than Ruby's mother, Amanda. One pregnancy term younger, if you looked at it that way. Was it evidence that Irene's and Theo's lives had continued to ricochet off each other?

'I have no idea if Theo ever knew he'd left Irene pregnant,' she said to Edna, who gazed meltingly back at her. 'Did they ever meet again? You don't have a clue, do you, sweet dog?'

Shutting the laptop, Ruby wrapped her cake in baking paper and took it outside to speed up the cooling. She wanted to offer Will a slice when he came in. He'd called her clear-sighted, which was flattering but inaccurate. She had no idea how her life would pan out. Hopefully, she'd sell the house quickly. But then what? A week ago, she'd have predicted herself back in Laurac, finding somewhere to live and developing a business idea. But here she was, making cakes for Philippa and Will and – damn it – *enjoying* herself.

Enjoying it all the more when Will came in, blowing on his fingers. 'Coffee? Life-saver.'

'And butterscotch cake.'

He gazed almost in disbelief. 'You just get it right, time after time.'

They spent an hour at the kitchen table, chatting comfortably. Will informed her that her roof was officially signed off. By him. He went on to tell her that it was Ronnie and Norman who had taught him most of his manual skills.

For her part, Ruby found herself telling him about her father.

Will gaped slightly. 'You really have no idea who he is?'

'Nope. He might be Irish, or a Breton poet Mum met at a festival in Finisterre. There's a slight possibility he's Italian, but I don't think so. I spent a year working in Florence and, though I loved it, I didn't feel "These are my people."'

'Can't you track him down – do you want to?'

'Mm, not really. Without a name, it's hard.'

There were those DNA sites, Will said. 'Spit in a tube, they find all your relatives.'

'But what if I don't like him – or worse, he doesn't want contact? I've made peace with not knowing.'

It was some time later, after Will had gone in order to check in on Philippa, that Ruby opened Messenger again. Nothing from Sabrina Robinson-Chase. She steeled herself for rejection. After all, how would she feel if a total stranger breezed into her world, claiming to know things about her father? To take her mind off the waiting, she started her decorating, and her hands were daubed white from painting the stairwell with a long-handled roller when she remembered that tonight, she had a date with Will at The Ten Bells. She turned the water on for a bath.

She was taking five minutes off, eating olives from a jar, when her phone rang. It was a foreign number and Ruby leapt to an assumption, swiping up eagerly. 'Hi, Mum, are you back in France now? What happened, did you and Charlie's new lady not hit it off?'

'Pardon me, am I speaking to Ruby Plait?'

The voice was mezzo, nothing like Amanda's quick, light

tone and the accent was American south. Ruby dropped her
olive. 'Sabrina? Ms Robinson-Chase? Professor Robinson-
Chase, I mean. Yes, I'm Ruby and my grandma Irene was
engaged to your father.' She added belatedly, 'Hi.'

'Hi. I got your message, and something made my fingers call
your number. I hope it's not too late for you to talk?'

'Not at all, it's only three in the afternoon.'

Silence hit, then they both started talking at once.

'You go first,' Ruby said.

'OK. Let me begin, Ms Plait, by saying that my dad, Theo,
passed away in 1987, and he and my mother were married for
thirty-six *happy* years.'

Ruby got the message: *Whatever you think you know, my
parents loved each other*.

She said, 'I'm glad, so very glad.'

'Thank you. My mother passed five years ago, and when I
was going through her things, I found letters among my father's
papers. Letters written to him when he was stationed in
England, from someone named Irene. From the style of the
writing, I supposed she was a teenage girl.'

Ruby winced. Irene's diary-voice often came across as
naive. 'My grandmother was Irene Boulter,' she said, 'later,
Irene Plait. She met your father after he came to build the
airfield a couple of miles from where she lived. She was a
farmer's daughter. Not a teenager, exactly, but maybe rather
unsophisticated.'

'That figures,' Sabrina said. 'The letters are headed "Westumble" and "Oak Apple Farm", like something out of a story
book.'

'They're real places,' Ruby assured Sabrina. 'I'm speaking to
you from Oak Apple's kitchen. Did the letters cause ructions
with your mother?'

'Did they cause a quarrel, are you asking me? No, ma'am.
My daddy was clear all along, he'd had a love affair with an

English girl. And you know what they say? What happens in Europe, stays in Europe.'

'I see.' Was that all it was to Theo, then, a European fling? Ruby kept her voice upbeat. Sabrina could not know that losing Theo had pitched Irene into a serious breakdown. 'I'm reading Irene's diaries,' Ruby went on, 'and they say a lot about your father's experience in Flixfield. He encountered bigotry, as did his comrades.'

Sabrina Robinson-Chase snorted. 'You don't say!'

'Not so much from the locals, though some were bastards, pardon my language. Mostly from—'

'From the white GIs. I know. Ms Plait, I have spent nearly a quarter of a century fighting to clear my father's name. He made a success of his life in two different worlds, music and politics, but he never got over being wrongfully imprisoned. I want to know why it happened and to have him exonerated.'

'Please call me Ruby... hello?' The signal was breaking up. 'Are you there?'

'Still here but – hey, I gotta whole pile of things to do today. I've got family coming to me for the holidays, so I better shoot. We're gonna talk more if that's OK with you, Ms Plait?'

'Ruby, please.'

'Call me Sabrina.'

'There's so much to say, Sabrina.' Ruby added, 'Before you go, did Theo write a song for Irene?'

'He wrote a song called "Irene", so I guess so. When's a good time to call you again?'

'Any time, I'm about five hours ahead of you, I think.'

'Fine. And, Ruby? I'm gonna send you something I want you to look at which might shed some light on things for you. It's a letter Irene wrote to my daddy when he was in Paris in June, 1950. When she was in Paris too.'

'Irene in Paris? That's not possible—'

Sabrina had ended the call.

All thoughts of a leisurely bath evaporated when a notification pinged on her laptop and Ruby found an email from ProfSabrina51. Sabrina had written, 'Hi Ruby, as promised. Can you fill in the gaps? We'll talk soon. Have a wonderful holiday.'

The attachment at the bottom consisted of pages of handwriting on shadowy-yellow paper. An address at the head of the letter reversed Ruby's presumptions about her grandmother.

In June 1950, Irene Plait, wife of Norman, had gone to Paris.

# IRENE

*Hotel Mercure*

*Rue des Petites Écuries, Paris*

*13 June 1950*

*My darling Theo, I cannot believe we are in the same city. When I got your letter, I felt sick, thinking you were so close and how would I ever get to see you? I know Flixfield is not so far from Paris, when you compare it to Georgia, USA, but it might as well be on the other side of the moon, for all the chance of me coming here. Then, what should happen, but the Flixfield and Medfold Women's Institute decides that nothing will do, but that we have a bus and boat trip to Paris, and then on to visit the mustard factory at Meaux. Have I spelled that right? Mrs Prentice says you don't pronounce the 'X' at the end of Meaux, it's pronounced like in 'Barley Mow'. Well, I'm not here for the mustard, I can tell you, and I don't fancy another long bus ride. Shall we be together at last? Dearest Theo, I have missed you every day since they took you. Why didn't you write before this? Seven years ago, we swore nothing would part us, then all these years of silence. Why? I had to make a choice, which I will explain when we meet and I hope you will forgive me.*

*Where shall we meet? I can't find my way around Paris to save my life, but there is a little place on the street where we are staying, Café de la Libération. I'm going to say tomorrow that I'm too unwell to go to the mustard factory. Which I am. I was seasick on the boat and my friend Joyce says only Mrs Prentice would suppose women who work in a jam and pickle factory would think it's a treat to go and watch mustard being made. I shall stay here. I'm sending this to the address on your letter, so please leave a reply at the desk of the Hotel Mercure. Don't call in person. Mrs Prentice watches me, smiling ever so brightly, but I know she thinks I'm a bad 'un. And maybe she's right. Café de la Libération, Theo, sounds like the right place for us to reunite.*

Theo did exactly as she asked, leaving a note with Madame who owned the hotel, and who policed the reception area in a black suit and demi-veiled hat. Unfortunately, Madame gave the note to Mrs Prentice, who pulled Irene to one side, as she, Joyce and two other WI members returned from the café where they'd had breakfast, including coffee in bowls. 'Like you'd give the dog,' Joyce had muttered, adding she could skewer somebody for a cup of tea.

'I cannot imagine who might be sending you notes, Irene.' The way Mrs Prentice kept hold of the small envelope put Irene on notice that meeting Theo was going to be difficult. 'Madame says that a Black person delivered it, Irene. I don't wish to think ill of you... but really?'

A familiar rage, dormant many years, exploded in Irene's stomach. How dare this woman speak to her that way? 'Give me my letter.'

Mrs Prentice handed it over. 'We're setting off for Meaux in twenty minutes. We mustn't be late.'

'I'm not coming.'

'Of course you are. It's why we've come.'

'I feel sick.' Irene had looked into the coffee in her bowl a short while ago, beige froth circulating on its surface, and had almost vomited. A cold block of fear sat in her stomach – fear she did not wish to probe. 'I'm going to lie down on my bed.'

'You cannot. Madame's women have to clean the rooms.'

'Then I'll find a park.'

'This is Paris; you can't just lie down in a park. You don't speak a word of French.'

'Leave me alone!' Irene pounded upstairs. She knew Mrs Prentice meant well, but it was like being a child again, all her decisions put under a magnifying glass, and the word 'no' constantly shoved in her ear. In the room she shared with Joyce and another Flixfield neighbour, she sat on her bed and waited for the sickness to pass. Finally, she opened the letter. It was too dark to read what Theo had written, even with the light on, as their room backed onto a tiny yard. She had to stand on a chair directly under the ceiling light.

*I'll be there, after rehearsal. Say, about two pm. Vive la libéra-tion! Theodore.*

She waited out a wave of emotion, wobbling on her chair. Theodore… where had Theo gone?

Joyce came in, gawping up at her. 'What are you doing on a chair? I heard Mrs Prentice asking Madame to help her book a telephone call to England.' Joyce breathed hard from climbing three flights. 'Someone's written to you, putting you in moral jeopardy, is that right? Tell me. I'm your friend.'

Irene got down and went to the sink. The room was spinning. 'Theo's in Paris, with a band.'

'Band – what, like Robin Hood?'

'Musical band. The Jake Hendrick Five.'

'Oh. How many of them are there?'

Very funny. Joyce could never resist a joke.

'He wrote to me a month ago.' Irene grabbed the soap beside the sink, and slathered her middle finger. She pulled off her wedding ring, dropping it into the soap dish. 'I was lucky; the new postman had just started so the village didn't hear that I'd had a letter with a French stamp on it, which they would have done with the last fellow.' Nor had the postie commented on the fact that the letter was addressed to 'Miss Irene Boulter' at Westumble Farm. He'd had the wit to come across to Oak Apple and hand it to her.

'Is this why you came on this jaunt? Oh, my woman.' Joyce came to stand behind Irene, and their eyes met in the mirror. 'What's the point, raking up that business again?' Joyce was the only person Irene had fully confided in about Theo. Uniquely in Flixfield, Joyce Fuller did not judge. 'What about Norman?'

'I don't love him.'

'Well, he loves you! The way he looks at you. All those little presents he buys.'

'I didn't want to marry him.'

'We all know that, but that's in the past. I tell you this, I often look at my Eric and wonder what on earth possessed me, but that's married life. You find a fellow, get put in calf and then spend the next forty years making the best of it. You've got it good, Irene Plait. Lovely farmhouse, part time at Ratty's. You don't know you're born.' Joyce tweaked Irene's earlobe. 'Besides, any fool can see you're in the family way.'

'I'm not. Why are you saying it?'

'Because your face is like new green cheese, that's why. God knows, I know what being pregnant looks like.'

'No. No. It can't happen.'

'What does that mean? You've got all the equipment dear,

and assuming Norman has too, you'll have babies like the rest of us.'

'I won't go through it again. Not for Norman.'

A tap at the door was followed by Mrs Prentice enquiring if everything was all right. 'We need to shake a leg, ladies, or we'll miss the train to Meaux.'

'Irene's not herself, Mrs P,' Joyce called back. 'She'll bide here.'

Mrs Prentice entered. 'That simply isn't possible. Madame expects us to be out until five this afternoon.'

'Tell her we don't need the room cleaned. Irene's not going anywhere. I don't see as she'll cope with the stink of a mustard factory. I only had to mention cheese a moment ago, and she was *that* close to retching.' Joyce mouthed at Mrs Prentice, 'Family way.'

Mrs Prentice closed her eyes momentarily. 'I see. In that case... I'll explain to Madame.'

They saw her to her bed, Joyce promising to buy a pot of mustard for her – 'To take home to your mum, like you promised,' and Mrs Prentice mentioning to Irene that she'd left her ring by the sink, and did she know, more rings were lost down plugholes than any other way?

Irene willed them to go and, after they had, she fell into a heavy sleep, from which she woke disorientated, staring at a ceiling that was smoothly painted, unlike Oak Apple's, and sparked no recognition. She remembered she was meeting Theo, though, and sat up in a panic, terrified she'd overslept. Her watch said it was one in the afternoon. Thank goodness.

She washed at the sink, ignoring her ring. The face in the mirror was whey-like. Pregnant? Why would it happen now, when six years with Norman had yielded no fruit? She'd always believed that the forceps delivery she'd endured with Theo's baby had wrecked her inside.

Her eyes looked enormous. Feverish. She applied eyeliner

and mascara to her lashes and brows. 'The bluest eyes' he'd once said of hers. She wished they didn't look so fretful.

He mustn't think she'd turned into a country bumpkin.

Only he would. Pushing and pushing during her labour six years ago had left broken veins in her cheeks. She used the swansdown puff from her compact, the one Mum and Dad had given her the Christmas she couldn't remember. Powder covered the spider veins. That time after Theo went was like a snapshot viewed under water. Ill-defined, half lost. A transport plane took off from Flixfield airbase. She cast herself onto the ground. And then she was in Thewell Park, being wheeled out onto the terrace in the blistering cold, smothered in blankets. *Fresh air is a wonderful cure.*

She brushed her hair, which she now wore in a soft bob, putting it in big curlers to give it height and shape. Her hair had darkened during her pregnancy and was more sandy than flaxen now. Not *Irene, fair as a dream* these days.

At the door of Café de la Libération, she made a quick, visual search of the interior. Not seeing Theo, she walked to the end of the street and pretended to consult her little red map. The women passing were matronly, in shapeless dresses and cardigans. In her check cotton dress with its nipped waist and turned-back collar, she felt she looked all right, though her straw hat and white gloves marked her out as a tourist. A girl in slacks and a baggy sailor top came along, carrying an artist's easel under her arm. She threw a few cheerful, incomprehensible words as she passed.

Irene imagined the girl heading off to sit in the sunshine, to ply her art. No wedding ring, no overalls to wash, no bloody chickens to feed. Lithe and free. Irene's last monthly had been in March. She'd missed three months, just like last time.

And there he was, crossing the road in front of her. Leaner than she remembered, wearing a natty linen suit and a dark trilby hat.

'Theo!' She held out her hands.

He took them in his grip and laughed at her gloves. She pulled them off and felt the pulse of his veins. She closed her eyes. At last.

'Say, did we agree to meet on the street corner? I was heading to the café.'

'I was too scared to go in.'

'Not too scared with me? I need coffee.'

As they walked into the Café de la Libération, she prepared herself for a frosty welcome from the waiter. Back home, there'd been a couple of occasions when publicans or shopkeepers had refused to serve Theo, though it had happened only after the white GIs had arrived.

To her astonishment, the waiter couldn't pull their chairs out fast enough. The man seemed overwhelmed to have Theo in his café. She listened in awe as Theo responded in French, getting them a corner table where they wouldn't be spotted from the street.

'He spoke to you like an old chum,' she commented as the waiter went to fulfil their order.

'Sure, he saw us at Le Hot Brick Club. Me, Jake, the boys, we're notables in Paris, didn't you know?'

'I – no. I don't know anything much, Theo. Not outside Flixfield.'

'We got a residency in a famous club, the Rose Noire in Montmartre, but we're free to do smaller places like Le Hot Brick in the afternoon, or late-late when we're done for the night on the Butte. Jake has us playing gigs in smoky dives, where we try out new numbers.'

The unfamiliar words hit her eardrums. Butte. Gigs. Numbers. 'That's good,' she said, hoping he wouldn't pick up her confusion.

Two cups of black coffee arrived. Theo asked, 'You hungry?'

She shook her head. The aroma of coffee and strong French

cigarettes being smoked at the next table were having a bad effect. She bent her fingers into her palm. Don't let her have to run to the ladies. There might not even be a ladies. At their breakfast café, there was only a primitive pit.

Theo said to the waiter, 'Ham omelette, *monsieur, s'il vous plaît*, with a tomato salad side.'

Tom*a*to, the way he pronounced it rolled back the years. He'd laughed when she'd corrected him once, when they shared the sandwiches she'd brought to St Margaret's, their meeting place: tom-*ar*-to. 'Makes no sense. You Brits make it up as you go along.'

She said now, 'Mrs Prentice calls waiters *"garçon"*. I don't think she ought because it means "boy".'

'Anybody who calls a grown man "boy" needs to be afraid what might happen when that boy grows up. Is that Mrs Prentice the wife of the reverend?'

'Yes. She organised this trip. She calls herself "Head Guide".'

Theo stirred sugar into his coffee. Two lumps, then another, and the way his spoon went round and round suggested he still relished the luxury of sweetness. 'I'm ravenous,' he told her. 'We've been practising since nine without a break except for a smoke.' He told her about the set they were rehearsing, with new songs and arrangements, including three of his own compositions. He spoke slower than she remembered, his accent a deep drawl which she had to listen to with fixed attention. He said, 'Tomorrow, we're back on the train.'

'You're leaving?' Panic at being abandoned again made her sit bolt upright.

'We've got a two-week guest slot in Marseille.'

That didn't tell her much. 'Where's Mar – Marseille?'

'It's a city. A port. In the deep south.'

'Of America? You're going back?'

'Deep south of France. You really don't know much outside of Flixfield, do you, Irene?'

Shame tinged her cheeks. 'No.'

Her left hand, knuckle-side up on the table, was bereft of its wedding band. There'd been no engagement ring from Norman. There hadn't been time. From the moment Dr Mickleson had brought him to her at Thewell Park, in late February 1944, events had set off like dogs out of a gate. A special licence, a word with the Baptist minister at Medfold because Irene refused to be married in the village church. She'd become Norman's wife wearing a skirt cut down from an old dress of her mother's with lots of material to make concealing gathers. Her belly had swelled. It was as if, by accepting Norman's gruff offer of marriage, she'd given the baby inside her permission to exist. Such a cold March day, nobody had questioned that she wore a heavy coat throughout the ceremony. Her witnesses were her parents and Aunt Elsie Binney, who was suffering from shingles and angry as a stoat all through it. Then back home on a haycart, for a lunch of bread, cheese and pickled cabbage. A boy sent by the photographic shop in town had taken hers and Norman's picture in the garden, and the bare stems of the roses behind them had felt about right. She hadn't been able to smile. Theo's locket, warm against her skin, had been the only thing stopping her screaming.

She said falteringly, 'Your letter... did I read it right? Do you want us to be together?'

'Do you want it, Irene?'

She answered with a nod. She'd do everything that Joyce and Mrs Prentice feared she'd do. Become the adulterous woman who went to Paris and never came home. She'd step off a cliff and hope she'd survive whatever lay at the bottom. She searched Theo's face for a glimpse of the funny, ardent young man she'd known. His hair no longer had to submit to the army razor, of course. It was thick and very black from its slick of styling grease. When he'd stirred sugar in his coffee, a gold ring had glinted on his right index finger and now, when he shrugged off his jacket, she saw a tailored blue shirt and silk tie. He wore patterned braces with suede leather button clips. She remembered the shabby uniform, the cold-bitten hands. But he wasn't just leaner of face; something else had happened. One of his eye sockets looked as if the bone had been broken, and reset itself at some point.

He gave a fine-edged smile, as if he'd wondered how long it would take her to see it. 'I got beaten.'

'I know, I was there.'

'A second time. The day I left England, I was flown away under guard to a base in Belfast, Ireland, where I was shut in a cell, chains on my legs. They beat me up against the wall. A Black sergeant who's whopped a white lieutenant earns special treatment, if you get my drift. I was put on a boat home, and I don't remember too much, only that I half-hoped we'd get torpedoed, so my chains would take me to the bottom. They locked me up a month in New York, took away my sergeant's stripes and when I reached my home base, I went on trial.'

'I wish you hadn't hit Lieutenant Macbeth, Theo.'

'Major Macbeth now, making lives a misery somewhere in the Philippines. I don't regret hitting him, but I paid for it.'

She reached inside her dress collar, and took off her locket, opening it up to reveal the ring inside. There was something else there too: a silky, dark sprig of hair. 'I never take it off.'

Theo swallowed. 'You're still Miss Irene Boulter, and waiting for me?'

'No.' She whispered the confession that had plagued her since she'd got his letter. 'I'm married. I had to, Theo.'

His omelette arrived and he waved it away. 'You *had* to?' He sat back.

The waiter looked pained. Omelettes were not to be kept waiting.

'OK, set it down,' Theo muttered, 'but forget the side salad. Irene, you're not drinking your coffee.'

'It's too strong.'

'Would you like something cold, and sweet?'

She nodded.

'*Citron pressé, mon ami.*' Theo waited until the waiter had gone. 'We said we would wait for each other. We swore it, Irene, in front of your parents. And that goddamn vicar.'

She leaned forward, pulling off her hat because its brim was in danger of colliding with Theo's forehead. 'I didn't hear from you. I didn't know what had happened to you. All Jake told me was that you'd been taken home. I tried to talk to him afterwards, but he and the others had moved on to lay runways at the other side of the county. And I couldn't wait.'

'Why not?'

She glanced around. The other café patrons were engaged with their food, their smoky conversations. 'I was pregnant. I had to marry.' A cloudy, lemony drink was put down by her elbow, and she took a long suck at the straw. She shuddered. It tasted like pure lemon juice.

'You're supposed to add sugar. Let me.' Theo stirred in a generous serving. She saw the lines across his brow, the dark circles under his eyes.

He asked, 'Whose child, Irene?'

'Ours.'

He bent his head. 'Yeah. I get it.' He picked up the ring which she'd placed between them, and balanced it in his palm. 'I was accused of stealing this, bringing the US military into disrepute. Got me an extra four months' jail time.'

'I'm so sorry.'

'Ain't your fault, sweetheart.' Their hair touched; their foreheads met. She smelled skin lotion of some sort. Added to the steam from the omelette and his coffee, she had to breathe slowly because it was triggering her nausea. 'I never did pay you back in full.'

'I don't care.'

'Now you're a married woman. Who is your husband?'

She broke eye contact. 'It doesn't matter. I don't love him and I don't plan to go home, not if—'

He cut in. 'What about the child – our child?'

'She... she—'

'We have a daughter? What's her name?'

'She...' Getting the words out was like pulling rocks from a dry place. 'She didn't have a name.'

'What? I don't understand.'

'I gave her a name, Theo, but there wasn't time to baptise her.'

'Because? I need to know it all, Irene.'

'I named her for you. I called her Theodora.'

'You should have got a priest in to baptise her.' Theo clenched his jaw.

She shook her head. How could he understand, unless she took him back to the events of March to July 1944?

On the 1st of March that year, she'd been formally discharged from Thewell Park. Dr Mickleson had driven her home. Later that month, she married Norman.

Theo closed his eyes. 'You married Norman Plait?'

Irene looked down at the table. In the saucer of her undrunk coffee was a paper mat, its white frill circling the base of the cup. Paris was good at little details. They just fell down on the views from hotel windows and the lavatories.

'Norman Plait,' Theo repeated. 'Who hated me and sold me out to Lieutenant Macbeth.'

What could she say? She'd believed she had no other choice. There had been no other choice. 'He made a deal. If I married him, I could keep the baby. He'd give it his name.'

'He'd give *our* baby *his* name.'

People looked up because Theo's words had ripped through the room.

'Please, try and understand, Theo. If I'd been single, I'd have been sent to a mother-and-baby home, and forced to give the baby up for adoption. I couldn't bear the idea.'

*And you weren't there.* The words manifested, hanging over their heads.

'Tell me about the birth,' Theo said.

On 23 July, almost two weeks before she was due, Irene's waters had broken. By then, she was married and living at Oak Apple Farm and she sent Philippa running to Westumble, to fetch her mum. Violet had rushed in, saying Little Flip had gone to knock on Dr Mickleson's door. 'I kept asking Mum, make up the cradle and get the nappies ready. I hadn't done it, because I thought I was good for another ten days.'

Her mother had replied, 'I will, don't fuss,' but she didn't do it. 'Not until I got right fretful. I was going to keep the baby. It was agreed; I wasn't going to change my mind. I wouldn't have married Norman otherwise.'

It had been a hideous, endless labour. 'At the end, I didn't know where I was.' The contractions had rolled in like battle tanks, pushing through flesh and muscle, sending her delirious with pain. Dr Mickleson had finally got the baby out with forceps, though she only heard about that afterwards. As the baby came out, Irene had haemorrhaged.

'Didn't they tell you anything? What she weighed? What she looked like?' A single tear was working its way down Theo's cheek. 'Didn't you see her?'

'I wasn't conscious; I'd lost too much blood. They told me later she'd died as she was delivered. Mum snipped off a little bit of hair, and kept it for me.'

'This is it?' Theo stared at the tiny strand in the locket.

Irene nodded. 'Hers, yes. Afterwards' – she bit her lips in a nervous, jabbing way that had become her habit – 'afterwards, I was taken to a convalescence home. And then somewhere else, another hospital.' That being Thewell Park again, this time for six months. 'I wasn't myself. I hated myself for failing our baby. I felt I had failed you too.'

'What did Norman do?'

'Visited me.' Irene had a brief mental image of sitting outside on the familiar terrace, a pad under her backside. Once again, fresh air was considered the best medicine Thewell Park could offer. Norman had arrived in his overtight Sunday suit, having walked from the bus stop, with nothing much to say other than, 'How are you doing, dear?' When she didn't answer, he'd told her about the farm, and how the fields were shaping up, and which hedges he'd taken out.

Norman was like a hawk, Theo said. 'Circling, waiting for you to break a wing.'

'I can't fault him as a husband, Theo. He does his best. It's not his fault I can't love him. And he didn't sell you out to Macbeth. It wasn't him reported on us for going dancing.'

'Then who was it? Tell me and I'll kill him.'

'Her. It was Mrs Scattergood, the landlady at The Ten Bells. I cheeked her, and she took her revenge. I only learned it a couple of years ago, after she died suddenly and her husband confessed. He'd felt awful about it.'

'But, still, you married Norman believing he had me beaten raw. What you went through, Irene, with that pig Macbeth. How could you go to church and take your vows with Norman Plait?'

'I don't know.' Right now, she hated Norman for planting a child inside her. *Clinging to my womb like a weed between the bricks of a house.* Empty of words, she opened her purse and took something out. A shiny disc.

'My silver dollar.' Theo turned it round in his fingers. His nails were buffed, his cuticles perfect half-moons. 'Where'd you find it?'

'On the lane out of Flixfield. It was torn off you and thrown, remember? One day I was cycling along the road and I saw it, glinting.'

'That's kind of a miracle. Only' – Theo gave a dark chuckle – 'this has to be the unluckiest damn dollar the US Mint ever struck. I'll give it one more chance.' He dropped it in his pocket before giving her a slanting look. 'Are we together now, or are you going home?'

Irene looked beyond him, at the walls of the café covered in cabaret posters. They said that when you died, your life went past you like a film at the cinema, sped up a thousand times. She had a lightning-fast replay of herself, walking home from Ratty's after a gruelling shift, hating her life and wanting something to happen. Theo and his friends, walking into the village hut on the first day of spring. *We hope you can find it in your hearts to welcome some lonely boys into your community.* Dancing with Theo. Dancing with Norman. Three steps forward. *Bash, bash.* Two steps the other way. *Bash, bash.* 'Not on that beat, Norman!'

Jitterbugging with Theo, swinging out, spinning, sliding through his legs, rolling over his bent back to music that made you want to make love under the stars and then dance some more.

Marriage in an ugly little chapel then home for cheese and pickled cabbage. Aunt Elsie sneering, 'She eats well for a sinner.'

Childbirth, excruciating pain, until blood loss brought blessed release.

Her mother bending over her. 'I'm afraid she died, my poor child. The doctor couldn't get her to take a breath. Norman's taken her little body to the mortuary, but I kept a snippet of her hair for you.'

Inserting fine black hair in the locket, with Theo's engagement ring.

'Perhaps it's for the best.' Who'd said that? Sally Mickleson, her so-called friend. 'Daddy says, perhaps it's for the best and Mummy agrees. After all, your poor husband could never have claimed it as his own.'

*Her*, not *it*. Her name is Theodora. Dora for short.

Dora for such a dreadful, short time.

'Irene? Irene?' Theo was massaging her hand, bringing her back. 'You OK, sweetheart?'

She gazed at him. 'What did you ask?'

'I asked if we're together now, or if you're going home. I need to know.'

'Why didn't you ever write to me, Theo?'

He moistened his lips, and now it was him recalling something ugly, unwelcome. 'Because of what I went through after they let me out of jail. I had lost everything and for a long while, my only friend was Mr Jack Daniel's.'

'Least you had a friend.' She squeezed his hand, not understanding why he laughed in a helpless way.

'Irene, if it hadn't been for my real friend Jake taking the bottle away and drying me out, I'd have been lost. I've wanted you every day and night since we were driven apart, but I didn't feel fit to look at you, or touch you. That's why I didn't write.'

She tried to speak.

Theo placed the engagement ring on Irene's finger. 'Are we together now?'

A harried English voice gave him his answer. 'No, you are not. I can't let it happen. I'm most awfully sorry, but it is completely impossible.'

Irene and Theo jerked away from each other, and Irene saw she'd been tracked down by the last person in the world who would support or encourage her in leaving her husband.

Mrs Prentice's jacket was far too heavy for the June weather, and she must have run because her high-browed face was red and perspiring. She dropped Irene's wedding ring into the empty ashtray on their table and again addressed Theo. 'Sergeant Robinson, you are not sitting with Miss Irene Boulter, but with Mrs Norman Plait, a married woman.'

'I know she's married. I'm no longer "Sergeant". Call me Theodore.'

'Theodore. Very well. Has Irene told you yet that she is expecting her husband's baby?'

Irene felt Theo's shock. A jolt of electricity straight to her heart. Anger, hurt and disappointment. It was all there in his face.

'Is this true, Irene? You're expecting?'

'Yes, but I don't want to be.'

'Unfortunately, that is not an option.' Mrs Prentice pulled out a chair and sat down, grabbing a napkin to mop her face.

The waiter approached. 'Madame?'

'No thank you, *garçon*. I'm not staying. Irene, I beg you to consider what you're doing. When a woman conceives a child, she may no longer follow her own wishes. Would you really alienate Norman from his own son or daughter?' Mrs Prentice seemed not to expect an answer, and turned to Theo. 'You have experienced a deal of trouble, my man. I see it in your face. A long time ago, you were warned of the danger of consorting with Irene. Then, it came down to what was acceptable, socially. This time, it would be a legal custody battle. Can you afford to lose everything again?'

Irene began to speak, but Theo raised his hand, asking her to stop. 'Would I give up the money I've earned, the little bit of fame I have, to be with Irene? My answer is yes, ma'am.'

Mrs Prentice shook her head. 'Irene, will you abandon your husband and your widowed mother, along with your child once it's born, to be with this man?'

Irene stared helplessly back. It struck her that Mrs Prentice was reciting a strange, upturned version of the wedding service. The whole café seemed to await her answer, the hum of voices, the clink of cutlery, suddenly stilled. She was being asked if she could leave Flixfield and Norman for Theo. The answer was yes.

But... her mother, widowed since the winter of '45, and worn out from nursing her husband for six years, could she abandon her? And darling Dad's grave where she laid flowers twice a week, could she choose never to visit it again? Yes, just about. For Theo.

What of the baby she was carrying? Because what Mrs Prentice had not actually said, but what they both knew, was that Irene would have to give up the child. Norman's rights as a father would trump hers as a mother.

Could she give birth in blood and pain, then hand the little mite over to others to raise? Her mother wasn't up to it, now. And Norman wouldn't have a clue. Philippa turned sixteen in a month's time, but she was too young and was courting Billy

Gifford's lad, Ronnie. Little Flip would want a baby of her own soon enough.

Irene knew then, with piercing clarity, what would happen to her baby.

Aunt Elsie Binney.

Age and ill-health had not dimmed Elsie's spite. Irene's mind went back to something she had discovered around the time Theo had been taken. Philippa had come to stay with them, because the old woman had gone down with chicken pox. Irene had been the one to wash and dress the child, and helping Flip out of her clothes and into the tub, she'd seen more of those ruddy-brown spots on the skinny little back.

'You've definitely got the chicken pox,' she'd said, and touched a spot. Philippa had winced and, looking closer, she'd realised it wasn't the chicken pox. The spots were burns.

'How d'you get those?' she'd asked.

'It's what Auntie do, when I'm bad,' the child had replied. 'She puts a hot poker on my back, to burn the Devil out of me. It hurts, Irene.'

She'd found more burns, some red, some scarred over. A whole childhood's worth. Had she told her mother? Yes, she thought so, but that time had been so strange and she'd thought she was dying. So perhaps she hadn't. Or perhaps Aunt Elsie had explained them away, like she had before, as being Philippa's own fault.

'Irene?' Theo spoke her name like a caress.

'My baby can't go to Elsie Binney,' Irene gasped.

'Who is Elsie Binney?' Theo looked perplexed.

Mrs Prentice sighed and laid a hand on each of theirs. 'Custody would be for a court to decide and I fear you would never be granted it, Irene. I know Norman well enough to say he would defend his paternal rights tooth and nail. You would have to give up your baby.'

'I would fight back. I won't lose another child.'

Mrs Prentice cleared her throat. 'Your, er, time at Thewell Park would also come out and would weigh against you.'

'What is Thewell Park?' Theo asked.

'Irene?' Mrs Prentice invited her to explain.

Irene shook her head, tears blinding her. Her fingers found something to squeeze for comfort. Later, she discovered it was the coaster with the café's name embossed on it, along with a coffee stain like a halo. Another image came to her inner eye: the cupboard in the sitting room at Oak Apple Farm with scratch marks on the inside. Little Flip, shut in, ''Cause I couldn't be a good girl for Auntie.'

Norman had refused to see those scratches for what they were when Irene had showed him. 'I expect Elsie lost her temper once or twice. You know how Little Flip can be.'

Wiping her tears, Irene asked Theo to hold out his hand. She removed the engagement ring from her finger and gave it to him. She picked up the locket and hung it around her neck. 'I have to go back. I can't leave a child to fend for itself at Oak Apple Farm.'

'Irene!'

'I can't, Theo. Were I not pregnant, I'd fly with you to the moon.'

She was aware of his chair scraping back, of his hand briefly on hers. An exchange in French as he paid the waiter. The door opened, shut and then his footsteps faded.


Later, at the hotel, Mrs Prentice brought her a note. Theo had sent back the engagement ring. The note had no address, but the following words:

> *I understand, sweetheart, and I don't blame you. Tide and*
> *time are against us, and I'm done with hoping. I always loved*

*you and I always will. I wish you joy in motherhood. Let us be*
*happy in the lives we make.*

*Theo*

Irene answered Theo's goodbye note some months later, after the baby she named Amanda was born and she had another breakdown. Back to Thewell Park she went for a third time while the baby was temporarily fostered.

While she was there, somebody in the hospital turned on the wireless and out poured a sad, lilting song by the Jake Hendrick Five.

*There's a face I see when I walk with the moon*
*Irene... Irene, fair as a dream*

She covered pages with wild writing, letting out her feelings, her regrets, and asked a nurse to mail the letter to Mr Theodore Robinson of The Jake Hendrick Five, Le Hot Brick Club, Paris, France. At the bottom, in brackets, she wrote: 'Please send on'.

She never knew if he got it, as he didn't write back.

## 49

RUBY

CHRISTMAS EVE 2022

So, the locket and ring had come back from Paris with Irene, along with a large pot of Moutarde de Meaux, the remains of which festered undisturbed on a top shelf of Philippa's pantry cupboard. How tragic, Ruby thought. Irene had let Theo walk away because it was a straight choice between him, and keeping her unborn baby safe.

Aunt Elsie Binney should have been locked up. And Norman – absolved by the skin of his teeth from the charge of informing on Theo and his friends – had closed his eyes to child abuse. Because what else had it been?

Poor Little Flip: isolated among adults whose eyes and priorities were elsewhere. No wonder Philippa was suspicious, prickly. A hoarder. And in denial about Norman. The adored brother who had never stood between her and a hot poker.

How much of this should she tell Will? He was picking her up for their date in an hour. He'd invited Mary Daker to sit with Philippa and promised the women fish and chips from the pub, which he'd collect and deliver. A cosy night in for the two old friends, with Edna making three, while she and Will... what? Held hands across a table, passing messages with their eyes through the flickering candlelight? Or discussing roof repairs and wood burners?

She just wanted him to kiss her again. With that in mind, what should she wear? She'd brought one dress with her, a black number from one of Laurac's *plus chic* boutiques. Too much for a village pub? It was either that or paint-splashed jeans.

By the time Will called for her, she'd made her decision. She'd already put on her padded coat, which reached past her knees, and because the temperature had dropped and it was icy outside, her feet were in three-quarter black leather boots. He too was dressed for the cold and he said, 'I advise a hat.'

She'd travelled to England wearing a beanie, also now paint-splattered. However, the other day she'd found a tweed flat cap in her grandparents' bedroom, which would do. She went up to fetch it. Will laughed when she came downstairs with it on.

'You look like one of Fagin's pickpockets.'

'Then keep your hand on your wallet, friend.'

Ruby was still looking forward to the meal, but a small fly had landed in the ointment, and she was worried that Will would blame her for it. While she was getting ready, she'd missed a call from her mother. Amanda's message had both confused and alarmed her.

Amanda was back in Laurac, unsettled from too much proximity to the ex she realised she still had feelings for, and his new wife. A misguided trip, she now admitted. 'And' – and this was pure Amanda-speak – 'I dreamed about the locket again. Philippa will find a message on her answer machine from me, telling her to look under the floor of her kitchen. I am convinced the locket is under the flagstones at Westumble Farm.'

Asking an eighty-eight-year-old to lift the flagstones in her kitchen? Ruby had called back, but either Amanda was somewhere without signal, or she'd let her phone battery run flat.

Ruby needed to let Amanda know that the locket was unlikely
to be at Westumble Farm as it had been with Irene until the
millennium and beyond. She had so much else to tell her
mother too. About Irene. About Amanda's own birth and the
choices Irene had made.

'Shall we go?' Will sounded upbeat. She deduced from this
that Philippa had not yet noticed that her answer machine was
flashing.


Ruby was sitting alone at a table for two in a corner, Will having
temporarily abandoned her to ferry the fish and chips home for
Philippa and Mary. A bottle of Malbec stood open in front of
her, and she sipped at a glass of the red wine. The Ten Bells was
authentic, she decided. A fire blazed behind a polished fender
and those wooden settles must date back a couple of centuries
at least. The bar had the patina of age, and Ruby imagined
Irene standing behind it, gazing at the front door, waiting for a
certain man to walk in.

'What goes into this beer?' Theo had asked Irene.

'Well, it's bitter beer with a lot of hop in it.'

'Hop... like the Lindy Hop?'

Ruby smiled. An opening joke, and the rest was history. No
– it was tragedy. Left to themselves, they'd have married, raised
a family and done whatever with their lives. Other people had
turned their love story into something ultimately scarring to
them both. Irene, three times an inmate of Thewell Park. The
first time after Theo left, the second after that appalling labour
and the stillbirth of hers and Theo's daughter. And the third
time straight after Amanda's birth.

Post-natal depression. Baby blues. Call it what you like. It
crushed Ruby to think of Irene separated from her living baby,
unable to care for Amanda. Ruby suspected the letter she'd
found on the bonfire was Irene's final discharge some time in

1951. Philippa would know about it, because she'd have been a young woman by then, quite aware of what was happening to her sister-in-law across the road.

Poor little Amanda. And people wondered why Irene and her daughter had never really bonded, never gained that close, loving relationship that Ruby had with her mother. 'If only they'd talked!' others would say.

The landlord came over, cheerful in a Christmas jumper. 'A romantic candle for you?'

'Go on, then.'

He put it on the table, lit it, and introduced himself as Craig. 'You're Will's friend? Nice earrings.'

Ruby was wearing shimmering sea-glass drops, her mother's creation. 'Thanks. And, yes, sort of Will's friend. I'm also Irene Plait's granddaughter. She barmaided here, in the Scattergoods' time.'

The landlord's response – a vague, polite smile – told Ruby everything. Who remembered the Scattergoods? Even the Plaits of Oak Apple Farm were the past.

'I'll bring over a couple of menus,' he said. 'Specials are on the board.'

Will came back soon after, and Ruby knew instantly that something had changed.

## 50

Will sat down, and Ruby saw him registering that she was wearing a dress. He'd left before she'd taken off her coat. Its neckline was cut to show the contours of her shoulders and a hint of cleavage. The sea-glass earrings caught the candlelight, and had he been the Will of half an hour ago, she guessed the effect would have been everything she wanted.

She spoke before he could. 'Philippa heard Mum's message.'

'I found her and Mary Daker trying to prise up a loose flagstone. What the hell, Ruby?' He shook his head when she tried to speak. 'Look, I know you didn't do it. It's your mum, but honestly? Is this obsession with Irene's life and a missing bloody necklace sufficient excuse to drive a damaged woman into some kind of mental hell?'

'No, of course it's not.'

'Then call off the dogs.'

She picked up her menu, mostly to hide her face. Will's anger was excusable, but it felt targeted and with her emotions drawn tight by reliving Irene's misery, she couldn't stop tears welling. 'Excuse me.' She put her menu down and got up. She caught the landlord's eye. He was polishing a glass behind the bar. 'Loos?'

Craig pointed. Ruby headed.

Locking herself in the loo marked 'Belles' – the other was marked 'Blokes' – she sat down and put her face in her hands. Crying like a five-year-old was not her thing. Hell, let the tears flow. Get them out. Five minutes later, she blotted her eyes with loo roll and left. A glance in the mirror over the basin told her that she'd smudged her eye makeup and it would be obvious to anybody but a robot that she'd had a weep. No, damn it, she thought. I'm not going to be this vulnerable. Will Keelbrook liked the moral high ground, but Ruby had forged her character under a string of chefs who could be case studies for anger management modules. She would go back out, head high.

Passing an open door on her way back, she peered in, drawn by the smell of fish and chips. Nice kitchen. Unlike the bar room, it had been modernised. White walls, stainless-steel tops. God, she missed that.

A yell and the clattering of metal made her step right inside before she could stop herself. A man in chef's whites had just dropped a tray of jumbo sausage rolls and was rather comically flapping his hands and sucking on them.

'You burnt yourself.' Kitchen injuries weren't actually funny.

'Forgot the sodding oven glove.'

'Under cold water, come on.' Ruby steered the man to the sink, ran the cold tap and shoved his hands under it. 'Let it run for twenty minutes.'

'I can't. I've got to do service.' He looked at her with a mix of despair and rage. He was around forty, going grey. 'I forgot the oven gloves.'

'Yes, you said. Keep your hand in the flow to stop the heat travelling through the skin.'

'I can't do this.' The man stared at the streaming water. He had the posture of someone who hadn't just burned their hands, but was emotionally burned out too. That same expression had stared back at Ruby from the mirror a few years back after she'd recklessly accepted a head chef's job in Toulouse and found herself running two busy venues on three hours' sleep a night.

The landlord, Craig, came in through a different door. He assessed the scene. 'Tarquin, sweetheart, what have you done?' He took his partner's hands. 'Blisters forming. Is that a good sign?'

'Keep the water flowing another fifteen minutes at least,' Ruby advised, and went to investigate the smell of burning carbohydrate coming from the oven. Padding her hands with tea towels, she pulled out a tray of rosemary focaccia. That was on the specials menu. It was scorched at the edge, but the middle was OK.

Will peered around the door. 'Hi, I was worried.' He saw the sausage rolls on the floor. 'Oh.'

'There are no disasters in a kitchen,' Ruby said crisply, 'only unplanned events.' The sausage rolls were cool enough to handle so she directed Will to sweep them up. 'They can't be served.'

'No, ma'am.' He was seeing her fully now, in her dress that showed quite a bit of leg, and the three-quarter boots. He swallowed. At last, the desired effect.

Shame they were on bad terms again.


They'd emptied the Malbec by the time their food arrived. Craig had sent Tarquin upstairs to their flat to have a lie-down and phoned in some emergency cover. 'Restricted menu now, sorry,' he'd said. 'Mrs Porter can only cope with four dishes at once.'

Both Ruby and Will chose the potted Lowestoft shrimp, followed by mushroom and pancetta pasta. Keep it simple.

They had talked about her roof, and her chimney flue, and he'd told her how he'd traded in the motorbike he'd parked at a friend's while he flitted between England and UAE, for the Volvo. 'Better for lugging building materials around, and it's low on the ground. Easier for Labradors and old relations to get in and out.'

She suspected he was trying to make up for spoiling the atmosphere, and the way he kept glancing at her suggested he realised she'd cried at some point. But Ruby wasn't giving ground. He was entitled to defend Philippa. She was entitled to discover her family's past. Amanda was entitled to have possession of the 'bloody necklace' she had been expressly promised in Irene's will.

'You know, they're looking for help in the kitchen,' Will said after their potted shrimp had arrived. It came with toast, over-crisp on one side, soft on the other. Mrs Porter was probably having a nightmare time of it.

She spread a lavish wave on her toast. It tasted wonderful. 'Ah ha,' she said.

'Is it something you'd consider?'

'No.'

She heard him sigh. He dug into his ramekin, and copied her, spreading shrimp pâté on his toast. 'Because you're not staying long enough?'

'I don't know how long I'm staying, but I made a vow in Laurac when I walked out of my flat for the last time. The flat came with the job, so I lost my partner, my work and my home at the same time.'

'I know. That's hard.'

'I vowed I would never, ever work for anybody else again.'

He bit into his toast, and nodded, and when he could speak, he said, 'Me too.'

'So we have something in common.'

'Ruby?'

'What?'

'I'm sorry. I'm hyper-sensitive about Aunt Flip. I'm terrified, actually.'

'What of?'

He didn't answer at once. She felt he was marshalling his words, fitting phrases to abstract feelings.

'I'm worried she'll lose her grip, mentally. She's getting frail physically and I'm scared that I, as her designated next of kin, will have to decide whether or not she goes into a care home. It would be my signature on a form, and it would crush her.'

'Just as Mum and I had to do for Irene.'

He had the grace to look self-conscious. 'Yup. You did. And I judged you.'

'You said it yourself, Will. Lives are messy. Look at mine, at Mum's. Yours. Your mum's.' He looked so unhappy, she reached out to put her hand on his.

'Was it me who made you cry just now?' He looked suddenly so stricken.

'Sort of. It was a culmination of stuff. Irene's life... was incredibly sad. She had to walk away from the love of her life, in Paris of all places. The capital city of romance. I think she left her soul there, and never retrieved it. I promise I'll have a word with Mum and tell her, on no account, to bother Aunt Flip.' They'd finished their starter, and Ruby picked up their plates. 'I'll take these through, save Craig a job.'

She was conscious in every fibre, as she walked away from the table, that Will's eyes stayed on her. When she'd bought the dress, the assistant had told her, 'It doesn't look much on the hanger, but it comes to life on the body.'

Maybe Will did too. Came to life... No, kill that thought.

By the time they'd declined dessert, and emptied half a second bottle of Malbec, the mood between them had shifted again. It had the edginess of desire hemmed with fear. Had they met on holiday, or in a bar somewhere, it would have been simple. But they were in Will's home village, and there was Philippa teetering on the edge of something, watching their every move.

Will had walked the five minutes back to the pub after delivering the fish and chips, and so they returned through the village street on foot, with a sky above them of starlit black. Flixfield had no streetlights. Christmas lights twinkled in shrubs and trees and it felt magical, and unworldly; the only sounds were a pair of hooting owls and hers and Will's feet, cracking the ice on the shallow puddles.

Will walked her to her door. And then, the decision. Thank you, goodnight or...

'Coffee?' Ruby suggested.

When Will nodded, she opened the door without a word. The logs she'd left smouldering in the wood burner cast a topaz mist around the dining hall. 'Isn't it beautiful? Don't turn the lights on,' she instructed.

'You can make coffee in the dark?'

'No. You're going to make it. In the dark.'

'Where are you going?'

'You'll see.'

She went upstairs and picked up a fake fur bedspread her mother had bought when they were here three Christmases ago. She wanted Will to make love to her, but not in the bed her grandparents had shared. Before going back downstairs, she took off her boots and tights.

She laid the rug in front of the wood burner and sank down on the fur, in a languid pose. She was thirty-four, and she was Amanda's child, and had never learned to simper.

Will came out of the kitchen, carrying two mugs. 'I made instant; no way I can grind beans in the—' He fell silent as he saw Ruby smiling up at him.

He put the mugs down fast and knelt beside her. The hurry left him then, and in a relaxed move, he peeled off his jumper, revealing a tee shirt that cleaved to his torso. When he stripped that off too, she saw a physique with wide shoulders and dark chest hair, a smattering from sternum to navel. Ruby gazed up at him, thinking, Wow, get you, tucked away out of sight in a barn.

'How come you're still single, Will?'

He shrugged and placed his hand on her knee, slowly moving upwards as he leaned down to kiss her.

Ruby was woken in the small hours by the chime of her mobile phone, coming from her coat pocket. She and Will had retreated to her bed. At some point, she had stopped caring if the ghosts of her grandparents minded. She got up to check it, thinking it could be Sabrina making contact.

It was a message from her mother. *Booked my flights, Toulouse-Amsterdam-Norwich. Already on my way, be with you for Christmas lunch. Did I tell you I was coming? Warn Philippa that my hair is purple.* Smiley face, smiley face, smiley face.

*Oh, Mum.* Ruby had faithfully promised Will that she'd call off the dogs. Course, she was thrilled her mum would be with her on Christmas Day, but this was the worst moment for Amanda to burst in, eager to stir the pot.

Will woke as Ruby was texting a reply. 'What's up?'

'Mum's flying into Norwich airport. She'll be here in a few hours. Happy Christmas, Will.'

'Happy Christmas, you.' A silence. 'Does she need picking up?'

'No. She can get a taxi. I'll duck out of lunch with you and Philippa and try to keep Mum caged here.'

'Course you won't. We can lay a table for four.'

'You don't know what you're saying, but you are such a kind man.'

'I'm not always, but for some reason, I'm in a good mood. Come back to bed, Ruby.'

## 51

CHRISTMAS DAY 2022

Ruby made bread sauce, leaving it on the hob, sealed tight under a lid with bay leaf and cloves. She was in Will's kitchen as they were having lunch at his place. The dining table had been extended and four places laid.

Will had taken Philippa to church for the Christmas morning service and they'd be back in an hour or so. He'd been perfectly accepting when Ruby offered to take over cooking dinner. 'So long as I get to do the canapés. I like doing *amuse-bouches*. We're having a three-bird roast,' he'd said, directing her to the fridge.

Opening the door, she'd got a dose of the Will Keelbrook sense of humour. On a tray were three dressed quails.

'Free range,' Will assured her.

'Good. Only, I'll have to make them stretch to four.'

'Philippa doesn't eat much. She could make a sparrow last two meals.' Will had made the comment as he lit candles which he'd fixed to an exquisitely gnarled piece of driftwood. He had carried the arrangement to the other end of the big room, next to a pile of presents. It was his sustainable answer to a Christmas tree. Before leaving, he'd said, 'Use whatever you like, drink whatever you like. I'd better go as I'm giving Mary a lift to church too.'

The outside temperature had improved, and the day was cloudy, the light through the huge barn windows nicely moody. Candle flames cast ever-changing figures on the white walls. With the gas stove shimmering, and Edna ranged in front of it, everything felt perfect. Complete.

Except that she hadn't heard from Theo's daughter, Sabrina, though she'd messaged, thanking her for sending that letter. Ruby knew Sabrina wanted some kind of explanation of its context; she wanted closure. But Ruby wasn't sure if it would help Sabrina to know that Irene and Theo's baby had died. Or that Irene had gone home to a marriage with a man she could never love, and whom she blamed for impregnating her just as the cage door had opened again for her.

Heartbreak was real. Within six months, Irene had been back in Thewell Park, and baby Amanda had been placed with strangers. Ruby wanted to give Sabrina something profound, while giving value to Theo and Irene's experience too. Only, she didn't know what that was.

She'd found a moment to send her mum a detailed text, warning of Philippa's fragility. *Can we forget about the locket for now?* She hoped Amanda would take note.

With time in hand before Will and Philippa came back, she opened her laptop again, plugging it into a socket because the battery light was flashing. She read again the scanned pages Sabrina had sent, and again they made her cry. She could understand how the discovery of Irene's final letter to Theo had caused a mini-detonation in the Robinson-Chase family. Nobody likes to uncover their father's secret love. And though it was pretty clear that Irene and Theo had parted forever in the café on Rue des Petites Écuries, Theo had married Sabrina's mother Millie very soon after. And penned a song called 'Irene'.

Ruby wrote a brief message, sending Sabrina Christmas Day greetings. The time by her watch was a little after eleven. She needed to get prepping for lunch.

She made apple, walnut and onion stuffing, basted the birds and got them in the oven; she peeled potatoes for roasting and trimmed the veg. As she worked, she thought of poor Tarquin, struggling with the pressure of a busy kitchen. Craig had said something interesting in the pub when he came to pick up their plates: 'Some of us have to move out to the country to discover how much we're suited to the town.'

Then she found herself wondering if Philippa would pick up on the changed chemistry between her and Will. Could she and Will continue what they'd started, or would it peter out? She flinched, remembering his response to his ex's killer question: *Do you love me enough to give up on your dreams?*

No.

The *peep-peep* of the door code sounded as she was mincing garlic for the gravy.

Will came in, alone. He frowned and said, 'You've been crying.'

She pointed to the board. 'This garlic is incredibly strong. Where's Aunt Flip?'

'Rounding up her stray cats for their Christmas breakfast. I've told her it's champagne and *amuse-bouches* at twelve forty-five. Hope that's all right.'

'Perfect.'

'And I need to warn you, we'll be expected to sit down to watch the King speaking to the nation.'

'Mum will love that. By the way, the correct term is *amuse-gueules*. *Amuse-bouche* is prissy. And, do you mind me saying?' Will had brought out a packet of pumpernickel as his base for the canapés and was laying the slices on the grill pan. 'Cut them into rounds before you toast them.'

'I wasn't planning to cut rounds. I don't have cookie cutters. I'm a man.'

She squeezed him. 'So you are. Did you tell Aunt Flip that my mother is due?'

'No.'

She looked at him, aghast. 'You didn't mention that Amanda has purple hair now, either?'

'That's your job. So why don't you go and see if Aunt Flip needs a hand with the cats?'


At the farmhouse, she found Philippa ready to join them. A dozen empty luxury cat food cartons lay on the kitchen surface. 'Some of my little stray moggies hoodwinked me into feeding them twice,' Philippa said. She sounded slurred and, catching Ruby's amusement, said, 'They plied me with mulled wine after the service and I reckon the vicar slipped some brandy in it.'

'Well, it's Christmas.' Philippa getting tipsy had more to do with her being undernourished, in Ruby's view. When had she begun starving herself? After her Ronnie died, or long before? The little girl who got wrong from Aunt Elsie, and was punished relentlessly, would have had few ways of asserting control in her world.

Ruby said brightly, 'Guess who's coming to dinner?'

'Wasn't that a film with Spencer Tracy?'

'Probably. But today, it's my mother. Amanda's on her way. In fact' – Ruby checked her watch, loving the feel of it on her arm – 'she's landed by now.'

Philippa scowled. 'Your mum sent me a very peculiar message yesterday, had me and Mary trying to dig up my floor.'

'As a rule, Aunt Flip, it's always best to take Mum with a large pinch of salt.'

'Hm. I hope her coming won't mean dinner is delayed.'

'No. We're eating at one thirty sharp.'

'I can't last that long!'

'Which is why we're having smoked salmon canapés first. Will's battling with pumpernickel as we speak.'

Philippa looked perturbed. Then her expression cleared. 'You've a funny way of talking, Ruby. You didn't get that from Irene nor my brother Norman.'

'I got it from my mother.'

Philippa pointed to her coat, meaning for Ruby to help her on with it. 'I lost my mother before I was old enough to blink my eyes. And my dad straight after.'

'I know. It was a cruel thing.' Pity always tempered Ruby's mistrust of Philippa, who, like a foundling cast into the river, had spent her life trying to survive. 'Can I bring anything else?'

'My walking tripod, please.'

Philippa had donned her wig for church, and a crushed velvet dress, vintage-style with little inserts of printed silk at the neck and sleeves. It was like a stained-glass window in fabric. Slightly undermining the look, she was wearing paisley pattern trousers underneath. Fine for inside a church, but she'd boil at Will's. Ruby pointed it out.

'I'll take them off when I've walked across.' At the door, Philippa stopped. 'Nip upstairs, would you, and fetch my perfume. It wears off so quick. My friend Mary says it's because I buy the cheap stuff. In the drawer, under the bathroom sink.'

Upstairs, Ruby turned off a dripping tap and opened the drawer, seeing the same mingled trove. Pastel-coloured goat's milk soap had been added to the clutter since the day she'd come up here to use Philippa's shower. Ruby had by now concluded that Philippa bought stuff as a comfort. Perhaps to fill up her loneliness. Rummaging for the perfume, Ruby uncovered the faux-tortoiseshell vanity case that she'd looked at before.

She was sure it was the one her grandma had used when she went to the airbase, desperate to charm her way past the barrier. And in Paris, to cover up the spider veins she was self-conscious about.

There was still powder in the compact, and the swansdown puff was there. Ruby smudged powder onto the back of her hand. Too light for her by three shades. Too light for Philippa. Definitely, this had to be Irene's.

'Why take it, Philippa?' Ruby whispered. 'Does your hoarding run to other people's things, or did you just want what Irene had?'

'You found it, dear?' came from down below.

'Er... yes.' Ruby picked out a diamanté-topped bottle. Hollywood Vamp. She sprayed a little into the air. Ooh. It smelled of aircraft seat. Hopefully, the Miss Dior Will had bought on Ruby's behalf yesterday would be considered an upgrade. When would they exchange presents? In Laurac, they'd done it on Christmas Eve.

Downstairs, Ruby watched Philippa spray Hollywood Vamp into the air, pinch her nose and walk through the mist. Philippa saw Ruby's expression. 'It's how you're meant to apply perfume. I saw it on telly; what's-her-name did it. Oh, I can't remember. Big shoulder pads. Fetch the key off the table, dear, and pick up that bag, the one with the presents in. I wrapped something up for your mother.'

'That's kind.'

A locket, by any chance? Life was never that simple. It occurred to Ruby that she should have opened the little compartments in Irene's compact case, on the off chance the locket was in one of them. Irene had written about finding a hiding place 'where no snooper' would find her locket. Would the compact case have been considered safe enough?

Ruby couldn't think of an excuse to go back upstairs.

As they left, she passed on her mother's message, about Amanda's hair now being purple.

Philippa grunted. 'Doesn't surprise me. Why does your mother dye her hair such a colour?'

'To my knowledge, this is the first time she has.'

'It isn't,' Philippa said heavily. 'She came home for her gran's funeral with hair like a dayglo beetroot. She called it "amethyst"; I called it disrespectful. Her gran was Violet Boulter.'

'Yes, of course.' It had taken Ruby a moment to catch on.

'Amanda was making a joke.'

'I doubt she was.'

'That's where you're wrong, dear. She turned up looking like one of those punk rockers and when I asked what she thought she was up to, you know what she did? Took a pair of scissors and cut it all off and sat in the church bald as a coot. Only the dye had soaked into her scalp, so she was still purple.'

Ruby had not heard that story before, but it sounded very like Amanda. She sent out a heartfelt energy-message. *Mum, tread carefully today, please.*

## 52

They found Will basting the quails. He had also parboiled the potatoes and put them aside to cool.

'Are we on target? Philippa is anxious to eat no later than one thirty,' said Ruby as she entered the kitchen.

Philippa called out from the sofa where she sat with a glass of sherry, 'It's so we don't miss any of His Majesty's speech. First time we've had a king in donkey's years.'

'We can always record it, Aunt Flip,' Will called back.

'Record it? That's unpatriotic.'

Will and Ruby's eyes met. She stifled a giggle, then took a platter of smoked salmon with dill mayonnaise on pumpernickel to the coffee table. He wasn't half good, she thought. He'd even cut the toasted rye bread in rounds. With a jam jar lid, he'd told her proudly. 'And you're right. It's murder if you've toasted the bread first.'

'First time king for me too,' announced Will, popping the cork of a bottle of sparkling wine. 'I only ever knew Queen Elizabeth.'

'Obviously, since we're the same age,' Ruby pointed out.

'When I was born,' said Philippa, 'we still had George the

Fifth, not that I was aware of it. Then Edward the Eighth for a bit, then George the Sixth, then the late Queen. That means I've seen five monarchs in my life. I shan't see another.'

'Sticking with sherry, or would you like a glass of English champagne?' Will asked, in a robustly cheerful voice.

'There's no such thing as English champagne,' Philippa replied. 'I'll stick with sherry.'

'Quite right,' Ruby agreed. 'The champagne region is French. No argument.'

'Give it a hundred years, with climate change, it'll be in Oxfordshire.' Will raised his glass. 'Cheers.'

'I've warned Mum by text to go carefully today,' Ruby murmured.

Will drew a soft line under her chin, making it lift so he could kiss her.

'Your dog's trying to eat the canopies,' Philippa shouted.

Ruby couldn't contain her giggling this time, until she saw that Philippa was watching them over the sofa back, with a knife-thrower's focus.

Will stepped away and called Edna. 'I'd better take her outside for a minute or two.'

With nothing to do in the kitchen for a moment, Ruby joined Philippa. Treading on eggshells got tiring after a while. 'I really like him, you know,' she said. 'And I think... I hope, he likes me. We're not an item; we have no plans. Do you mind?'

'I'll mind if you hurt him.' Philippa still wore her wedding ring, and other rings too, with chunky stones that knocked together as she wove her fingers. Ruby thought about Irene's jewellery, the taking and hoarding. Pointless, as none of it would have suited Philippa.

'I'll mind if you make him think you're staying, and then flit off back to France, girl.'

'I'm not a flitter, Auntie.'

'Your mother is.'

'My mother is not me. Besides, I'm thinking of getting my sofa shipped over here from France. Owning an eight-foot sofa is like having a dog. It ties you to a home.' She was being glib, but actually, that antique bergère piece would suit Oak Apple Farm.

'You're selling, you said.'

'True. Auntie, can I ask a straight question?'

'You can. Don't promise to answer.'

Ruby glanced towards the door. Will was still outside, giving Edna a loo break. 'I have a feeling Mum might ask you about Grandma's locket.'

'Here we go.'

'The one Theo gave her. You remember Theo, the man she was engaged to during the war.'

Philippa shook her head. 'That was a fairy tale.'

'Well, that's your take, but Irene's father, John, my great-grandfather, promised them three acres of land.'

'Three acres! You can't farm on less than fifty, Norman used to say. He was a Yank – that Theo was – and they had a short fling then he went. There was a lot of that going on, girls falling for Yanks and being left high and dry. More than one child was born here who didn't look like their father, after their father came back from war, if you get my meaning.'

Yes, yes. 'The only thing Irene had left of Theo's was an engagement ring and a locket. Because their baby died.'

Philippa pushed herself up, using the sofa arm. She stumped to the kitchen, washing out her sherry glass and splashing the drainer. Ruby followed. She'd done it again, begun in good faith to communicate with Philippa, and ended up digging herself into a hole. 'It upsets you and I don't want to push you back into a panic attack, but Mum is desperate for the locket and though I've asked her not to mention it, she likely will.'

'I got a panic attack, if you call it that, because you made me think of all the people I've lost.' Philippa dragged her wrist across her forehead. It was hot in the kitchen, and she was still wearing the trousers under her dress. Had she forgotten she had them on? 'You're too young to understand what it is to be the only one left.'

Ruby acknowledged that. Being the last of your generation must be tough. 'I understand you were angry with Irene because she didn't love your brother enough.'

Philippa's response was like a tongue of flame. 'Angry? I could have torn her apart. Seeing Norman's eyes follow her around the room, for a scrap of attention, the littlest smile to make his day, it was humiliating. I hated her sometimes. She had everything.' Philippa ran water into her sherry glass and drank it down in one. 'Every damn thing on a plate. Loving parents, a nice home, friends—'

'Not everything. Her mother made her work in a place she hated. Did you know, she wanted to be a hairdresser? Her dad had to sell off his land. It wasn't a life of ease by any stretch.'

'Nobody's life was, back then. But Norman and Oak Apple dropped into her lap. But that wasn't enough. Oh no. Irene had to fish in a different pond. A darkie. I ask you!'

'That isn't an acceptable word, Philippa. Theo Robinson was a clever, gifted man who happened to be born in a cruel age of discrimination. He suffered for loving Irene, and she thought the world of him.'

'He left her, all the same, with a baby in her belly and no ring on her finger. Norman stepped in, doing the decent thing. Gave her his protection, and the baby when it was born only it was too—' Philippa stopped. They could hear Will on the other side of the door, whistling to Edna.

'Too what?' Ruby pressed. She was being unethical. Aunt Flip had consumed a schooner of sherry on top of mulled wine, giving her an appetite for confession.

'Too premature to live.'

Ruby wasn't letting that pass. 'Irene went into labour ten days early. That's not too premature.'

'Well, it died.'

'She. The baby was a girl. Irene called her Theodora. Dora for short.'

Philippa leaned towards Ruby. 'If you want your grandma's wedding ring, the one my brother gave her, walk down the fields behind Oak Apple, towards the little river. Halfway down is an old horse pond, full of weed and stink. She lobbed it in the afternoon Norman died.'

Somehow, that didn't surprise Ruby. 'You saw her do it?'

Philippa nodded. 'The undertakers had come to fetch Norman away, but they wouldn't do it without Irene being there as next of kin. I went to find her. She was by that pond and she showed me her finger and you could see where the ring had been all those years. I asked why and she said... she said...'

Ruby held her breath until it ran out. 'Said what?'

'"A prisoner will throw off his manacles, soon as he can!" She was rabbiting on, making out she'd been hard done by, when all my brother did wrong was love her. So, if you want that wedding ring back, you need to buy one of those detectorist things.'

'A metal detector?' Did they even work in ponds? Ruby had one last question. The door was opening. 'If you knew where her locket was, Auntie, would you tell me?'

Philippa's answer, when it came, was revelatory. 'Last time I saw it, I ripped it off her, broke the chain and I'm not sorry.' Philippa opened one of Will's kitchen cupboards, staring at the tins and jars. 'D'you think he has camomile tea? I know he drinks camomile. He can't sleep sometimes, on account of that girl he was with. Chummy, or something.'

'Kimmy.' Ruby suspected Philippa was playing games.

Irene had written of putting her locket where nobody would find it, but that was when she was living at Westumble

Farm. Had she found an equally good hiding place at Oak Apple? In 2001, two days after Norman's death, Irene had taken the locket to Lubbock's, asking for it to be welded shut. To keep safe whatever was inside. Safe from Philippa. And Maple Court hadn't included it on the inventory of Irene's possessions.

Will brought Edna back in as Ruby stood in the kitchen, mentally moving through every room of her home. So many places to hide a piece of jewellery. Under floorboards, within the timber-framed walls. Behind wardrobes, under the bath.

'I've got a lovely slab of local cheese at home,' she said on impulse. 'I'll fetch it. Aunt Flip, would you like me to pick up one of your herbal teas while I'm out?'

'I'd like my fig leaf, please.' Philippa held out her door key.

Ruby took it, thinking, I can be sly too.

## 53

Ruby found the fig leaf tea, then took down the French mustard pot from its high shelf. She ought to have looked inside it before. Philippa hoarded. And she liked keeping trophies. She dug out grey, solid scraps of mustard with a spoon, pitching it into the bin, but found nothing but the bottom of the jar. Clearing up, she went up to the bathroom and took out Irene's vanity case. All thumbs, she opened its secret compartments. Not very secret, they slid open easily enough. Empty, except for one thing.

A tatty, stained paper circle with a frilled edge. Staring at it, she recognised Irene's souvenir from the Café de la Libération. A dainty mat, put under a cup to stop the coffee slopping in the saucer. Ruby put it back and returned the compact case too.

In Philippa's bedroom, she searched the top of the wardrobe, the drawers and the bedside table. Nothing but reading glasses and sleeping pills. She should resign herself to never finding the locket. Unless she bought a metal detector and set about emptying that horse pond...

.  .  .

Back at Will's, clutching a wheel of local English Brie, she found him making toast for Philippa, who was sitting up at the breakfast bar. She shot Ruby a narrow glance. 'Were you caught short, dear?'

Ruby thought, Either she's psychic or a brilliant psychologist. 'Caught me, bang to rights. I went upstairs in your house, to the bathroom.'

'I know you did. Will took me outside to stretch my legs. Not for the same reason as Edna, but because I get aches in my calves. I saw a light in the landing and I thought – she can't stop poking and nosing. Can you, dear?'

Ruby accepted the charge. 'I had a sudden thought where Grandma's locket might be.'

Will shot her a sharp look.

'Did you find it?' Philippa asked.

'No. And it's not about being nosy, it's about justice. Aunt Flip, did you know Irene's Theo was given four years in a tough penitentiary in America?'

'No. Why would I?'

Will frowned. *Not now.*

Ruby climbed onto one of the bar stools. 'Sabrina Robinson-Chase, Theo's daughter, intends to clear her father's name and I want to help. What happened was, he thumped a senior officer who goaded him, and beat him. And then, for good measure, after they'd beaten him again, they threw a false charge of theft at him.'

Will put the toast in front of Philippa. 'This can wait, Ruby.'

'Sure. Sorry.' The champagne had got to her, Ruby realised. She was talking with the handbrake off. She changed the subject. 'Did the birds come with giblets?'

'What?' Will stared.

'The quails, did they come with their innards?'

'Oh, yes, they're in neat little vacuum-packed bags, in the fridge. I wasn't sure what to do with them.'

'You don't have to do anything. I'll make a red wine *jus* and, afterwards, the choice bits can be chopped up as Edna's festive treat.'

'We haven't opened our presents,' Will reminded them as Ruby cut open the vacuum pack and began the delicate task of slicing the contents. He refilled her champagne flute. 'I want to know what you've got me. D'you think your mother will be here soon?'

'Amanda's always late. Nobody ever holds dinner for her. Do you have any cooking wine?'

The clanging doorbell took Will away and Ruby heard him jab in the code. 1988. His birth year, and hers.

She heard, '*Bonjour, bonjour*, you are William? Is Ruby here?'

Hurriedly rinsing her hands under the tap, she ran to the door and flung herself into the arms of the extraordinary vision, loaded with bags, standing on the step. 'Mum!'

## 54

When Ruby had said goodbye to her mother in Laurac, Amanda's hair had been silvery grey, flowing over her shoulders. Now it was aubergine and worn in a style that could only be described as unicorn horns, one above each ear. Ruby tried to imagine how Amanda's fellow passengers had felt, sitting behind that on a plane.

'How was your flight?'

'Who cares, I'm here.' Amanda folded Ruby into another embrace, then stroked her hair. 'Beautiful girl.'

Next, formal introductions were made. 'Amanda Plait, crazy mother extraordinaire. Will Keelbrook, kind neighbour.' And lover extraordinaire.

Amanda hugged Will and Ruby saw him wince.

'You'll get used to it. When Mum hugs you, you stay hugged.'

They took Amanda's travel case into the utility room out of the way, and the French champagne she'd brought was put in the fridge. The cork on a second bottle of English sparkling popped as Amanda went to greet Philippa.

'Darling Aunt Flip, *comment ça va?*'

'If that means, am I all right, I'm fair to middling.'

Amanda had leaned down to kiss her aunt. Philippa had planted herself on the sofa again. Ruby had often noticed that Philippa's mobility fluctuated. At times she got about quite well with her tripod walking aid, and a few hours later she'd be leaning on furniture.

Amanda emptied some of the bags she'd brought in with her, and the pile of gifts next to the candlelit driftwood expanded. She apologised for the lack of gift-wrapping. 'I had to buy everything at Amsterdam airport.'

Will suggested they open their presents now and began by handing Ruby a weighty rectangular box wrapped in minimalist silver. He passed Philippa a squishy parcel.

He'd bought Ruby two bottles of Bekaa Valley wine. 'Nice,' she said. 'Thank you.'

Philippa cooed over her gift, which was a turquoise pashmina. 'You know my taste, lad. I like proper colours. Feel this.' She held out the shawl to Ruby.

'Gorgeous.'

'I never see the point of wishy-washy shades. Like red wine, do you?'

'Love it. Open yours from me, so I'm not on tenterhooks.' As Philippa unwrapped the Miss Dior, Ruby held her breath.

Philippa held up the rectangular bottle to read the label. 'Goodness. All the way from Paris?'

'No, from Boots in Hollesford.'

'It's lovely, dear, a real treat. French perfume, look, Will.'

'I see it.' He didn't mention that he'd actually bought it, and that Ruby had transferred the cost of it to his account. 'You mustn't spray that in the air and walk through it; it's too good.'

'I only do that with the ones I get off the market stall in Beccles. Thank you, Ruby.'

Will opened his gift from her. Artisan chocolates. His eyes

gleamed, a warm, amused message in them. 'You know I struggle with my sweet tooth.'

She returned his look, a flash of shorthand that promised they'd investigate the subject some time.

Philippa gave them identical boxes. 'I always buy chocolates too,' she said, before they'd even started unwrapping. 'Everyone likes chocolate and Mary Daker got them for me from a farm shop she goes to. If I'd known earlier that you were coming, Amanda, I'd have bought you some too but you'll have to make do with this.' Philippa handed Amanda a squat, cylindrical package.

Amanda unwrapped it, and smiled angelically. 'Greengage jam. Home made? Delicious, thank you.'

There was one last gift from Philippa. It was wrapped in shiny pink paper with a ribbon rosette on the top. 'For a special girl,' Philippa said. 'Ruby, fetch it up, would you?'

The box weighed little and when Philippa said, 'It's something I had in my jewel box, which I'd forgotten about,' Ruby couldn't help looking at her mother. Amanda, catching her eye, sat forward.

'Let Will open it,' Philippa said.

Ruby handed the box over, impatient because Will unwrapped it without ripping the paper. A small, hard-shelled box appeared, the kind an old-fashioned watch would be kept in. He couldn't work its finicky catch so he handed it to Ruby.

She flipped it open and saw inside a small gold disc. Picking it up, holding it to the light, she could see that something was inscribed on it.

'It's for Edna,' Philippa said. 'To hang off her collar. She was a puppy farm bitch before Will rescued her and got her spayed. I reckon she deserves a medal.'

The disc had Edna's name on it and the words, 'I'm Done'.

Ruby couldn't stop laughing.

Next, Amanda handed the bags she'd brought to each of

them. Will's contained a Lego set, a Bugatti Chiron sports car to assemble from pieces.

His mouth fell open. 'Wow... incredible.'

He meant it too, Ruby saw.

Philippa's gift was a carved teak wood box. 'That's very special, dear. Thank you.'

Ruby's was a bracelet set with crystals. 'Because you are my shining star,' Amanda told her.

'It's lovely,' Ruby breathed. How much had her mum spent in one airport shopping sweep?

'And one last little thing.' Amanda handed her a paper bag from a shop called The Ancestor People. Inside was a DNA testing kit. 'I thought it was time you found out who your father is, Ruby. I would like to know too.'

Talk about a conversation stopper. The ensuing silence was so profound, they could hear Edna breathing and the quails browning in the oven.

'Good thought,' Ruby managed.

'I had always imagined myself undergoing deep hypnosis to remember the night I conceived you,' Amanda went on blithely. 'But I had drunk tea laced with who-knows-what, so no hypnosis was ever going to bring back the memory of your father.'

Ruby knew Will was looking at her. She met his eye. 'I warned you, didn't I?'

He burst out laughing. 'But not quite enough.'

Amanda bent down and hugged Edna, who was sniffing her knee. 'I did not know about you, beautiful girl, or I would have bought you something.'

'Like a toy drone, or a full-sized Toblerone?' Will asked.

'I've got her something.' Ruby remembered the beef jerky. It had fallen behind Will's driftwood sculpture.

It was after they'd gathered up all the bags and given Edna one piece of jerky that Ruby noticed a voice message on her phone. It came from a number she didn't recognise and she went into the utility room to listen to it in peace.

'Hi, erm, uh. This is difficult. Probably shouldn't have drunk three glasses of Baileys post-lunch.'

The caller was a mature-sounding woman, with a London accent.

'I got your number from Sabrina, who is... hang on. Sorry—'

The message was interrupted as the caller shouted to someone else in the room, 'Alex, get your head out of your tablet and help your brother put his model together. What? Because I'm your gran and my word is law. No, your mum can't – er, because she's breastfeeding twins? Yeah, I know, lamest excuse ever.'

The voice came back to the phone. 'Sorry, domestic chaos. Where was I – no, drat. I have to go. I'll call later. Oh, and my name is Parkinson. Barbara Parkinson. And I'm the one who got adopted. I'm the daughter of Theo Robinson and Irene Plait.'

## 55

Irene and Theo's daughter had died at birth. Irene had told Theo so. It's what Philippa had said too. Barbara Parkinson. Who the hell?

*'I'm the one that got adopted.'*

Ruby walked slowly into the main room and played the message to Will, first beckoning him into a corner of the kitchen where they wouldn't be seen by Philippa or Amanda, who sat each end of the long sofa, each locked in their own thoughts. Ruby hardly let Will listen, because she was on hot bricks with impatience. 'It's a London accent, right?'

He agreed, it sounded like it. 'Let me listen through.'

She saw him smile at the interaction between Barbara and Alex – a grandson? Then he jolted. 'Your gran's baby with Theo was adopted. I thought it—'

'Died.' Ruby nodded. 'Me too. Sabrina Robinson-Chase sent me Irene's last letter to Theo, after their last meeting. Did I say? He was in Paris, performing there, and she managed to see him. She spilled out her sadness. She also described giving birth to a stillborn child in a bedroom at Oak Apple Farm.'

'You didn't tell me that.'

'I'm never sure how much you want to know. Irene was in labour far too long – she should have gone to hospital, but I suppose it was before the days of proper neo-natal care. Doctors simply struggled on... She bled out and nearly died. And Philippa told me point blank that the baby – Irene and Theo's daughter – was too premature to live.'

'Who is Barbara Parkinson then?'

'She says she got my number from Sabrina... Robinson-Chase, presumably. If she'd made contact with Sabrina, then it's possible Barbara is who she says she is. Sabrina's half-sister. Theo and Irene's daughter.'

'Your mother's half-sister, too.'

Ruby leaned against the kitchen countertop. 'It's insane. I thought I'd had all the shocks I was owed for one year.'

'Will you share this with Amanda?'

Ruby shook her head. 'Not this minute. I know Mum so well, even a hint of an adopted half-sibling, she'll go into overdrive.'

After listening to the message again, Will identified Barbara Parkinson's accent more closely. 'South London, somebody who has lived within the Black community for a while, I'd say. I did my degree at Goldsmiths, in south-east London, so I got familiar with the accents.' He handed her phone back. 'Will you return the call?'

Ruby blew out her cheeks. What if it turned out to be a scam? Or a case of mistaken identity? 'This isn't the day to open the closet and invite the family skeletons to tumble out. I'll tell Mum tonight, then I'll call the number. Just not now.'

Will put his hands on her arms. 'You're shivering. Shall I turn up the thermostat?'

'It's more than warm enough. I'm thrown. It's too much. Will, give me something else to think about.'

'Like this?'

She ended up with her back against a cupboard, poleaxed

by a desire that threatened their self-control. She clung to him, her hands finding an anchor against his shoulders. The fact that Amanda and Philippa sat only at the other end of the open-plan room gave the situation an edge of tension.

Will pulled back and looked deep into her eyes. 'I could bundle you into the pantry, but I'm not going to.'

She laughed anxiously, keeping the sound inside, so he felt rather than heard it. 'I've just had a thought,' she said.

'That we run over to Oak Apple?'

'No! I'll call Sabrina and check Barbara out.' She reached for her phone. 'What time is it in Savannah, Georgia?'

Will took the phone off her. 'It's Christmas morning over there. They'll be having breakfast, or going to church. Or enjoying a lie-in. You can't call Sabrina now.'

Ruby gave a deflated sigh.

'Later, you can go up to my office and use the landline. It's more private. For now, I agree, we keep this quiet. The day's going really well.'

Lunch was a triumph. Too full after the main course to go straight on to cheese, coffee and chocolates, Will suggested a quick walk, 'Before the King.'

Philippa demurred and it was he, Ruby and Amanda who took the dog out for a bracing fifteen minutes. They met at least a dozen other dog walkers and Amanda's unicorn hairstyle caused quite some interest, and she introduced herself to everyone as 'Irene and Norman's prodigal daughter, from Oak Apple'.

Ruby picked up a wistfulness in her mother's tone. Did Amanda regret that for most of her life she had seen Flixfield as a trap containing only painful memories? On impulse, Ruby said, 'If I were to live here, you could come every spring and autumn. You always said those were the best seasons.'

Amanda raised an eyebrow. 'But you won't live here, darling. There's no work here. Oh – I forgot to say. I have your knives.'

Ruby stopped dead. 'My chef's knives? How?'

'I knew how much you missed them, so I called on Didier on my way to the airport. He was so shocked to see me. I think because I had a suitcase, he was terrified I'd come to move in with him. I let him believe it for a few minutes, for fun. After that, he boxed up your knives just to get rid of me.'

'How did you get them through customs?'

'They went in my suitcase, into the hold. That's why I was a little late, waiting for it to clear at Norwich. Didier wants something in return.'

'Let me guess. The figures for Maurice Bouchard?'

'I said you would send them.' Amanda turned her eyes on Will, who was throwing a stick for Edna on a patch of green. 'It's time to move on.'

'If you mean Will, we're enjoying the moment.'

'Voilà! In the moment is a good place to be. Take off your glove – no, the left one.'

Ruby did as she was asked, confused.

'See?'

'What, Mum?'

'No engagement ring. That tells me there is no place in your life for sulky Didier and his overpriced jumpers. Yes?'

Ruby pulled her glove back on. 'Yes. All right. You win.'

## 56

They got home as the light began to fade.

Philippa was fretful, because the King spoke at three and it was seven minutes to.

'It's all right, Auntie. Televisions don't need twenty minutes to warm up these days,' Will said, finding the channel. 'I'm going to get the cheeseboard out.'

Amanda offered to do that, and make coffee. 'I don't mind your king, but listening to any man talk uninterrupted for twenty minutes makes me edgy.'

'He's your king too,' Philippa snapped back. 'You aren't French, Amanda, however much of an accent you put on. You were born and bred here in Suffolk. And why have you put your hair up in Devil's horns? And the colour. I'd have thought you'd have known better, after that business with Violet's funeral.' Philippa turned to Ruby. 'Your mother turned up with bright purple hair, which upset the whole family.'

'You told me, Aunt Flip.'

'Amethyst,' Amanda corrected. 'And it was you who convinced everyone I'd done it to insult my grandmother's memory. It wasn't meant to come out so bright; it was a mistake.'

She explained to Ruby, 'I cut it all off, and went to the funeral looking as if I'd had a terrible accident,' then shook her head at Philippa. 'If you had let me alone, nobody would have minded.'

Philippa wasn't having it. 'Your mother minded. Irene never forgave you.'

'Because you went on and on about it.'

Ruby squeezed Amanda's arm warningly. 'Go make that coffee.'

Will cleared his throat. 'The King's about to start.' He sat down next to Philippa.

Amanda touched Ruby's shoulder.

'What, Mum?'

'Is this a good moment to visit Oak Apple Farm? I'd like to take my first step inside, get it over with.'

Ruby nodded. 'Let's leave these two in peace,' she said. 'I'll take you over the road and show you my new woodburner.'


In the dining hall, Amanda strode to the inglenook, stroking the holly wreath Ruby had hung there. 'The stove is lovely.'

'Thanks.'

'Those books on the table...'

'Grandma's diaries. I found them, half burned outside.'

'Outside? Go on.'

Ruby said, 'They were in a suitcase and I thought maybe my tenants had decided to use them for a Bonfire Night blaze, but now I'm not so sure.'

'Philippa. Course it was.' Amanda went to the table, and picked one of the diaries up. 'After you went back to France and Mother went to Maple Court, I couldn't get rid of her. Poking about, putting things in the bin, as though she wanted to erase everything about Mother. Not my father, no, no, not Norman. Just Irene.'

'It figures, but she has her reasons.'

'Oh?' Amanda shot Ruby a wry look. 'Is love softening your heart? Philippa is poison, always was. Do you know, many, many years ago, she said something that completely upended my life. She changed everything I believed in, and I'm not being dramatic.'

Of course, Ruby needed to know more.

Amanda pulled out a chair, sat down and picked up another of the diaries. She turned the book in her hands, like an oversized worry-bead. 'I'd be about fourteen. Difficult age. Philippa found me crying down in the fields. I was in trouble with Mum and frightened to go back in the house. Philippa didn't comfort me, and bear in mind, she was a grown woman by then, married. She said to me, "You know your mother doesn't love you."'

'God.' Ruby pulled out another chair, sitting so that her knees touched Amanda's.

'I knew that well enough anyway. But she went on, "Want to know why? Because you're the wrong baby. You spoiled her life and that's why she can't love you. It's why my brother, Norman, never looks at you." "My brother, Norman", not "your father". "You ruined their marriage." And that wasn't fair! My dad adored me. He was the one who picked me up as a toddler and bathed my knees when I fell over. Mum hardly touched me, except to brush my hair, too hard. Dad let me ride on his shoulders. He called me "Mandy", which Mum hated. But after Philippa said what she said, I couldn't look him in the eye. With those few words, she destroyed everything.' Fiercely brushing away tears, Amanda took a long, sweeping glance around the dining hall. 'You want me to be kind to her, Ruby, and I am trying, but some things are hard to forgive. She is cruel.'

'Come and look at this.' Ruby took her mother into the sitting room, opening the little cupboard, shining her phone torch on the scratches inside. 'Touch them; they're quite deep.'

Amanda crouched down, hitching the flowing skirts of her pinafore dress. 'What made these? Ugh, not a rat?'

'A child. Philippa was shut in there by her guardian, Elsie Binney.'

'Elsie, that old lady who died when I was about ten? She was unpleasant.' Amanda peered into the cupboard. 'But you couldn't get a child in there.'

'"Little Flip", remember. And there is worse. Elsie used to burn Philippa's back with the tip of a poker, where it wouldn't be seen.'

'But that's terrible!'

'It's why Philippa has her demons. Abuse can make people cruel, and desperate.'

Amanda stood up. 'Close that door.' They walked back into the dining hall, and Amanda returned to the table, this time opening one of the diaries. '*Mon dieu*, you need a magnifying glass for this!'

'I have one.'

'This is all my mother's work?'

'Yes, Irene's private diaries, from when she was in her late teens, to the day she married Grandad.'

'Does she say where she hid her locket?'

'I haven't got there if it does.'

'It is under stones. I know it.' Amanda tapped her brow. 'I keep seeing it in my dreams and I want it, Ruby. Can you understand? I got no love from my mother, and the fact that she meant me to have something so precious to her, it means everything! I can wear it and pretend I mattered to her, just a little bit.'

'You mattered an awful lot more than that to Irene.' Ruby put her arms around Amanda's waist and they leaned into each other. 'Did you know that Irene – Grandma – fell in love with a Black soldier during the war?'

'Sort of. People in the village whispered about it, so I picked up the rumour. She never spoke a word. Is it in the diary?'

'Yes,' Ruby said. 'In graphic detail. When I can, I'll transcribe every page for you. But there's something I need to say.' She had told Will she wouldn't break the latest news but with her mother's tears in her hair, she couldn't hold back. 'Did you know she had a baby by Theo, the soldier? Well, he was an engineer, but also a soldier.'

'What?' Amanda stepped back. Her face beneath the horns of twisted hair grew round with astonishment. 'I knew she'd had a stillbirth. Village gossips know everybody's business, even their medical records. It was the soldier's baby? Mixed race, then.'

'I guess so. Yes. But it died.'

'I would have a brother or sister! Ruby, how sad.'

'A sister. Only...' Ruby hesitated. If Barbara Parkinson was a hoaxer, or a confused fantasist, she was about to muddy the waters even further.

'Only what, *chérie*?'

'I had a phone message today from someone who might be her.'

'How, if she died?'

'What if she didn't, and somebody made a mistake at the time of her birth... or lied?' A pulse drummed in Ruby's ears. It would have been more than a lie to tell Irene after that gruelling labour, 'Your baby was too premature to live.' It would have been a grievous abuse.

'You're saying the baby girl lived?' Amanda bit the side of her finger, as if this was too much to take in.

'It's possible. Would you be OK if I follow up?'

Amanda gaped. 'You're asking permission to find my sister? Of course you have it. Who is she, what's her name, where does she live?'

'Her name is Barbara.'

'Barbara!'

'I don't know yet where she lives. London, I think. And, Mum, please, before you go completely wild with excitement, she is six years older than you.'

'I have an older sister called Barbara!'

'Which makes her seventy-eight years old. We have to be sensitive. She's spent a lifetime not knowing her birth parents.' Ruby corrected herself. 'Not knowing who her mother is, anyway.'

Amanda waved that away. 'If she has any sense, she will have done a DNA test and discovered her father's relations at least.'

'I'm sure that's how she found Sabrina, Theo's daughter from his marriage.'

'Theo had a daughter too?' Amanda hugged herself and spun. 'And I never knew it. Ah, Ruby, I should have done a test years ago, then my DNA data would have been there, and Barbara could have tracked me down.'

'Well, she seems to have done so now.' Ruby's phone buzzed. A message from Will:

*The King has finished. Coffee is made.*

They left, locking up.

'When will you call Barbara?' Amanda asked as they crossed the unlit road.

'Soon,' Ruby promised. 'But Mum, please, Philippa doesn't know. So keep this quiet.'

'Yes, yes, I promise.'

As they approached Westumble Barn, Ruby voiced two questions. Who had smuggled a baby out of the house as Irene lay slipping in and out of consciousness from blood loss? And who, when she was in a fit state to be told, had said brazenly, 'She died. So sorry.'

'Who do you think?' Amanda said bitterly. 'It is always family. They forge secrets, then take them to the grave. There's only one person left alive who can tell us the truth.'

## 57

Will brought the cheeseboard to the table. 'Not merely selected but *curated*,' he told them. 'I suggest you work clockwise from Suffolk Gold to Baron Bigod by way of the maple smoked goat's cheese.'

He opened a bottle of cognac and, after one mouthful, Amanda forgot her promise of discretion. She fixed her gaze on Philippa. Ruby mouthed, 'Not now. Please.' Amanda seemed to get the message and the peace might have lasted, had Philippa not also been coming down off her sherry-fuelled high.

The trigger was Amanda cutting a slice of the Brie and saying, 'English cheese has improved a thousand times since I left Suffolk. It used to be hard and yellow or hard and orange and both tasted the same.'

'I don't like people talking down their country.' Philippa sniffed.

'I'm not talking down my country, and by the way, I have dual citizenship, like Ruby.' Amanda added a smile to reassure Ruby she wasn't going to take Philippa's bait. 'I have never underestimated British produce. People in Gascony fight to get

English and Welsh lamb. But even you must admit, Aunt Flip, Suffolk cheese in the 1970s was uninspired.'

'Ram some pickle on, it tasted all right to me.'

'You win. I will admit, with an inch of pickle on top, it was fine.'

'We drank English champagne earlier,' Will reminded Amanda. 'You were impressed.'

Amanda agreed. 'It was very good but give me a bottle of ruby-red Gascon wine any day of the week.'

'Is that why you called this girl Ruby?' Philippa threw at her.

Still holding her good temper, Amanda laughed. 'No! I called her Ruby because "Ruby Tuesday" by the Stones was the first single I ever bought. It's about a girl who is free. She comes and goes. I wanted my daughter to choose her life, and not for one moment imagine she was second-best.' *Second-best* was emphasised.

'Lucky her,' Philippa said.

'Yes. You and I were not so lucky.' Amanda had light blue eyes, but they gained a piercing focus. 'My gift to Ruby is never to have confined her or shut her in.'

'Mum, stop it,' Ruby said.

Philippa fixed Amanda with an equally steely gaze. 'You might go a bit further and tell your daughter who her father is.'

Ruby clamped her teeth together. Couldn't Philippa recognise an olive branch when it was offered?

'You saw me give her a DNA testing kit,' Amanda said lightly.

'Well, I don't know what one of those is, but I do know that Ruby deserves to know who fathered her.'

'The passion that created my daughter came after a night of dancing at a festival in the West Country, where it gets very dark. That, and forest flora, ensured I didn't see him too well.'

'I don't know what you're saying.' Philippa was impatient.

'She means magic mushrooms,' Ruby said wearily. 'I know how I got conceived, Auntie, and it isn't a problem.'

'Well, it ought to be and it's sinful, mushrooms and dancing and making babies out of wedlock.' Philippa knocked her fist on the table. 'Sinful.'

Will got to his feet. 'Aunt Flip, if you're tired, I'm happy to take you home. Would you like your bed?'

'No. I'm not a baby.'

Will sat down. He glanced at Ruby, seeking help.

She said, 'I'll make you a fig tea. How about it?'

On her way to the kitchen, she gave her mother a light jab on the shoulder. Button it.

But Amanda was past picking up hints. 'There's a woman living in London who might have liked to know her mother when she was a child, Philippa.'

Ruby turned to see what damage that remark had caused. A flush was coursing through Philippa's cheeks.

'What do you mean?' Philippa gasped. 'What are you saying?'

Ruby said to Will, 'Can I put on some music?' Thinking it might help divert attention away from this dangerous subject.

'Sure. Ask the Bluetooth for whatever you'd like.'

'None of your modern stuff,' Philippa said instantly. 'It hurts my ears.'

'Classical?' Ruby suggested.

'Not that either. It goes on too long.'

Ruby instructed the Bluetooth speaker to play music from the '40s and '50s. That ought to hit the spot for Philippa.

'Playing relaxing tracks from the golden age of swing,' the speaker obligingly responded. The air filled with a crooning clarinet over the steam train chug of saxophones. 'Moonlight Serenade'. It worked. Philippa slipped into a different state of consciousness. 'That's what I call proper music.'

When it finished, she said, 'I remember that coming over

the wireless at Oak Apple, Irene sitting in her chair with her eyes closed. She was very pregnant, not moving around much.'

'Pregnant with me?' Amanda asked. 'Or with Barbara?'

Philippa recoiled.

'Who was on clarinet?' Will asked, in a desperate attempt to steer the ship from the rocks. 'Benny Goodman? Ask the speaker.'

For the first time in Ruby's hearing, Philippa snapped at Will. 'Glenn Miller, of course.' She'd misunderstood his question. Bluetooth gave the answer as Wilbur Schwartz.

Will got to his feet and, between them, he and Ruby cleared the table. He ran water over the plates and muttered, 'Would it be unethical to inject them both with some kind of tranquiliser?'

'I keep telling Mum to shut up.' Ruby made more coffee and they went back to the table as the radio station host lined up another song.

'I love a rummage in the archive and I've got a special treat for you now,' went the man's whispery voice. 'Taking you back to the early fifties with a piece that's my current all-time favourite... until the next favourite comes along. It's by a band who went by the name of the Jake Hendrick Five—'

Ruby stiffened. No. Surely not.

Philippa looked as though she had seen – or heard – a ghost.

'—and the song is called "Irene".'

*There's a face I see when I walk with the moon,*
*A feeling I get of a hand dragged from mine.*
*Irene... Irene, fair as a dream.*

Will placed his hand on his godmother's shoulder. 'Ruby, could you grab Philippa a glass of water.'

From the Bluetooth speaker, the host announced, 'That was "Irene", written by Theo Robinson, arranged by Jake Hendrick.

The Jake Hendrick Five played in Paris in the summer of 1950, at the famous Rose Noire nightclub in Montmartre, and at Le Hot Brick Club too. Oh, to have been there.'

As if lightning had struck, Ruby was suddenly certain that she knew where Irene had hidden her locket. She rose from her seat only for Philippa, who had been silent all through the song, to say something that made leaving impossible.

'I was there when Irene had Theo's baby,' Philippa said as clearly as if giving a statement in court. 'I was there.'

## 58

## PHILIPPA

The midwife was murmuring encouragement as Irene panted in disjointed rhythm. It was mid-afternoon and stifling in the bedroom. They weren't allowed to open the window because of the flies. Irene, hours now in labour, was red-faced and sweating. Her lips were pulled back with pain, her eyes unnaturally bright.

Philippa, just ten years old and scared, had been summoned to take over for a while from Violet, who had been with her daughter since seven o'clock the previous night. Philippa knew the midwife was worried from the way she kept telling Irene, 'Just you do your breathing, my angel. Baby's keeping us waiting, but I've seen this many a time. Hannibal got his elephants over the Alps, so we'll get baby out in due course.'

A pretty rotten thing to say, Philippa thought, elephants and Alps, when Irene was trying to push a real baby out from her down-below. She'd never known before now how babies came into the world, but then, she was little and nobody told her anything.

This baby didn't want to be born. No surprise since everybody knew it was going to be a coloured cuckoo in Norman's nest. She'd heard some women saying it, after church last week. They hadn't noticed Philippa crouching behind a stone cross, earwigging. Norman kept saying that because Irene was so fair, the baby wouldn't be all that dark-skinned. It would quite likely have blue eyes too. 'It'll be a bit swarthy, like me,' he'd said only last night. 'Like me, after a summer working out in the fields.'

Ronnie Gifford, who was a sneaky little rat, had said as how the baby would be black and white, like a carthorse. Either way, Philippa didn't want it around. She liked it here at Oak Apple Farm, looking after Norman because Irene was too pregnant and too sick. Even when she wasn't big as a barrel, Irene wasn't much of a hand at housekeeping. Norman would sometimes say, 'I don't know how we'd manage without you, Little Flip.' Horrid Aunt Elsie had moved into Westumble, to help Auntie Violet look after Uncle John, and that meant she, Philippa, was free of her. For now, anyway.

Everybody said these days what a poppet she was. Norman talked to her properly, now. Only, once the baby was here, and everyone was pointing at it and calling it a cuckoo, they'd stop noticing her again. It always happened.

'Is she having it yet?'

Irene was thrashing her head side to side and the midwife was asking her if 'another contraction' was coming.

'It's my back,' Irene groaned. 'Feels like someone's splitting my spine open with nutcrackers. When's it going to stop?'

'Soon, my angel, soon enough.' The midwife said Irene wasn't anywhere near fully dilated. Whatever that meant. Philippa was sent down to make them a cup of tea and when she brought it up, the midwife forgot to change her worried look for a cheery one. She turned to Philippa and said, 'Fetch Dr Mickleson. Tell him, nothing too urgent, just a little check-up, to be on the safe side. Would you hurry, dear?'

Philippa hadn't gone immediately because as she turned away, she noticed the lipstick-and-powder case Irene had been given last Christmas. It was on top of Irene's chest of drawers. Philippa couldn't resist a peep to see if that locket was inside, the one Irene had worn on her wedding day. Philippa had sneaked quietly into Irene's room when everyone was waiting for Irene to come downstairs, and had watched her fasten the clasp behind her neck. Irene had moaned in a voice like a hurt animal, 'I'm sorry, Theo.'

Philippa had told Norman about it and he'd said, 'Something old, something new, something borrowed. That's what it is. Something borrowed, for luck.'

The vanity case was empty, but for face powder and a puff. To Dr Mickleson's she went. He was at home and, on seeing her, he nodded. 'Come along, hop in the car.' And so Philippa had her first ever ride in a motor vehicle. Only about one minute's worth, but exciting.

Once the doctor was there, Philippa was kept out of the bedroom. Sitting on the bottom stair, she heard Irene screaming. *Blorting* was the word, like a cow birthing an oversized bullock. A terrible sound. Violet came down for some water, without wiping her tears away. Norman paced in the dining hall, only stopping to ask Auntie Violet, 'How's it going?'

'Not good, Norman,' Violet had whispered, not realising Philippa had moved closer. 'Doctor's using forceps and I can't bear my girl in such pain.'

'The baby?'

'Any minute.' Violet filled her jug and hurried back upstairs.

No sooner was she gone, they heard the wail of a newborn. Norman had rushed to the stairs, telling Philippa, 'Bide here.'

She got up on a chair so she could hear through the floorboards what they were saying in the room above. She heard the baby crying. Then Norman came down, blood down his shirt sleeves, running out and not even closing the door. Later,

Philippa discovered he'd gone to the doctor's house, to telephone for an ambulance. The ambulance came after a while,
bells jangling. Irene went out on a stretcher, eyes tight closed.
Violet went with her.

The midwife had come down carrying the baby wrapped in
a shawl. It was like a little doll, with dark, wispy hair and eyes
black as liquorice twists. Philippa asked what the funny dents
were, either side of the baby's face.

'Forceps marks, dear. This little one didn't want to arrive.' A
tiny fist clenched above the shawl. Skin smooth and brown, the
fingernails like pink shells.

Dr Mickleson had followed the midwife down the stairs,
and Philippa trailed him to his car. 'Where's the baby going?'
she asked.

'To the best place. Run along, dear.'

Later, Auntie Violet came back from the hospital, where
Irene had to stay. When Philippa asked where the baby had
gone, she said, 'I'm afraid the poor little dear died. It's God's
will and for the best.'

Philippa replied that she'd seen the baby with its eyes open.
Seen it move its hand.

'She died.' Auntie Violet grew very stern.

Later, when Philippa said the same thing to Norman, he
didn't answer for a long time. Then he told her to come out with
him, and to bring a carrot for the horse. By the stable door, as
the big Suffolk horse crunched and dropped bits onto the
ground, he said, 'Baby couldn't stay here, Little Flip. It wasn't
possible.'

'Because it's going to die?' She was pleased the baby had
gone, but felt sorry for it too.

'No, because baby wouldn't have been happy here. She's
going somewhere to be looked after, by people who will love
her.'

'Until she dies?'

Norman stroked the horse's broad nose and the creature breathed contentedly at him. 'That's right. Until she dies.'

'How do you know they'll love her?' Aunt Elsie didn't love *her*, Philippa knew well.

'Dr Mickleson will make certain of it. He knows how things work.'

Philippa said that Auntie Violet thought the baby was already dead. 'Only I saw it open its little hand. It has pink skin under its fingers but the creases are brown.' She showed Norman her own palms. 'Is that why it can't live here?'

'We're not going to talk about it, Flip. When Irene comes home, we have to be kind and not mention it. Not ever. If she asks, you will say it died. Do you understand, Little Flip?'

She didn't, really, but because Norman asked her, she agreed and soon, the liquorice-black eyes, the tiny coral-shell fingernails, were something she supposed she'd imagined.

Irene had cried. Dear Lord, how she had cried. And for a while afterwards, she had to go to a place called Thewell Park. Irene always believed her baby was stillborn because Dr Mickleson had said so.

Philippa had eventually believed it too. Until a fine May morning many years later.

## 59

SATURDAY 23 MAY 1987

Philippa was married to Ronnie by then, and living at Westumble Farm. She had walked over to Oak Apple that morning as Norman had hurt his leg falling over the grass harrow. The injury had formed into an ulcer. Irene needed help changing his dressings.

They were in the lounge at Oak Apple Farm, where a bed had been set up as he couldn't make the stairs. Philippa was watching Irene bathe the wound with warm salt water, when she heard a car coming up the drive.

'That'll be the postman,' Norman grumbled. It annoyed him that the postie only drove to the gate these days, then reversed back down the drive again, rather than walk to the house.

When they heard a rap at the front door, Philippa said she'd go. 'Probably wants something signed for. Irene, don't you make that wound too wet.'

Only it wasn't the postie standing on the brick path but a woman, maybe in her late thirties or early forties. A stranger at any rate, and Philippa gaped at her. See, you never saw a Black person in Flixfield. Not since the war, not really.

This lady wasn't exactly Black, not like, say, Floella Benjamin on the telly. This visitor was what folk called 'mixed race' and because she was wearing a suit and a white blouse, Philippa reckoned she was canvassing for the general election in June. She looked to see what colour rosette the woman was wearing, but she wasn't wearing one. Nor did she hold out a leaflet.

*Oh, no*, Philippa thought. Not one of the 'End Is Nigh' brigade, trying to convert me. She began, 'Sorry, dear, we're strictly Church of England,' when the woman made a nervous movement of the hands. A clench of the fists, opening them up to show a glimpse of pink palm. Philippa knew. She just knew.

'I'm Barbara Parkinson.' The woman's accent wasn't from round here. 'That's my married name, but I was raised Barbara Leach. Are you...' She gazed up at the farmhouse's uneven windows and staunch chimney pots as if they made no sense. 'Are you Irene?'

Philippa had dreaded this moment for over four decades, knowing at some deep level that it would arrive. A lifelong lie, exposed to the light.

Irene would curse them. Irene would break. It would be Thewell Park all over again, except that that place had been knocked down. So goodness knows where Irene would be sent this time.

Philippa made a choice on the spot. 'I'm Mrs Philippa Gifford.'

That stalled Barbara Parkinson for a moment. But she had the gumption to press on. 'Do you know of Irene Plait, though? This was her address. I was born here. The adoption people gave it to me.'

'When?'

The woman gave a jerky, embarrassed smile. 'More than ten

years ago. I've only just plucked up the courage to come. This is where Irene is... was?' The question shivered with hope.

Philippa slowly shook her head. 'I don't think so, dear. My family's been here six generations, so I reckon I'd know Irene Plait if she'd ever lived here.'

'But this is Flixfield? I know this is Oak Apple Farm, because I read the sign on the gate. I was born here, but I was adopted from a children's home in Hollesford, a few miles away.'

'Like I say, there's no Plaits here. D'you suppose there could have been a mistake? Why don't you ask at the place where you say you were adopted?'

'It's gone. It was run by the church and closed down eight years ago.' A bleakness entered the woman's eyes. Eyes dark and troubled. 'This is the address on my file.' She turned a sheet of paper, so Philippa could see. It was an official letter, rather crumpled, and Philippa could easily imagine it sitting in this woman's drawer for ten years – taken out, breathed upon, put back again a hundred times. 'Please, try to think,' Barbara urged her.

Philippa looked down the drive, at the car parked halfway up. She needed this woman gone before Irene came to see what was keeping her. 'Sorry, dear. The last baby born in this house was me in 1934.' She shut the door, leaving no room for doubt.

'Have we got a letter?' Irene asked as Philippa came back into the lounge. For a moment, Philippa saw again those slim brown hands holding out the proof of her birth. *Irene Plait, Oak Apple Farm.*

'No letter,' Philippa said. 'It was someone asking if she could rely on my vote next month. I said I'd vote for any party that cleared the ditches on Hut Lane. How are we doing for saline dressings, Irene? No, don't wrap that bandage too tight! Let me go again with it. You go put the kettle on.'

· · ·

Rosemary Clooney was singing over the Bluetooth speaker. 'Stay with me...'

Will told the speaker to shut up. 'Let me get this right, Aunt Flip. Irene's child came looking for her mother and you told her she'd got the wrong house?'

Philippa looked wretched, but she'd gone past the moment of panic and meekly nodded. 'Yes, I did.'

Amanda spoke in a voice dry as splinters. 'My father told my mother that her baby had died? You, my grandmother, the doctor, the midwife – you all conspired.'

'Not me. I was a child.'

'You all lied in the cruellest way possible.' Amanda was struggling to maintain composure.

Ruby laid her arms around her mother's shoulders.

'We had to!' Philippa shrilled. 'You can make something true if you tell yourself often enough. Even Norman began to believe it, and so did Auntie Violet till the day she died.'

'But *you* knew,' Amanda said, her voice cracking. 'You looked into that baby's eyes and met the same baby forty years later. And lied again!'

'What could I do? It was for the best. The little scrap wouldn't have thrived here.'

'That's bullshit.' Will sounded disgusted. 'Say it how it is, Aunt Flip. She was given away because she was too Black.'

Philippa's voice rose to a beseeching pitch. 'It wouldn't have been happy, that's what Norman said. It was found a lovely family.'

'You don't know that!' Something in Will's voice made Ruby stretch out to touch his arm. Will controlled himself, but only just. 'That baby might have gone to a children's home, left in a cot to cry herself hoarse. She might have been abused. Norman invented a cosy falsehood to make himself feel better. He didn't want a cuckoo in the nest, a child people would look at and say, "We know what your missus was up to."'

'That's right,' Philippa answered desperately. 'That's exactly what people would have said.'

'But he married Irene promising to protect her baby. When it came to it, he backed out.'

'He was human. Will, don't get up.' Philippa tried to get up too but hadn't the strength. 'Oh, my boy, don't go.'

Will went upstairs where Ruby found him, in his office, switching his computer on.

'Do you want to be alone?'

'Come in, shut the door.' He looked as though he'd been punched. With one finger, he typed in his password and opened up a search engine. 'This is not the side of me I want you to see.'

'I want to see all sides, Will. But look – whatever she's done in her life, Philippa loves you like her own. Don't lose sight of that.'

'She lied all those years, Ruby.'

'I know.' There was no excuse, no rabbits to pull from hats. Philippa had always sided with Norman and seeing the baby go had suited her too. 'She's caused massive destruction and not only to poor Barbara, but listen.' Ruby perched on the edge of the desk, pressing three fingers lightly against Will's shoulder. He was shaking, she discovered. This went deep. 'She was a child of ten. Those making the decisions, the grown-ups, they're all dead. Let's not crucify Philippa because she's the only one left standing.'

He nodded. 'It's how things were done. I know. Spirit the baby away, get it adopted, pretend it never happened.' He typed into the search line, summoning Theo Robinson's Wiki page. 'Don't you see, Ruby, that if Philippa had spoken the truth to Barbara in May 1987, she'd have had the chance not only to meet her mother, but her father too.' He pointed to the side bar: 12 November 1987. The date of Theo's death. 'It's too late now for her to know either of them. If I were her, I would be incandescently enraged.'

Ruby said, 'Barbara is in communication with Theo's other daughter. And now with me. It's not all hopeless.'

He rubbed an eyebrow. 'I suppose. Barbara is still looking for Irene, and if she's talked to Sabrina since you spoke to her, then she knows Irene is dead. Happy Christmas.'

'It could yet be,' Ruby said. 'She'll find another half-sister – my mum. Barbara has a family, from the sound of things, so we get a new set of relations too. We're still here.'

'Yeah.'

'Philippa only has you, Will.'

'I know.' He gripped her hand in both of his, more tightly than he realised. 'What I can't stop thinking is, if Philippa lied all those years to Irene, did she lie to me?'

'About what – about your mother?'

'Not about Mum. I was nearly eleven when Mum died, so I know how it was. About my father. Vince Keelbrook from Manitoba, Canada, the no-hoper who didn't want contact. Only, what if he did? What if he wrote to me and Aunt Flip burned the letters?'

What could she say? 'You need to find your dad, then, Will.'

'How?'

'Facebook. Or you can use my DNA test. Plug away, till you get a result.' Ruby stroked Will's head, kissing the place where a distinct crown was forming on his scalp. 'Barbara managed it.'

Will got up abruptly, making his chair swivel. 'I've just thought. About two months ago... early November, after Storm Marion... Your tenants had left overnight. The postman told Aunt Flip, "They're gone, leaving windows open." She and I went to check. She had a key, naturally.'

'I know she did.'

Will drifted for a moment, then found his thread. 'We went in and closed the windows. Emptied the fridge. They'd done a bunk, basically, left dog food in a bowl on the floor and the bath filthy. They'd also left the heating on full, so I went to reset the timer. I was tinkering with the dial when I heard the landline ring. This weird, old-fashioned jangling through the house. Philippa answered and I heard her say, "Oak Apple Farm, who's speaking?" Then a silence until she said, "There is no Irene Plait here. You have the wrong number." I sorted the thermostat and found her shaking like she'd seen a ghost. She said she'd had a nasty turn and I totally forgot about the call. Later, I rationalised it. She hadn't wanted to say that Irene was dead, because it was too painful. Only, surely, under those circumstances you'd say, "I'm afraid she's passed on" or similar. You wouldn't say, "There's no Irene Plait here."'

'You think it could have been Barbara ringing?'

He drew a breath. 'Possibly. What I do know is that I took her to the doctor's because her heart rate was all over the place, and she started losing her hair. Just like she did when Ronnie died. After that phone call, her hair pretty much dropped out.'

'Shock and fear.'

'Or lies catching her up.'

'Mum reckons Philippa burned all Irene and Norman's papers and tried to destroy the diaries. I think it, too.'

'But she didn't anticipate you salvaging them and getting obsessed.' Will closed down his computer. 'Come on, I'm fit for company again.'

Downstairs, they found Philippa lying on the sofa, plucking at the turquoise pashmina Amanda had wrapped around her.

Sensing their presence, she opened her eyes. 'Will?'

He went slowly to the sofa. 'I'm here.'

'Don't hate me. I've got nobody else.'

'I don't hate you, but I'm angry.'

'I know.' Small, bent fingers sought Will's hand.

He flinched, then allowed them to weave with his. Crouching, he said, 'Aunt Flip, this has to be put right. You have to call Barbara Parkinson.'

'I can't.'

'Then I will, or Ruby. Or Amanda. No more lies.'

Ruby found her mother in the kitchen, waiting for the kettle to boil.

Amanda looked over her shoulder. 'She wants fig leaf tea. Is that a metaphor?'

'No, it's a real thing.' Ruby pointed to the packet she'd brought from Westumble farmhouse. 'I'll make it. I've been trained to do it right.' That done, she turned on her phone, and tapped the most recently stored number, before handing it to Amanda. It was dialling. 'Go stand by the door. That's where the signal is best. With luck, you're about to speak to your long-lost sister.'

Leaving her mother to start that conversation in private, Ruby let herself out and pointed her feet towards Oak Apple Farm. She was going to prove her hunch about the locket's hiding place.

## 60

## RUBY

Ruby had left lights on at Oak Apple, never wanting a repeat of the darkness that had greeted her on her arrival fourteen days ago. Unlike then, the dining hall was toasty warm because she'd left her stove banked up. She went towards it, convinced she was about to solve a mystery.

'Ruby?' Will came in, closing the door behind him. He wasn't wearing his coat and a shiver ran through his voice. 'When I saw you'd gone, I was worried I'd chased you away.'

'Course not. I don't blame you for your feelings. And all told, you've been remarkably tolerant.' She stepped away from the fireplace to put her arms around him. 'Thank you for Christmas.'

'It still has a few hours to run. Anything could happen. You know, Kimmy told me once, during an argument, that the first time she met Aunt Flip she knew she and I would never make it. Philippa would drive us apart, she said, and that I'd stand by and let it happen. But I won't do that. I'll fight to keep you, if you want me.'

'Are you afraid Philippa will scare me away?'

'It crossed my mind.'

'Well, uncross it. We're family, Will. Blended, but family. We'll stick together because we can't let the past strangle the future. Philippa needs help, and the older she gets, the more help she'll need. So does Amanda and so will Barbara.'

He accepted her words. 'Why were you staring at the stove when I came in? Waiting for Father Christmas?'

'I was thinking about the Parisian jazz joint where the Jake Hendrick Five played.'

'They're not up the chimney, Ruby. It's been a long day.' He pulled her against him and put his lips to her hair. 'I just want to go to bed.'

She leaned into the embrace. 'I've been searching for Irene's locket since I arrived here. She gave Theo his lucky silver dollar when they met in Paris. And the wedding ring that Norman put on her finger lies at the bottom of a horse pond, somewhere behind this house.'

'Makes sense. So far.'

'But the engagement ring and the locket came back here.' Uncoupling herself from Will, she ducked under the fireplace bressummer, pushing her hand into the niche where, traditionally, the salt pot had lived to keep its contents dry. After Bob Oaks had mentioned it, she'd looked 'salt nook' up online. 'It was the mention of Le Hot Brick Club through the Bluetooth speaker that made me think—' She felt inside the niche, finding a fingerhold in the mortar between two bricks. 'Irene started wearing her locket again the day after Norman died, only Philippa tore it off her in rage. So... Irene took it to the jewellers' for repair. And to have whatever was hidden inside sealed away for good.'

Ruby pulled out one of the bricks, placing it on the hearth. In the crumbly surface she'd exposed, her fingers discovered a shallow pit. Something hard and cold lay inside it. 'Hallelujah.' Backing out carefully, she held it up to the light.

Will took it from her. 'It's a horseshoe nail. It was a local superstition, to bury one at the back of the fireplace to keep the witches away.'

Above their heads, a ceiling light flickered, on, off, on, off.

'Power lines must be overloaded,' Will said, glancing up. 'Often happens at Christmas.' He bent cautiously and put the nail back in its bed, replacing the brick. The lights shone brightly again.

Ruby made a noise of frustration. 'I was so sure! Mum dreamed it was encased in bricks, or under flagstones.'

'The other night, I dreamt my Volvo was made of sponge cake.' Will pulled her into his arms again. 'You know the real reason I ran over here just now? Your mum was saying to Barbara on the phone that you'd both be heading back to France. She seemed so sure.'

Of course. Amanda expected her to return to France and relaunch her career, Ruby realised. That's exactly what Ruby had told her and anyone who'd listen. 'Will?' She locked her hands around his neck until he lowered his lips to hers. 'I'm going to send for all my furniture.'

'What are you telling me?'

'That even if I sell this house, I'm not going. I'm not leaving Flixfield.'

He lifted his head, enough for her to see the glimmer of hope, of relief in the hazel eyes. And something more... it was nothing less than joy. They kissed and held each other as the fire in the wood burner gently whispered.

Eventually, Ruby tipped back her head. 'But where is that bloody locket!' She called into the space beneath the bres-summer beam, 'Irene, what did you do with it?'

'What did she write in her diary?' Will asked.

'That she'd put it where nobody would find it. Rather, "Where no snooper would find it." She was in Thewell Park when she wrote that, and was expecting to go home to Westum-

ble. But I bet she found a similarly secure hiding place here,
after she married Norman.'

'Who were the snoopers?'

'Snooper, singular...' Ruby walked over to the table and
picked up Irene's 1943 diary, turning to the flyleaf. 'She
declaimed, "Property of Irene Boulter. If ever I find you reading
this, Little Flip, I'll turn you into a frog." It was Philippa she had
to hide everything from,' she said, her voice deepening with
emotion. 'Remember what Flip said just now, how she spied on
Irene putting the locket around her neck on her wedding day?
And went straight downstairs and told Norman.'

Will did a good impression of Norman's voice: '"Something
old, something new, something borrowed. That's what it is.
Something borrowed, for luck."'

'Exactly. Norman heard Philippa out, and refused to delve
into Irene's secrets. Not for him opening her diaries or stealing
things the way Philippa did. Irene wasn't hiding stuff from
Norman—'

'No. From Philippa.'

'So where would Irene put a locket to keep it safe, beyond
any shadow of a doubt, from Little Flip?'

Their eyes met. The answer flashed up in their minds at the
same moment and they raced to get through the door to the
lounge.

The little cupboard next to the fireplace smelled of damp,
and long-ago mice. Ruby shone her torch and Will levered up
the bricks that made the cupboard's floor. And there it was, in a
bed of grit, curled like a baby snake. He lifted it out, blew the
dust off it, and placed it in Ruby's palm. A tarnished silver
chain with a heart-shaped locket at its end.

She stared at it. 'I need to know what's inside.' But Irene
had gone to great lengths to protect whatever lay within and
when Ruby tried to open it, she found that Grimmonds and

Sons, of Hatton Garden, London, had done a sterling job of welding it up all those years ago.

'It should be opened by a craftsman,' Will advised, 'otherwise, you'll break it.'

'I'll go to Lubbock's first thing in the morning.'

'Boxing Day? You'll have to be patient.' He suggested they go back to the barn, uneasy at leaving Philippa and Amanda alone for too long.

They walked back, hand in hand. When they got there, Philippa was watching TV, half asleep. Amanda was waiting for them anxiously.

'Ruby,' she said the moment the door closed behind them. 'I have spoken to Barbara, and she's lovely! We connected so beautifully, and she wants to see me. Can we go to London today? Is there a taxi driver in Flixfield these days?'

'No, Mum, and the nearest Uber is miles off. No way are we heading to London. But hold your hand out and close your eyes.'

Amanda did so, like a trusting child. Ruby placed the locket in her mother's palm.

Opening her eyes, Amanda gaped in delight and astonishment. For once, she could find absolutely nothing to say.

## 61

TUESDAY 17 JANUARY 2023

Clement Lubbock looked up as they entered his shop. He put down the brass clock pendulum he was carefully polishing to shake hands with Ruby and Will. 'And who is this?'

Ruby introduced her mother. 'Mum is Irene's daughter and she's delayed her return to France because she's so excited about the locket. Did you get it open?'

Mr Lubbock laughed. 'I did, and I feel I ought to whisk off a tartan blanket for a big reveal. Sadly, I haven't got one of those. I'll bring it through.'

He returned moments later and placed an open jeweller's box on the counter. On a bed of cream satin lay Irene's locket, cleaned to a glinting shine. 'Removing the welded seal was a fiddly business and involved actually sawing through the metal. We had to replace the hinges.'

Ruby was hardly listening. 'What did you find, though?' There had to be something. Why else would Irene have had the locket sealed in the first place?

Clement Lubbock moved the box towards her. 'You can open it and see for yourself.'

Ruby took out the locket, pressed the catch and it sprang open. Inside was a plain gold band. Irene's engagement ring.

Amanda said, 'May I?' She picked out the ring, holding it to the light. 'It's so small. My mother's fingers were very slender. This wouldn't fit me, nor you, Ruby.'

'I could put it on a gold chain,' Mr Lubbock offered. 'Or rings can be enlarged, you know.'

Ruby said, 'We should give the ring to Theo and Irene's daughter. To Barbara. Mum?'

'Oh, yes.' Amanda nodded eagerly. 'My sister. Your aunt. She'll be pleased.'

'There was something else inside, which fell out during the work, so I took the liberty of preserving it.' Clement Lubbock put a tiny envelope on the counter, one that might once have contained beads or precious stones. 'Remember when I showed you that Victorian locket when you first came in, Ruby?'

'The one with the gentleman's lock of hair in it?' Ruby was busy opening the tiny envelope.

'Careful, shake the contents out onto this paper.' Mr Lubbock moved a sheet of letter paper across the counter, so Ruby could empty the envelope onto it. Out fell two curls of hair. One was silky and black. The other was bright purple and both were tied together with strands of blonde.

'My hair!' Amanda cried, indicating the purple curl. 'From when I cut it off before Grandma Violet's funeral. Does this mean my mother kept some of it?'

'Looks like it. And this...' Ruby held the magnifying glass she'd brought with her to hand back to its owner over the dark snippet of hair. 'Could this be Barbara's?' In Paris, Irene had shown Theo a sprig of their daughter's hair, saved for her by her mother. 'She'd have treasured it.'

Will asked, 'Whose is the blonde? Is it Irene's?'

'Yes,' Amanda breathed. 'It's how I remember it, when I was young.'

'She kept your hair bound together, hidden away,' Ruby said. 'Her two girls.' Choked, she couldn't say more.

It was Will who asked Clement Lubbock, 'Would you do what you suggested, and put the engagement ring on a chain?'

Barbara was coming to Suffolk in a couple of months, when her son would be able to drive her and her husband to meet them all. She hadn't felt confident about coming on her own, to a place that had rebuffed her so heartlessly on her previous visit. 'Barbara should have something her father paid such a high price for.'

'Speaking of which...' Clement Lubbock placed two faded carbon-copy receipts on the counter. They dated from August 1943. One was the proof-of-sale for a silver locket. Eight shillings value. The other was for a twenty-two-carat gold band. Fifteen shillings value.

Written across both were the words, 'Paid in full'.

Clement smiled at Ruby's reaction. 'My brother Basil had the time of his life, searching our archives. You made him very happy.'

'We'll send these to Theo's daughter in Georgia,' Will said. Sabrina was still campaigning to clear her father's name and have his military record reinstated. 'At least the charge of theft can be challenged.'

As they left the shop, heading to a café for a late breakfast, Amanda said shakily, 'I suppose my mother must have loved me a bit, to keep my hair all those years.'

'Course she did,' Ruby said fiercely. 'It broke her heart, but when it came to a choice, she chose you. She loved you, Mum. She just didn't know how to express it, she was so damaged.'

While they waited for their croissants and cappuccinos to

arrive, Amanda and Ruby cried unashamedly. It was as though by opening the locket, trapped emotions finally found their voice, as the following months proved...

# EPILOGUE

A hundred acres of pale blue sky stretched over the abandoned Flixfield airbase. The half-grown wheat rippled under a fresh breeze where, eighty years ago, Theo Robinson and his comrades had laid concrete runways. Ruby jumped out of Will's car, putting her shoulder to the rusty barrier to open it so he could drive through. A people carrier followed, parking behind the Volvo on some hard standing.

Ruby watched everyone get out of their vehicles. Amanda's silk scarf lifted like a parachute as she emerged from the Volvo. Barbara Parkinson and her husband, Graham, stepped cautiously out of the people carrier, avoiding a puddle. Barbara's son, Terrence, jumped out, pocketing his car keys. Looking around him, bemused.

Two of the Parkinson grandchildren, fourteen-year-old Alex and Quincey, six, were the last out. Will gave Edna the full lift-down from the Volvo's rear.

A party of eight, they trooped over to the memorial to the men of the 699th Bomb Group. Someone had laid fresh flowers but the Remembrance Day poppies that Ruby had seen last year were gone. The lawn was neat, the granite stone newly washed. Barbara stepped over the chain that marked the plot and read the words on the memorial. The others watched silently. Ruby had been surprised, meeting her for the first time, to discover that Barbara's hair was completely white. So much time had passed since she'd first come to Flixfield, as a woman in her forties, looking for her mother.

Barbara took a pouch from her pocket and sprinkled the contents on the grass. A few of Theo's ashes, sent by Sabrina. 'Can we walk?' she asked, and Ruby suspected she was uncomfortable in front of a tablet that made no mention of the men who had laboured to build the airbase.

They spent an hour walking the perimeter.

'Is this all there is?' Terrence asked.

''Fraid so,' said Ruby. 'It was all bulldozed after the war and ploughed for crops. But the concrete you're walking on was laid by your grandfather and his friends.'

Will took a mortar chisel from his pocket and hacked a few pieces where a crack had opened. He gave pieces to the two young boys. 'A bit of your family history. Maybe your great-grandfather laid it.'

Edna scampered off after a rabbit. Will whistled for her to come back, as the wind soughed around their ears and buzzards wheeled overhead.

That evening, all eight of them sat down to dinner at The Ten Bells. So much to talk about. They learned that Barbara had been adopted by a professional family, the Leaches, and had grown up in Kent. She'd trained as a teacher, married and moved to Lewisham in south-east London – not far from Goldsmiths where Will had studied.

Her husband, Graham, had worked in local government. They were both retired now, and had a daughter, Simone, as well as their son, Terrence. Simone was Alex and Quincey's mother and had recently given birth to twin girls. 'She thought her family was complete, but life is never what you plan.' Barbara smiled. She'd been happy, she said. Loved by the mum and dad who adopted her. 'It was only after my adoptive mother passed away that I felt the need to look for my birth parents.'

They talked through three courses, several bottles of wine and copious cans of Lilt. Their meal was cooked by a stand-in chef and served by Craig, the harassed landlord. Will and Ruby had been daunted to see, on arriving at The Ten Bells, a 'For sale' sign outside.

'Don't say we're losing our village boozer.' Will was upset at the prospect. 'Where else can we go to drink and then walk home?'

Philippa had been invited to join them that evening, but had declined, saying, 'This lazy old wind is too cold for me. I'll stay home and look after Edna.'

They had accepted the polite fiction. Philippa could be forgiven, excuses made for her, but nothing could alter the fact that maintaining the lie over Barbara's birth had robbed Irene and Theo of the chance to know their daughter, and their daughter of any possibility of meeting them.

As Amanda had said, Philippa had colluded in erasing Theodora, Irene's name for her daughter. 'But we can change the present, if not the past.'

That summer, Amanda and Barbara were heading to Savannah, Georgia, to meet Sabrina and her family.


FRIDAY 8 SEPTEMBER 2023

An enormous removals van inched down the village street, stopping abreast of Ruby and Will as they walked with Edna towards The Ten Bells. The driver leaned out. 'Oak Apple Farm?'

Ruby pointed down the road. 'On the right, where the oak trees are.'

As the lorry rumbled away, she took Will's hand.

'Sad day?' he asked.

'Autumn's always sad. Change of season, leaves turning. Nights drawing in.'

'I mean, selling the family pile.'

'No. Oak Apple Farm will live on. The new owners want to raise their family there and that's what it needs. It's Philippa who minds most.'

'She's fine,' Will said. 'I left her and Mary Daker riding the stairlift to heaven.' He'd finally persuaded Philippa to have an electric stairlift installed, so she could stay as long as possible in her home. 'I had to tell them, it's not a toy, you know.'

Turning into Church Lane, they were in time to see an estate agent's 'Sold' sign being removed from the front of the pub. Craig and Tarquin had returned to London to run a City wine bar. Ruby and Will walked up to the front door where a notice announced: 'Closed for redecoration. Reopening October'.

Above the door was a sign declaring, 'Ruby Plait, licensed to sell intoxicating liquor for consumption on or off the premises'. She had bought the village pub after selling Oak Apple Farm, completing the purchase in August.

Standing behind the bar, Ruby rested her palms on the worn oak. This place was going to be her home-from-home. She'd moved in with Will that summer, but here, where Irene had come in a bid for freedom and independence, she'd build a business, running a free house and making The Ten Bells a locally renowned pub restaurant. She smiled, recalling that before she'd posted the memory stick to Didier, concluding her side of a bargain, she'd taken a copy of the spreadsheets it contained. The figures she'd laboured over for many a long night in Laurac were the foundation of her business plan, here in Flixfield.

As Edna nosed around the shelves under the bar, Ruby looked at Will, who was standing by the door, watching her, his eyes soft with love and pride. She placed a hand on her chest, a secret signal. Irene's locket hung around her neck, warm against her skin, reminding her that, like her grandmother, she had found the love of her life.

Amanda had wanted her to keep it. 'It belongs with you, darling, because your story is an echo of poor Mum's.'

In her case, one with a happy ending. Unlike Irene, Ruby was able to make a future with her chosen man, right here. There would be no harsh goodbyes for her. Ruby cherished the belief that by loving and living true to their values, she and Will could lay the troubled past to rest.

# A LETTER FROM NATALIE

To my dear readers,

Thank you for reading *The Locket*, and I hope you enjoyed following Irene and Theo's story, and that of Ruby and Will. If you enjoyed it and want to keep up to date with all my latest releases, just sign up at the following link. Your email address will never be shared and you can unsubscribe at any time.

*www.bookouture.com/natalie-meg-evans*

When you compare the two couples, Ruby and Will had it easy! In our society, where we get to make our own choices about who and how we love, it's shocking to think that only three generations ago, people could be driven apart by prejudice.

Yet love is the most persistent human emotion. It *will* grow, even if it will struggle for life. And it can spring up between people who would never have imagined they'd be brought together. I doubt Theo had ever heard of Suffolk, UK, before he was shipped over, and Irene could not have found his home state of Georgia on any map.

Suffolk lies on the furthest eastern edge of Britain and as war broke out in Europe in 1939, life here kept to its gentle pace. Then suddenly – the 'friendly invasion' arrived. Our US allies came over to occupy the airbases that had been built fast and furiously by their compatriots, the cohorts of Black engineers who came here first. Everybody knew an American, and cordial relations broke out – and not a few romances.

However... As Theo says to Irene: attitudes travel more easily than men. The racist beliefs of many white aircrew, who arrived in number from the summer of 1943, introduced conflicts into small communities which were completely unprepared for it. While segregation never became British policy, it was in force within the US army, and it created divisions which led to injustice and pain for the Black servicemen who had done nothing more than their duty in difficult conditions.

For those who fell in love with local women, and the women who loved them back, the full force of racial segregation swept them into a political reality that was almost certain to overwhelm them. In telling the story of Irene and Theo, I hope I have done justice to those who were criminalised for falling in love.

As *The Locket* is published, I am working on another story of love-against-the-odds in the time of war. There are so many tales to tell. If you have enjoyed *The Locket*, or other novels of mine, do please tell your friends, as it helps me to reach out to more readers. Meanwhile, if you'd like to get in touch, my contact details are below.

Once again, thank you for reading,

Natalie Meg Evans

Suffolk 2023

www.nataliemegevans.uk

facebook.com/NatalieMegEvans
twitter.com/natmegevans